COURT
OF
THE
VAMPIRE
QUEEN

KATEE
ROBERT

sourcebooks
casablanca

*To everyone who was Team Damon, Team
Spike, and far too into Dimitri Belikov.*

Court of the Vampire Queen is a dark and incredibly spicy book that
contains dubious consent, blood play, patricide, pregnancy, blood,
gore, murder, explicit sex, vomiting (caused by pregnancy), discussions
about abortion, abusive parent (father, historical, off-page), attempted
sexual assault (alluded to, nongraphic), and attempted drugging.

Copyright © 2022 by Katee Robert
Cover and internal design © 2022 by Sourcebooks
Cover design by Stephanie Gafron/Sourcebooks
Cover image © Magdalena Wasiczek/Trevillion Images
Internal design by Laura Boren/Sourcebooks
Internal illustrations © Aud Koch
The publisher acknowledges the copyright holders of the individual works as follows:
Sacrifice © 2020 by Trinkets and Tales LLC
Heir © 2021 by Trinkets and Tales LLC
Queen © 2021 by Trinkets and Tales LLC

Sourcebooks and the colophon are registered trademarks of Sourcebooks.

Published by Sourcebooks Casablanca, an imprint of Sourcebooks
PO Box 4410, Naperville, Illinois 60567-4410
(630) 961-3900
sourcebooks.com

Cataloging-in-Publication Data is on file with the Library of Congress.

Printed and bound in the United States of America.
LSC 10 9 8 7 6 5 4 3 2 1

ACT I
SACRIFICE

1

I DON'T WANT TO BE HERE.

Rain slashes my face, the wind turning my long hair into whips. I feel like I've been walking for hours, but I suspect in the light of day, I'll discover it's a mere half mile from the tall iron gate to the front steps of the house looming in front of me. It looks like something out of a gothic novel, towering peaks and narrow windows, all dark and vaguely faded as if it's stood on this hill for time unknowing.

Probably because it has.

I readjust my grip on my suitcase and march up the steps. There's no point in turning and running as far and fast as I can. I already tried that and it got me a brand-new scar on my knee and a limp that made the hike up here agonizing. The only reason my father healed me the little bit that he did was to keep me from being fully damaged goods. The man in this house won't care about a few scars. He's interested in what lurks beneath my skin.

Specifically, my blood.

I don't knock. The vampire in this house knows I'm coming. There's no point in playing the courteous guest or pretending I want this. I make it three steps inside before the door slams shut behind me, sealing off the roar of the storm and leaving only eerie silence in its wake. I glance over my shoulder, but I don't expect to see anything.

Vampires move faster than the human eye can see. And while I'm only 50 percent human, I'm tainted by that lineage enough to not be able to see more than a blur of movement. Another way I'm seen as damaged goods. At least if I had full vampire reflexes and strength, it might make up for my lack of magic. As it is, I'm barely better than a human. Barely better than prey.

The knowledge sticks in my throat, preventing a shriek of surprise when I turn around and find a man looming close. No, not a man. A *vampire*. It's there in his pale skin, the barest hint of fang pressing against his bottom lip. It's the slightest loss of control, and it makes me wonder how long it's been since the last sacrificial lamb was sent to this house.

He's gorgeous in the way all vampires are, flawless beauty and hidden strength. This one has dark brown hair that falls in a sleek wave to his shoulders, fathomless dark eyes, and a muscular body slightly too thin for his frame. He holds himself stiller than any human ever could. "I apologize."

I blink. Of all the things I expected him to say, that didn't number among them. "What?"

"Cornelius sent you."

It's not a question, and I can't quite stifle the flinch at my father's name. At the reminder of who I can blame for my current circumstances. "Yes."

"You know why."

Now his stillness makes sense. He's barely preventing himself from attacking me. My heartbeat kicks up, and I can see well enough in the dark to note how his nose flares as he inhales my scent. I'm running out of time. I want to stay silent, but there's no point. Despite my best efforts, my voice wobbles a little with nerves. "He gave me to you."

"Yes." It's hardly more than a sigh. "We'll discuss this... after."

"After—" This time I can't stop the shriek of surprise. One blink he's a few feet away, and the next he hits me with the force of a runaway truck. He still manages to control our fall so I don't bash my head on the marble floor, but I don't have a chance to appreciate the consideration. Not when he surges forward and bites my neck.

"Fuck!" My curse turns into a breathy moan. I knew to expect this, but being lectured on the pleasure of a bloodline vampire's bite does nothing to translate how *good* it feels. It's as if every pull of his mouth is connected directly to my clit, pulsing through my body and turning my resistance liquid. I don't *want* to want this, but my body doesn't care. I arch against him, reaching up to pull him closer to me.

One of his hands is in my hair, using the leverage to keep my neck bared to him, and the other snakes around to press against the small of my back, urging me closer to him. As if I wasn't already straining against him.

I have the distant horrified thought that I'm going to come if he doesn't stop. "Wait!"

"I'm sorry." I feel more than hear his murmur. His tongue strokes my neck and then he moves to the other side. "I can't stop."

"But—"

He bites me again and I whimper. Fuck, that feels good. My dress is tangled up around my hips and I wrap my legs around his waist, arching closer. I can feel my blood warming his cool body, and evidence of his bite is already hardening against me. He rolls his hips and growls against my skin, but he doesn't move his hands from their spots. He doesn't touch me like I'm suddenly desperate for him to do.

"More," I moan.

He gives a hard pull to my neck and I slide my hands down his back to his ass, holding him close as I roll my hips, grinding myself on his hard cock like a wanton thing. It doesn't matter I'll regret this later, I'll hate both him and me for this loss of control. I need to come more than I need my pride. It will still be there on the other side of this.

I work myself against him, and I have half a thought to reach for the front of his pants, but it would mean stopping this delicious friction, and I'm not willing to do that. Another time.

It's what I'm here for, whether I chose this role or not.

I realize he's stopped sucking my blood, but the endorphins have nowhere near worn off. I should stop. I know I should stop, but the subtle pressure of his fingertips against the small of my back urge me on. Pleasure winds through me, tighter and tighter, and for one breathless moment, I think I won't get there, that I'll be poised on the brink for an eternity.

My orgasm hits me even harder than the vampire did earlier and I come more intensely than I ever have before, crying and panting as I hump him like I really do want this. The last wave crests and I slump back to the cold marble floor, my head feeling fuzzy and too light. "You took too much," I murmur, my words coming as slowly as taffy.

His tongue strokes my neck and he gives another of those growls I don't want to enjoy. "You don't taste like a human."

It's strange to be having this conversation on the floor while he's pressing between my thighs, but I can't seem to find the energy to shove him off. "I'm not." I lick my suddenly dry lips. "I'm half bloodsucker."

"Ah." He inhales and slowly, oh so slowly, he releases me and sits up. There's a new flush in his pale cheeks and his eyes are blazing with power. He kneels between my legs and his gaze strokes over me in a way I can almost feel, lingering on my lips, on my bloody neck, where my breasts are nearly escaping this ridiculous dress, where said ridiculous dress isn't covering my panties any longer. My panties that are *soaked*.

I start to cover myself, but he catches my wrists, easily overpowering me. He does another of those long inhales and I know beyond a shadow of a doubt he's scenting my arousal. He shifts my wrists to one hand and reaches for my panties with the other.

"Wait!"

The vampire's eyes are pure black and his fangs are on full display. The little glimpse of control from earlier, of regret, are nowhere in evidence. Gods, I'm in trouble. His gaze drops to my panties again. "You know why you're here." His knuckles brush the wet fabric, lightly stroking against my pussy. Despite just coming, I have to fight the desire to lift my hips in invitation. I *know* it's the aftermath of the bite, but I hate myself a little for it.

He pauses, his hands shaking as if he's fighting himself. He could have broken my wrists, could do so much more damage, and there's nothing I could do to stop him. "Say it."

I don't want to. I very much don't want to. But the words spill from my lips, almost as if he compelled them with his low voice. "I'm here to satisfy your hunger."

"Hunger*s*, little dhampir. All of them." He strokes me again. "Lift your hips."

I obey even as I argue. "You said we'd talk."

"Yes, after." Still, he hesitates. A drop of blood drips down his chin and I dazedly realize he's bitten himself. "Say yes."

The fact that he isn't simply taking what he obviously wants confuses me even as I hate him for making me say it. Would he really stop if I tell him to? I'll never know. "Yes."

His eyes flash to my face as he grips the crotch of my panties and tugs them down my legs. He could have just ripped them off—it probably would have taken less effort—and that little show of restraint almost makes this worse. Or better. I'm honestly not sure.

I didn't choose to be in this house, to be a sacrificial lamb, but that doesn't stop my body from shaking with need. I bite my bottom lip as he moves down my body and I know I should argue more, should never have let the word *yes* leave my lips, but he gives my pussy another of those light strokes and the touch short-circuits my brain.

"Please," I whisper. I don't know what I'm begging for, for him to stop or not stop. It doesn't matter. He shifts slightly to the side and strikes, quick as a snake, sinking his fangs into the sensitive skin of my upper thigh.

I come again instantly.

I keep coming, wave after wave, until I'm sobbing and begging, but I can't begin to guess what I'm begging for. For him to stop. For him to fuck me. It doesn't matter. Before I can decide, he lifts his head.

And then he's gone, a flash of motion up the curving staircase, and I'm left alone in the entrance hall. Wet. Bleeding. And filled with enough confusion that my head feels like it's spinning wildly on my shoulders. "What the *fuck* just happened?"

2

I THINK I BLACK OUT. I MUST, BECAUSE ONE MOMENT
I'm lying on the cold marble floor and the next I'm blinking up into
a darkened bedroom. I go perfectly still out of habit, forcing my
heartbeat to slow and my breathing to stay even. I can see well in
the dark, courtesy of my vampire blood, and I pick out the features
of a bedroom that must have been the height of luxury sometime in
the last few hundred years. It hasn't been kept up in the meantime.
There's dust on every surface of the heavy wooden furniture and the
canopy overhead is filled with holes and worn nearly transparent.

I count to one hundred slowly and then do it again.

Nothing moves in the room except for the steady rise and fall
of my chest.

I can't lie here forever, no matter how much part of me wants
to curl into a ball and wait for this all to be over. Maybe another

woman in my position would. Maybe the last sacrifice sent to this place did.

It's not who I am.

My life has been hell since I was old enough to realize my position within the vampire colony my father rules. I am the worst of all things. Magic-less. Bastard. The product of my monster of a father and one of his human mistresses he pretends is there of her own free will, rather than an exotic pet he likes to keep to prove his power. Unlike other dhampir children of bloodline vampires, I have no magic to speak of. I fit nowhere, so every move I made was an insult deserving punishment.

For years, I didn't understand why he resisted killing me and getting me out from underfoot once and for all.

Now, I do.

This is where he planned to send me all along. A sacrificial lamb. A womb just waiting to be filled with one of the failing vampire bloodlines my father holds so highly. And if I die before accomplishing that? He'll lose no sleep over it.

Under other circumstances—mainly, if I'd inherited his magic like I should have—my getting pregnant would make me his heir. Now, he wants me to serve as a vehicle to bring another bloodline under his control. It seems particularly cruel, but I've long since stopped expecting anything resembling kindness from my father.

I let rage propel me to sit up and gingerly touch my neck. The bites are small puncture wounds. The vampire didn't so much as tear my skin, though I'm not about to thank him for it.

Him.

Malachi Zion.

If my father is to be believed, this vampire can trace his bloodline back to one of the original seven vampires. There are only two types of vampire: turned and bloodline. Over time, the number of turned vampires has far outnumbered the bloodline ones born—something rare even before vampires withdrew and hid away from humans, and now practically nonexistent—which means those family lines are in danger of dying out.

Which is supposedly where I come in.

I sigh and climb carefully off the bed. My thigh aches, but my busted knee aches worse. The hike did me no favors. I limp to where my suitcase is tucked near the door. It appears untouched, but when I lay it down and open it, I find things rifled through. "Nosy ass vampire," I mutter. A quick search finds what I feared. He's taken my knife. I glare at the mess of clothing in the suitcase. "What's the fucking point? You're like two hundred years old, and I'm half human. I couldn't kill you with that knife if I tried."

If he's lurking close enough to listen to me rant, he makes no appearance to reveal it. It's just as well. Even with my vampire side accelerating my healing, I'm a little light-headed from blood loss. I need to eat something, but I might as well wish on a star as hope that kitchen is stocked.

Still.

The alternative is hiding in my room until the vampire starts wanting a snack and seeks me out again. My body hums at the thought, entirely too on board with the idea. I'd heard blood-line vampires had a pleasurable bite, had even seen it play out during my father's *services* when he moves through the room and bites a few of his chosen followers, but I chalked it up to vampire-on-vampire nonsense. The few times I haven't been fast enough to avoid one of the turned ones' fangs, it *hurt*.

I glance at the bed, at the reminder I'm here as more than blood donor. All part of my father's grand plan to bring the vampire race back to supremacy or some bullshit. He never asked me what *I* want, but then a bastard magic-less dhampir is more tool to be utilized than actual person from where he's standing. I clench my fists.

The house will be watched. My father is too smart to leave anything to chance. He figures if he throws me in this place, it's only a matter of time before Malachi either knocks me up or kills me. Either will suit his purposes. If I *do* get pregnant, I suspect I won't live past the live birth. It won't matter if my child manages to inherit powers or if they are born without magic like their mother. I'll have served my role.

Fuck that.

I'll find a way out of here, even if I have to carve my way through Malachi and every vampire guarding this house. I need to bide my time and wait for the right opportunity. I doubt I can kill them, but I should be able to find a way to incapacitate them long enough to get the hell out of Dodge.

First things first. I won't be worth a damn while I'm dizzy and exhausted.

I glance at the bed again and shake my head. Even without the sheer amount of dust and moth-eaten fabric, there's no reason to make it easier on the vampire. *No reason to tempt myself, either.* I won't be sleeping there.

I dig a power bar out of my suitcase. I only stashed a handful, which means I *do* need to figure out food at some point.

Starving to death is not on my agenda. A faint sliver of light trickles through the window. I push wearily to my feet and move to look outside. Dawn is here. And I'm on the second floor. I try to open the window, but it's been painted shut. Great. Not that I expected much else. If this house has been updated since it was built, I haven't seen any evidence of it.

Now I'm stalling.

I grit my teeth and open the bedroom door. Nothing happens. Just like nothing happens when I step out into the hallway. It looks just like the entranceway and the bedroom—old and dusty and threadbare. The carpet beneath my shoes is black or purple or maybe gray. It's hard to determine in the low light and with age fading it. The walls are equally faded, though I can tell they were originally green. Paintings line them, but I ignore the art for now. Getting caught up in curiosity isn't an option.

I find the front stairs easily enough. This place seems laid out logically, which is a relief in a way. Not that I know what I'm supposed to *do* with that information. For all my dreams of running, there are several harsh realities standing in my way.

First and most insurmountable is the vampires themselves. They're faster than me. Stronger than me. And all of them, from Malachi to my father to the guards no doubt lingering at the edges of the property, have a vested interest in me staying trapped exactly where I am.

But it's more than that. The only things I know about human society are what I've gleaned from the few servants my father keeps and the books my mother somehow managed to smuggle into the colony. It might be enough to whet my appetite for freedom, but I'm not naive enough to think I'm anywhere near prepared to slip into their world.

Knowing all that won't stop me looking for an escape, but it's enough to keep me from doing something truly reckless. Like trying to flee right now, this morning.

The kitchen is slightly more updated than the rest of the house. The appliances look like things I recognize, and there's power when I flip on the lights. I study the dusty hanging lights. "So the bloodsucker likes a little modern convenience after all." Apparently he has some way to order in resources, which is useful knowledge to have.

"Such charm you have, little dhampir."

I startle like a cat, straight up into the air and over a good six feet. The vampire doesn't move from where he's standing against the doorframe I just walked through. He looks...amused. And healthier. There's a flush to his pale skin from *my* blood.

The thought sends a pulse through my body, directly to my core. I didn't hate being his snack as much as I want to, and even as I tell myself I'll fight him to a standstill before I let him bite me again, part of me wants it and wants it now.

Part of me wants *more*.

I glare, hating that now *my* face is flushed. "If you drink any more from me, you'll kill me and my father will probably make you wait another twenty-five years before he sends a replacement."

The vampire—Malachi—pushes off the doorframe and takes a purposefully slow step into the kitchen. He looks like he's concentrating, as if it's more natural for him to move too fast for me to really see. "You're here for a reason. Don't forget that."

"Why not tattoo *sacrifice* on my forehead in case I forget?"

His brows inch up. "The last one wasn't so mouthy."

"And look what happened to her." I don't know much about the stranger who occupied this position before me. Only that she was chosen to continue Malachi's bloodline and my father was infuriated by her inability to breed—and stay alive. I'm not even sure how long ago it was. "Thanks, but if I'm going to die in this house, I refuse to cower for the time I have remaining."

His sensual lips curve, and I loathe I notice they're sensual at all. "Are you mad I didn't fuck you earlier?"

My jaw drops. "You're out of your fucking mind!" I throw my hands up when he drifts another step closer. "I didn't even want you to bite me."

"Mmm." Another step. I retreat and he stalks me through the kitchen. He's edging me back into the corner of the counter, and there's not a damn thing I can do about it. He finally stops a bare six inches from me and braces his hands on the counter on either side of my body. This close, it's impossible not to notice, no matter how run-down the house, *his* clothing is new and smells faintly of tobacco and something spicy. He wears a pair of fitted pants and a shirt that would be at home on some historical romance about a pirate. It leaves a slice of his pale chest bare, and I can see a number of raised scars there.

It looks like someone tried to hack out his heart.

"I've tasted a lot of humans over the years." He sounds almost like he's musing to himself. "Even a few dhampirs before you." His gaze coasts down my body, lingering on my breasts. "None of them tasted as good as you."

I blink. "Is that supposed to be a compliment?"

"It's a fact." He shifts another inch closer. "It intrigues me."

"Back off." My voice comes out hoarse. My skin is tingling and I wish I could say it's tingling with danger or fear. It'd be a lie. I'm fighting not to press my thighs together from the remembered pleasure.

Malachi leans down a little until he's looking directly into my eyes. His eyes are so dark, they seem to draw in the light of the room. There's a hunger lurking there, and I can't stop the horrified suspicion he's seeing that hunger reflected right back at him when he looks into my eyes.

His lips curve slowly. "You don't want me to back off."

"Wait."

"You keep saying wait, little dhampir. Not stop. Shall I slow down further?" He lifts his right hand with agonizing slowness. I stand perfectly still as he traces his thumb over my collarbone to the thin strap of my dress. Now's the time to say stop. I don't know if he'll respect it, but I should voice it all the same. Should tell him how much I loathe his touch. How much I never want him to lay hands on me again.

I don't.

I hold my breath and lift my chin.

He eases the strap off my shoulder and down, tugging it until the fabric falls to bare my breast. The cool air of the kitchen pebbles my nipple. Or that's what I tell myself as he stares down at me. Using that same exaggerated slowness, he moves to my other shoulder and gives it the same treatment until I'm naked from the waist up.

Malachi's gaze flicks to my face, and whatever he sees there has him licking his lips. "You know why you're here."

He said the same thing to me multiple times last night. As if he's checking in with me, which is laughable. He's no different from my father, from all the other vampires I've been forced to interact with over the twenty-five years of my life. He wants what he wants, and he'll mow down anyone who gets in his way. Including me. *Especially* me.

My anger blooms again, ready and waiting for the least provocation. I glare. "Just call me your resident blood bank and womb. Suck me, fuck me, do whatever you want. It's not like I'm a real person to you. I'm just a *little dhampir*, after all."

"You're *my* little dhampir now." He brackets my waist with his hands, his fingers digging in the slightest bit.

I have the borderline hysterical thought he could literally rip me limb from limb right now and there's not a damn thing I could do about it. Wouldn't *that* ruin my father's day? I laugh. I can't help it. It comes out angry and derisive. "I might have been traded like a possession, but I'm not yours. I never will be."

"I suppose we'll see, won't we?" He closes the last bit of distance between us and I lose my grip on my rage. It shudders out of me in a sigh that's almost a whimper. Malachi's so *strong*. I don't know why that surprises me. All vampires are stronger than they look. Hell, so am I, even if I can't compare to a full-blood. But there's something about the way he touches me, as if tempering that strength so he doesn't harm me sends my body into a dizzying spiral into desire.

I am so fucked.

3

"I'M FEELING GENEROUS."

I stare up at Malachi's handsome face. "What?" I should be fighting right about now, but the only thing I'm fighting is my desire to arch against his hard body.

He flashes a little fang in a quick grin. "I'll let you choose where I bite you this time, little dhampir. But only if you speak quickly."

"You can't." I sound like I'm asking a question rather than giving a command. I lick my lips, achingly aware of the way he follows the movement. "Unless you really do want to kill me."

"I'm not hungry for your blood." He leans down and his lips brush against the shell of my ear. "I want to feel you come again."

I open my mouth, but not a sound emerges. I expected a lot

of things when my father laid out my fate in that cold way of his. Pain. Torment. Maybe even death. I didn't expect this. I'm not even sure what *this* is. "What?"

"I can bite you here." He gives my neck a slow kiss, dragging his mouth over the spot where he bit me last night. Malachi keeps moving down, stopping at the top of my chest. "Or here." His gaze flicks to my face and he descends to flick his tongue out and stroke my nipple. "Or here."

"Do it." I don't even sound like myself. I sure as hell don't feel like myself. It takes everything I have not to reach for him as he holds my gaze and sinks his fangs into the soft skin of my left breast just above my nipple.

Pleasure bows my back and I cry out. Gods, it shouldn't be *so good*. And then his mouth closes around my nipple and it gets even better. He cups my other breast and loops his free arm around my waist, pulling me tighter against him. He strokes me with his tongue and I'm lost.

I barely register letting go of the counter. One second I'm clinging to it for dear life and the next my fingers are tangled in his long dark hair, holding him to me. My knees buckle, and he eases us to the floor with me straddling him. Careful. He's so fucking *careful*. He's not really taking blood right now, not more than a few drops. His hold on me is tight, but nowhere near tight enough to hurt me.

Like before, each pull of his mouth sends a bolt of lust directly to my clit. I whimper and arch closer. "Please." I'm so empty. I need to come. I need to fuck, hard and quick. I simply need.

He shifts his grip around my waist, urging me down until

I'm pressed against his cock. He's hard again, and I have the dazed thought that he's massive, but I can barely cling to it. Not when he rocks me against him, sliding my pussy along his length through his pants. It's not enough, but it feels too good to stop.

Over and over again, building my pleasure stroke by stroke, pull by pull of his mouth.

He releases my breast and I cry out in protest, but Malachi moves to my right one. This bite is a little rougher, and it propels me into a brutal orgasm. I cry out and grind down on him, coming so hard he has to tighten his hold to keep me from collapsing. He licks my nipple one last time and lifts his head.

I look down and find twin bite marks marring my breasts. Thin trickles of blood run from each puncture wound, and the sight threatens to ramp up my desire again. Especially when he leans down and drags his tongue over my skin, cleaning me.

Now's the time to say something. To remind him again I'm not here because I chose to be. I don't actually want this, humping him in the kitchen notwithstanding.

Malachi looks up at me and gives that slow smile. "Don't worry, little dhampir. I *will* fuck you, and soon. This was simply a little taste of what it will be like."

There's no point in protesting. He *will* fuck me. It was inevitable from the moment I walked through the door, but it feels almost like fate in this moment. A fate I'm not quite sure I want to fight. If it's this good with a bite and most of our clothes on, will it be better when we're both naked and I'm entirely at his disposal.

Will I survive it?

Vampires can go into a frenzy when they fuck. It doesn't happen often as long as everyone's getting regular feedings, but Malachi has been alone in this house for at least as long as I've been alive. I don't know why he doesn't hunt, but the last sacrifice my father sent was before I was born. No matter how good his control right now, it might not hold.

He might kill me.

"Let me go," I say quietly.

He slowly releases me and leans back to prop his hands on the floor. He's studying me like I'm a puppy who's done something unexpected. "You enjoyed what just happened."

Yes, I did. A lot. I also want it to happen again as soon as possible. I have too much self-preservation to admit as much, though. "Your bite is orgasmic. Of course my body liked it."

"Ah."

I need to get up, especially when I can feel his cock pulsing against me, but my legs aren't cooperating. Or that's what I tell myself as I glare at him. "And stop ambushing me. I get you need blood, and that's what I'm here for, but unless you want this sacrifice to be short-lived—literally—you need to knock that shit off."

His brows inch up, and he's back to looking like he's half a second away from laughing at me. "I'll take that into consideration."

"I'll need food, too." I brace my hands on his shoulder to push to my feet, but somehow my wires get crossed and I rock my hips against him. Just a little. I bite my bottom lip. "What are you *doing* to me?"

"Nothing." He very slowly, very gently, replaces his hands on my hips. "Nothing at all."

"I don't believe you." My desire is spiking again, my body hot and pliable. I have to get out of here, and I have to do it now. Otherwise I'm in danger of doing something unforgivable, like reaching between us to free his cock and taking him deep inside me. I want it. I want it more than I want my next breath.

I shove to my feet.

Or at least I try.

My bad knee buckles halfway up, and Malachi catches me before I make harsh contact with the floor, his hands beneath my knees. I barely have a chance to register what happened when he moves us, lifting me up and setting me on the counter. He pushes my dress to bare my knee and frowns at it. "This is recent."

No point in denying it. The truth is written right there on my skin in ugly purple scars. "Yes."

"I was under the impression dhampirs heal quickly."

"Not as quickly as vampires."

"That is not an answer."

He's like a dog with a bone. I don't understand where he's headed with this line of questioning. "Yes, I heal quickly."

"And yet you have an injury like this." His face takes on a forbidding look. "Explain."

Oh, for fuck's sake. I shove at his shoulders, but I might as well try to shove a mountain. Frustration bubbles up inside me, hot and cloying. "As I'm sure you've probably figured out, I didn't exactly volunteer for this gig. I tried to run. My father made sure I wouldn't be able to again."

He goes still in that predatory way that makes every instinct I have scream at me to flee, which might be laughable under other circumstances. Flee. Sure. That'll work out great.

Malachi's thumb traces the most prominent bit of the scar, the spot where my father beat my knee again and again until the bones were little more than pebbles. "There is no quick fix for this type of injury."

"Thanks for that, Doctor Malachi, but I'm already aware. Even with my accelerated healing, I'll never walk right again." It's something I can't think too closely about or it might be the thing that breaks me. My entire life has been spent running, even if it was contained within the colony walls. I've escaped beatings and worse because of my ability to flee. No longer.

He presses a hand to the center of my chest. "Stay."

"I am not your dog to command."

"Stay," he repeats.

I don't know why he bothers to tell me what to do. He moves so quickly, I barely have a chance to tense before he's back between my thighs again, this time holding a knife. I freeze. "A vampire with a knife. How novel." Which reminds me. I narrow my eyes, trying to ignore the blade glinting between us. "Return *my* knife."

"When I'm sure you won't try to carve out my heart, I will."

"Looks like someone already tried and botched the job." I jerk my chin at the mangled scars on his chest. "I'm more than happy to do it properly."

He chuckles, a dry rasping sound. "What's your name, little dhampir?"

As much as I want to dig in my heels instead of answering, it won't serve any purpose. I'm here for the foreseeable future. Might as well be on a first-name basis with my captor, willing or no. "Mina."

"Mina." He says it slowly. "It suits you."

"If you say so."

Malachi reverses the knife in a smooth move and presses it to the side of his throat. "You seem like a smart girl."

I blink. "Um."

"Too smart to deny yourself a tool, even if I'm the one giving it to you."

I don't know he's right about that, but I can't help staring at his throat as he drags the tip of the knife over his skin, leaving a thin trail of blood in its wake. My fangs ache in response. I might not require blood the way actual vampires do, but the desire is still there. "What are you doing?"

"Blood is power, little dhampir." He leans in, pressing against me, until his neck is a few spare inches from my mouth. "Drink from me enough and your knee will mend itself."

"Impossible." I throw the word out like a life preserver. "It's healed already."

"Not impossible." He tilts his head to the side, baring his neck completely. "Drink."

I shouldn't. It's another tie linking me to him. His bloodline's power might not be glamour like my father's, but sharing blood back is what vampires do to mind-fuck humans. I've never drank from a vampire before. I don't know what will happen if I do.

But if he's not lying... If it *can* heal my knee...

My tongue snakes out without permission and drags over his neck. That small taste feels like a nuclear bomb going off inside me. I stop thinking, stop trying to rationalize my way through this. I simply act.

I bite him.

I have no finesse, like he demonstrated even when he was tackling me to the floor that first time. I'm too desperate for more.

His blood is like lightning on my tongue. It lights every nerve ending up. I swear I can actually feel the power rolling through my body. I want more.

Malachi digs his hand into my hair and gently pries me off him. "That's enough."

"But—" I can't take my eyes off his neck. Even as I watch, the wounds close. "More."

"Not today." He steps back slowly, as if it pains him to put distance between us. "Get some sleep, Mina. You're going to need it."

I inhale. Even the air tastes different with his power flowing through my veins. "I don't want to sleep. I want to..." I look at him. He really is sexy in a brutal sort of way. I can appreciate that, appreciate his strength and the way his eyes bleed to black when he looks at me. "I want to fuck."

"Not that, either."

"Why not?" Is this what being drunk feels like? It's completely different from the bliss of his bite. That's a physical thing and it eases almost as soon as his fangs leave my skin. This feeling is in my veins, searing me right to my very soul. I shiver. "It's what I'm here for, isn't it?"

"Yes." He's studying me, but I'm too loopy to read his expression. "But not yet. If you still want my cock when you wake up, you're more than welcome to it."

"I want it now." I hop off the counter, but the world shifts, turning topsy-turvy on me. My bones go liquid and the last thing I feel before darkness claims me is Malachi's strong arms closing around me.

4

I WAKE UP IN THE SAME BED AS BEFORE. UNLIKE LAST time, I don't feel like I've been hit by a truck. I feel *great*. Like I've had a full night's sleep and a month's worth of well-balanced meals. I sit up slowly and look down. My dress is back in place, but a quick check shows the bite marks are healed as if they never existed.

I prod my knee, but though the pain is fainter than normal, I don't feel much different. Maybe it was all bullshit, but I can't deny I feel better than I have in months.

Maybe that's the point, though.

Biting him drugs me as much as his bite does. The first dose was free, but he'll demand I fuck him for another.

The thought should fill me with horror. Having sex with Malachi means playing out the scheme my father put into motion. But the thought feels distant. Malachi isn't anything like

I expected. Oh, he's vampire through and through—arrogant and predatory and sure that might makes right. But if he was as much monster as my father is, he would have taken *everything* he wanted from me that first time in the foyer. He'd have chained me to a bed somewhere and gotten down to business until I'm knocked up or dead.

But just because Malachi is taking a softer route doesn't mean he's a better person. I have to remember that. Even if part of me feels a thrill of anticipation at the thought of his hands on me again.

I climb carefully to my feet, and my knee doesn't buckle the way it sometimes does first thing in the morning. A few careful movements bring some pain, but my mobility is already better than it was.

Maybe he wasn't shitting me after all.

The thought rocks me back on my heels. *This*, out of everything, doesn't make sense. I'm here. I'm more or less willing to play my part. I might hold out as long as possible, but it's inevitable I end up in his bed at some point. Especially with that bite of his. He has absolutely no reason to heal me. None. Not when I've already admitted my father pulverized my knee because I have a history of running.

I don't understand this vampire, and that scares me more than anything else that's happened.

I make a circuit around the room. My suitcase is gone, which initially fills me with panic, but I find it tucked in the wardrobe, along with all my clothing, which has been unpacked. I frown at the neat row of shirts and pants and dresses. "Pushy."

The thought of putting clean clothes on without cleaning my body first makes me leave the wardrobe and go check the second door I didn't bother with this morning. Sure enough, it leads to a bathroom. I don't have high hopes for the plumbing, but when I turn the faucet on the large copper tub, the water comes out clear and hot.

I eye the door. I could try to block it, but what's the point? If he really wants into the room, he'll end up here, chair in front of the doorknob or no.

Will he see me *not* locking the door as an invitation?

I refuse to examine that thought too closely as I strip and step into the tub. The water is hot enough to make me hiss out a surprised breath, but I sink down into it all the same and lean my head back. I didn't realize how cold I was until now, when heat begins soaking into my body.

The creak of a floorboard has me opening my eyes to find Malachi leaning against the wall across from the tub. I narrow my eyes. "Did you make a sound on purpose?"

"You seem opposed to me surprising you."

"Gee, I wonder why?"

He crosses his arms over his chest, which leads me to realize he's changed since I saw him last, too. Now he's wearing a pair of low-slung pants...and nothing else. His body is too lean for his wide shoulders and sturdy frame, confirming my suspicion he's gone without regular feedings for a long time. And he's covered in scars. The one over his heart is the worst of them, but there are slashing and stabbing marks and more than a few bullet holes. And that's just what I can see from my position.

I frown. "If your healing power is so superior, why are you scarred up?"

"I'm surprised you don't know. If the wound is made with silver, it doesn't always heal properly." He touches the one over his heart. "The scarring is mostly surface-level, though."

I *hadn't* known that. Why didn't I know that?

I study him. "Are you here to collect your daily feeding?"

"You don't seem particularly opposed to the idea."

No, opposed isn't the word I'd use. Damn it, but even the sight of him has desire coursing through me. There's no point in denying it, either, because his senses are acute enough to pick up on all the signs. "Might as well get it over with."

Malachi's lips curve. "Such a noble sacrifice."

"You're stronger than me. Faster than me. And your bite ensures I become a willing victim the second you get your fangs into my skin. Fighting you is pointless, and I try to save my strength for battles I can win." It sounds logical enough, even if I feel anything but.

The bastard laughs. It's just as rusty as the last time. "No, Mina. I'm not here to take my *daily feeding*."

I draw my knees to my chest and refuse to categorize the sinking feeling inside me. "Then why *are* you here?"

"I suppose I owe you an apology." He studies me for a long moment. "All the others who've come through that door felt differently about the role than you do. If I hadn't been half-starved, I would have realized it."

Half-starved. *I knew it.* "Why wait for your meal to come to you? You're more than capable of taking care of it yourself."

He ignores the question and taps his fingers against his forearm. "I suppose if you want your freedom, you're more than welcome to leave."

Ah, so this is just another game. I glare. "You should really work on your sense of humor. You know as well as I do I can't leave."

"Do I?" He doesn't move. "Walk out the door. I won't stop you."

"And the guards my father has posted around the property?"

His mouth tightens. "I'll handle it. I'm more than capable of keeping them distracted long enough for you to slip away."

For a moment, I almost believe him. Freedom is what I crave more than anything else in the world. If there's a chance...

But then reality raises its ugly head.

I have nowhere to go. No money. No way to pass among the humans without raising some eyebrows and doing something that puts me on the government's radar. From there, it's a short trip to a padded cell, at best. At worst, to some scientist's lab to be experimented on for the rest of my life. With enough preparation, I might be able to slip into the world without a ripple, but I don't have that knowledge or the resources required.

Not to mention the fact that my father will not let me leave in peace. If he realizes I've run, he'll send his hunters after me. There's nowhere I can hide they won't find me, and when they drag me right back, I'll be worse off than I started.

No. No matter how much I dream of running, it's not really an option. It never was.

I close my eyes and fight against the burning behind my lids.

I don't know if he's doing this on purpose, but it feels particularly cruel to offer me what I've always wanted and force me to reject it. "I'm staying."

"The offer stands."

I press my lips together, hating the way the bottom one quivers. My anger feels so far away right now. *Everything* feels far away right now. "You are such a bastard."

"I've been accused of worse."

I finally look at him again. Desperate to focus on something else, I go back over what he said. How he apologized. How he dodged my one question. Why he'd be so starved even though he seems more than capable enough of hunting. I frown. "You're stuck here, too, aren't you?"

Malachi lifts a single shoulder. "It's complicated."

Complicated. Smells like vampire politics to me.

I push it away. It's a mystery for another day, and I'm suddenly too exhausted to poke at him any longer. "I suppose we might as well fuck since you've rubbed my nose in the fact that I'm stuck here."

He barks out a laugh. "Enjoy the rest of your bath, little dhampir." A blur of movement and he's gone, the door closing softly behind him.

Every time I think I've managed my expectations, he does something to pull the rug out from beneath my feet. I don't understand what's going on, and I don't feel like things are going to change any time soon.

It takes three minutes to acknowledge the relaxation of my bath is ruined. I wash quickly and get out. After some consideration, I pull on a pair of yoga pants and a baggy shirt before I leave the room. I need food.

And maybe part of me wants to provoke another encounter with Malachi. He's so unexpected, I never quite know what he'll do. Attack. Seduce. Apologize. He's brought my most unforgivable trait to the fore.

He's made me curious.

I make my way back to the kitchen and stop short in the doorway. It almost looks like a different room from the one I visited earlier. Every surface gleams and it smells faintly of lemon. The only thing that remains from yesterday is the faded paint of the walls. I walk to the fridge and pull it open, my jaw dropping at the sight of it filled to capacity with a wide variety of food and drink. "What the hell?"

I slept through the majority of the day, and I expected Malachi did the same. Sunlight is barely an inconvenience for vampires, no matter what the human legends say, but most of them prefer to keep nocturnal schedules to avoid the irritating brightness. Either there's someone else in the house with us... Or he cleaned the kitchen and stocked the fridge for me.

How the hell did he stock the fridge if he's trapped here?

"Tricky vampire," I murmur. I shove down the weird warmth in my chest. Of course he's ensuring I can feed myself. I'm no use to him if I starve to death, and no matter how much power his blood carries, I still need actual food to survive. The blood bank dries up if I die. Surely that's why he did this. Believing anything else is a fool's thought.

Refusing to eat out of spite is silly, so I grab the makings for a light breakfast that's heavy in protein. It feels strange to sit at the kitchen table and eat slowly rather than shove food in my mouth before someone decides to deprive me. My father always allowed me meals in a begrudging manner, as if my very need to eat inconvenienced him. It didn't seem to matter there were other humans in the colony who had the same biological requirements I do. Every reminder of my human side irritated him.

At least until he found a use for me.

I blink down at my empty plate. I'm not sure how long I've been staring at it. I give myself a shake and clean up my dishes and put everything away. I look around the kitchen again and frown. What am I supposed to *do* for all the hours in between Malachi biting me? In the colony, after breakfast, I'd immediately be put to work at whatever menial task I was assigned that day. Before my knee injury, I'd sneak in a workout at some point, too. The younger turned vampires loved to spar with me because it gave them an excuse to beat the shit out of me. They'll always be faster, but I picked up plenty of skills in the process.

With nothing else to do, I go exploring. The house is more or less what I expect. Room after room on the verge of decay, all with peeling wallpaper or fading paint. Dust covering everything. The whole house needs an update in the worst way.

I stop at the back door and stare out over the fields behind the house. A ring of trees mask the fence I know circles the entire property, a tall imposing iron monstrosity designed to deter even the most curious explorer. I'm reasonably sure I can wander anywhere within that fence without worrying about running into the guards, but I'm not willing to test it out. Not yet.

Instead, I turn around and head upstairs. More rooms, most of them bedrooms, but I hit the jackpot in the back corner of the house. I walk through the door and have the strangest feeling I've walked into a different building entirely. It's been converted to a passably modern gym. The walls are painted a new-ish white and the dusty carpet has been torn up and replaced with wood floors that are only moderately beat up. A free-weight set looms in the back corner, stacks upon stacks of weights on the bar. A fancy treadmill is pushed against the other wall, angled to look out the window. In the center is a mat similar to what we had in the colony for sparring.

Huh.

I poke at the treadmill, a bittersweet feeling rising in my chest. There was a time when I would have given my left arm to have access to equipment like this. A chance to properly *train*. My knee might feel okay right now, but I suspect it's a false feeling created as a side effect from taking Malachi's blood. No matter what he seems to think, even vampire blood can't fix something already healed. He'd have to rebreak my knee, and even then I doubt there's enough structure left to ensure it'd heal properly the second time. No, he's simply acting the way all vampires do naturally—with casual cruelty.

My neck prickles and I speak without turning around. "I thought you weren't going to sneak up on me anymore."

"It's not my fault your dhampir senses aren't acute enough to hear me coming, even when I'm not trying to mask my steps."

I turn to find Malachi's changed again. He's wearing a pair of loose pants, and he's foregone a shirt again. He's even tied back his long hair. Obviously, he's here to work out. I clear my throat. "Don't let me interrupt you. I was just checking out the house." I hesitate. "Um, thank you for the food. And for cleaning the kitchen so I can actually make it without worrying about giving myself some kind of lead poisoning or some shit from whatever old paint is on the walls."

He moves a few steps into the room. "Would you like to spar, little dhampir?"

5

I BLINK. HE WANTS TO *SPAR*? "WHAT?"

"It would be useful to see your skill level."

His words are logical, but that doesn't mean they make sense. "Why do you care what my *skill level* is? I'm only here for two reasons." Maybe that's what his offer is about. A reminder of my place here. I'm not foolish enough to nourish the false hope he's different from every single vampire I've ever known. The odds of that are astronomically not in my favor.

"Indulge me." The steel in his tone informs me this is less a suggestion than a command.

I could try to push back, but it'd just end in us sparring while I attempt to escape the room. The thought of him getting his hands on me again has my traitorous heartbeat kicking up a notch. "You just want to bite me again."

"If I want to bite you, I'll bite you." He moves closer, backing me onto the mat. "Surely your father didn't leave you completely defenseless. Show me what you can do."

I snort. "You have a heightened opinion of my father he doesn't deserve."

He clenches his jaw. "Trust me. He deserves everything I think of him."

Not sure what I'm supposed to say to *that*, but it doesn't matter because he strikes. He slows himself down enough that I can see him coming—but only barely. I jerk back, and I can actually feel the air displacement against my cheek where his fist moves. "What the hell?"

"Stop arguing and spar, Mina."

I try for a right jab, but he shifts out of the way. He's fast, and it feels like I'm moving through water by comparison. "Even a dhampir can't hold their own in a fight against a vampire."

"Sounds like an excuse to me." He hits me in the stomach. It's barely strong enough to knock me back a step. "Again."

I glare. "This is pointless."

Malachi arches a brow. "Is it? I already know plenty about you." When I glare, he jerks his chin at my body. "Your form is abysmal, you have no formal training, and you favor your injured knee even though it's not bothering you as much as it did yesterday."

I drop my hands. "Like I said, this is pointless."

"Are you going to flee from every single confrontation, Mina?" The question is quiet and strangely serious. "Are you so sure you know everything there is to know about the world at…what? Twenty-five years old? Can you truthfully say there's nothing left to learn?"

I open my mouth to argue but stop myself before any of the angry words can escape. It's like he's found a wound I didn't know existed and he's digging his fingers around in it. Finally, I say, "Why do you care?"

"You have potential."

That isn't an answer. Not really. "What does that mean?"

"There was a time when dhampirs were far more common than they are now. I don't know what your fool of a father told you, but you haven't begun to reach your upper limits." He's watching me closely, each word a precision missile aimed at the heart of me. "With proper nutrition and a steady diet of vampire blood, you'll be easily as strong and fast as a turned vampire. Possibly as a born vampire, albeit without the magical abilities."

"Don't lie to me." I sound too harsh, but I don't care. What he's saying… I know all too well how hope can become a weapon used to break an opponent. That has to be what Malachi is doing right now. It *must* be. "I know my role in all this. You don't have to be cruel."

He watches me for a long moment. "Give me a chance to convince you."

"*Why?* Even if what you're saying is true, why would you want me stronger? Then I could fight you off, possibly even kill you."

His lips curve. "I have my reasons."

Reasons that no doubt include tormenting me. I shake my head. "No. You get to fuck with my blood and my body. You don't get to fuck with my head."

"And if I offer you a bargain?"

It feels like my feet have sprouted roots, each one holding me in place when I just want to run away from this vampire and this conversation. But then, what would be the point? Even without my knee injury, he's faster than me. He'll *always* be faster than me. I swallow hard. "What bargain?"

"Train with me. Exchange blood. As long as you're doing that, sex is off the table."

I stare. "You're lying."

"I think you'll find, Mina, I never lie." He shrugs a single shoulder. "Sometimes I withhold the truth, but I give you my word I won't fuck you while you're meeting your end of the bargain." He flashes me a hint of fang. "Unless you ask nicely."

"It'll never happen," I shoot back, even as part of me wonders. I can't deny I want him, whether it's bite-induced lust or pure lust. He's gorgeous and strong and there's a sly intelligence in those dark eyes that draws me despite myself. I can't blame all that on his intoxicating bite, no matter how much I'd like to.

"Then you have no reason to say no to the bargain."

It's too good a deal. Why would he offer this? I frown. "Every time you bite me, I orgasm."

"I can't control that."

"And if I beg you to fuck me while I'm all drugged up on your bite?"

Another of those quick flashes of fangs. "I won't fuck you until you ask me nicely while my fangs aren't inside you."

I don't know if I believe him, but I'd be a fool not to take this bargain. What if he's *not* lying? "You have yourself a deal."

"Then we can begin."

I don't know what I expected, but Malachi immediately begins correcting my stance and then we proceed to spar in slow motion while he critiques me. I had thought I'd learned something in the colony, but with every word, he flays my confidence down to nothing at all. After an hour of it, he stands back. "That's enough for today."

I'm covered in sweat and shaking like a leaf. I'm not sure I have the strength to make the trip to my bedroom, but I'll be damned before I admit as much.

Malachi stalks to a low stool set against one wall and motions me closer with an impatient flick of his fingers. I tense. I know what comes next. The biting. "Why can't we do it standing?"

"Because you're going to collapse again and I have no interest in accidentally ripping your throat out."

My face flames. My embarrassment is made more overwhelming by the fact that he's right. I can't seem to control my body when he bites me. I pad to him slowly and don't argue when he takes my hand and pulls me down to straddle him on the stool. He runs a broad hand up my back to fist in my hair and tow my head gently to the side. I don't have a chance to brace myself before he strikes, sinking his fangs into me.

Gods, it's so good.

I clutch his shoulders and relax against him. His strength will hold me up, keep me caged, and I can't decide if it's a good thing or a bad thing. Why am I fighting this? It feels so good, it's hard to remember my reasons.

Each pull feels like he's stroking my breasts, my clit, my pussy.

His free hand lands on the small of my back, urging me closer, and I'm only too eager to obey the silent command. I *need*. I roll my hips, rocking against his hardening cock. It feels so good. Too good. If Malachi stripped us and bore me to the floor, I'd welcome him happily. Knowing that, somehow trusting he won't... It makes me bolder. I dig my fingers into his hair and moan.

Malachi growls against my skin, but instead of sucking harder, he lifts his head and drags his tongue over the spot where he bit me. "You taste too fucking good. I don't understand it."

"Keep going."

"No." He leans back, easily overpowering my hold, and reaches up to grab my chin. He runs his thumb over my bottom lip, urging my mouth open, and presses the pad of his thumb against one of my canine teeth. They're a little more prominent than a human's but nowhere near as long as a vampire's. He frowns. "I don't think you can break skin effectively with these little things."

"Wow, I didn't realize you were a size queen."

His grin is quick and nearly knocks me on my ass. "We'll have to improvise." As I watch, he drags his tongue over his tooth, cutting it. Malachi shifts his grip to the back of my neck. "Come here."

He doesn't even have to pull me. I'm already moving, diving down and taking his mouth. He tastes of blood and man and, *gods*, I can't get enough. I wish I could say it's because of the blood zinging across my tongue and setting fire to my veins as if he's poured lightning down my throat. That would be less unforgivable than the truth.

I like kissing Malachi.

He holds me easily to him and plunders my mouth. Tongue and teeth clash, this moment as much a battle as our earlier sparring. Maybe I shouldn't like that. Maybe I should crave a softer touch, something like my single kiss before this. A tentative brush of lips against mine. A stolen moment filled with yearning. At least on my side... At least until I realized Darrien only kissed me on a dare from his friends.

That slams me out of this moment. No matter how devastating this kiss is, Malachi isn't kissing me because he's so overcome with lust he had to have my mouth on his. No, he's playing a game of chess and I'm already seven moves behind.

I force myself to lift my head. It's only then I realize I can't taste his blood any longer. He healed while we were kissing. If I hadn't pulled away, would he have stopped me on his own? I look down into his handsome face, his eyes violently dark with desire, and I just don't know.

I lick my lips, tasting him there. "That's enough."

"As long as you're satisfied." His voice is as rough as I feel. He strokes the small of my back, the slightest touch that almost seems to urge me to keep riding him.

I want to demand he bite me again, do the one thing guaranteed to override my spiraling thoughts long enough for me to orgasm like this. Worse, I almost don't care if the bite is even involved. I want him to keep touching me, to keep doing this until neither of us can think anymore.

That's the problem, though. *I* might lose myself, but Malachi won't. I can almost guarantee it. Aside from that first time in the foyer, he's been perfectly in control during every encounter. Unlike me.

I shove to my feet and nearly land on my ass. For once, Malachi doesn't move to catch me, merely watching as I stumble back until I'm steady. I press my fingers to my lips. "Give me the knife back and you won't have to *improvise* again."

He smiles, flashing a little fang. "No."

"So this is all a trap. You say you aren't going to sleep with me and then you cross lines all over the place the first chance you get." I'm trying to work up a good mad, but my body is still crying out from the loss of his. I *ache* in a way I'm terrified only he can fix.

"Don't be naive, Mina. A kiss is not the same thing as sex." He leans forward and props his forearms on his knees. The position should look relaxed, but every one of my prey instincts is screaming he's half a second from pouncing on me. "When I fuck you, it won't be with a little tongue." Another of those slow smiles. "But if you're feeling needy and want me to kiss your pussy better, I'm more than happy to."

I take a measured step back. Now is the time to retreat, to take the out he's offered me and put some distance between us. It's what a smart woman would do in my position. But then, a smart woman would have run the second she had the chance and damned the consequences. I'm here. For better or worse, I'm choosing this. I lick my lips. "Prove it."

6

THE WORDS BARELY LEAVE MY MOUTH BEFORE HE'S ON
me, bearing me to the ground. Once again, he makes a cage of
his body and protects me from any impact. Malachi takes my
mouth in a rough kiss. His fangs nick my tongue. Or maybe it's
his tongue. Hell, maybe it's both. All I know is I taste blood and
add a bolt of sheer lust to what's already a tidal wave of desire.

He's already moving down my body before I have a chance
to sink into the sensation, kissing my breasts through my thin
shirt before he settles between my thighs. I prop myself up on my
elbows, breathless and a little shocked. "Um."

He trails his finger down the seam of my yoga pants, stopping directly over my clit. "Changed your mind?"

"No." The word bursts out before I can think about the intelligence of waving a red flag in front of a bull.

"Good." He does something, moving too quickly for me to follow. One second we're staring at each other and the next he's ripped my pants in half. The movement jerks my hips closer to him and then his mouth is on me.

I tense, expecting a bite. *Anticipating* a bite. But instead of the sharp pleasure of his fangs, it's the soft heat of his tongue. He licks a long line up the center of my body. It feels so wrong and so right at the same time. His growl vibrates through my pussy and my arms give out. "*Fuck.*"

That's when he moves up to drag the tip of his tongue over my clit. Over and over again. I thought this would feel different from when he bites me, and it does... But not as different as I expected. It's too good. Desire drugs me, molten and fluid, winding tighter and tighter through my body.

I don't make a conscious decision to move. One second I'm trying to get my equilibrium back and the next my hands are in his hair, pulling him closer even as I lift my hips to grind against his mouth. "Oh gods, that feels so good."

He makes another of those hungry noises and then his tongue is inside me. He spears me with it, and the intrusion has me crying out in surprise. Malachi withdraws a little and lifts his head to look at me with eyes gone dark and feral. For a second, I could swear I see flames licking in their depths, but I blink and the illusion disappears. He drags his thumbs down either side of my pussy. "Mina." My name sounds like a sin on his lips.

I have to swallow hard before I can speak. "Yes?"

"Are you a virgin?"

I really, really don't want to answer that question. It's too loaded, too filled with implications I want nothing to do with. Vampire culture doesn't place the same importance on virginity as human culture does—at least according to the media I've consumed—but it remains a *thing*.

He watches me closely. "Answer me."

"Yes." The word feels dragged from my lips against my will.

Malachi presses his forehead to my lower stomach for a long moment. "Okay." He exhales harshly. "Okay."

I don't know what he means. I just know I might die if he leaves me on this ledge. "Please."

"Give me a second."

Give *him* a second? What the hell kind of game is he playing right now?

My breath sobs from my throat. "Malachi." I dig my fingers into his hair, but I'm not strong enough to move him on my own. "Malachi, *please.*"

He hesitates and then his mouth is back at my pussy. He picks up right where he left off, spearing me with his tongue and then moving back to my clit. Each little circle he makes ratchets my need higher. He has to pin my hips in place to keep me from writhing too far from his tongue.

Between one gasp and the next, I orgasm. I cry out, the wave crashing over me strongly enough to leave me breathless. It feels so good, so incredibly good, just as good as his bite but at the same time better. And then he bites me and I lose my fucking mind.

I think I might be screaming. I can't tell. All I know is I manage to haul him up my body or maybe he's already moving up on his own. He claims my mouth and then he's between my thighs and thrusting, grinding his cock against my pussy, his thin pants the only thing keeping us from fucking.

I want them out of the way. I want him inside me. I *want.*

I open my mouth to tell him, but his tongue is there, stealing my words, my thoughts, my very sanity. One of us is snarling. It might be me. I can't stop, rolling my body up to meet his every stroke. I taste myself and blood on his tongue, and it only drives my frenzy higher. *More, more, more. Don't stop.*

I come again and he goes still against me. He lifts his head and this time I know I'm not imagining the flames in his eyes. I'm breathing so hard, I'm gasping. "Malachi?"

He strokes a hand down my thigh, hitching my leg up around his waist. His pants are wet, but I can't tell if it's because of me or because of him. He drops his head to my neck and keeps moving against me, rocking in an almost decadent motion. I cling to him, barely managing to keep from begging him to fuck me.

The first sign something's gone wrong is the heat flickering against my arm.

I open my eyes and shriek. "*Fire.*"

Malachi doesn't stop moving against me. He doesn't seem to notice the flames licking at the floorboards in almost a perfect circle around us. It's not getting closer, but *the room is on fire.* I yank on his hair. "Malachi." Still no response.

In a panic, I do the only thing I can think of. I squirm my hand between our bodies and grab his cock in a ruthless grip. He rears back, his eyes entirely black. Smoke burns my throat. "*Fire, Malachi.*"

He blinks and gives himself a shake. A brief wave of his hand and the flames smother themselves. "Sorry."

I stare at the burned floor. I know all seven of the bloodlines have different magical properties associated with them, but my father decided I didn't need to know more than that. He never saw fit to inform me that Malachi's is *fire*. I swallow hard, tasting ash. "Is that going to happen every time we make out?"

He slumps on top of me and gives a hoarse laugh. "No. I lost control."

That's not nearly as comforting as he seems to think it is. "Let me get this straight. We didn't even have sex and you lost control enough to set the room on fire."

He still seems to have no desire to move off me. "Your blood is intoxicating, little dhampir. It's easy to lose myself in you."

I blink at the ceiling. "So it's *my* fault you lost control and almost killed us both?"

"No." He finally sits back and pulls me up with him. "It's simply the way things are. But you were never in any danger. I wouldn't have let the fire touch you."

There *is* a perfect circle around us of untouched floor. "I can die from smoke inhalation. Or the floor could have collapsed and given us both an inconvenient stake in the heart. So yeah, I think I might have been in some danger."

He frowns at the charred boards as if he never considered those outcomes. But then, why would he? No matter that he keeps calling me dhampir, he keeps drinking my blood, he seems to forget sometimes I'm not operating on the same level he is. I think it might be a compliment if it wasn't likely to get me killed on accident.

Finally Malachi shakes his head. "It won't happen again."

"But—"

"It won't happen again," he repeats firmly.

Maybe I should let this go, but I can't quite manage it. "You've drank my blood several times in the last couple days and this hasn't happened before." He also wasn't licking an orgasm out of me before now, either, but surely *that* isn't enough to undermine his control so thoroughly. I have never heard of a vampire losing it like this during sex, let alone foreplay. Granted, my information is incomplete, but surely people would talk about it if it was a real risk? Vampires might be immortal, but that doesn't mean they can't be killed. Any of the seven bloodlines have powers strong enough to kill. If they lose it every time someone orgasms, their lines all would have died out a long time ago.

Malachi sits back on his heels and drags his hand over his face. "I underestimated the strength of your blood. It's increased my strength as a result."

I pull my legs to my chest, acutely aware my yoga pants no longer cover the essentials. "I thought you've drank from dhampirs before. Why didn't you expect this?"

"Because none of the dhampirs I've tasted before had this effect on me." His dark gaze turns contemplative, and I notice his pupils have retreated to their customary shape, no longer bleeding over the entirety of his eyes. "It's strange."

When it comes to vampires, *strange* is not an asset. Something akin to panic bleats through my veins. "Stop it."

"What?"

"I don't know what game you're playing, but stop it. I am not special and I am not a mystery and I'm not any of the other shit you're about to spout." It *has* to be a game. It's the only thing that makes sense. Rejecting his musings is the only thing that will keep me sane. The mystery he paints is too tempting by half.

Everyone wants to be special. To be unique. Me more than most. When you're a dhampir, especially one without a lick of magic to speak of, you can never measure up no matter what you do. Never strong enough, fast enough, just flat-out never *enough*. Malachi acting like this is just cruel. "Don't you think if my blood was some kind of magical booster, someone would have figured it out by now?"

His expression is painfully serious. "Have many vampires fed from you more than once?"

A fair question, but it stings all the same. "No. Of course not. I think my father had me destined as a sacrifice from the moment I was born, so he didn't exactly pass me around to his people." I look away. "I've been bit a couple times during sparring." And a couple times outside it. "But it was rare."

"By turned vampires."

"Yes."

"Then how would you know if your blood boosts a bloodline's power?"

I open my mouth but close it without answering. Again, a fair question. It doesn't make it less cruel. "I am not special."

He frowns. "Yes, Mina. You are. Even without the blood element."

That's about enough of that.

I shove to my feet and start for the door. I barely make it one step before Malachi sweeps me into his arms. He glares at my sound of protest. "You'll burn your feet."

"I just drank a bunch of your blood. I'll heal."

"All the same." Except he doesn't set me down once we're out of the room. He just keeps moving at that dizzying pace until we arrive back at my room. Malachi pauses in the doorway and sets me on my feet. He frowns at the bed. "I'll order new things for the room."

That startles a laugh out of me. "Oh, you're just now remembering maybe I don't want to sleep in a dusty old bed? Lovely."

He gives me a long look. "Are you angry about the fire or something else?"

It's so, so tempting to confess what has me twisted in knots, but if I honestly believe he's playing games with my mind, then telling him what I'm feeling is just opening a path for him to fuck with me further. I can't risk it. "I'm tired. Good night, Malachi." I shut the door in his face.

Even so, I clearly hear him through the thick wood. "I am not the enemy."

I want to believe him. I want it so badly I can taste it like the coppery tang of blood on my tongue. But there's one lesson my father taught me, one I cannot afford to forget. Not even with Malachi. Especially not with him.

Everyone is the enemy.

THE REST OF THE WEEK FALLS INTO AN INCREASINGLY familiar pattern. I wake up, wander down to the newly shiny kitchen for a meal and coffee, and then explore the house. At some point, Malachi shows up and drags me to spar and train. When I'm shaking with fatigue, he bites me. I always orgasm. I always bite him back.

But he doesn't kiss me or offer to *kiss it better* again.

Even as I tell myself to be grateful, my irritability rises with each passing day. I want him and I don't want to want him, and it was easier to live in my head when I told myself I didn't have a choice. Malachi is effectively undermining that narrative, and I'm not in the mood to be grateful. More, I'm mad at myself. I shouldn't want this. I shouldn't want *him*. Desiring Malachi is just playing into my father's plans, which is the last thing I want.

I'm so distracted by my tumultuous thoughts, I don't realize I'm not alone in the library for a moment too long. I catch sight of the blond vampire and jump off the couch I was sitting on, but I barely make it a step before he's on me. He digs his fingers into my hair and shoves me back onto the couch, following me down. He gets a knee between my thighs and grins at me. "What a delicious little thing you are."

Fear clamors in my throat, but I refuse to show it to this stranger. "I don't know who you are, but you have five seconds to get off me or I'm going to cut your fucking head off."

"So vicious." He says it slowly, like he's savoring it. "I like it."

In the flickering light of the fire, his features seem exaggerated. High cheekbones. Hollow cheeks. Freakishly pale eyes that still seem encased in shadows. His blond hair is cut into a short mohawk, and though he's smaller than Malachi, he's still stronger than me.

I am so fucking *tired* of everyone else being stronger than me. "Who the hell are you?"

His grin is a little deranged, flashing fang. "You can call me Wolf."

Wolf. The name tingles a memory, but I can't quite grasp it. Not when I'm in immediate danger of getting my throat ripped out. He's not one of my father's, though. I know that much. Which means he's a wild card and I can't anticipate what the hell he's going to do.

Except bite me.

That's all but guaranteed with the way he's watching my pulse thrum beneath my skin. "Malachi will kill you."

"Nah." He laughs. "We're old friends." Wolf raises his voice. "Aren't we, Malachi?"

"Wolf." I didn't see Malachi enter the room, but then I've been more than a little distracted. I turn my head as much as I'm able and find him standing a few feet away, his hands casually tucked into his pockets as if he's not witnessing a trespasser pinning me to the couch. "It's been a long time."

"Your choice. Not mine." Wolf transfers my wrists to one hand and turns to keep Malachi in his line of vision. "Imagine my surprise to find you're accepting sacrifices from that jackal Cornelius again. Tsk, tsk, Malachi. No one likes a hypocrite."

"Extenuating circumstances." Malachi's gaze flicks to me. "You have something of mine."

Wolf laughs again. The sound is downright sinful. It sounds like good chocolate tastes, decadent and a little bittersweet. "You've been alone too long, my friend. You've gotten greedy and forgotten how to be a good host." He licks his lips. "I'm positively *parched*."

Malachi hesitates for a long moment, and a traitorous hope whispers to life in my chest. Surely he won't let this stranger bite me. Surely he can see how much I am not on board with this idea. Surely...

"Help yourself." He drops into the chair across from us. "Biting only."

Wolf looks back at me, and the cruelty in his pale eyes is matched only by the amusement lingering there. "Did you think he'd step in? Poor thing, you've really done a number on her, Malachi."

"Wolf." The warning in Malachi's tone seems not to register. Wolf runs a single finger down my neck. His eyes flick to mine, and his grin softens the tiniest bit. "Don't worry, love. It'll feel good."

Which means he's a bloodline vampire, too. I don't care. "A chemical reaction. That doesn't mean a single damn thing. I don't want it."

He contemplates me, pointedly ignoring the way Malachi tenses in the chair at the edge of our vision. He inhales and goes still. "Ah. Not a human at all, are you? Dhampir." He settles down on top of me, using his body to keep me in place. He smells faintly spicy, like cloves and cinnamon or something similar. I hate that I don't hate it.

Wolf nuzzles my throat, and then his voice is in my ear, so low I can barely hear him. "Look how quickly he gave you away. Doesn't that make you angry? Do you see how still he sits? He doesn't want me to bite you, and yet he's not going to stop me. How does that make you feel?"

"Angry," I bite out.

"Thought so." His breath ghosts against the shell of my ear. "I'll do what he didn't. I'll ask permission. Let me bite you." He chuckles, low and decadent. "It'll piss him off something fierce."

He's trying to manipulate me, but even knowing that, it's working. I am *furious* at Malachi. Furious at myself for looking to him to be my savior when every other experience I've had with a vampire proves they can't be trusted. I forgot, and the sting of that knowledge is what prompts me to do something I never would have otherwise. "Do it."

"Wicked girl." He doesn't give me a chance to brace. He strikes, sinking his fangs into my throat. Instantly, pleasure pulses through me, heady and intense. Wolf's grip on my wrists keeps me from reaching for him, which is just as well. It doesn't stop me from arching against him and moaning. I'm angry enough that I don't try to fight it.

Malachi wants to give me to this vampire like a host offering a selection of wine? Well, he can damn well watch it happen.

I expect Wolf to pull something shady, but even as his cock hardens against me, he keeps his hands exactly where they started: one around my wrists and another braced next to my hip. The only move he makes is to stroke his thumb along the exposed skin at my side where my shirt has slid up during my struggle. It feels like he's touching me somewhere else. Or maybe that's the bite doing all the work for him, each pull as if he has his mouth all over my pussy.

I moan again. Distantly, I hear something crack, but I'm too invested in Wolf's bite to try to look. He presses a little more firmly between my thighs. Not quite a stroke, but it doesn't matter because it's enough to send me hurtling into orgasm. I come hard, panting out each breath. Distantly, I'm aware of him slipping his fangs from me and a little zing at my neck I can't identify. Then his tongue is there, cleaning the last of my blood from my skin.

Finally, a small eternity later, he releases me and sits up, flopping back against the other arm of the couch with a groan. "Malachi, you've been keeping secrets."

I turn my head, wondering at the lack of pain from the motion, and see that Malachi has completely demolished the arms of the chair where he's sitting. It looks like he exploded them; there's little more than kindling on the floor.

Petty satisfaction buoys me. There weren't good options in this scenario, but I chose this and I hope he fucking choked on the sight of Wolf on top of me. I ease up and lean against the other arm of the couch. My head is a little fuzzy from blood loss, but when I lift my hand to my neck, there are no wounds.

Wolf gives me a grin that's, well, wolfish. "You look surprised, love. Doesn't Malachi close the bite marks with his blood when he tastes you?"

"No." He lets me drink from him, which accelerates my healing. But I'm not in the mood to talk about this. I start to climb to my feet. "You are both assholes."

"Stay." The amusement disappears from Wolf's voice. "We have something to discuss and it involves you."

Even as I curse myself, I look at Malachi. He nods the tiniest amount. Not a command but a request. It doesn't change the fact that I'm pissed at him, but I relax back against the couch and pull my knees up. Wolf is still too close, and his spicy scent is all over me. It makes me want to simultaneously purr and scream, and I don't understand why I can smell him so intensely. He's not wearing any scent. There are no artificial tones in there that would signify perfume. But my nose has never been this sensitive before.

Wolf props his feet on the coffee table. I belatedly notice he's wearing a strange outfit. Fitted pants tucked into bulky black boots I suspect are steel-toed. A graphic T-shirt and a jacket that has a gothic feel to it complete the picture. He catches me looking and winks at me before turning his attention to Malachi. "You know the reason he sent her here instead of another one of those hapless humans is because he wants your bloodline."

Malachi doesn't move. "I'm aware."

"The second you knock her up, Cornelius is going to come collect his daughter, and then he'll have your child under his control—and as leverage."

It's exactly what my father has planned, but I can't help looking at Wolf more closely. He's given the impression of a vampire who's been around long enough to lose some of his sanity. Now he's lost the deranged tone and sounds nearly as serious as Malachi does normally. He taps his fingers on the arm of the couch. "You need to break the ward."

The ward?

What's he talking about?

I look at Malachi, but he's acting like I'm not in the room. He leans back against his chair as if the demolished remains of its arms aren't littering the floor at his feet. "Careful there, Wolf. One might start to think you care."

"That bastard having access to more bloodlines is bad news for all of us. His success with you has made him bold. He's hunting some of the others."

"You mean he's hunting you."

Wolf gives a blood-tinged smile. "He's trying. Unlike *some*, I haven't let honor get in the way of power."

I sit perfectly still, my mind racing to catch up and fill in the blanks. Some of it is easy enough. My father is responsible for Malachi being unable to leave. I'd wondered at that, but not as hard as I should have. Vampires are eccentric creatures under the best of circumstances. It seemed entirely within the realm of possibility that Malachi was more than happy to stay in this house and have his meals delivered to him. Yes, there was some starving in the intervening years, but it seems strangely logical to suffer that than try to step out into human society with all the technological upgrades they've made in the last generation. I suspect that's the main reason humans have driven vampires back, knowing about their existence or not.

Humans adapt and evolve. Constantly.

Vampires don't. Oh, they're capable of it, but it's harder for them because their very nature is as entrenched as their immortality. Or maybe all immortals face the same challenges of being unable to evolve. I don't know.

What Wolf is saying, though, contradicts my assumption. It sounds like my father trapped Malachi here with more than vampire guards to ensure he could take control of his bloodline. That he plans to do the same to the other bloodlines in danger of dying out.

Which means Malachi's as trapped as I am.

Surely not. Surely I'm misreading the situation. "If there's a ward, why not just burn your way out?"

Wolf's the one who answers. "That's not how wards work, especially not the ones your father uses." He says *father* like it's a curse. "He used a blood ward, and it would take a human sacrifice or a being more powerful than a vampire to break it."

Human sacrifice. Being more powerful than a vampire.

My mind is spinning, or maybe it's the room. I'm not certain. I'm not certain of anything anymore. "You killed the last woman he sent. Why not use her death to free yourself?"

Malachi makes a move that's almost a flinch. "I didn't kill her. She killed herself."

"What?"

Wolf stretches and yawns. "Blood wards won't hold me, which is the only reason that bastard hasn't managed to trap me yet."

If blood wards don't hold him, that means...

I thought I was afraid before. I really did. Now, I can barely breathe past the terror clogging my throat. Even if I was never officially taught about the bloodlines and which power goes with which or the members of the families still alive, I was taught *this*.

Seven bloodlines. Seven powers. The elementals: earth, air, water, fire. They're dangerous, can turn the very world around a person against them. But the other three? Body, blood, spirit. My father is the latter, and I've seen what he can do with glamour and illusion when he's angry. I've *felt* it, had my deepest, darkest fears dragged forth and shoved in my face. Had my very mind turned against me. If he can do that kind of damage with only the mind, what more can Wolf do with the blood?

I'm trapped in this house with two deadly predators, and right now they're both looking at me like I'm a tasty snack.

8

"I'M GOING TO BED." I PUSH TO MY FEET, BUT WOLF IS
there before me, moving so fast, I have to scramble back to avoid
running into his chest. I end up back on the sofa, staring up at him.

His pale eyes flicker red. "I don't think so."

"Wolf."

He takes a slow step toward me. "You are too careful,
Malachi. This girl tastes sweet and feels sweeter, and it's playing
with your head because you've been alone too long. She's a sweet
trap and you damn well know it. Kill her and free yourself."

He's not joking now. He means every word. He won't lose
sleep in killing me, and I don't know why that surprises me. Why
anything surprises me anymore. "Wait—"

"Back the fuck off, Wolf." The flames in the fireplace crackle
in a way that can only be described as menacing. "Now."

For a second, I think he won't do it. The red in his eyes edges into crimson and he looks downright feral for a moment. Just a moment, though. Between one blink and the next, he relaxes and grins down at me. "Ah well. Another time."

I can't move. I should fight, should scream, should do *something*, but it's all I can manage to draw in harsh inhale after harsh inhale. Malachi is dangerous, but even if I don't understand him, he's got some kind of reason for what he does. Wolf is a rabid dog, a chaotic gale-force wind that whips back and forth unexpectedly. Just when I think I might have a read on him, he turns around and tosses me off a cliff.

"Out." The quiet menace in Malachi's voice has goose bumps rising over my skin.

Wolf finally nods. "We'll talk more tomorrow." He turns and strides out of the room, moving at a human pace. I don't know why that's scarier than if he blurred away, but it is.

Between one blink and the next, Malachi is out of the chair and pulls me into his arms. "Mina."

"Get off me." I mean it to come out like a command, but it's a whispered plea. I can't stop shaking. What the fuck just happened? I don't understand what's going on, don't understand the players, don't even understand the game.

Instead of obeying, he scoops me into his arms and sits on the couch, tucking me into his lap. "I'm sorry."

"No, you're not. Stop saying that when you don't mean it." Oh gods, my voice sounds watery and my throat is burning. I will *not* cry in front of this vampire, will not expose yet another weakness in his presence. He already has me outmatched in every way measurable; I won't give him this, too.

But my body hasn't gotten the memo. Something hot and wet escapes the corner of my eye. I lower my head, and Malachi allows me that much, but he uses the opportunity to tuck me more firmly against his chest.

"I'm sorry," he repeats. "No one is going to kill you."

That draws a ragged laugh from me. I hardly sound like myself. "If not you, then Wolf. If not him, then my father will once I've played out my role." I thought I'd have more time, more opportunity to find a way out. I lied to myself about how outmatched I really am. There's no point in lying any longer. I am a pawn in other peoples' power games, destined to be moved from one side of the board to the other without any agency of my own.

Malachi's arms tighten around me. "I won't let it happen."

"What are you going to do? You're trapped by a blood ward, and the only way to get out is to kill me." There goes that laugh again. Gods, I sound deranged but I can't help it. "Checkmate."

"No." He strokes my head with a surprisingly gentle touch. "There's another way. I just haven't found it yet."

I want to believe him, but my life has taught me otherwise. There is no hero waiting in the wings to sweep in and save me. There is no convenient plot twist that will let the good guys win. The only thing that matters is power, and I have none. Even Malachi, a bloodline vampire, doesn't have enough to get out of this mess.

That's not the only thing weighing me down right now, though. I might be smarter if it was, if the only thing I cared about was getting out and being free. But there's a hurt deep inside, a betrayal I hate myself for feeling. "You gave me to him."

He tenses and then sighs. "It's complicated."

"It doesn't seem complicated from where I'm sitting. I thought..." But no. I can't put *that* foolishness into words. No matter how blurred the lines have begun to feel, the truth is Malachi is a predator and I am prey. He might insist on boundaries and bargains, but they're illusions. Just like with my father, he holds all the power and I hold none.

I try to straighten, but he keeps me pressed against him. I glare at his chest. "How far do *guest privileges* go? If Wolf gets an itch, should I expect him to show up in my room and fuck me? Since I'm a resource to be shared and all."

Malachi says something in a language I don't recognize, but the tone sounds like a curse. "*No.*"

"If you say so." I try to stop talking, but I can't seem to put the brakes on my mouth. The hurt and frustration and rage well up and morph into poison dripping from my lips. "Maybe I'll let him. Since you're not interested in sex, I might as well do it with someone else. Wolf's scary, but he's hot, and I'd hate to die a virgin."

The only warning I get is Malachi tensing beneath me. One second I'm cradled in his arms, and the next I'm straddling him and he's gripping my hips nearly hard enough to hurt. His eyes are edging toward black and I know enough now to recognize the flames they contain aren't the same ones reflected by the fire. It doesn't matter that I'm technically on top. I have no more control in this position than if he pinned me down onto the couch the way Wolf did earlier.

He glares up at me. "What the fuck part of me giving you

space to find your feet translates into that thick head of yours as I don't want to have sex with you?"

"*My* thick head? You're the one who laid down that ridiculous bargain!" I'm yelling and I don't give a fuck. "And yeah, I thought maybe you weren't a total monster but then Wolf shows up here like some kind of horny punk phantom and you're just like 'help yourself, my dhampir captive tastes really good.' It's bullshit. What am I supposed to think, Malachi? You don't fucking talk to me. We spar and we bite each other and that's all it's been for a week."

"A week," he grinds out through clenched teeth. "Seven fucking days. You spent your entire life under the thumb of Cornelius and then he shipped you off here where you're just as trapped. Forgive the fuck out of me if I wanted you to choose me instead of just going along with it because you had no other option."

I laugh in his face. "Choose you? What the hell are you even talking about? Choosing you means I get my heart broken in the bargain. The *best case* scenario is that you never manage to knock me up and I die of old age in a hundred years or so while you keep living forever in this house my father has trapped you in. I get wrinkled and gray and you stay exactly as you are now? Tell me how that's not just another kind of hell."

Something around his mouth softens. "You've thought about it."

"No, I haven't." It's not even a lie, not really. "But it's just how things are. I'm not that lucky. It's more likely to be a worst-case scenario and you know it. Either I get pregnant and my father comes to collect me, keeps me locked up long enough to have the baby, and then kills me, or I don't get pregnant and he decides he's tired of waiting and comes here and kills me. Do you understand what I'm saying, Malachi? No matter which way you look at this situation, I end up dead."

"I won't let that happen." The quiet confidence in his voice almost makes me believe him. Almost.

"Are you a god instead of a vampire?" I shake my head. "We're both trapped here. You should have told me the circumstances of your side of it."

He starts to speak and shakes his head. "You're right."

I blink. I didn't expect him to actually agree with me. "What?"

"You're right. I've played this all wrong." His grip softens on my hips and he nudges me closer to him, pressing us more firmly together. Impossible to ignore that his cock is rock hard. Apparently the regular feedings mean he doesn't have to bite me to get it up. I shiver.

Malachi dips his thumbs beneath my shirt and strokes my skin. "I should have been honest with you."

"Uh-huh." I lick my lips.

"Why don't we try some honesty right now?" He holds my gaze. "The reason I stopped doing anything but biting you is because I don't trust myself not to seduce you into having sex with me before you're ready. I fucking ache for you, Mina, but I want you to choose me because you want me. I don't want it to be coerced because you're out of your mind with bloodlust."

He said something to the same effect before, but part of me believed it was just another manipulation. It doesn't feel like that right now. I carefully set my hands on his chest. "And what about Wolf?"

Something like guilt flickers over his expression before he locks it down. "We're friends. Sometimes more."

Friends. Sometimes more.

The truth reaches out and slaps me in the face. "You want to share me for more than just blood."

He holds my gaze. "Wolf and I fuck, Mina. We have since we were teenagers."

I don't ask how long ago that was. The bloodlines have been dying out for a very long time. Malachi could be a hundred years old, or he could be five hundred. The gap between us already feels miles long without adding age to it.

I try to think, try to understand what he's saying and not saying. "So you're going to keep fucking Wolf, but you want to fuck me, too, and you'd be into me also fucking Wolf," I say slowly.

"More or less."

"I—"

"You don't need to say anything now." He releases me, and despite the fact that he's still pressed against me, I feel unmoored. "I just wanted to clarify where things stand."

"Are you going to fuck him tonight?" The question pops out before I can think too closely about why I want to know.

Malachi carefully lifts me and sets me back to my place on the couch. "That'll depend on what Wolf has to say when I talk to him later."

That wasn't a yes, but it wasn't a no, either. Something like jealousy flickers to life in my chest, even if it's a foolish emotion I have no right to. Malachi isn't mine. I didn't choose him. Even if I *did*, Wolf has a claim that precedes my birth, let alone this week.

It's too much. I don't know what to think, what to feel. "Oh."

He tucks a strand of my hair behind my ear. "No matter what Wolf acts like, he won't touch you without permission."

"Permission from you," I say bitterly.

Malachi snorts. "How quickly you forget *you* told him to bite you, little dhampir." When I open my mouth to protest, he beats me there. "It doesn't matter why you did it. The fact remains that you did, and so he bit you. If you hadn't, he would have backed off."

It seems to defy belief. "He had me pinned to the couch."

"Mmm." He looks at the fire. "It changes nothing. Wolf will manipulate if it suits his purposes, though, so if you don't want him to fuck you, be careful what you say when his fangs are inside you."

This conversation has taken too many strange turns for me to keep up. I study his profile. "And if I have sex with him?"

Malachi meets my gaze. "Someday, you'll believe I'm not your father. I have no desire to own you, Mina." His hand snakes out and he grasps my chin. "I simply want you."

"You don't even know me."

"I know enough."

I don't know why I'm so determined to push him, to shove my way through his carefully cool exterior, but I can't seem to stop. I lean into his grip on my chin. "And what happens if Wolf knocks me up, Malachi? If he gets there first because you're too busy being noble to take what you want?"

His eyes flare and I hear the fire hiss behind me. "Do you want me to fuck you, little dhampir? All you have to do is ask. All you've ever had to do is ask." He leans forward, easily holding me immobile. "But you *do* have to ask. We started things poorly, and I'm not interested in playing the part of marauding beast any longer. If we do this, it's because you're choosing it, not because I forced the issue. Until you're ready to admit that, it's not happening."

Damn him. That's exactly what I'm not quite ready to admit. No matter how much I hate it, it's easier to pretend I don't have a choice. How else am I supposed to hold on to my rage, the only thing that's kept me alive this long?

To avoid answering, I say, "You really were starving when I got here, weren't you?"

"Vampires can't starve to death."

No, they just turn into dried-out corpses without blood. It's one of my father's favorite ways to punish the vampires that cross him. When I was ten, he freed one that had been locked up for nearly a hundred years. I had nightmares for weeks. "Not to death, no, but you can starve."

Malachi looks away. "My condition is no excuse for attacking you."

Maybe not, but it creates a bridge of understanding I'm not sure I wanted. If Malachi is trapped here with a blood ward, he's entirely reliant on my father for blood. The last sacrifice was sent before I was born. Even if she lasted a few years, when I showed up, Malachi had gone without blood for at least twenty years. The fact that he had the restraint not to drink me dry, to try to prepare me for what was coming, is a little astounding when taken with that perspective.

He strokes my bottom lip with his thumb and drops his hand almost reluctantly. "Go to bed, Mina."

It's on the tip of my tongue to ask him to fuck me. I want it. I'd be lying to myself if I said I didn't. I might even like this vampire, though it seems impossible to wrap my mind around. But in the end, I can't speak the words that will unlock us from this stalemate.

I climb to my feet on shaky legs. "Good night, Malachi."

"Good night, Mina."

9

I CAN'T SLEEP. I SHOULD HAVE KNOWN IT WAS A LOST cause before even trying, but hope springs eternal. Even now. I can't stop thinking about all the new information this night brought, trying to puzzle through it to figure out what's true and what's manipulation. The possibility it might *all* be true is...

I don't know what to think.

Even though I know I should stay in the relative safety of my room, eventually my rushing thoughts demand movement. If I can just work off some of this frantically circling energy, then maybe something will make sense.

Or that's what I tell myself as I pad barefoot down the hallway. Dawn already lightens the horizon, another night having passed with us at a standstill. I press my forehead to the thick glass of the window and breathe slowly. The coolness does nothing to douse my thoughts, my feelings.

I want Malachi.

It takes *so much* to admit that truth to myself. I don't like it. It's inconvenient and messy, but it *is* the truth. I meant what I said before—there is no way for this thing between us to play out that doesn't end in heartbreak. It's an impossible situation.

But then, my entire life is an impossible situation. I've had no choice, no recourse, *nothing* that was mine and mine alone. Every single thing I've done is a reaction with the intent to survive.

What if I simply...said yes? Took what Malachi is offering? Took my chances with this small slice of pleasure?

I lift my head and sigh. I'm looking for an excuse to fuck him. Maybe I just need to stop trying to reason my way through it and simply *do* it.

I don't make the decision to head for the stairs. My body simply moves on its own, each step taking me closer to Malachi's bedroom on the third floor. Am I really going to do this? I don't know. I just don't know.

A sound cuts through my inner turmoil. A soft grunt. I stop short. It almost sounds like someone's in pain, but even without much personal experience with it, I know what fucking sounds like. I should turn around. Should take the humiliation heating my cheeks and let it increase the distance between me and Malachi's room.

I don't. I walk down the hallway. The door is cracked, which feels almost like an invitation to press two fingers to the thick wood and push it open a few inches more. Just enough to see his bed. Just enough to see what he's doing to Wolf in it.

My breath stalls in my chest and my feet sprout roots to hold me in place. Both men are naked. Wolf is on his hands and knees, each muscle in his lean body looking carved from stone as he shoves himself back against Malachi. No. That's not what he's doing. He's shoving himself back onto Malachi's cock.

And Malachi?

Gods, he's a masterpiece. His thick hair is flung over one shoulder and his big body is one hard line, his ass flexing with each thrust as he takes Wolf's ass. It's brutal and they both look angry, as if they started a fight and ended up fucking despite themselves.

I should leave. Should walk away. Should do anything but stand here and watch like the worst kind of voyeur.

I wait for hurt or betrayal to rise, but there's nothing. He told me, after all. He and Wolf are friends who are sometimes more. No matter what Malachi wants from me, he obviously wants Wolf, too. I don't understand their history, don't really get how they can be so antagonistic and still seem to care about each other.

Wolf turns his head and meets my gaze. His eyes are the same crimson they were in the library and he grins, flashing fang. He opens his mouth, but I don't wait around to hear whatever he's about to say.

I turn and flee.

Each step brings a recrimination with it. Coward. Fool. Weakling. I say I want Malachi, but then the second I get the hint of an invitation to join in and I'm fleeing like a scared little girl.

I stop short at the top of the stairs. What am I doing? I make a decision and then instantly backtrack? Is that really what I'm made of? I close my eyes and take several deep breaths. I'll just talk to Malachi about it tomorrow like a reasonable person. That's a logical way to proceed. A nice easy pace.

"What a little coward you are."

I startle and start to tip down the stairs. My stomach goes weightless and I start to curl in on myself to minimize the damage I'm about to receive.

Rough hands grab my upper arms and yank me back to the relative safety of the third floor landing. Back against a naked chest. I don't have to look to know it's Wolf. He's shorter and leaner than Malachi. And even after only one encounter with him, I recognize the casual cruelty in the amused tone of his voice.

"Let me go."

"Is that any way to say thank you? You might be hardier than a human, but a broken neck is still a broken neck." Wolf doesn't release me. He buries his nose in my neck and inhales deeply. "Gods, you smell good. Or rather, your blood smells good. How you managed to survive this long while walking around like the best kind of candy is beyond me." His lips brush my throat. "Someone should have sucked you dry by now."

I swallow hard, the movement pressing my throat more firmly against his fangs. "Wolf."

"I like the way you say my name, love." He doesn't move back, but he also doesn't close that last minuscule distance between us to draw blood. "Makes me think I'll like it even more if you say it while I'm inside you."

I shiver. "You seemed busy."

"I am. Malachi and I just hit pause for a brief moment." He gentles his grip on my upper arm and then his thumbs brush the sides of my breasts. "It'd be a shame if you got the wrong idea. That look back there was an invitation." He eases me back more firmly against his chest. His cock presses against my ass, which is right around the moment when I realize he's still naked. "Join us."

Join us.

Climb into bed with those superior predators and hope I live long enough to enjoy the consummation. I lick my lips. The unforgivable dark part of me wants to do exactly that. I don't think I like Wolf, and I'm not sure I trust Malachi, but my body doesn't care. It craves pleasure in a way that scares me. One hit might be enough to chain me to them forever. I can't risk it. I refuse to. "No."

"Mmm." He keeps stroking my arms, a relatively innocent touch if I could ignore the naked body and giant cock pressing against my back. "Malachi's made his wishes clear. Your precariously short life is safe with me." His lips brush my throat with each word. "Life. Body. Pleasure."

The man weaves a spell with his words, and it's like my pulse responds to him, each beat of my heart a surge of desire I don't want to feel. If I didn't know better...

I jerk away, and he releases me easily. The feeling doesn't get better with a few feet of distance between us. It's as if he's stroking my body without touching me, sending heat to my breasts and pussy. I press my hand to my chest, realization dawning. "Blood."

"Hmm?"

I stare. "Your bloodline's power is actually *blood*." I suspected as much, but this confirmation staggers me. He could kill me *so easily*, all without raising a finger. A thought and he could send all the blood in my body surging free, draining me in seconds. I shudder. "Stop it."

"If you insist." He shrugs. "I hear it's quite pleasurable."

It is. That's not the problem, though. I am outclassed and outmatched and every second I spend in this house only reconfirms the truth that I'll never have the upper hand. Malachi's fire is scary enough. How can I battle against the very blood in my body? "Don't do that again."

"Fine." Another of those put-upon sighs, but then he grins, his pale eyes lighting up. "I promise not to do it again...until we fuck."

"Who says we're fucking?"

He smooths a hand over his short mohawk, his grin widening. "Fun little side effect of my powers is I can sense blood. Do you know what gets the blood flowing, love?" He doesn't wait for me to answer. "*Desire.*"

Impossible to argue when he already has evidence of it. Especially because I can't blame a bite for it this time. No, it's just my fucked-up head that looks at two men who can easily rip me limb from limb and decides *that* is what'll get me off. "Feeling desire and acting on it are two very different things."

"So they are." Another shrug as if he couldn't give a fuck.

Somehow, in the midst of all this, I forgot he's naked. Now that the shock of his powers has faded a little, it's impossible for me to keep my attention on his face. His skin is several shades lighter than Malachi's, a pale that almost looks unreal. Though he's built leaner than Malachi, too, there's plenty of muscle definition drawing my eye down, down, down, to where his hard cock juts forth.

Fuck.

"Another perk." His amusement is cutting. "With a little blood in my body, I can keep it up for days if I want to. Think of all the pleasure I can give you, love. Come back to the bedroom with us."

I shake my head slowly. The thought of fucking for *days* blows my mind. I can't... I shouldn't... I swallow hard. "I said no."

"So you did." He turns and starts ambling toward Malachi's bedroom. "Ah well, consider this an invitation to watch, then. I promise to be on my best behavior."

"Do you have a best behavior?"

He laughs. "Not even a little bit." Wolf pauses in the doorway. "But Malachi does. He's got enough for all of us." He disappears into the room before I can form a response.

What is there to say?

Walking into that room is a mistake. It's a *choice*. I can't pretend someone forced my hand or I was influenced by anything but my own lust. If I cross that threshold, there's no uncrossing it.

Isn't that what I came here for tonight, though? I didn't bargain on Wolf, but I should have. Malachi as much as told me he and Wolf have a long and complicated history. I might not have fully comprehended they were a package deal. But that doesn't change the fact that apparently they *are*. Can I live with that?

I don't know. There's so much I don't know.

Except...

All I'm doing is stalling, putting off the inevitable. I made my choice already. It might be the first fucking choice I've *ever* made, but it's mine. I close my eyes and inhale slowly. I don't think I'm ready to jump into bed with both of them. But the idea of watching?

I want that. I didn't realize how much I wanted it until Wolf offered that option. A way to dip my toes into the water. I know I'm making excuses to do what I want, but it doesn't matter as I retrace the path to Malachi's door.

The men have their heads close together and are speaking in low voices. They turn as one and I have to fight the instinctive urge to flee. I swallow hard. "I'd like to...watch. If that's okay with both of you."

Wolf grins. "You know it's more than okay with me, love."

I glare at him, but it feels half-hearted. Against my better judgment, I'm starting to like his irreverent attitude. Kind of. I don't know what it says about me, but I'm nowhere close to a place where I want to analyze that. I lick my lips and focus on Malachi. "Is that okay?"

He searches my face for a long moment but must find whatever he's looking for because he nods slowly. "Yes, it's okay."

10

I DON'T KNOW WHAT I EXPECT, BUT IT'S NOT FOR THE vampires to start making out as if I'm not in the room. I look around and finally move to the chair near the bed and sink onto it. Wolf digs his fingers into Malachi's hair and wrenches his head back, deepening the kiss. They're like two titans clashing, powerful predators at the top of their game and grappling for dominance.

It's really, really sexy.

They seem totally lost in each other, which allows me to settle into the strangeness of this situation. To begin to enjoy myself. Malachi shifts in one of those blurring moments and bears Wolf to the bed hard enough to make the other man grunt. The sound reaches across the distance and sends a bolt of pure pleasure through me.

I shift in the chair, pressing my thighs together. It doesn't alleviate the pressure at all. If anything, it makes it worse. Gods, I need to get control of myself.

Except...

Do I?

Malachi brackets Wolf's neck with a big hand, forcing his head to turn to face me. "Look what you've done." He hardly sounds like himself, his voice deeper and containing a rumble that nearly makes *me* moan. "Started something neither of us can finish tonight."

Wolf grins, completely unrepentant. "Speak for yourself. Not all of us have that inconvenient noble streak of yours."

He growls. Literally *growls*. "Mina, stroke your clit or I'm going to come over there and do it for you."

I jolt. "What?"

"You heard me."

I am seriously tempted to call his bluff, but I'm not sure it *is* a bluff. I'm also not sure I want to pull the tiger by his tail. Malachi's managed to restrain himself until now, but if I keep poking him, he might finally force me to put my money where my mouth is.

I reach down beneath the hem of the oversized shirt I'm wearing and touch myself lightly. My breath hisses out before I can stop myself. The evidence of my need wets my fingertips and it's a wonder I haven't soaked through the chair. I lean back against it and drag my middle finger over my clit. This time, I can't stop my moan.

Both men give moans of their own, the merging sounds making me look up and freeze. They're both staring at my hand, their eyes gone molten with their respective magics. Malachi drags his thumb along Wolf's jaw. "Pull your shirt up, little dhampir. Show us."

We're dancing on a bladed tightrope. One wrong step and this will blow up right in our faces. Or maybe only mine. How far can I push these two before I end up in bed and we all throw my hesitance right out the window? Do I *want* that?

I pull up my shirt before I can admit the answer to that question, baring myself from the waist down. After the slightest hesitation, I spread my legs a little, angling so they can see everything. Wolf starts to sit up, but Malachi pins him down and reaches between them with one hand. I can't see exactly what he's doing, but a few seconds later, Wolf tenses and moans. Malachi begins moving and... Oh. *Oh*. He's fucking Wolf.

Oh my gods.

I stroke myself faster, watching the roll of his hips, watching the way Wolf's muscles flex as he tries to take Malachi's cock deeper. Wolf curses softly. "He's got a giant cock, love. Feels so fucking good inside me." He grins, his eyes going crimson. "Just imagine how good he's going to feel inside you."

I don't know if I *can* imagine it, but my mind is only too happy to make a liar out of me. Desire spikes and I have to force myself to slow down, to draw this out. I don't want to come too fast. "I'm imagining it," I whisper.

Malachi slows down, seeming to give me his full attention despite being seated deeply in Wolf's ass. "We aren't fucking you."

"Pity," Wolf murmurs.

"We aren't fucking you," Malachi repeats more firmly. A slow smile pulls at the edges of his lips, an expression downright wicked. "But you're welcome to Wolf's mouth while I fuck *him*."

That's a mistake.

I ignore the voice and nod. "Yes, I want that."

"Thought you might." He pulls out of Wolf and takes the other man's jaw in a tight grip, forcing him to meet Malachi's eyes. "One wrong move and I gut you."

Wolf laughs. "It's always gutting with you. That shit *hurts*, Malachi."

"Which is why it's a deterrent and a punishment." He leans back and slaps Wolf's side. "On the floor in front of her."

He moves slowly, obeying but doing it on his own timeline. Wolf kneels in front of my chair. He looks at me for a moment and then moves in a rush, grabbing my shirt and hauling it over my head. I'm naked in an instant and he bands his arm over my lower stomach as I lurch forward, instinctively grabbing for the shirt. "Ah ah. Give our Malachi something to look at." Another of those infectious grins. "He's a breast man and yours are superior."

I'm still trying to form a response as he lowers himself and takes my pussy with his mouth. There's no other way to describe it. Wolf doesn't ease into it. He doesn't taste. He simply devours me. I moan, every muscle going molten even as every nerve ending lights up.

Malachi moves to kneel at Wolf's back. I catch sight of a bottle of lube in his hand and then he's fucking Wolf. It must feel amazing, because the other man moans and starts fucking me with his tongue.

I don't know where to look, what to feel. Wolf's hands gripping my thighs, his eyes crimson as he edges me closer and closer to orgasm. At the lean strength of his body, which flexes with each thrust Malachi makes.

Or at Malachi himself.

He has one hand on Wolf's hip and the other on the opposite shoulder, holding the other man in place as he fucks him in short, brutal strokes. But his eyes are on me. His gaze touches on my mouth, my neck, my breasts, before moving down my stomach to where Wolf's head is buried between my thighs.

"She tastes divine, doesn't she? Just as sweet there as she is in her veins."

Wolf makes a sound of agreement but doesn't lift his head. He works my clit with his tongue, finding the touch that has me clenching in response and repeating it mercilessly. I reach back over my head to grip the chair. The position puts my body on display, and the way fire flickers in Malachi's eyes speaks to how much he likes the sight.

Words rise up, words I'm not sure I won't regret.

I changed my mind. Fuck me. Fuck me until we forget all the reasons this might be a mistake.

My orgasm hits me before they can slip free, barreling into me and bowing my back. I cry out as the pleasure goes on and on and on. Malachi finally curses and grabs the back of Wolf's neck, wrenching him off me. Or trying to. The other man drags me with him, taking me half out of the chair. I let loose a startled cry, but then it's too late. I'm on the floor with them.

Malachi curses and Wolf pins me beneath him.

I freeze at the feeling of his cock pressed against me, at his face so fucking close. His beauty is downright otherworldly, and I know I should be scared, but I can't quite manage it. I lick my lips, and he follows the movement. One thrust and he'll be inside me. I can feel Malachi holding his hips, holding him back from that last little bit of distance.

"I'll hold still, love." His voice is pure sin, as tempting as Lucifer himself. "Rub yourself all over me while Malachi fucks my ass."

Reckless doesn't begin to cover agreeing to this, but I'm already nodding. My body doesn't care about the risks. His hard length pressing against my pussy is a temptation I can't resist. "Yes."

Malachi grips Wolf's throat and bends him back a little, shifting so his face is nearly kissably close to me. He looks at me, but his words are all for Wolf. "That virgin pussy is mine, Wolf. If you fuck her tonight, I'll rip your goddamn throat out."

Something like shock flares on Wolf's face, but it's gone in an instant, replaced by what I'm coming to recognize as his default expression: a mocking smile. "And here I thought we were sharing the pretty toy."

"We will." Malachi says it so casually, as if it's a foregone conclusion. I'm not sure he's wrong. "But not the first time."

I swallow hard. "Do I get a say in this?"

His expression goes downright forbidding. "Not tonight, you don't."

I start to argue, but what's the point? He's honoring my wishes, even if I'm questioning my own fortitude to maintain those lines. I reach past Wolf to brush my fingers against Malachi's mouth. He holds perfectly still, letting me drag my thumb over his bottom lip. I shift my touch over his jaw. "Okay."

"Not arguing?"

"No, not arguing." I shift a little, all too aware of Wolf's body against mine, of Malachi very carefully not adding his weight into the mix. "Thank you."

He grabs my wrist and turns to press a kiss to my palm. "Now be a good girl and rub your pussy all over Wolf's cock until he comes." He starts moving again, resuming his fucking, each thrust making Wolf jolt against me a little. It's beyond sexy.

I arch up as Wolf bears down, closing the distance so there's no chance of him slipping inside. I roll my hips, rubbing myself up and down his length. It's positively decadent, the sensation heightened by the feeling of playing with fire. One wrong move and we cross the line Malachi drew in the sand. I don't necessarily *want* to cross the line, but the knowledge it's there heightens my pleasure.

Wolf catches my hips, urging me into longer strokes that send my thoughts scattering like flower petals in the wind. "I bet you feel empty right now, don't you? Needy."

He's right, but I can't catch my breath to tell him so. Each stroke has me dancing closer to the edge. "Gods, Wolf."

He goes stock-still. "Fuck, but I like it when you say my name." He kisses my neck. "What do you need, love?"

I answer before I can think about the wisdom of it. "Bite me."

He doesn't hesitate before sinking his fangs into my throat. I grab his hips and frantically chase my orgasm. One stroke. Two.

Then I'm coming, crying out in a ragged breath as I do. Except it doesn't stop. The orgasm rolls over me again and again, and I can't stop writhing, rubbing against him, trying to get closer, desperate for something I can barely conceptualize.

"*Wolf.*" Malachi's snarl slams me back into myself. He's farther away than I expect. I catch sight of him standing in the bathroom doorway, a cloth in his hand.

Wolf and I both go still. My heart is beating so hard, I feel dizzy. Or maybe that's the danger screaming through my veins at the feeling of the broad head of Wolf's cock pressing against my entrance. "Wait."

"She's so wet." I can't see Wolf's expression with his face buried against my neck, but his voice is downright feral. "So tight, Malachi. So needy for a cock." His hips flex, pushing into me the tiniest bit. "Might be worth getting my throat torn out." He strokes a hand down my side, but I can't tell if he's trying to soothe me or hold me down.

Another of those tiny flexes and he pushes farther into me. It feels good and bad and, oh gods, I don't know if I want him to stop.

I don't get a chance to decide. A blur of movement and then something hot and wet hits my chest and stomach. I freeze, my fangs aching at the copper scent filling the air.

Wolf slumps to the side of me, bleeding from his throat. Even as I watch, the wound starts healing, fusing together faster than I could have imagined possible. That doesn't change the fact that Malachi just...ripped out his throat.

And then Malachi is there, covering me with his big body.

Wolf's blood slicks our skin against each other, the scent of it only heightening my desire. I reach down with a shaking hand and drag my fingers through where it coats my breasts.

Malachi catches my wrist as I raise my fingers to my mouth. "Not yet."

"But—"

"I said I wouldn't do this." He curses long and hard, looking like an entirely different person, a creature more beast than man. "Say yes, Mina."

No mistaking what he means. No pretending I don't know what I'm going to get if I agree. I don't know if he'll let me walk out of this room if I tell him no, but I believe with my entire heart he'd try.

I don't want to say no.

I take a shuddering breath, allowing myself to be lost in the flames in his dark eyes. There are so many things I once believed I should want, but there's no place for *should* here. There is no future, no past, nothing but this moment where the two of us perch poised on the precipice of no return. Wolf, too.

I lick my lips, tasting Wolf's blood there, too. It zings through me, just as potent as Malachi's but different. His tastes as hot as his flames do. Wolf's is spicy and somehow barbed. It tastes better than alcohol, but I knew my answer before it hit my veins. "Yes."

11

MALACHI KISSES ME. IT'S JUST AS CONSUMING AS EVERY other time, and I dig my bloody hands into his hair as I lose myself in his taste. I'm only vaguely aware of him moving our bodies, hitching one of my legs up and around his waist. He drags his cock over my pussy and then his broad head is pressed against my entrance.

I tense, but he doesn't shove inside. He leans back enough to meet my gaze. "The first time can be painful."

Trying to think past the buzzing in my veins is almost too difficult. "I know that."

"I'm going to bite you to negate that." He hesitates, suddenly looking more like the man I've been spending so much time with rather than the monster who just ripped his friend's throat out so he could fuck me first. "Are you sure, Mina?"

I pull on his hair, frustration getting the better part of me. "I've never had a choice, Malachi. Not once in my fucking life. I'm saying yes, choosing this. Stop questioning it and fuck me."

Wolf gives a wet laugh from where he's leaning against the side of the bed, his hand against his healing throat. "You heard her."

"I'll deal with *you* presently."

"With more orgasms, I hope."

Malachi gives an exasperated rumble. "Shut up, Wolf."

"Yes, Sir."

I whimper. "Malachi, *please.*"

He hesitates for so long, I think he might have changed his mind. But before I can say anything else, he curses and strikes, sinking his fangs into my throat on the opposite side of where Wolf did. At the same time, he drives into me. I get a blast of pure agony and then the pleasure of the bite takes over, washing it all away in a tidal wave of need. I think I scream. Maybe I black out. I don't know.

The next moment, I come back to myself, my legs locked around Malachi's hips and my fingers tangled in his hair as I rise to meet each slow thrust. Pain and pleasure dance together in an elegant symphony. "Oh *fuck.*"

Malachi slows down and lifts his head a little. "Stay with me."

I run my hands down his broad back and dig my nails into his ass. "Don't stop." I moan. "Don't you dare stop."

His pace hitches, but he recovers quickly, kissing me as he resumes that slow fucking. He's big, and he feels bigger inside me than he did when he was pressed against me. I revel in the fullness, in the way my body stretches to accommodate him.

"Malachi."

We go still at the warning in Wolf's tone. Malachi shudders out a breath. "I have it under control."

"Do you? Because I have no desire to die in a fire because you're so lost in our Mina's sweet pussy that you burn the house down around us."

"I have it under control," Malachi repeats.

It's right around then I notice the flames behind him are roaring high enough it looks like they might burst out of the fireplace at any moment. I should care, but I really don't. I dig my fingers into his ass again. "Don't. Stop."

"I won't, little dhampir. I won't ever stop." He kisses me again and resumes moving, driving me higher and higher.

Part of me wishes I could blame this on the bite, but it's pure Malachi. He's overwhelming, and the fact that we're fucking while covered in Wolf's blood only makes this more depraved, more perfect.

I catch sight of the pulse thrumming in his neck and bite him without thinking. It's messy—my fangs really *are* too small to serve their purpose—but Malachi shoves his arms between my body and the floor, lifting me closer to him so I have better access to his neck. So he has better access to my pussy. He shifts the angle just enough that, combined with his blood coating my tongue, I scream my way through another orgasm.

It's like lighting a match in a room full of gunpowder. He crushes me to him and then he's driving into me just shy of brutally, rumbling my name as he comes.

We slump to the floor and I stare at the ceiling, wondering

if the stars themselves have been rearranged. It feels like they should be. The world is no longer the same as it was an hour ago. Nothing will ever be the same again.

"Malachi." Wolf's tone is dry. "Control yourself."

I twist just enough to see the fire has escaped the hearth and is snaking its way toward us. Malachi curses and it immediately reverses course, shooting into the fireplace and returning to a normal-sized flame. He eases off me. "Did I hurt you?"

"Not in any permanent way." I ache all over, but it's nothing compared to the pleasure pulsing in time with my heartbeat. I lift a hand to my mouth. I feel...different. Strange. I give myself a shake. Of course I feel different. I just had sex for the first time. More, I just all but agreed to have sex with *both* these vampires in the near future. I am a stranger to the woman I was two weeks ago.

Malachi sits up and leans over to peel Wolf's hand off his throat. The skin there is new and pink but intact. "Sorry."

"No, you're not."

"No, I'm not." He grabs Wolf's chin and pulls him forward into a quick kiss. "Maybe one day you'll be able to resist pushing."

"Unlikely. If it hasn't happened yet, it's not going to."

The fact that they're joking after Malachi ripped out Wolf's throat is so purely *vampire*, I almost laugh. But the events of the last hour are catching up to me quickly and I'm starting to shake. Malachi notices first. He stands, scooping me into his arms. "On your feet, Wolf."

"So bossy." Wolf staggers up and follows us into the bathroom. Malachi's bathroom is even bigger than mine, with a tub large enough to be termed a pool. Wolf moves to turn the tap on without prompting, but Malachi heads directly for the shower. I understand the moment he sets me on my feet and I get a good look at the three of us. I knew we were covered in blood, of course, but seeing it now that the adrenaline and lust are fading hits differently. We look like we've just survived a massacre.

I let Malachi tow me beneath the spray, but then I try to pull my hand from his. "I can wash myself."

"Hush."

I blink. "You did not just *hush* me."

"He did." Wolf steps into the space behind me, and suddenly the roomy shower feels almost crowded. He catches my hips. "Malachi is feeling guilty. Let him make it up to you."

I look up at the vampire in question and I'm shocked to find that Wolf's right. There's something akin to remorse in those dark eyes. He and Wolf guide me farther into the water and the blood runs off my skin in waves. I'm so busy trying to process the guilt, I let them wash me.

It feels...good. For once, it's not sexual, but the sensation of skin against skin is almost too much for me. I've been touched more tonight than I have in the past five years combined. Gods, that's depressing, but after I turned eighteen, touching meant a beating or some other kind of torment. Better to avoid it altogether. I didn't realize how much I missed it until now.

Once they're satisfied, Malachi shuts off the water and they guide me to the tub, now filled with steaming water. It stings as I step into it, but the heat quickly soaks into my bones and I sink down with a groan.

I don't know why I'm surprised the men follow. They take up positions across from me, creating a little triangle with the three of us. The tub is so large, there's still plenty of room, which might make me laugh if I had the energy for it. As it is, I'm suddenly so exhausted, I can barely keep my head above water.

Malachi sighs. "Come here, Mina." He doesn't wait for me to respond, just reaches over, grabs my wrist, and tows me over to half float in his lap. He guides my head to his shoulder, and the position allows me to relax fully. He carefully sets his hands on my hips, keeping me anchored in place. "I didn't mean for it to happen like this."

"There he is." Wolf laughs. "So eager for that guilt. She said yes. That's consent."

"I promised I wouldn't."

I give in to the feeling of gravity weighing my eyelids down. "I wouldn't have come to your room if I didn't want to end up in some variation of what happened." It's the truth, even if I couldn't admit it to myself until the moment Wolf tempted me with something I hadn't realized I wanted. Worrying about doing this the *right way* is silly. There is no right way when you live in a world of vampires and blood wards and sacrifices. Which reminds me... "Is there another way to break a blood ward beyond killing someone?"

Both men go still and I open my eyes to find them exchanging a look. Wolf finally shrugs. "There's a theory other supernatural creatures might have ways to do it, but I've never seen it first-hand. You'd have to fill the space with so much power the ward couldn't contain it, but without a sacrifice, it's impossible for a vampire to do it."

That's what I'm afraid of.

It's not that I think Malachi will kill me. Foolish or no, I trust he means me no harm. But as long as that blood ward is up, we're both trapped here. Now that we've crossed the line of no return, it's theoretically only a matter of time before I get pregnant and my father comes to collect me. No matter how powerful Malachi is, he's no match for my father and his turned minions. They have numbers on their side, and my father is also a bloodline vampire. Malachi won't win, which means I'll be carted back to the colony until I give birth and they decide they no longer need me.

There has to be another solution. There *has* to be.

"Don't worry about that, Mina." Malachi's chest rumbles at my back as he speaks. "You're safe here."

Safe.

What a foreign concept. I'm not safe here. None of us are. Not while we stay where my father can reach us.

I close my eyes again and relax back against him. "We'll find another way out."

"We, huh?" Wolf's tone is lightly mocking. "She gets one cock inside her and we're all a big happy family."

"You're free to go whenever you want, Wolf." Malachi rests his chin on top of my head. "Nothing's keeping you here."

A pause, and I have a feeling they're doing one of those silent exchanges. I don't open my eyes. No matter what I was feeling in the moment, I'm honestly *not* sure of Wolf. I won't ask him to stay, especially since he's not trapped here like we are.

Finally, Wolf gives a dramatic sigh. "I suppose I'll stick around for a bit." A calculated pause. "Rylan mentioned he might meet me here at some point, but you know how he is."

Malachi tenses beneath me. "You're just *now* telling me?"

"It slipped my mind."

"I'm sure it did." Malachi curses. "Convenient, that."

"Isn't it?"

I finally drag my eyes open. "Who's Rylan?"

"Another bloodline."

That shocks some of the exhaustion from my system. "*Another* bloodline? I thought most of you were scattered or loners?" Three of the bloodlines, including my father's, are still in power in their respective territories, even if their numbers are low. But I was under the impression the remaining four were scattered to the winds.

"We are." Wolf's got that strange smile on his face, as if he's telling an inside joke. "But the vampire community isn't so large that any of us are strangers, especially those of us who have been around for a few centuries."

There's more there, more he isn't saying, but I don't have the energy to drag it out of him tonight. I twist a little to look at Malachi. "Is Rylan a problem?"

He hesitates, clearly torn. "No," he finally says. "We have a complicated history, but he's not an enemy."

"So confident," Wolf murmurs. "I wonder if Rylan feels the same way. Especially now you have this delicious little dhampir riding your cock."

"Fuck off, Wolf."

"Tempting."

I look at them both. "Another ex?"

Their silence confirms my guess hit right on the mark. I barely resist the urge to sink beneath the surface of the water and scream. It's not exactly surprising Malachi has people who care about him, complicated history or no, but I don't look forward to another conversation about sacrificing me to get his freedom. And yes, maybe there's a little jealousy there for these two vampires that have known him long enough to *have* a complicated history.

I rise on shaking legs but brush off Malachi's hand raised in an offer to help. "I'm very tired."

"Mina—"

Wolf moves, blurring out of the tub. I barely get a chance to tense before he wraps me up in a large towel. He grins down at me, obviously enjoying the minor chaos he's stirred up. "What our darling Malachi won't say is that he wants you to stay."

"He's more than capable of speaking for himself." I slant a glance in his direction. "Or ripping out throats when words don't work."

Wolf gives a deep, happy laugh. "I like you, Mina. Most mortals would be rocking in a corner after all that bloody fucking. You're interesting."

"I'm pretty sure you're certifiably insane."

"Guilty." He grins and shrugs. "You learn to enjoy the ride."

Against my better judgment, I find my lips curving. "I'll keep that in mind."

"Do." He squeezes my shoulders, hands curiously gentle on me despite his irreverence. "Stay, love. We'll be on our best behavior."

"I don't believe that for a second."

"Guilty again."

I hear Malachi rising out of the tub and the water draining, but I don't look over. My instincts are to retreat and lick my proverbial wounds until the ground feels steadier beneath my feet. But I can't deny the thought of letting these two ground me is attractive. Maybe it's weak, but I can't really bring myself to care. "Okay. I'll stay."

12

I WAKE UP BETWEEN TWO MALE BODIES. I KEEP MY EYES closed and fight not to tense, waiting for my brain to catch up with my circumstances. As sleep fades away completely, the events of the last twenty-four hours comes back to me.

Gods, things keep happening too fast. It feels like the entire world has changed its shape around me. It's so incredibly tempting to pull the covers over my head and hide away to avoid thinking about it, but I haven't survived this long by ignoring the reality of my circumstances. It's better to deal with the hard truths up front than to ignore them until they're literally ripping your throat out.

Wolf's back is pressed against mine, and when I open my eyes, I find Malachi watching me. I lift a brow. "Creepy of you."

"You were thinking hard over there." He presses a finger to the spot between my brows. "Regrets?"

"No, nothing like that." It's even true. I don't make a habit of regretting my choices, but this goes beyond that. My feelings for Malachi are a pulse in my blood I can't ignore. It's more than desire, more than lust, even more complicated than something as ridiculous as love. I don't understand it, but I don't have to fully understand it in order to acknowledge its existence.

I worry my bottom lip. "How are we going to get out of this?" Will there even be a *we* after we do? Or will he grab his freedom with both hands and ride off into the sunset, happy to no longer be chained to a cranky dhampir with rage issues. "And after—"

Malachi twines a strand of my hair around his fingers. "When you've lived as long as I have, you learn to recognize the important things."

"Like freedom."

He snorts. "Like *you*, Mina. I've never met anyone quite like you."

"You mean you've never tasted anyone quite like me." I don't know why I'm being so stubborn about this, but what he's saying is impossible. We've known each other a little over a week at this point. There's no way he's feeling some kind of mystical connection to me. It's far more likely he finds me valuable in a different way. That's how vampires work, after all. Power and ambition above the softer emotions. Always.

"I mean what I said." He tugs lightly on my hair. "But I respect it'll take you longer to trust me, given your history."

"That is remarkably patronizing of you."

He chuckles. "I'm trying to tell you I like you."

Like feels too tame a word to use for what flares between Malachi and me. I'm not sure what to say to that, so I swallow hard and change the subject. "So how do we get out of this mess?"

"If Wolf is to be believed—"

"I am." Behind me, Wolf turns around and slings an arm over my hip. He doesn't *quite* press his hard cock to my ass, but I can feel the tension of it behind me.

Malachi snorts. "Then Rylan will be here shortly. Between the three of us, we can figure out a solution." He shoots a sharp glance over my shoulder. "A solution that *doesn't* involve your death, Mina."

"Tsk, tsk, after last night, I'm not particularly fond of the idea of our Mina bleeding out for your freedom. Why waste all that *delicious* blood on something as mundane as freedom?" Wolf's breath ghosts the back of my neck. "We'll find another way."

"As simple as that."

"As horrendously complicated as that." Wolf sounds like he relishes the challenge, but even after knowing him such a short time, I'm not surprised he's perverse like that.

I relax against him, soaking up all this skin-to-skin contact. It's heady and intoxicating, nearly as much as the sex was last night. I can *touch* these men as much as I want. I lightly stroke my hand down Malachi's impressive chest. "I suppose we'll have to keep ourselves occupied until then."

His muscles jump beneath my fingertips. "You need to eat something." He searches my face. "I've also ordered you some iron supplements. Even with the blood exchange, you're paler than you were when arriving here."

Something in my chest warms even as my logical side points out he's just looking after his food source. I'm no good to them if I pass out constantly from being anemic. That's the most likely reason Malachi is acting like a mother hen. Despite my reasonable explanation, the feeling in my chest gets warmer. I find myself smiling. "I'm not quite ready to get out of bed yet."

Behind me, Wolf blurs. One moment I'm on my side, facing Malachi, and the next Wolf is on top of me, settling between my thighs. He grins down at me, flashing fang. "No point in worrying about anything until Rylan appears. There are better ways to occupy our time."

It's against my nature to push worry aside when I can poke and prod at a situation until I find a way forward. But it's hard to remember with Malachi's brooding presence next to me and Wolf's warmth pressing me into the mattress. I stare up at him, tracing the carved lines of his cheekbones and those eerie colorless eyes. He's beautiful. I registered it before, but there's something about the softness of sleep still lingering in his expression that pushes him from being terrifying to just being breathtaking.

I reach up with a cautious hand and stroke my thumb along his cheekbone. "You're very, very pretty."

"I know." His grin widens. "I'm going to kiss you now."

It's not quite a question, but I want to kiss him. I don't know what it says about me that I had Malachi last night—have him right next to me right now—and all I can think about is kissing Wolf again. But then, Malachi seems just as into this as I am.

They're right; there's nothing to be done right now. Or maybe that's the excuse I cling to as I nod slowly. "Okay."

He starts to lean down and pauses to glance at Malachi, who's watching us with a small smile on his lips. Wolf gives his hand a pointed look. "Are *you* going to behave?"

"Do you want me to?"

Wolf laughs. "As enjoyable as it was to watch you fuck her while covered in my blood, I'd like to feel Mina coming on my cock more than I want a repeat right now." He settles more firmly between my thighs and thrusts a little. "Sore?"

"No." In fact, I feel better than I have since the first time I took Malachi's blood. Energized and downright glowy. I'm sure if I had access to a mirror, I'd find I look a mess, but it doesn't matter right now. I'm not sure what it says about me that I desperately want to fuck Wolf just as much as I wanted—still want—Malachi, but I'm past questioning these things. Everyone is obviously into this and it's not like vampire culture is overly monogamous. That whole mates-for-life thing is nice in theory, but when your life spans centuries, even the most intense love can shift and change. I've noticed partner hopping just from watching the way the vampires in my father's colony operate. There's no reason to think this is abnormal.

Again, I feel like I'm grasping for a reason to do this. It only means what I let it mean.

My life has been so devoid of pleasure up to this point. Is it any surprise I'm desperate to grab on to any bit of it I can touch, to glut myself on it with these two devastatingly gorgeous men? Maybe I'll wake up in a day or two and wonder what the hell I'm doing, but I don't care right now. I just want to feel good.

And yet...

I press a hand to Wolf's chest. For all his pushiness, he goes still immediately. I glance at Malachi. "Are you okay with this?"

He raises his brows. "Why wouldn't I be?"

"Um." When he says it like that, I feel silly for even asking. "Because we had sex last night?"

"And I fucked Wolf last night."

Right. I'd almost forgotten about that particular detail. I worry my bottom lip. "Still."

Malachi props his head on one hand and looks down at me. "Stop worrying about what you *should* want and focus on what you *do* want."

"Like it's that easy."

"It's exactly that easy." He sifts his fingers through my hair and then over Wolf's arm. "When you're immortal, the reasons for not taking what you want don't hold up."

The reminder that they'll live on forever while I age and eventually die is almost enough to dispel the lust Wolf is weaving around me. I could swear he hasn't moved, but he's got my leg hitched up around his waist and his cock is pressing against me in a way that feels so good, I can barely stand it. I lick my lips. "I'm not immortal."

"Not yet." Malachi kisses me before I can ask him what the hell he's talking about. Humans and dhampirs can be turned, but I'm an anomaly. A dhampir with no power of my own. I might be an anomaly when it comes to the other rules, too.

I could break the kiss, could argue, could demand more information, but I am so goddamn tired of running around like a hamster on a wheel. No matter how hard I fight, how many scenarios I run, I am still trapped. My fate is still in the hands of other people.

I really am a coward, because I push away those thoughts and grab the pleasure the two of them are offering me with both hands. Malachi moves back and then Wolf's there, nipping my bottom lip. He tastes just as spicy as he smells, something that defies explanation. The why doesn't matter, though. It's enough that it simply is.

He reaches between us with his free hand and begins dragging his cock through my folds. Up and down, spreading my wetness around, teasing me even as he kisses every thought out of my head. Just when I'm about to pull back to beg him to just fuck me, he notches his cock at my entrance.

And then he's inside me.

I was too distracted by Malachi's bite to fully appreciate that first stroke last night, but being filled by Wolf is an experience I don't have words for. He's big, but he feels different from Malachi. I exhale in a rush as his hips meet mine, sealing us together.

"Fuck, she feels good, Malachi."

"I know." His voice has gone deep, gained a little of that sexy growl that I'm starting to crave. He's still got my hand in his and he laces our fingers together as his friend starts to fuck me in slow, rolling strokes. The feeling makes me go soft and molten, each thrust rubbing against something inside me that has the top of my head in danger of spinning off.

Wolf moves back, bracing his hands on either side of my ribs, and looks down our bodies. I follow his gaze, and *fuck*. The sight of his cock sliding in and out of me, of his body rolling with each thrust, of the way I spread to take him deeper... "*Wolf*." I moan.

He shortens his strokes, rubbing that spot over and over again. "Malachi."

I blink up at him, a part of me wondering why he's saying Malachi's name while he's inside me, but then Malachi shifts closer and snakes a hand down my stomach to stroke my clit. Did I think the sight of Wolf fucking me was enough to send me to the moon? Malachi's fingers lightly rubbing my clit in the way I love, Wolf's cock inside me hitting that spot... Gods, it's too much.

I dig my heels into the mattress as I orgasm, but they hold me in place. And they don't stop. The pleasure just keeps rolling over me again and again, until Wolf's strokes hitch and he drives into me with a rough curse. I swear I can feel him coming, filling me up, but I don't get a chance to wonder if it's my imagination because Malachi gives his shoulder a light shove and Wolf flops onto his back next to me.

Before I can mourn the loss of him, Malachi drags me over and turns me so my back is to his chest. He hitches one of my legs over his hip and then his cock is wedging its way inside me. He's broader than Wolf, and even though we were just fucking, he has to work to sink all the way into me.

"*Fuck.*" I reach out to claw at the sheets, but Wolf is there, catching my hands and moving to nuzzle at my breasts. He palms them as Malachi grips my thigh with one big hand and spreads me farther, sinking deeper yet.

"Don't bite her."

"Spoilsport," Wolf murmurs against my nipple. He works his way down my stomach, trailing lightly teasing kisses. I tense as I realize where he's going, but neither I nor Malachi stop him as he settles at my hips and leans forward to lick my clit.

I arch back against Malachi and then moan. This feels dirty and decadent and I can't quite believe it's happening.

Malachi begins to fuck me. It's nothing like last night. Not brutal at all. It's almost...lazy. As if he plans to memorize every inch of me. Wolf's licking me in the same way. It's as if they have time now they got the first orgasm out of the way. As if they want to enjoy this as much as I'm enjoying it.

I can't afford to think too closely about that. I'm not capable of it right now anyway. All I can do is take what they give me.

Then Wolf's mouth is gone and Malachi jolts behind me. I lean forward enough to see the other man biting his thigh, mirth lighting his crimson eyes. Malachi curses and then he's driving into me in rough thrusts. "You fucking bastard."

Wolf gives one last pull from his thigh and then his mouth is back at my pussy. This time, he isn't messing around. He sucks on my clit as Malachi pounds into me hard enough that they have to hold me in place between them to keep us from inching across the mattress.

And then I'm coming and nothing else matters. Malachi thrusts again and again and then yanks me back onto his cock as he grinds into me. We exhale as one, but he makes no move to pull out of me. Wolf kisses my lower stomach and then moves up to flop down beside us. "That was a fun appetizer."

I blink at him. "Appetizer."

"Yes." He turns onto his side and props his head in his hand. "I haven't fucked Malachi in years, and you're a delightful new snack." He leans forward, his eyes still crimson with lust. "I said I can go for days, love, and I meant it."

Malachi curses and plants a hand in the center of Wolf's face, shoving him back. "She's half human. She needs to eat."

"Pity." Wolf throws his arm over his eyes. "Fine. Go do your human things."

"Wolf." Malachi grips my hip, keeping me from moving. "Go put something together for breakfast."

Wolf lifts his arm enough to give us a long-suffering look. "If you insist, but I'm getting my cock sucked when I come back."

"Go."

He huffs and rolls off the bed. Even though I don't know him well, I can still tell he's putting on a show as he walks out of the room, well aware we're watching him walk away.

The door barely shuts behind him when Malachi strokes his hands up my body to cup my breasts. "Tired?"

As if I can't feel him getting hard inside me again. I shiver. "Don't stop."

13

"MINA."

Gods, the way this vampire says my name. I start to twist to try to see him, but he blurs, pulling out of me just long enough to push me onto my back and then easing his cock into me again. His eyes are pure black. Malachi thrusts a little, his gaze going to my mouth when I moan. "Mina," he says again.

I don't know what he's going to say. I'm just not ready for this to be over. At some point, we're going to have to talk about plans and blood wards and my father, but not yet.

I dig my hands into his hair and arch up to kiss his jaw. "Don't stop."

Malachi growls and then we're moving again. This time, he keeps us sealed together as he rolls onto his back and takes me with him, leaving me straddling him, his cock still seated deep inside me. "Ride me."

The new position makes me feel almost exposed. He's still got a grip on me, but it's light as I roll my hips, moving slowly until I find a rhythm that feels good. Fuck, what am I talking about? Everything feels good.

Having Malachi beneath me, seeing his powerful body spread out as if for my pleasure... It's intoxicating in the extreme. We don't need to speak at all. Not when my body already knows what to do, not when he's filling me so perfectly. I plant my hands on his chest and begin chasing my own pleasure.

I'm almost there, so close to coming, when an unfamiliar dry voice cuts through my pleasure. "So *this* is why you haven't bothered to find a way out of this cage."

I freeze for half a second and then scramble off Malachi. He lets me, sitting up to shield me with his big body. Has he gotten bigger in the last couple days? I hadn't really noticed, but now I'm sure of it. I look over his shoulder at the man standing in the doorway. He's a white guy with a close-cropped beard and short dark hair, and he's wearing an honest-to-god suit.

Malachi tenses. "Rylan."

Rylan, the one Wolf said would show up at some point. He couldn't be more different from the wild blond vampire. He looks like some kind of CEO, and I swear the room dropped ten degrees when he entered. I shiver, and he flicks a look at me. His blue eyes go even colder. "Leave while the grown-ups talk, little girl."

My shiver turns into a full-out shudder and goose bumps rise across my skin in a wave of warning. Even without knowing he's a bloodline vampire beforehand, the sheer power in his eyes would tell me an apex predator has entered the room. I start to inch toward the other side of the bed, but Malachi reaches out and grabs my hand. "Stay."

Rylan raises his brows. "Keep your pet if you insist, but you know she's a trap in a pretty package. You were about to come inside her." His upper lip curls. "Idiot."

"Make sure to tell Wolf how you really feel because he filled her up not thirty minutes ago."

The crass words make me flinch. I'd forgotten. Gods, how could I have forgotten? Rylan scares me, but he's not wrong. Imagine my father's delight if he manages to trap Wolf with a child. He might love that even more than Malachi since Malachi is chained to this property by the blood ward, and that kind of cage could never hold Wolf.

I yank my hand out of Malachi's, and this time he lets me, but he starts to turn in my direction. "Mina—"

"This pretty trap is taking herself elsewhere." It's too late. Far too late. Unless it isn't? I snag my oversized shirt off the floor and yank it over my head. I have to catch Wolf before he gets back to this room. *He* can leave without an issue, can get me what I need to make sure this isn't a mistake of epic proportions.

I stop a few feet away from the door Rylan still hasn't shifted away from. "Move."

He stares me down. "I should kill you now and solve all our problems. Can't breed if you're dead."

The fire has nearly died down to ashes, but it flares high as Malachi climbs to his feet, eerily slow. "Watch your words or, friend or not, you'll lose your head."

Rylan's eyes widen just a fraction. "You fool."

"Fool or not, it stands."

He shakes his head and finally moves back. Even knowing those couple of feet won't make much difference if he decided to make a grab for me, I inch out the door and take off running for the kitchen. I find Wolf staring at a pot of water suspiciously. It's odd enough that it almost distracts me. "What are you doing?"

"How long does water take to boil? I mean, honestly, this is just plebeian." He glances at me and narrows his eyes. "You're scared. What happened?"

"Rylan is here." I jump forward when he starts to blur toward the door, barely getting there before him. "Wait!"

Wolf stops short. "He and Malachi need a referee or they're going to rip this house down to the foundation."

Even with that risk, this is too large to ignore. Especially when every hour counts and we're quite a ways from the nearest human town. "Wolf, wait."

He narrows his eyes. "What's going on?"

I don't know how I'm supposed to handle this, so I just blurt it out. "You came inside me." When he starts to smirk, I rush on. "If I get pregnant with your baby, my father will use it to collar you. I can't let that happen. Not to you or Malachi." I lift my hands but let them drop before I touch him. "The humans have something called the morning-after pill. Or Plan B. Or something like that. I need you to get it for me. The sooner, the better."

He searches my expression, looking uncharacteristically serious. "You'd go to such lengths?"

"It's a pill. It's not like I'm agreeing to surgery with no anesthetic." When he keeps staring, I wrap my arms around myself.

"Look, I know why I was sent here, and I know there's no happy ending for this for me, but at least I can make sure I don't screw you guys over. Malachi can't go. Neither can I. It has to be you."

He reaches out and catches my chin lightly. "You know if you did end up pregnant, I'd simply whisk you away to somewhere your father can never find you."

That's vaguely comforting as a plan of last resort, but that doesn't create a fix for all our problems right now. "What about Malachi?"

"When you have forever, it gives you time to figure out alternative solutions." He shrugs. "Most likely, once I secure you, I'll snatch up some human and haul them back here to break the blood ward and free Malachi."

"Let's just shelve the idea of murder for the time being." I hesitate. "And maybe get condoms, too? If you want to keep fucking?"

His grin is quick and wicked. "Oh, love, we are *definitely* going to keep fucking." He kisses me, and then he's gone, moving so fast my hair lifts in the breeze of his passing.

I exhale slowly. There's nothing to do but wait now. I know I should eat, but my stomach is tied up in knots. I'll just grab something and take it back to my room. Barricading myself in sounds like a good plan right about now. I know it's more emotional comfort than actually a deterrent for a murderous vampire, but it's better than nothing.

I feel the cold as I shut off the burner. It's the only indication I'm not alone. The desire to curl into a ball is so strong, I almost lose it. Gods, I thought Wolf was scary. He's nothing on this new vampire. I turn slowly and find Rylan standing in the doorway, watching me with those icy blue eyes. A quick glance over his shoulder confirms we're alone.

Great.

"Malachi seems to think you're something special." His tone conveys his doubt of *that* pretty damn clearly. Rylan steps into the room with exaggerated slowness. "You sent Wolf away. I'm surprised he listens to you."

"I've known Wolf a grand total of twenty-four hours and even I know he does what he wants, when he wants."

He raises a single eyebrow. "You don't know him. You don't know Malachi. You sure as fuck don't know me."

If he lifted his leg and peed to mark his territory, I wouldn't be surprised at this point. Fear is still threatening to clog my throat, but anger rises in steady waves, battling the chill I feel just from standing in the same room as this vampire. I narrow my eyes. "How long have you been harboring a sad, unrequited love for Malachi? Centuries? It's got to sting he's shacking up with a dhampir now."

He flinches, the tiniest of movements, one I would have missed if not for my dhampir senses. When Rylan speaks, it's with a dry tone that raises the small hairs on the back of my neck. "You're bold."

"I was doomed the second I was born." I force myself to shrug, as if the painful truth of the sentence means nothing. "If not you, then someone else. The fact that I've made it this long is, frankly, surprising. My father hates me."

"A likely story."

Anger is quickly surpassing fear. I glare. "Yes, you're right. Fathers who love their daughters definitely ship them off to Gothic mansions haunted by famished vampires to be a resident blood bank and womb. Totally."

I blink and he's in front of me. Holy shit, he's fast. I didn't even see him move. This close, it's strange to discover he's only a few inches taller than me. His suit shows off a great body, but he's not nearly as huge as his presence makes him seem.

Rylan's hand whips out and closes around my throat. "I don't care about your sad little life. I care about Malachi, and I care about Wolf."

"Quite the exhaustive list." Gods, why can't I stop talking back? It's like rage has hijacked what little verbal brakes I had. "Should I be impressed?"

He stares at me with something akin to surprise. "Do you want to die?"

"Not particularly."

His dark brows pull together in a frown. "Why are you baiting me?"

"I don't like you." When he keeps frowning at me like I'm a disgusting but vaguely interesting insect, I snarl. "Either rip out my throat or get the fuck off me."

"Malachi says you taste different." He's not talking to me. He almost sounds like he's thinking aloud, musing to himself. "But he's young. There's so much he doesn't know. I suppose there's one way to find out."

Comprehension dawns. "No. Don't you dare."

It's too late. Rylan shifts his hand from my throat to my hair and wrenches my head to the side. I jerk back, but the counter is in my way, and even if it wasn't, he's too strong. They're always too goddamn strong. He bites me, sinking his teeth into my throat. He tenses against me. "What *are* you?"

I don't get a chance to answer before he bites me again. His free hand lands on the counter next to my hip and he presses his entire body to mine. Instant pleasure hits me in a wave. I grit my teeth, trying to fight it. I don't want it from *him*. I refuse to orgasm as a result of this asshole's bite, bloodline vampire or no.

But, fuck, it's good. Each pull tingles through my body, a sensual touch that doesn't care if I like this vampire. Pleasure winds through me, tightening with each movement of his mouth. I find myself clutching the front of his suit with no memory of moving my hands. I bite down hard on my lip, but the pain only spikes the pleasure hotter.

It doesn't matter if I fight it. My body doesn't care about how I feel when it comes to this vampire. It's too good. *He* feels too good. Rylan grabs one of my legs and hitches it up around his hip, opening me just enough so he can shift between my thighs. It lines us up perfectly, and then his cock is there, pressing against where I suddenly need him.

I whimper as I orgasm, hating myself. Hating him.

He lifts his head slowly and blinks down at me. His eyes have bled to a pure silver that looks otherworldly. "I see."

"Get. Off. Me."

He licks his lips. Slowly, oh so slowly, he releases me and takes a step back, and then another. "You sent Wolf for birth control?"

I reach up with a shaking hand to press my neck where he bit me. Two perfect puncture wounds. At least he didn't tear the skin. I shudder. "It's a temporary fix."

He nods, expression still contemplative. "I see."

"Stop saying that!" My head feels a little woozy. I really shouldn't have gone so long without eating. Really shouldn't have spent the morning fucking and forgetting exactly how much danger I am in. "Either kill me or get out."

"You're going to collapse before you take two steps."

I'm not sure he's wrong, but that doesn't mean I'm going to lower myself to ask for help from *him*. I don't want him to touch me again. I don't... I try to push past him and the room turns into a sickening swirl of color and then goes black.

14

"SHE'S NOT HUMAN."

"Get the fuck out of here, Rylan."

I keep my eyes closed and maintain my slow breathing. I'm lying on a bed, and the lack of dust smells means it's likely Malachi's. I also don't seem to have acquired any new aches and pains, which means Rylan didn't let me face-plant in the kitchen. Honestly, I'm surprised. He seems the type to let me crumple and then leave me there for someone else to find. Or maybe just kick me a few times while I was down.

"Listen to me, you idiot. She might be half vampire, but her other half isn't entirely human."

What's he talking about? The ice has cracked in his voice and he sounds almost... Excited isn't the right word. Intense. Incredibly intense.

Malachi curses. "You've done enough, don't you think?"

"Mal—"

A low whistle. "I leave for an hour and look what trouble you two get into." Wolf. The crinkle of a plastic bag. "Did you kill her?" He sounds only mildly interested, and I might be hurt if I didn't recognize the question as so incredibly Wolf. He's pure chaos in motion. I'm honestly a little surprised he actually made it to the store and returned rather than wandering off to get into trouble elsewhere and reappearing in a few days—or a few years.

"He bit her." The accusation in Malachi's quiet statement is nearly enough to make me open my eyes.

"She's fine. She just needs to eat something."

"She's mortal."

"Not as mortal as you think."

There it is again. Rylan still hasn't elaborated on what the hell he's talking about. I finally give up and open my eyes. Malachi and Rylan stand over the bed, a bare six inches between them. They look half a second from fighting or fucking, and as I blink up at them, I'm honestly not sure which outcome is most likely. The intensity in the room makes it hard to breathe, or maybe that's because I'm so light-headed.

Wolf has a plastic bag dangling from one finger and looks distantly amused like he always seems to. He sees me first and crosses to drop the bag on the bed next to me. "I got what you asked for."

I leverage myself up to sit, ignoring the other two men for now. This is the priority. I dig out the pills and raise my eyebrows at the vanilla protein drink he also purchased. Not to mention the dozens of boxes of condoms in every variety and...flavor. "Huh."

"Covering all the bases, love." He plucks the pill package from my hand and opens it, but he hesitates when I reach for it. "Are you sure?"

"What is that?"

I don't look at Malachi. "We didn't use protection." We didn't even *talk* about using protection. Stuff like diseases might not be an issue—vampires heal everything, even that—but we should have been smarter when half the reason I'm here is because my father wants a little bloodline vampire baby to control. Reckless. So fucking reckless.

He catches Wolf's wrist and snags the box out of his hand. The more he reads, the harder he frowns. "What is this?"

"It's Plan B. It's a..." I wave my hand vaguely. "A concentrated form of birth control." I heard a group of the humans talking about it when they didn't think any of the vampires were around. No one in my father's compound used protection, but they were whispering about a way to avoid getting pregnant by the turned vampires. They all had their eyes set on the bloodline ones and didn't want a dhampir baby without any powers. None of them seemed to worry their *bloodline* dhampir child might not have powers. Another way I'm a freak, an eternal disappointment.

"Will this hurt you?"

I hadn't really thought about it. "No?" I honestly don't know. It's made for humans, and while my system seems to function nearly identically, there's really no telling. "I don't think so?"

"But you don't know."

I reach for it, but he holds it just beyond my grasp. "Malachi, give it here. Worst case, something goes wrong and you just give me blood to heal me. It's fine." I'm sure it's fine. I don't sound quite as confident as I want to, but I'm rattled and I can feel Rylan's gaze drilling a hole into the side of my head. I turn to him. "Tell him! This is what you want, isn't it?"

A muscle in Rylan's jaw twitches. "Have you taken human medication before?"

I blink. "Not you, too. You've been petitioning for my death since you showed up. What do you care?"

"Circumstances have changed."

I blink again. "Yeah, I'm going to need you to elaborate on what the hell you mean because you aren't making any sense."

Rylan crosses his arms over his chest. "You're not human."

"I'm dhampir."

He glares. "That's not what I'm talking about. These two don't recognize it because they're babies." He motions at Malachi and Wolf. "By the time they were born, we'd already started retreating and so dhampirs became more and more uncommon outside colonies like your fathers, places we don't go."

I'm still trying to comprehend how old Rylan must be if he's calling Malachi and Wolf *babies*. I'm still not quite sure how long they've been around, but it's long enough to get stuffy and mad, respectively. If I lined the three of them up, I'd assume Rylan was the youngest based on how he acts. Shows what I know.

Malachi's looking at Rylan with something other than antagonism. "What are you saying?"

"Who cares? Regardless of what I am, I have no magic to speak of, so it doesn't matter." I try to grab the box again. "*None* of this matters or has anything to do with the potential pregnancy."

"Ingesting chemicals the humans have thrown together is dangerous. There's no guarantee our blood would be enough to counteract it."

I am half a second from shrieking in frustration. "Then you get your wish and I'm dead. I still don't see why you're arguing."

Rylan leans down and looks at me. Silver flashes over his eyes and the sight of it holds me immobile despite my anger. "You really don't know, do you?"

"Rylan," Wolf drawls. "You're not usually such a tease. Spit it out and tell us what she is."

"I don't know."

Malachi curses and Wolf laughs. "All that buildup for nothing. Pity."

"If I knew what she was, this would be simpler to navigate." Rylan still hasn't taken his gaze from me. Finally, he shakes his head. "We can't risk it."

That's about enough of that. I start moving to the edge of the mattress. I can't let myself believe what he's saying. When I was young, I dreamed someday my magic would present itself and I'd be able to cast illusions like other dhampirs of my father's bloodline. Those dreams have long since turned to ash. It's not happening. Wanting it despite all evidence pointing to the contrary is a recipe for hating myself, and there are already enough people in this world who hate me. I don't need to add to their number. I'm not about to start now. "Yeah, you're still not making any sense, so I'm going to need that pill now."

Malachi tosses the box to Wolf and catches my shoulders. "Let's hear what he has to say." His expression is carefully neutral. "If, when he's done talking, you still want it, you can have it."

Frustration sinks its claws into me, but I do my best to stifle it. At least they're talking to me and no one has set the damn pill on fire or something, so I suppose that's progress. "Fine."

"And drink that." Wolf points at the protein drink. "You're looking peaky, love."

"Thanks," I say drily, but I *am* feeling dizzy still, so I make myself open the bottle and take a few drinks. It's warm and less than appetizing, but it's better than nothing. I twist to look at Rylan. "It doesn't matter what other theoretical supernatural blood I carry because I have no magic. I'm not even particularly strong or fast for a dhampir. I am utterly average in every way, aside from apparently being particularly tasty."

Instead of answering, he moves back to lean against the wall and studies me. "What do you know about other supernatural creatures?"

Little more than rumors. My father is so hyperfocused on vampires, he doesn't care about the other things out there that aren't human. Why would he? They don't bother him, they can't help him accomplish his goals, and so they're beneath his notice. "Next to nothing. Other than apparently some of them would be strong enough to break the blood ward." Understanding dawns. I frown. "But again, for the millionth time, I have no magic. I can't break a blood ward. I wouldn't even know how to try." And I don't want to try. Not when it won't change anything. I spent countless hours focusing so hard I got piercing headaches because I was sure if I just focused hard enough, I could manifest my magic. It didn't work then. It won't work now.

"Some of them mature late. A quarter century is nothing."

My chest gets tight and I have to fight to speak through it without yelling. "Stop it."

His brows draw together and he looks actually confused instead of just icy and terrifying. "I don't understand why you're fighting this. It's a fact. Your blood is not just vampire and human. There's something else there. It's familiar, but I can't place it. The fact that it's strong enough to be tasted means it's strong enough to manifest." He tilts his head to the side. "It would explain your lack of magic. The other blood is more powerful than the vampire half of you."

"You're crazy."

His blue eyes are merciless. "Why not try? What do you have to lose?"

I close my eyes and strive to think instead of reacting emotionally. It will hurt if this is all bullshit and nothing changes. It will hurt a lot. But it won't kill me. If I don't get out of this house, if *Malachi* doesn't get out of this house, my father might.

Really, it's a simple decision when I lay it out like that.

I exhale slowly and open my eyes. "What do I have to do?"

Rylan glances at Wolf and Malachi and then refocuses on me. "There are two ways. Pain or pleasure."

I wait, but he doesn't offer anything more. "So you want to torture me."

Malachi snorts. "No, little dhampir, no one is getting tortured."

"It might be the only answer." I glance at him, and gods, my chest aches just looking at him. It's too soon to feel something so strong, but hell if I can push the feeling away. "I've *had* pleasure since I've been here, especially in the last twelve hours. Nothing's happened."

"Pleasure." Wolf drops onto the bed beside me and laughs in that slightly unhinged way of his. "You haven't seen anything yet, love." He grins, flashing fang. "But it'll be fun to blow that pretty little mind of yours."

I had already planned on grabbing every bit of pleasure possible, so I suppose this isn't exactly a trial. Still... I look over to find Rylan still watching me too closely. Every instinct I have says the other shoe is about to drop. "What am I missing?"

"Those two can't do it on their own." He doesn't move, doesn't seem to breathe. "I have to be involved."

I blink. "You wanted me dead—literally dead—twenty minutes ago."

"Things change."

"You don't like me."

His lips twitch the tiniest bit. "Are you really that naive you think sex and fondness have anything to do with each other?"

No, of course not. But there is a large distance between *fondness* and wanting to murder someone. Isn't there? "No. I guess I'm not." I guess if he can handle his side of things, all he has to do is bite me to get me on board.

And Rylan is sexy. I really hate that he's sexy. He's like some ice king that's wandered in and letting him touch me might freeze me right down to my bones, but I can't quite forget how good it felt to have him pressed against me.

Apparently now I've gotten a taste for sex and bloodline vampire bites, I'm in danger of getting addicted. The thought should worry me, but I'll deal with the consequences later. If there's a way to get us out of this trap my father's constructed, I'm going to do it.

I look up at Malachi. He doesn't seem particularly pleased by this turn of events, but he's not exactly *dis*pleased, either. I can't read the expression on his face. He motions to the box in his hand. "Will you agree to hold off on this until we try?"

"The longer I hold off, the less effective it is."

"All the same."

I search his face, but it's like the first few days here. I can't tell what he's thinking. "If this works, you'll be free." He'll have no reason to keep me around.

That should make me happy, right? After all, the only thing I want is what I've wanted since I was old enough to watch my hopes turn to ash. Freedom. No vampires to speak of. A chance to figure out my own way. And hopefully not stumble right into a government facility that will spend the rest of my life doing experiments on me.

I drop my gaze, but Malachi plants his hand on the bed and leans down until it's more awkward to avoid his gaze than to look at him. I still can't read the expression on his face. "We won't leave you hanging."

Something like hope flutters in my chest and I want nothing more than to squash it. "You've been locked up here a long time, Malachi. You're not in any position to offer me protection." Which isn't what he's offering anyway. He said they won't leave me hanging. *They.* I shake my head. "And you can't speak for them."

"No, I can't." He doesn't move. "But I'm speaking for me. I want you to stay with me. If that's not what you want, we'll figure out a way for you to land safely. I give you my word."

There's no reason to trust him. We've known each other a tiny fraction of a moment and he might be a liar in addition to everything else. I can't help trusting him all the same. "Okay," I whisper.

"Okay?"

Gods, why does he always make me say it? I know, though, don't I? "Okay, let's try this."

15

I EXPECT US TO GET RIGHT DOWN TO BUSINESS, BUT apparently that's not the plan. Rylan leaves, muttering something about preparations. Wolf plants a devastating kiss on my mouth and then he leaves, too. They couldn't be more obvious if they'd hand painted a sign saying *We'll give you two time to talk.*

Malachi holds out his hand. "Let's go find you something to eat."

I'm starving, but I'm so nervous, I don't know if I can eat. It's more than the sex that has my stomach tying itself in knots. They're putting a lot of hope in something that's barely more than a theory. "This might not work."

He tugs me off the bed and across the room to the door. "If it doesn't, we'll figure out something else."

How can he be so calm at a moment like this? His very

freedom is on the line. "Malachi…" I dig in my heels a little and he slows to a stop. "You're just going to do this on Rylan's say-so? The longer we put off me taking that pill, the less likely it is to work." I don't know what the odds are that I'm pregnant. I know how cycles work in theory, but I hardly track mine closely enough to tell if I'm ovulating right now or in the near future. And really, all my information is related to full humans. I don't know how a dhampir's reproductive system might differ, especially when there are vampires and magic involved.

I don't know if the damn pill would work even if we use it under the best case circumstances.

"Mina."

Gods, I love it when he says my name. It's like I'm a tuning fork thrumming just from the sound. "I'm not being unreasonable."

"I know." He gives my hand a squeeze and pulls me closer so he can wrap his big arms around me. I have absolutely no business feeling safe right now just because he's holding me. The list of things to worry about is longer than my arm and seems to be growing by the minute. A hug doesn't solve anything.

It feels really, really good, though.

I close my eyes and relax against him. "If this doesn't work, Rylan is going to start in about killing me again."

"No one is killing you."

"If not me then some innocent human Wolf snatches up. Better to be me." It's not that I want to die. The exact opposite is true. But I don't know if I can live with myself if someone innocent dies in my place. Being that ruthless would make me no better than my father. It would make me a monster.

"Mina." Malachi digs his hands into my hair and tugs until I lift my face to his. "Rylan is very, very old. He's also not in the habit of spouting off the way Wolf likes to. If he says this can be done, he's likely right."

"You don't seem to like him very much."

"Our history is…"

"Complicated?"

His lips curve. "Complicated."

There seems to be a lot of that going around. I sigh. "A lot has changed in a little over a week. It seems like it's too much, too fast. I shouldn't feel—" I barely manage to cut myself off before I say something I can't take back. Like confess I've gone and done the unforgivable. I *like* Malachi, even when I find him infuriating. I might even be falling for him, though it's not like I have much experience with that sort of thing.

"I feel it, too." He brushes his thumbs over my cheekbones. "When you've lived as long as I have, you learn not to question these things. Some feelings transcend logic."

"That's just it. I'm not going to live as long as you, not by any stretch of the imagination."

"Trust Rylan."

I snort. "Yeah, he was calling for my head not too long ago, and then he pulled a full one-eighty between one bite and the next. Trust takes longer to build."

"Then trust me."

I open my mouth to repeat what I just said. Trust takes longer to build. But the truth is I *do* trust Malachi. Not only do I trust him not to hurt me, but I trust him to keep his word. It's a little disconcerting, to be perfectly honest. I've spent this long relying only on myself and the only truth that held steady was I couldn't trust anyone.

I take an unsteady breath. "I do trust you. Even if I shouldn't."

The smile Malachi gives me is nothing like I've seen before. It's a small smile, but it lights up his dark eyes with something akin to happiness. "We'll get free, Mina."

I kiss him. It's not even a decision. I simply hook his neck and go onto my toes as I pull him down to me. He comes more than willingly. The second our lips touch, it's as if an inferno lights inside me. I need more. I dig my hands into his hair and Malachi hooks the back of my thighs and lifts me so I can wrap my legs around his waist. One step and my back meets the wall. Gods, this man is addicting in a way I don't know if I'll ever have a defense against. I don't know if I want one.

He kisses me like I'm the best thing he's ever tasted. Like he'll never get enough. We devolve into tongue and teeth and little sounds that mean everything and nothing.

Malachi pulls back a bare inch. "You need to eat."

"Later." I'm already reaching between us to push at the waistband of his lounge pants. "I need you more."

He curses, the sounds sweet against my lips. "You're hell on my self-control."

"Sorry?" I delve into his pants and wrap my fist around his cock. The feeling of him pulsing against my palm has my whole body clenching. I need him and I need him now. "Please. I'll make it quick."

He gives one of those rough laughs. "I think that's supposed to be my line." But he leans back enough that I can push his pants down and free his cock. I start to guide him to my entrance and then hesitate. "We're supposed to be using condoms, I think?"

He's breathing as hard as I am. For a moment, I think he might argue, but he finally gives himself a rough shake. "They're too far away."

I don't have a chance to argue. He shifts his grip and sinks to his knees before me, holding me aloft as if I weigh nothing at all. I yelp a little. "Malachi, I want your cock."

"Too bad. You get my tongue." And then his mouth is on my pussy and I forget everything but the slick feel of him licking me to orgasm. It feels so fucking good I never want it to stop. He's not rushing, either. He's licking me like he relishes my taste, this moment, as much as I do. Under his tongue, my body coils tighter and tighter with pleasure, ascending toward a peak that will send me hurtling into oblivion.

I'm gasping. I think I'm speaking, but I can't make out the words. It seems beyond comprehension that he can do this to me without biting me. That there are no vampire tricks or magic involved. Just Malachi's overwhelming strength and the desire weaving a spell around us.

I barely register we're in the hallway until I look up and realize we aren't alone any longer. Rylan and Wolf stand at the top of the stairs, watching us with identical looks of lust in their eyes. Wolf's have bled pure crimson. Rylan's only flash silver, but there's no animosity in the way he looks at me now. No, there's pure need.

It's too late to wonder how I feel about that. I'm too far

gone. I dig my hands into Malachi's long hair and roll my hips, grinding myself against his mouth and tongue as I come. He bites me, sending my orgasm to new heights. I scream and slam back against the wall, damn near convulsing with the sheer amount of pleasure pouring through me.

He gives my pussy one last long lick and then rises easily to resume the position we started in. He looks down at me with eyes gone pure black. For a moment, I'm sure he'll fuck me right here, condom or no. I almost hope he does. Even after coming so hard, I crave the feel of him inside me.

But he just turns with me still in his arms and stalks down the hall to the stairs. Rylan and Wolf edge out of the way as he carries me down to the kitchen and sets me on the counter. I blink and weave a little. "I thought..."

"Food, Mina. Or you're going to pass out before we get to the good stuff."

What we just did *was* the good stuff. What we did this morning and last night was good stuff. I can't quite comprehend how it can get better than *that*.

Rylan and Wolf walk through the door a bare second later. Wolf veers toward the fridge and Malachi, but Rylan walks to me. Without so much as a word, he flicks up my shirt and looks at my pussy. "He bit you. You need blood."

"I'm fine." I don't know why I'm arguing. I also don't know why I flash hot at the hungry way he looks at me before he lets the shirt drop. "And *you* bit me first."

He doesn't respond other than to lift his wrist to his mouth and bite down. It's not a polite little bite. No, he rips his own flesh as if it's nothing. As if he doesn't feel the pain. Rylan grabs the back of my head and lifts his wrist to my mouth. "Quickly, before it heals."

I want to argue. I do. But his blood makes my fangs ache so intensely, I could weep from the sensation. Even as I tell myself I'll only have a taste, I cover his wound with my mouth. When I took Malachi's blood, it felt like lightning shooting into my body.

If Malachi's blood is lightning, Rylan's is a hurricane.

The taste of it explodes on my tongue and I swear every hair on my body stands at end as if I've stuck my finger in a light socket—except a thousand times more powerful. I whimper but I don't know if it's in pain or pleasure. I can actually feel the blood moving through me, down my throat, into my stomach, the magic there shooting out to the tips of my fingers and toes.

And then it stops.

I drag my tongue over his newly healed skin, and I've almost lost myself enough to start gnawing on him like a goddamn animal.

"That's enough."

I blink my eyes open and stare at him. He was dangerously handsome before, but now he's reached another level. The entire room has. It feels like I'm seeing a new level of detail my eyes couldn't discern before. I look at Wolf and Malachi and they practically crackle with energy, though it looks different on them than it does on Rylan. In fact, it looks different for each of them. I lick my lips, tasting Rylan's blood. "How old are you?"

"It's considered rude to ask."

I finally look back at him. After he bit me earlier, I was feeling woozy and exhausted. Now, I feel like I could run a record-breaking marathon. "Even Malachi's blood didn't make me feel like this."

"Like I said, he's a baby." He releases me slowly and steps back. When he speaks, it's aimed at Malachi. "We will go over what breaking the ward entails while she eats."

I slide off the counter and bounce on my toes a little. Yeah, I feel better than great. I belatedly realize my knee doesn't ache; it hasn't today at all. It's probably a good thing Rylan doesn't like me that much because I could get addicted to drinking his blood. I give myself a little shake. My thoughts are buzzing at twice their speed and I'm having trouble focusing. "I'm not hungry anymore."

"All the same, you need to eat." Malachi sets a plate with a sandwich on the table and points at the chair for me to sit. Two glasses join it, one with water, one with orange juice.

I make a face, but I know he's right so I sit down. My stomach chooses that moment to growl, so I pick up half of the sandwich and obediently start to eat. The vampires take up positions on the other three sides of the table. Rylan plants his elbows on the table. "The goal is to fill the blood ward with so much power that it bursts."

I take another bite of sandwich to avoid pointing out I don't actually have power. It'll just start an argument, and I suspect the only way they'll believe me is if we go through with this. And if it works...

No.

Easier to shut down that thought before something as

unforgivable as hope can take root. I told Malachi I trusted him to not drop me like yesterday's trash the second he gets free, but that's as far as I can stretch this new trust. Letting in that old hope, the fragile belief that maybe I *am* special... It's too dangerous. I don't know if I'll recover from it when this invariably fails after I let myself believe it'll succeed.

As if he can hear my thoughts, Rylan shoots me a sharp look, but he keeps going. "We do that by boosting Mina's power with our blood and then making her come so hard, it overrides the blocks in her mind."

I blink. "What?" He said pain or pleasure could do the trick, but I didn't really think about what it would entail. "Why do we need all three of you to make that happen?"

Wolf laughs. "Three cocks are better than one, love. Trust us. You'll have a good time."

Even when I had sex with both Wolf and Malachi, it wasn't at the same time. Adding in Rylan? I shiver. "That seems like it's going to be overwhelming."

"That's the idea." Rylan's cold gaze flicks over me.

Malachi has that strange look on his face again, the one I'm not sure how to define. I can't tell if he's looking forward to this or dreading it or something infinitely more complicated. "You'll enjoy yourself. Trust me."

There it is again. That demand that I trust him. I take a tiny sip of water, but it does nothing to combat the closed feeling in my throat. "I do."

16

THROUGH SOME UNSPOKEN DECISION, THE MEN DECIDE tonight is the best time to do this—I hesitate to call it a ritual. But I'm not sure what other word applies. Rylan leaves again, though this time he gives no information about where he's headed.

I'm not sure how I end up back in Malachi's room. I had every intention of going back to mine, but it seems like I blink and the last few days start catching up with me. And then I'm on the bed, sandwiched between Wolf and Malachi, and my eyelids feel like someone's attached weights to them. "I should…"

"Rest." Malachi smooths my hair back from my temple. "We have a few hours."

Even as I know I'm not going to win this fight with sleep, I keep trying. "My things…"

"I'll get them packed." His lips brush my forehead. "Sleep, Mina. We'll wake you when it's time."

It feels like one moment I'm trying to form words to argue and the next a hand on my shoulder is shaking me gently awake. I open my eyes and squint at the darkness coating the room. It was late morning when I fell asleep. "What time is it?"

"It's almost time to begin."

I sit up. Malachi is on the bed next to me. Wolf and Rylan are talking softly on the other side of the room. It's happening. It's really happening. Something like panic flutters in my throat. "I need a shower. To brush my teeth."

"Be quick."

I slip out of the room before they can argue. As promised, my suitcase is sitting on my bed, packed nearly identically to how I originally had it. Despite everything, I smile a little. "Pushy vampire." I grab the stuff I need and take a quick shower and brush my teeth. Though I'd hoped the time would give me a moment to calm down, being away from them has panic bleating even louder.

This isn't going to work.

I don't care how old Rylan is, how knowledgeable, how much the other two seem to trust him. If I had some hidden power, I would have brought it forth before now out of sheer desperation. I wanted it *so* badly; surely if it existed, it would have appeared before now?

I stare down at my suitcase. Am I supposed to get dressed again? We're just going to end up naked, right? It seems weird to put on clothes, but it seems even weirder to just walk in there without anything on me at all.

After calling myself seven different kinds of fool, I pull out a short, thin robe and shrug into it. It's as close to a reasonable compromise as I can come up with, but I still feel incredibly vulnerable as I pad back to Malachi's room.

They've turned off the lights and added a scattering of candles around the perimeter of the room. I don't know if it's meant to be romantic, but it feels like I'm about to play sacrifice in some kind of arcane ritual. All three of the men wear lounge pants and nothing else. Apparently they were as hesitant to start out naked as I was.

All three of their attentions narrow on me as I step into the room and softly shut the door behind me. It feels different than it has up to this point. I am painfully aware this trio are apex predators and I am one measly step above human.

I might not survive the night.

They're going to have to be very, very careful to ensure I do.

The thought has a borderline hysterical laugh bubbling up, but I clamp my jaw shut to keep it inside. Malachi crosses to me, and I appreciate he's walking human-slow instead of blurring. I don't think my nerves can handle being startled right now.

He takes my shoulders and smooths his thumbs over my collarbones. "Rylan says condoms will affect things."

I blink. Of all the things I expected, that wasn't on the list. "What?"

"There's magic even in our semen," Rylan says from his spot next to the window. "It can't hurt to add it in, along with the blood."

I blink again. "That sounds like one hell of a line."

Did he smile? It's hard to say. Wolf nudges him with his shoulder. "You're playing fast and loose, old friend."

"No, I'm not."

Wolf laughs. "Whatever you have to tell yourself." He turns to me. His eyes are already crimson and his smile is more than a little deranged. "You ready, love?"

No. I'm not even close to ready.

Malachi steps between me and the other vampires. "Breathe, Mina."

"I'm breathing." I sound more like I'm wheezing. This is a mess. How am I supposed to get to some point of magical orgasm-to-end-all-orgasms when I feel so skittish, I'm half a second from turning around and running out of this room like my hair is on fire? I look up at Malachi. "Bite me?"

His eyes widen just a fraction and it's as if my nerves trigger something in him. The strange expression he's been wearing since Rylan showed up disappears and he gives me a slow smile. "Where's the fun in that, little dhampir?"

It seems like it's been forever since he called me that, but I can't help leaning toward him in response. "This isn't fun. This is serious."

"I'm going to kiss you now." He makes no move to close the distance between us farther. "And then Wolf is going to touch you. And then Rylan. Okay?"

Is he asking permission *now?* I've already agreed to this. There's no reason to walk me through this like I'm an innocent. Except I *am* damn near an innocent when it comes to this kind of stuff. Having sex a handful of times does not prepare one for whatever this is supposed to be. "Okay," I say softly.

"If at any point you want to stop, we stop."

Behind him, Wolf laughs. "She won't want to stop once we get going."

Malachi ignores him. "Do you understand?"

Does *he* understand by constantly putting this in my hands, he's stripping me of the ability to fully let go? I can't pretend I'm just a butterfly being swept along before a gale-force wind, praying that it doesn't rip me to pieces. It's so much easier when you don't have a choice, and Malachi insists on giving me one, over and over again. I kind of hate him for it. I kind of love him for it, too.

I take a shaky breath. "Yes, I understand."

Instead of pressing me further, he leans down and brushes a light kiss to my lips. And then another one. I'm so tense, a soft touch might make me shatter, but the third kiss comes with a hint of his teeth against my bottom lip. I jump and the motion presses me to his chest. He wraps his arms around me, and I relax into what's becoming a familiar sensation of being held by Malachi. He's so fucking *big*. He makes me feel weirdly fragile in a way that isn't entirely unpleasant. Maybe it's because he's so careful with me, careful with our respective differences in strength. I don't know. I just know I whimper against his mouth and slide my hands up his chest.

That's when I feel Wolf behind me, lifting my hair off my neck. His lips are cool as he kisses the newly exposed skin, and I shiver when his fangs lightly scrape me. Malachi shifts his arms a little and then Wolf's gripping my hips in the newly created space. They buoy me between them until I feel pleasantly dizzy from Malachi's drugging kisses and Wolf playing with the sensitive skin at the base of my neck.

Malachi tenses and the scent of blood teases me. He breaks our kiss and leans his head to the side, baring his neck. I catch sight of a long cut and of Rylan behind him, holding a knife. It's almost enough to jar me out of my pleasure-soaked state, but Wolf uses his body to press me closer to Malachi, uses his mouth on the back of my neck to guide me to the fresh cut.

I moan at the first taste. Rylan's blood might be more powerful, but I don't think I'll ever get tired of the way Malachi's zings through me. I drink from him until the cut closes and then I can't quite help giving his skin one last lick. It feels like my nerve endings are sparking and I lean up to try to catch Malachi's mouth.

He turns me in his arms and then Wolf's there. He kisses me before I can fully register they're moving me around like a toy between them. Malachi coasts his hands over my sides and around to my stomach. He cups my breasts through my robe, lightly pinching my nipples.

I moan against Wolf's mouth and his fingers clench harder onto my hips. Not hard enough to really hurt, but the faint ache grounds me in a way I desperately need. I nip his bottom lip the same way Malachi did to mine, enjoying how he jerks a little in response.

For the first time since Rylan put forth this plan, the nerves settle a little. It will be okay. As long as we keep touching, everything will be okay.

Malachi traces the opening of my robe, tugging it until it falls open. As if they planned this, Wolf kisses his way down my neck to my newly bared breasts. He makes a sound of appreciation and then he pulls one nipple into his mouth while Malachi keeps up that delicious light pinching with the other. I stare down at the sight of Wolf's mouth on me, of Malachi's hands on me at the same time. It's just like before, when they drove me to orgasm together, and yet it's entirely different.

I never want it to stop.

Movement behind Wolf draws my attention. Rylan sits on the bed, idly toying with the knife in his hand, his attention entirely on us, his eyes fully silver. I tense, but Malachi uses his free hand to cup my jaw and urge me to bend backward so he can kiss me again. I know it's a distraction technique, but I eagerly arch to accept his mouth.

Wolf uses his mouth to keep parting my robe until he gets to the tie and yanks it open. The blood pounds through my body, but I don't think he's to blame. It's this situation, it's Malachi's blood inside me, still sizzling through my veins. The feeling has settled a little, as if I've absorbed it. It must be what's happened before, but I've never felt the transition as acutely as I do right now. "More."

Both men pause. Malachi lets out a slow breath. Wolf looks up at me and grins, flashing fang. "You heard the lady."

Malachi moves first, pulling the robe off my shoulders and tossing it aside. He lifts me into his arms and starts for the bed.

Wolf snorts. "Things were just getting interesting."

"You can have your turn later." Malachi sets me on the bed on the opposite side from Rylan, and there's no way it's coincidence. I'm still uneasy about Rylan, and even more off-center because of my reaction to him. I don't like him, but I can't deny part of me is drawn to him. It's uncomfortable and I don't like it, but ultimately he's right. This is just sex, and the purpose of it tonight is to somehow awaken my theoretical magic. The orgasms are just a convenient side effect.

Better this than torture.

Malachi nudges me onto my back and moves down my body to wedge himself between my legs. He went down on me in the kitchen and again in the hallway, but somehow this feels a thousand times more intimate. His broad shoulders force my thighs wide and the way he looks at me...

I shiver and lick my lips. "Please."

Wolf drops down next to me, planting himself between us and the edge of the bed. He grins at Malachi. "You stole my turn and now you're teasing. Rude."

Malachi presses an openmouthed kiss to my thigh. "You can have a turn later."

There it is again. That feeling of being a toy between them, something to be passed around. I expect to hate it, but the feeling never comes. How can it when they're being so careful with me? Not a toy after all. A *treat*. I shiver.

Malachi drags his tongue over my pussy and the fire behind him flares higher. Wolf tenses. "Keep it locked down."

"Mmm." Malachi ignores the other man and keeps licking me. It's not like before in the hallway. He's taking his time. It feels so fucking good, but the feeling he's savoring every little taste? It only makes this hotter.

I try to roll my hips, to guide him up to my clit, but he uses one arm to pin my lower half to the bed without missing a beat. I moan. I can't help it. Desire drugs my senses, and a hot, hard knot starts to pulse inside me. Close. I'm so close.

Malachi chooses that moment to slow his kisses until they're the barest brushing of his lips to my heated flesh. Nowhere near enough to get me off. "Please!"

Wolf traces a lazy finger up my stomach and between my breasts. "We're just getting started, love. Don't get impatient." His crimson eyes flick to the other side of me. "Now."

I follow his gaze and tense. I was so focused on Malachi, I hadn't realized Rylan now lay on the other side of me. He reaches over my chest and takes Wolf's wrist. The knife flashes and a wide cut opens on Wolf's forearm. Rylan holds my gaze as he guides Wolf's bleeding arm to my mouth. "Drink deeply."

I obey without thinking. Wolf's blood is like drinking pure fire. I might find that ironic later. Maybe. Right now, it's yet another sensation on the heels of so much. The lightning from Malachi isn't completely gone and the fire dances with it, sending shivers through me. I gasp, belatedly realizing Wolf's wound has healed. I start to look at him, but he's already moved down to my breasts again. He pulls one nipple into his mouth as Malachi shoves his tongue inside me.

The dual sensations bow my back. "Oh gods."

I reach for Wolf, but Rylan catches my wrists and presses them back to the bed. It causes him to loom over me, and I might be out of my mind, but I swear his gaze drops to my mouth for a long moment before he drags it back to my eyes. "I'm going to touch you now."

It takes two tries to form words. "You're touching me right now."

"Not like this."

Malachi swirls his tongue around my clit and I have to close my eyes for a long moment. When I finally drag them open again, Rylan is still bent over me. Waiting for permission, I realize. I've already agreed to this, to all of it, but I nod slowly. "Okay."

I don't know what to expect. Most of my body is covered with Wolf and Malachi right now. There isn't much space left for Rylan. But he surprises the hell out of me when he leans down and kisses me.

Just like that, everything changes.

17

MALACHI KEEPS LICKING MY PUSSY AS IF HE'LL NEVER get enough, but every time I get close to the edge, he retreats. It's agonizing. It's glorious. Wolf lavishes my breasts with attention, but it's as if he and Malachi can communicate without words. Every time Malachi backs off, Wolf does the same, gentling his nips and kisses to almost nothing.

And Rylan?

Rylan kisses me like he never needs to breathe. The slow slide of his tongue against mine mimics Malachi's against my clit, almost perfectly in sync. It's so good and nowhere near enough.

They overwhelm me, moving with such synchronization, it's as if they've done this before. Maybe they have. And through it all, Malachi's and Wolf's powers thrum through me, making me feel weightless and yet all too present in my body. I have the frenzied thought that I could fly, just levitate directly off this bed and shoot out the window to dance with the stars.

Malachi brings me to the edge again and lifts his head. I fight against Rylan's hold, fight to reach for Malachi and force him back to my aching pussy. I arch back, breaking the kiss the tiniest amount. "Please." My voice is rough and I'm damn near sobbing. "Please, no more."

The vampires pause. Wolf drags his mouth along the underside of my breast. "Dibs on her ass."

"*What?*"

But they aren't listening. Rylan shifts back, using his grip on my wrists to pull me up from the bed. Malachi rolls onto his back, taking me with him, and I end up perched above his face with Rylan kneeling in front of me. I blink at them. "Um."

"Trust me." Malachi gives my pussy one last thorough kiss and then retreats.

The mattress dips as Wolf moves to my back and Rylan releases one hand to press it between my shoulder blades, easing me down until my face presses against the mattress. The new position leaves my ass in the air, leaves me completely vulnerable, but I can't bring myself to care. My body pulses in time with my heartbeat. I'm so wound up, it won't take much to shove me over the edge. I've never been denied like this, never been *played with* like this.

I think I love it.

Something cool and wet spreads down my ass, and I barely have a chance to understand what's happening when a hard cock presses to that tight entrance. I tense. I can't help it. "Wait."

Wolf—because it is Wolf at my back—hesitates. "Relax, love."

Yeah, not likely. I start to lift my head, but Rylan shifts his hand to my hair. I tense further, expecting... I'm not sure what I expect. It's not for him to run his fingers through my hair. It feels good, almost like comfort, but surely I'm misunderstanding. He keeps doing it and gentles his grip on my wrist. "Breathe, Mina. Relax. Let him in."

I take a breath, and then another. Slowly, oh so slowly, my muscles relax one by one. Wolf strokes my hips, my ass, the small of my back. "That's it, love. Let me in." He eases a little more into me.

I'm not sure if I expect pain, but it's more of a strange fullness. Nothing like when he and Malachi fucked my pussy. But not unpleasant. I take another breath and relax completely, giving myself over to this.

Rylan keeps stroking my hair, Wolf keeps touching me, keeps murmuring meaningless words in a low voice as he works his cock farther and farther into my ass. And then his hips meet mine and he exhales harshly. "Fuck, that feels good."

"Hold it together." This from Malachi.

I turn my head to find him kneeling on the other side, watching us with fire in his eyes. Behind him, the flames remain safely in the fireplace but they've flared so high, they fill the space completely. How much of that is from when he ate my pussy and how much is from watching Wolf's cock sink into my ass? I don't know if I care.

"We're moving, love." Wolf hands an arm around my hips and rolls carefully onto his back, taking me with him. It makes him shift inside me, and I can't stop myself from whimpering. Wolf kisses my temple. "Does it hurt?"

"No," I gasp.

Malachi moves to kneel between my thighs. His cock looks even bigger than it did this morning, and I lick my lips as I stare at it. It couldn't be clearer what their plans are, and I'm not sure I'm going to survive it. I'm not sure I care. I glance at Rylan and frown. "What—"

"Not yet."

Malachi braces one hand beside me and Wolf and wraps a fist around his cock. He drags his blunt head through my folds and up to circle my clit. I whimper and writhe, but Wolf grabs my hips and forces me still. His breath is harsh against my temple. "It feels too good when you do that."

"Thought you could go for days," Malachi says, but he's too focused on the sight of his cock rubbing my pussy for the comment to sting. He notches himself at my entrance and then he's pressing in, in, in.

I can't breathe.

It's too much. I'm too full. They're too big.

I open my mouth to tell them that, to beg them to... I don't even know. Hurry up? Stop? Something.

Rylan kisses me before I can give the words voice. He devours my whimpers and pleas as Malachi works his thick cock into me in short, steady strokes. I think I'm sobbing. I don't know. The sensations are so intense, it feels like I'm floating above my body, watching the scene play out. Malachi's muscles flex as he works himself into me until he's fully sheathed. And then he goes still, aside from the little tremors that shake his body.

Only then does Rylan lift his head. He moves back enough

to grab the knife and use it to slice a deep cut into his forearm, deeper than he cut Wolf or Malachi. He looks at Malachi as he presses his forearm to my mouth. "Now."

Malachi moves the moment Rylan's blood hits my tongue. He begins to fuck me in slow, deep thrusts, never quite pulling out all the way before he drives into me again. Beneath me, Wolf doesn't move, but he doesn't have to. His cock fills me, adding to the sensation every time Malachi thrusts deep. And the power of Rylan's blood surges through me, until it feels like my hair is floating around me.

Except...my hair *is* floating.

And so is Malachi's.

I can't see Wolf, and Rylan's hair is too short to tell, but there's a weightless feeling to the room, as if we've somehow decreased the force of gravity. But that's impossible. No, this is magic. I can *feel* it thrumming inside me in time with Malachi's thrusts. So close to the surface, but not there yet. Something...

Something's holding it back.

I'm holding it back.

I claw at Malachi's shoulders. "I need more." His brows draw together as he looks down at me and then he glances at Rylan. I follow his gaze. Desperation claws its way through me and I find myself reaching out to Rylan. "It's not enough. I need more. I can't let go."

Rylan hesitates. "If—"

"Fuck my mouth." Under different circumstances, I might enjoy the way his eyes blaze even brighter as shock suffuses his handsome face. Right now, I'm too intensely focused on that feeling of *almost*. I nod to myself. "Yes, that's what I need." If he does that, it will overwhelm me, I'm sure of it. Then maybe this horrible feeling of being almost there will burst. I glare up when I realize Rylan is still hesitating. "*Now*. Hurry."

He curses, but then he's shoving out of his pants and moving to kneel over us. It's a little awkward, but I don't care. I wrap my fist around Rylan's cock and reach for Malachi with my other hand. "Don't stop."

Malachi's expression is almost feral. "I won't."

I arch up and tug on Rylan's cock at the same time, guiding him into my mouth. He's not quite as long as Malachi and Wolf, but he's thicker, thick enough I have to work to suck him down. His low curse has me clenching around Malachi, but it's not enough. I can't get him deep enough.

Rylan, thank the gods, seems to understand. He touches my jaw. "Relax. Let me do the work."

Yes, that's what I need. I make a sound of assent and give myself over to all of them. Malachi smooths his hands up my thighs, pressing them up and out, splaying me open. "Her clit, Wolf." As Wolf snakes his hand around my hip to stroke my clit, Malachi picks up his pace until he's pounding into me. Rylan doesn't take quite as punishing a pace or depth, but as he starts fucking my face, I have to relax completely and let him lead. I have to submit. I have to become a receptacle for their bodies, for my pleasure. Wolf's clever fingers stroke my clit. This time, they aren't backing off. All four of us are cascading toward one inevitable ending.

The feeling inside me rushes higher, pressing against something invisible holding it in place. With each thrust, it surges. Again and again. Higher and higher. More and more.

Something tears deep in my soul as it ascends. It feels like someone shoved their hand into my chest and wrapped it around my bloody heart, squeezing, squeezing, squeezing until it bursts from my chest in a rush that has me crying out around Rylan's cock.

Glass shatters. A great pressure pushes against my skin. In the distance, I think I hear screaming.

And then Rylan curses and he's coming down my throat. I drink him down without thought, sucking on his cock even as he begins to ease away. Malachi shudders between my thighs and then he fills me in great spurts that have me moaning. Holy shit, what is happening? He barely moves out of the way before Wolf flips us, pinning me to the bed as he drives into me. I'm too loose to do anything but take it, and I have the distant thought that even this feels amazing. He pulls out a bare second before he comes across my back and then he slumps down beside me.

For a long moment, only the sound of our ragged breathing filled the room.

Then Malachi gives a choked laugh. "It worked. It fucking worked." He pulls me up and kisses me hard. "You did it, Mina."

I barely have the strength to cling to his shoulders as he pulls me into his arms and grabs someone's shirt to wipe down my back. "Are you sure?"

"Yes. The blood ward is gone."

Wolf stretches and his fingers feather along my thigh. "He'll have felt the rebound of it shattering. It'll put him out of commission for at least a few hours."

Him. My father.

I shiver in Malachi's arms. My body doesn't feel like my own. My skin is so sensitive I simultaneously want to shove him away and also rub myself all over him. "I don't think I can walk."

"You just got fucked to within an inch of your life. No shit you can't walk." Wolf laughs. "That was work well done, if I do say so myself."

"Malachi." For the first time since I met him, Rylan sounds... shocked. "Do you recognize what she is?"

I twist to look at Rylan. His eyes are still blazing silver and he's staring at me like I'm a poisonous snake that just slithered into his bed. It stings, but I try to rationalize my response; it's not as if he liked me to begin with. I take a shaky breath. "What am I?"

"Seraph," he says the word like a curse.

"A *seraph*?" Wolf throws himself onto his back and laughs so hard he has to clutch his stomach. "Our little dhampir is a fucking *angel*."

Seraph.

Malachi's arms tighten around me. "Are you sure?" He doesn't sound particularly happy about this, either. When I look up at him, his expression is tight.

"Can't you feel it?" Rylan rubs his chest. "Focus."

Malachi goes still for a long moment, but it's Wolf who speaks first. "Fuck."

I look from one of them to the other. "What? What are you talking about? What's going on?" My body has started to feel more like my own now, but the strangely light feeling inside me is still there. I clutch Malachi's arms. "Malachi?"

"A long time before I was born, the seraphim were hunted to extinction by the other supernatural creatures." Malachi's arms tense around me. "Or so everyone thought."

I'd heard of seraphim, of course, but I thought they were just another fictional part of the humans' religion. No one ever talks about them as if they were *real*. "Why?"

"Among their abilities is one that links them with their partners." Once again, it's Rylan who answers. "It might have started out as some kind of mating bond, but they used it to create courts of supernaturals around them. A seraph could do whatever they wanted to a bonded supernatural and that supernatural couldn't fight back, couldn't harm them in return, couldn't break free. Vampires, in particular, are susceptible."

"I heard they had godlike powers." Wolf sounds uncharacteristically serious. "There's a reason they scare the shit out of the humans, even if history has defanged them out of sheer self-preservation."

I start to pull away from Malachi, but he hugs me tighter to his chest. His voice lowers, deepens. "It doesn't matter."

"The longer she lives, the stronger the bond will grow." Rylan scrubs at his chest as if he can dig through flesh and yank the bond out by its roots. "The best bet we have is to scatter and get as far away as fast as we can before she calls us back."

What they're describing is a monster. If I'm a seraph, that means *I'm* a monster. The only thing I've ever wanted is freedom, and if what they're saying is correct, then freedom is the very thing I've stolen from them. "I'm sorry," I whisper.

"It's not your fault." Malachi climbs off the bed, taking me with him. "Can you stand?"

"Yes." I'm not sure if I'm lying, but I lock my knees to ensure I stay on my feet when he releases me.

Malachi points at the other two vampires. "Don't move."

Rylan shakes his head as Malachi leaves the room and looks at Wolf. "Run. This is going to be your only chance."

Wolf sits up and eyes me. "Nah, I'm good. This is the most excitement I've had in centuries."

"It will be your downfall."

"You're all doom and gloom. Look at her." He waves a hand at me. "*Think*, Rylan. I heard the stories of seraphim, too. The bond is annoying, but only in the hands of a tyrant. Think about what else she'll be capable of if she lives long enough."

"You're making some large assumptions."

I wrap my arms around myself and try not to shake. "Rylan's right. You should leave. I don't want..." My breath hitches. "I know what it's like not to have your freedom. I don't want to do that to you."

"See." Wolf laughs. "Not so tyrannical, is she?"

Rylan seems unmoved. "People change."

"Then run." Wolf shrugs. "Me? I'm tired of being hunted. Cornelius only has two other kids; neither of them have managed to pop a baby vampire out and become heir. With her seraph blood, I'll bet she's just as fertile as her mother was."

I blink. "Um, what?" I realize what he's suggesting and shake my head. "It'll never work." Sometime over the history of vampires, the tradition began that in order for a bloodline vampire to officially become heir, they had to procreate to prove they could continue the line should it fail elsewhere. That was back when they were slightly more plentiful, when three of the bloodlines hadn't been pruned down to one or two vampires. My father still holds to the tradition, but I've never really worried about it too much because it doesn't affect me. "I'm a bastard."

"Only because you didn't have a recognized magic until now. If you show up with a baby and start flashing seraph magic about, all we have to do is kill him to take over the colony." Wolf grins. "That's my kind of fun."

Rylan shakes his head. "She's right. It'll never work."

Malachi walks through the door, my suitcase in hand. "Sounds like the beginnings of a plan."

"More like a dream." Rylan looks at me and then away, as if he can't stand the sight of me. "We have a narrow window to get out of here unscathed. Let's not waste it. We'll deal with this later."

Guilt clamps around me. I want to be happy that I was wrong, that I really *do* have magic, but the price seems too high. I never wanted to tie these vampires to me, not in a way that defies their free will.

I never want to be my father.

I slowly dress in the clothes Malachi hands me. No answers have presented themselves by the time I pull on my boots. "Rylan's right. You should leave me. If there's some kind of geographical limit on this—"

"There's not," Rylan says flatly. "As long as you're alive, there will be a pull on us to return to your side."

I spin on him. "This was *your* idea. I didn't ask for this. I didn't set out to trap you or bond with you or whatever the hell has happened. Stop looking at me like this is my fault."

He opens his mouth and I half expect him to cut me down with a few icy words. Instead he sighs. "You're right. Sorry."

I blink. Holy shit, that was an actual apology. I glance at Malachi, but he looks just as taken aback as I am. He gives himself a shake. "Get dressed. We leave in two."

Rylan and Wolf blur out of the room. I take a deep breath and turn to Malachi. "You—"

"Stop telling me to leave you behind. It's not going to happen." He dresses in a pair of jeans, boots, and a long-sleeved shirt. Malachi pulls me into my arms, which is right around the time I realize I'm shaking again. "Not because of a mystical bond, either, so get that out of your head."

"You don't know what I'm thinking." That was exactly what I was thinking.

He gives me a squeeze. "We'll figure out a plan once we get out of here. Give me that long, okay?"

"Are you asking me or telling me?"

His lips curve. "Would you rather I toss you over my shoulder and just take you with me?"

Kind of.

Except, no, I wouldn't. I wanted a choice, and now I have one. Really, there's only one option. If my father realizes what I am, he'll try to kill me. Or, more likely, he'll try to break me so he can use me to boost his own power. Neither option is good for me. At least with these three, I have a chance. Hell, I have more than a chance.

First, we have to get out of this house.

Two minutes later, we're at the front door. Malachi tosses my suitcase to Wolf and hefts me into his arms. When I start to protest, he gives me a look. "Seraph or not, you can't keep up."

Damn it, but he's right. "Okay."

He looks at Wolf and Rylan. "Where to?"

"New York." Rylan glances at the sky. "We can get there in half a day or so, and even if he sends his trackers, it will be difficult to find us among that many humans."

Malachi nods. "Lead the way."

He moves at a quick lope across the grounds, not quite blurring. When we reach the edge of the property, Wolf leaps over the seven-foot iron fence as if it's nothing. Rylan follows suit. Malachi hesitates and then we're airborne. He tenses as we pass over the top, but nothing happens. The blood ward really is broken.

He gives that rusty laugh of his when he lands on the other side. "Freedom."

"Not quite," Rylan says.

"Close enough for me."

We take off into the night, the cool air whipping against my face. I look over Malachi's shoulder in time to see flames licking through the windows of the house we just abandoned. They spread preternaturally fast, consuming the roof in giant bites. Something gives way and a piece of the house collapses. There will be no rebuilding that particular cage.

Malachi and I really are free. Or as free as we can be while my father still lives.

I open my eyes, resolve settling over me. No matter what else happens with these three men, one thing is certain.

For us to be safe, we have to kill my father.

And I have to be pregnant before we can do it.

ACT II
HEIR

1

I CAN FEEL MALACHI'S HEARTBEAT. IT THROBS IN MY chest, a steady thump that would be reassuring if it wasn't so foreign. After all, it's not as if I'm lounging with my head on his chest the way I have many times in the last month. Malachi isn't even in the house.

He's across the county, the miles stretching between us.

I rub the back of my hand against my sternum, but if the last four weeks have taught me anything, it's that the sensation of multiple hearts nestled up against mine is magical in nature rather than physical. Malachi assures me that I'll get used to it eventually, which might actually be reassuring if his dark eyes weren't worried every time he looks at me. Better than Rylan, who won't look at me at all. I still don't understand why he hasn't left our little nest and taken his chances on his own. I don't understand him.

And Wolf?

Wolf, true to form, offered to carve open my chest to relieve me of the sensation.

"Stop it."

I don't look over as Rylan's icy words cut through the stillness of the loft. "You're talking to me now? How novel." I drop my hand and then have to curl it into a fist to resist going back to rubbing my sternum when Malachi's heartbeat kicks up a notch. The feeling in my chest intensifies, signaling proximity. "He's coming."

"About time," Rylan mutters.

At that, I finally face him. "It's been a month. Leave if you hate it with me that much."

"I would if I could." He practically hurls the words at me. His hand goes to his chest, mirroring me. He looks just as perfectly put together as he has from the moment I met him, his dark hair cut short on the silvered temples, his endless supply of suits without a wrinkle out of place. The only time I've seen him remotely rumpled was the night we all fucked, subsequently awakening my powers and landing us in this mess.

Together.

Whether we like it or not.

"Just kill me then. It's what you wanted from the beginning."

His eyes flash silver, the only sign that I've gotten beneath his skin. I shouldn't be so petty as to enjoy aggravating Rylan, but he's like a wall of knives I brush against with every movement. Malachi and Wolf might not be overly comfortable being tied to me, but at least they *like* me a little. Rylan's hated me from the start—a very mutual sentiment—and now we can't escape each other.

"Would that I could." He turns and stalks to the balcony doors, pausing to strip and systematically fold his clothing over the chair set there for what I assume is entirely that purpose.

I know what's coming, and as such, I should look away. But I've had so few pleasures in my life that I find myself unable to resist a single one, no matter the source. A naked Rylan is a pleasure, what comes next even more so.

He's gorgeous in an entirely different way from Malachi and Wolf. His suits do a good job of masking his strength, but out of them, he looks nearly as big as Malachi. He also has little dimples at the top of his ass that, despite myself, I want to lick. As much as I'd like to blame the bond for that, the truth is that I found this asshole attractive even before the night the bond snapped into place.

He steps out the doors and there's—I'm not sure how to explain it—a ripple, almost. As if reality gives a little shudder, a tiny tear, and then Rylan is gone and a giant black bird perches on the balcony in his place. A flap of its massive wings and he's gone, flinging himself out into the darkness.

He's moving quickly in the opposite direction Malachi is coming from, putting miles between us with ease. I feel each one like a nail driven into my chest. I hate it. I *want* him gone, but the more distance he puts between us, the greater the urge to demand he return.

To force him to return.

I stomp down on the urge and turn away from the balcony. I don't care what Rylan says about seraphim. I don't care that I can no longer deny that I'm one of them. I don't care about their history of bonding with and abusing vampires. Doing that intentionally would make me no worse than my monster of a father, and *that* is something I'll never do.

Death is preferable.

I can feel Wolf downstairs, likely painting again. The man holds multitudes and while I can appreciate the beauty behind his art, it's highly disturbing. Wolf is chaos personified, and that truth is even more apparent when he paints. He might kiss me or try to cut my throat on our next meeting. I never know. He scares me, but a small, secret part of me likes it. I feel particularly *alive* when I'm dancing on the blade edge with Wolf.

I don't want that right now. I'm too tired, too frustrated. Wolf, predator that he is, will pick up on it immediately, and he won't be able to resist testing me. Testing the bond. It exhausts me just thinking about going a round with him right now.

We might have spent the last month together, but I should know better than to lean on these vampires. Even Malachi, for all his declarations of intent, hasn't known me nearly long enough to actually mean anything he says. More, considering the possibility of a future together is a far cry from agreeing to a bond that only death will sever.

I am surrounded by men, but I'm just as alone as I was in my father's compound. Separate. Other. Alternatively a threat and prey, depending on who's around. The only thing I ever wanted was freedom, and it's the one thing I'll never have.

Gods, I'm a little ray of sunshine tonight.

I move through the upper floors of the house that is our most recent lodgings. Despite Malachi's intentions of losing ourselves in the city, the plan fell through almost immediately. It took my father's people less than twelve hours to find us the first time. Since then, we've had to get increasingly creative, avoiding any properties directly linked to Wolf or Rylan and moving regularly. It still isn't enough to grant us true peace, but at least we're staying ahead of my father's hounds.

Barely.

The air shifts behind me, but I don't need to look to know who it is. Malachi. When we first met, he had a habit of surprising me by appearing unexpectedly without a sound. Now that we're bonded, he'll never be able to sneak up on me again. None of them will. That knowledge should reassure me, should offer some kind of layer of safety, but it's simply a reminder of how much has changed in such a short time.

"Do you think he knew?"

Malachi doesn't ask who I'm referencing. "I doubt it. Even if she was like you and tasted different than humans do, there are a lot of monsters in our world. Knowing your father, he wouldn't have risked bedding her if he suspected she had even a hint of seraph blood."

She. My mother. The source of my seraph powers that awoke a month ago in a bed filled to the brim with sex and blood, the chain that now binds me to these three bloodline vampires.

Not every vampire in our world is graced with magic. Those turned might get the near-immortal life spans, but that's the best of it. Even those naturally born barely have a leg up over the turned vampires.

No, the true power lies with the seven bloodline families, each with a specialization they pass from parents to children. There are other perks, including pleasurable bites, but the real focus is the magic. My father can get anyone to do anything he wants as long as they're in the same room and he's able to speak. He can also use his glamour to shift his appearance.

And now I have three bloodline vampires linked to me. Malachi with his fire. Wolf with his blood magic. Rylan with his shape-shifting. Practically an army of three, all vested in keeping me alive, because if I die, there's a decent chance I'll drag them all to hell with me. Aside from my father, little can touch me now. If I were a different person, maybe I'd be elated.

I never wanted any of it.

Malachi closes the distance between us and wraps his arms around me, tugging me back against his large body. If not for the way he sometimes looks at me, I might allow myself to sink into these little intimate moments. To believe that the future holds even a sliver of happiness for me.

"You're thinking too hard." Malachi rests his chin on the top of my head. "You and Rylan have been sniping at each other again, haven't you?"

"I didn't want this," I whisper. I can feel Rylan winging his way farther and farther from the house—from me. Eventually, he'll reach the limits of our bond just like he has countless times in the last month, and it will snap at him until he turns back. "Why can't he understand I hate this even more than you all do?"

"He's got a long and complicated history with the seraphim. When your memory is as long as Rylan's, it's difficult to get past old beliefs. Old fears." Malachi delves his hands beneath my shirt to bracket my waist. I try to resent that the feel of his hands on my skin instantly unwinds some of my tension. I try...and I fail. I want to blame *this* on the bond, too, but my attraction to Malachi has been there from the moment we met and only seems to grow stronger with time.

With a sigh, I lean back more firmly against him, letting him coast his hands up my sides. "I didn't want this."

"I know." He shifts to press a kiss to my temple, my cheekbone, my jaw. "Mina."

"Yes." An answer and permission, all rolled into one. Rylan may be staying as far from me as he can manage. Wolf is as changeable as the wind, wild for me and avoiding me by turns. Only Malachi is consistent in this.

I wish I could believe that it's simply because he wants me.

If I were anyone else, maybe I could. But I'm not. I'm the daughter of Cornelius Lancaster, the last bloodline vampire of his line. Up until a month ago, I was a freak, a powerless dhampir. Half human, half vampire, somehow missing the power that should come along with that mixing of vampire with human. Useless except as a pawn in my father's schemes, as a womb to fill with another bloodline.

I have power now, but that doesn't make me safe.

If my father discovers that I have not one but *three* bloodline vampires linked to me, he'll use me as a tool to bring them to their knees. I might not want to take their freedom and willpower, but he'll be only too happy to in order to boost his own power. Killing him might be possible, but it won't solve the problem, not when I have other half siblings who are ready and willing to step into his shoes.

We have one chance to avoid being hunted until the end of time.

I have to become my father's heir.

The only way to do *that* is to get pregnant before any of my half siblings do. Not exactly an easy feat when some of them have been trying since before I was born. Not to mention I don't even know how vampire and seraph and human mix together. Rylan claims it's possible—even probable—that I can conceive and quickly. I'm not so sure.

"Mina." Malachi's lips brush my throat. "It will work out."

"You don't know that."

"No more than you know that it *won't* work out." He kisses my neck. "Let me make you feel good for a little bit."

Let him make me feel good. Let him have another go at getting me pregnant.

I exhale slowly. At this rate, my racing thoughts aren't going to slow down without extreme measures. "Bite me."

Malachi, gods bless him, doesn't hesitate. He sinks his fangs into my skin. Just like that, every thought turns to mist in my head. I melt back against him. Every pull as he drinks from me has pleasure curling through my body. Yes, this. This is what I crave right now.

I reach back and fumble at his pants. I need him inside me and I need it now. "Please."

He withdraws long enough to pull my shirt over my head and skim off my pants. His clothing quickly follows, and he wastes no time carrying me to a nearby couch. It's as sturdy as all the other furniture in this house, as if it were built for giants instead of regular people. Malachi sets me down and goes to his knees in front of me.

In this position, he feels even larger than he is. Broad shoulders that taper down to a slim waist. Muscles strong enough to punch his way through concrete walls without breaking a sweat. Scars upon scars, his outsides matching my insides. I reach out and press my hand to the mangled flesh over his heart where someone tried to carve it out. He still hasn't told me that story. Maybe he never will.

I abandon that line of thinking and dig my hands into his hair. It's just as long and dark as mine, though he's got a bit more wave in it. "I need you."

"Not yet." He presses me back against the couch and kisses his way down my stomach, his beard scraping against skin already overly sensitized by his bite. "I'm ravenous for you, Mina."

This. This right here is why I can't quite believe Malachi is only in this because he has no choice. We might be trapped together, have been trapped since the moment we met: first in that old house by my father's blood ward and now by the bond that strums between us with every beat of our hearts. If it was only the bond, Malachi would fuck me and nothing else. I'd hardly complain if that was all we did.

Instead, he's bringing me pleasure in a multitude of other ways every chance he gets.

In particular, he loves eating my pussy as much as I enjoy his mouth on me.

His breath ghosts against my clit and I shiver. "Well, if you insist."

Movement behind him has me startling. I was so focused on Malachi, I didn't feel Wolf approaching. He stands outlined by the doorframe, his lean form clothed in his normal eccentric mix of dark pants, a graphic T-shirt with a band I've never heard of, and suspenders. He gives me a feral grin. "You started playing without me."

Malachi doesn't lift his head, each word vibrating against my heated flesh. "Get over here, then."

2

WOLF'S ALREADY MOVING. HE STRIPS SLOWLY, HIS GAZE sliding over Malachi's ass, his bare back, to me. He looks at us like he can't decide if he wants to eat us or fuck us. Apparently I'll be dancing on the bladed edge with Wolf tonight after all. "So many toys, so little time."

Malachi ignores him and then his mouth is on me properly, his tongue sliding between my folds. Kissing my pussy just as thoroughly as he kisses my mouth. A moan slips free and the last of my worry slips away. It will still be there when we're finished. I tighten my grip in his hair, lifting my hips to rub myself against his tongue. It feels good, but I know Malachi. It's about to feel even better.

As if he can hear my thoughts, he bites me, his fangs on either side of my mound. Pleasure surges through me, as if the first bite readied me for exactly this moment. I come so hard, I scream, bucking against him. He grabs my hips and pins me in place, each pull making my orgasm crest higher and higher until my very voice gives out.

Only then does he give me one last lick and lift his head.

Wolf is there in an instant, claiming Malachi's mouth. I lie there and watch them kiss, a savage meeting of predators that should scare me but only turns me on more. They're not mine, no matter what the bond and Rylan think. They're not mine...but in this moment, they almost feel like they could be.

Wolf tugs Malachi's head back and licks the blood and me off his lower lip. He shudders. "Exquisite."

"You first." Malachi stands and pushes Wolf down on the couch next to me. "Suck my cock while you're at it."

Wolf's grin is...well, *wolfish*. I'm reminded yet again that these men—including Rylan—have a history that precedes my birth by centuries. Friendship and more, even if they had some sort of falling-out that I still don't have the details on.

I don't have the details on a lot of things when it comes to these bloodline vampires.

There's no time for my worries to take hold, though. Not with Wolf hauling me to straddle him and wrapping a fist around his cock. He doesn't hesitate to guide his blunt head to my entrance. I'm ready, more than ready, but I still have to work myself down his length in small strokes to take his size. I brace my hands on his shoulders as I do, looking down into his pale eyes that are already edging crimson the way they do when he's feeling strong emotions... Or drawing on his power.

I feel an answering pull in my clit, my blood rising to his call as he guides it to further my pleasure. I gasp and sink the rest of the way onto him. "I love it when you do that."

"I know."

Malachi barely waits for Wolf to seat himself entirely within me before he leans over the couch and then Wolf's sucking him down. I rock my hips as I watch him fuck Wolf's mouth, so turned on I can barely think straight.

He won't finish like this. They never finish anywhere but inside me these days.

I push the thought away and focus on riding Wolf's cock as he uses his power to call blood to my clit and nipples. It makes me so sensitive, it almost hurts, but I drink up the near pain with the same fervor that I consume the pleasure. I need more. Endlessly more.

I look up to find Malachi watching me. He doesn't break his stride, his fingers digging into Wolf's pale blond mohawk as he keeps up that punishing rhythm that demands a submission I don't know the other man is capable of. In these moments, I'm reminded that no matter how soft Malachi can occasionally be with me, he's truly the one who holds our little foursome together.

Not me.

As if he can sense my mood shifting, he reaches down and hooks the back of my neck, towing me closer to Wolf. "Drink from him."

"But—"

"Do it, little dhampir." His voice is slightly ragged as he fucks Wolf's mouth, but his eyes are intense on me. "How are you going to get stronger if you shy away from this?"

How indeed?

The worst part is that I *liked* drinking from them before the bond snapped into place. Whiskey is great, but bloodline vampire blood is like bottled lightning. The problem is that we don't know what exchanging blood is doing to the bond. All I know is that I crave drinking from all three of them with an intensity I can't blame on the pleasure I get from their blood. "But..."

Wolf makes the decision for me. He pulls a knife from somewhere and slices a long line down the length of his neck. Blood gushes and I'm closing the distance to press my mouth to the wound before I have a chance to reconsider.

Fucking Wolf is amazing.

Fucking Wolf while drinking his blood is like going from 2D to 3D. Every nerve ending lights up, even ones I'm pretty sure don't actually exist in the physical world. His power surges into me even as he grabs my hips and fucks up into me. It's so good. Too good. I try to hold out, to make this last, but my control is less than nothing when it comes to these men. I orgasm hard, crying out against his skin, his blood on my tongue.

He follows me over the edge, his fingers pressing so hard into my skin that I know I'll have bruises...at least for a few minutes before my increased healing abilities take care of them.

It's only when I'm being lifted off Wolf's cock that I realize Malachi stopped fucking his mouth a few moments ago. And then *he's* inside me, wedging his cock into me. Malachi doesn't give me time to recover, to move, to do anything but take him. He braces one hand on my hip and one on the couch next to Wolf's shoulder, and then he fucks me against the other man's chest.

Wolf grabs my hair and uses his hold to maneuver my head to

the side, baring my neck. It's all the warning I get before he bites me. I orgasm instantly, already primed from everything we've been doing up to this point. The bastard doesn't stop, though. He keeps sucking, timing it with Malachi's thrusts, driving my orgasm higher and higher.

My body gives out before they do.

I collapse, held in place between them as they finish. Wolf licks my neck, a sizzling feeling there telling me that he used his own blood to heal the bite. Malachi grinds deep into me and curses, filling me up.

Maybe this will be the time I get pregnant.

I know that's the goal, but part of me can't help hoping that it takes a little longer. Selfish. So fucking selfish of me. I'll feel bad about the thought later. Right now, I don't have the energy to do more than lay against Wolf's chest and relearn how to breathe.

This should be enough.

I have two sexy as hell vampires who have just fucked me within an inch of my life. The echoes of that last orgasm are still settling in my bones. Wanting more, craving more, is so beyond selfish.

Wanting *Rylan* is the height of foolishness.

I close my eyes, and even without trying, I can feel him down the length of the bond. He's miles away now, winging a circle with the house at the center. I might loathe the man, but my magic—my body—craves him with an unholy strength.

I wish there was someone I could talk to about seraphim. I didn't even know they existed until a month ago, and the only one of the three vampires that seems to know anything is Rylan. Unfortunately, he isn't talking. Or, rather, if it involves anything but icy silence or cold comments, he's not interested. He hates the seraphim, which means any information he has will be tainted by that emotion. It might be justified—hard to argue that it isn't—but that doesn't mean it's helpful.

But if there's a seraph left alive, they're deep in hiding. I can't pin my hopes on finding that needle in a haystack, especially when I'm not even certain it exists. No, there's no easy solution for me. I'm going to have to muddle through as best I can.

Malachi eases out of me and drops down on the couch next to us. A faint sheen of sweat glistens on his skin, and even as exhausted as I am, I want to lick him. Gods, I can't get enough of either of them.

He looks at us and gives that slow smile of his. "You're both a mess."

"It's your fault." I leverage myself up enough to press my fingers to the blood coating my chest from where I was rubbing against Wolf. It's already going tacky. "Both your fault."

"Guilty." Wolf stretches beneath me, lifting us a few inches off the couch. "I'd say I meant to be more careful with the knife, but—"

"You'd be lying." Despite everything, I find myself smiling at him.

"Yep." He drags his pale gaze over me. "Besides, you look good in my blood. You should wear it more often."

I blink. I'd say he's joking, but the way he's looking at me isn't amused at all. We just fucked, and he's staring at my body like he wants to clean me up with his mouth. "Wolf?" I don't mean for his name to come out as a question, but it happens anyways.

"You can take more, can't you, love?"

"Wolf." The word is carefully neutral, Malachi watching us both closely. I can't decide if he's trying to encourage the other man or deter him.

Wolf grins, flashing fang. When we first met, I thought it was a lack of control that causes him to do that. Now I know that it's just pure Wolf. He wants to flash fang so he does. It's as simple as that. He cups my breasts, dragging his fingers through the blood coating my skin. "Don't play so restrained, Malachi. We both know you'd like nothing better than to spend a month straight with her on your cock, filling her up over and over again until you plant a babe in her womb." He lowers his voice, speaking as if intent on seduction. "It makes you crazy that I'm fucking her, doesn't it? That I might be the one to father the child that makes her heir."

"That's enough."

"Is it?" Wolf lightly pinches my nipples. "Malachi, so calm and collected and in control." He laughs. "What a liar you are. She might believe you, but I know the truth."

Tension winds around us, tighter and tighter and having nothing to do with sex. No, there's the threat of violence on the air. "That's enough," I say, echoing Malachi's words.

"Would you kill me to get her to yourself?" Wolf hasn't stopped touching me, but all his attention is on the other vampire. I might as well be a cup of tea he's using to keep his hands busy. "Would you betray our history for *her*?"

Malachi hasn't moved. It doesn't seem like he's even breathing. "Would you?"

Just like that, the tension bleeds out of Wolf and he grins. "Time will tell, won't it?"

My desire has gone up in smoke, leaving only ashes in its wake. Bond or not, I am a fucking person and they're talking over my head like I'm a toy they're not inclined to share. "Let me go." I grab Wolf's wrists and pry his hands off my breasts. He lets me, which is just as well. I'm not sure what I'd do if he kept touching me while I'm this angry. "I'm done."

"Mina—"

"No." I struggle to my feet and point at Malachi. "I don't want to talk to you, either. I'm going to take a shower and then I'm going to bed. Alone." I make it one step before my anger gets the best of me. "I don't know if you need to fight or fuck your way to the end of this conversation, but you obviously don't need me here for it. Good night."

Neither of them say a word as I stalk out of the room. Of course they don't. I'm not required for this pissing match. I'm not required for *anything* important.

Except, oh yeah, I'm the reason we were able to break the blood ward keeping Malachi trapped in that house for decades.

And my damned womb is going to be the thing that unseats my father and allows them to finally stop being hunted by him and his people.

None of that matters, though. Bond or not, I'm still not convinced they see me as more than a tool for their endgame. Even Malachi betrays that when he gets like this, snarling and snapping over me like I'm a piece of meat in his possession.

No one gives a shit what *I* want.

3

I STALK INTO THE ROOM THAT I'VE CLAIMED AS MY own. Most nights, Malachi shares it. Wolf's here more than half of the time, too. Not Rylan. Never Rylan. He alone doesn't seem to have a use for me, which should irritate me, but right now it's almost a relief.

Almost as if my thoughts summoned him, the curtains billow out from the window and then he's there, a dark silhouette against the full moon in the shadows of the room. The shadows clothe him well enough, but I know he's naked. He always is after shifting back to human.

I stop short, planting my feet against the nearly overwhelming need to go to him. To run my hands up his bare chest and rub as much of my skin against his as I can manage. To take him into my body and ride until we're both sweaty and sated.

It's the bond. I *know* it's the bond.

The feeling in my chest isn't a tug any longer. It's a riptide, and I'm losing ground. I stagger forward a step. "What are you doing here?"

"I...couldn't stay away." He sounds like he's speaking through gritted teeth. "I tried."

My body takes me another step closer to him. It's like something else resides within my skin, a force I can't fight; I don't even know how to try. I grab the footboard of the bed. "Leave. I don't..." The surge in my chest gets stronger. "I can't control this."

"I can't leave. It won't let me." He says the words with such finality. As if pronouncing a death sentence.

It's only then that I notice how his body shakes. He's fighting this as much as I am. My fingers release the footboard without my permission and I stumble another few steps closer. "I *hate* this."

Rylan catches my elbows, and even that touch is enough to dim the pressing magic a little.

I exhale shakily. "I'm sorry."

"Stop saying that." He tightens his grip. "Stop fucking apologizing to me."

I shouldn't find his anger reassuring. It shouldn't feel like a bridge forming between us, a shared experience that neither of us want. I can't help it. I rest my forehead against his chest and close my eyes. "I guess there are limits to this, too. Can't fly too far from me. Can't go too long without...this."

"Tell me to stop and I'll find a way."

I open my eyes and drag in a breath. "It will hurt both of us if you do."

"Still," he says through gritted teeth. "Wolf can cause injuries serious enough that regenerating will take up all my strength. It'll buy time."

I blink. "Would you rather we do that?" I'm not sure how I feel about the idea that he might prefer to be maimed than to have sex with me, but I'm not exactly frothing at the mouth to fuck him, either. Still...

Rylan's muscles clench beneath my palms. I don't even remember putting my hands on his chest. He curses. "No, I don't want that. I resent the hell out of this bond—out of *you*—but that doesn't change the fact that I want you. Fucking you is no hardship, Mina."

"No hardship." My laugh comes out jagged. "It is if we don't choose this."

"Tell me to stop and I'll find a way," he repeats.

That's the thing. I don't want him to stop. I can blame the bond, but the truth is that I've been drawn to Rylan since I first saw him. I've hated him, resented him, but neither of those feelings have been enough to combat the sheer desire that licks at me every time we get too close. "I won't ask that of you," I whisper. I'm not even sure which outcome I'm talking about.

Rylan doesn't ask.

He yanks me against him, plastering us together. He takes my mouth. It can barely be called a kiss. It feels like an attack I'm only too happy to meet halfway. This is what I need. If we must do this, we'll do it our way. Angry. Just shy of violent.

I shove him back, and he twists just enough that he hits the wall instead of the open window. The impact still shakes us both.

Not enough. It's not fucking *enough*. Every time I turn around, I'm being reminded of how little control I have, how very much I'm at the whims of powers far beyond me. These vampires. The bond. Even my father. All have power where I have none.

I just want to forget.

Rylan spins me around and I barely catch myself on the window ledge. He doesn't give me time to recover, kicking my legs wide, and then he's there, shoving his giant cock into me. He's almost too big to make it work, even after fucking Malachi and Wolf earlier. Not that he cares. Not that *I* care. I press back, taking him deeper. "More."

His hands land on my hips. Sharp pain makes me jump. I twist to find that the tips of his fingers have...changed. Into claws. "Rylan?"

"Sorry," he grits out. "Can't control it."

He hesitates, but I'm having none of it. "Don't stop."

Rylan takes me at my word. He pounds into me, each stroke relieving a layer of pressure on the bond. I didn't realize how intensely his absence weighed on me until we're as close as two people can be, his body invading mine. The relief has me nearly giddy, which only stokes my anger hotter. "Harder."

The sharp pain of his claws digs in and then he's doing just as I command. Fucking me just shy of violently. Taking his frustrations out on my willing body.

Because I am willing.

I didn't choose the bond, but I choose *this*.

Pleasure instead of violent pain.

I look out over the grounds around this house. Trees crowd

close to the house, giving the impression of us being cut off from the rest of the world. Overhead, the moon is the only witness for what we do in the dark. Pleasure builds in time with the pounding Rylan's giving me. It feels so good that I want it to go on forever.

He has other ideas.

He loops an arm around my waist and hauls me away from the window. To the bed. I get a glimpse of his bloody claws, and for reasons I'm not inclined to examine, the sight makes me clench around his cock. Rylan growls and then he pulls out of me, flipping me around and shoving me down to the mattress.

The only other time we had sex, he was distant for the whole experience. He practically orchestrated it, overseeing things to ensure my power awoke and I broke the blood ward. Even when he was fucking my mouth, he was restrained and in control. There's none of that control now.

He covers me with his body, wrapping his claws around my wrists. "I can't stop."

"Don't." I lift my hips, angling to take his cock again. He shoves into me, and we release twin shaky breaths. This isn't enough, though. I knew it wouldn't be upon the first stroke. I tilt my head to the side. "Bite me."

"Mina." On his lips, my name sounds like a benediction and a curse, all wrapped up into one. He bites me with the speed of a striking cobra. Too deep. I can tell that from the moment his teeth sink into my skin. They're larger than normal, sharper. A predator's teeth meant for ripping and tearing.

Fuck.

This is bad.

The sharp spike of fear is instantly swallowed by the pleasure of his bite. I orgasm hard, wrapping my legs around his waist in an attempt to get him closer, deeper. To make this wave last forever. He keeps fucking me in a borderline frenzy, his mouth latched onto my neck. My blood is flowing freely, too freely, but I can't quite bring myself to care. Not when he's so close.

His strokes lose their steady rhythm and he grinds into me as he comes. I hear shouts in the distance, but I don't really care about that, either.

At least I don't until Rylan lifts his head and snarls. The sound is beastly and far too deep to have come from his throat. In fact, he feels bigger all around right now, as if he's put mass onto his muscled frame while I wasn't paying attention.

He pumps into me almost leisurely, but his eyes—now fully silver—are on something outside the bed. I start to turn my head but stop when pain flares to life with a strength that makes me gasp.

That brings Rylan's gaze back to me. His eyes drop to my neck and he licks his lips. Blood covers the lower half of his face. It covers everything. Him. Me. The bed. Too much blood, even for me.

"Rylan!" That's Malachi's bellow. Close enough to rattle my bones.

Rylan gives himself a shake. He's moving strangely, as if not quite at home in his body. Slowly, so so slowly, he releases one of my wrists and uses a claw to cut his neck. His blood joins mine on his skin, but I can't quite make my body obey my command to lift my head and drink.

Something akin to true fear flashes over his face. "Fuck."

"Feed her, you idiot!" That's Wolf. He sounds almost... worried.

Rylan carefully slides his hand under my head, his claws tangling in my hair, and lifts me as he lowers himself down. My lips touch his neck and fire lashes my tongue. Another swallow and I'm able to latch onto him. Not as well as he could with his superior teeth, but enough that I can drink freely from him. Each mouthful of blood chases away the cobwebs that had sprouted in my head. I swear I can actually feel my body knitting itself back together, muscle and veins and skin.

Gods, he really fucked me up.

He's already hard inside me again, and he starts to withdraw, but I dig my heels into the small of his back. I manage to lift my head enough to say, "Just a little more."

It might be my imagination, but Rylan makes a sound that's filled with relief. "Consider it done." His grip on my head goes gentle and he moves against me, in me, leisurely as I drink from him.

This time, when my orgasm comes, it's softer and nearly sweet and Rylan follows me over the edge immediately. He eases out of me but doesn't move away entirely. I'm shaking. Or maybe he's shaking. I can't tell.

Malachi and Wolf descend on us. Malachi yanks Rylan off me, his big hand wrapped around the other vampire's throat and murder on his face. I struggle to sit up, but Wolf is there, climbing behind me and pulling me between his legs to rest against his chest. He has a knife in one hand and presses the blade to his forearm. "You need more."

"Malachi." My voice is hoarse. I'm not sure if it's from fucking or damage done by Rylan's bite, and I don't care. "Get your hands off him."

"He almost killed you."

"*Let him go.*" My words ring with a foreign power, making my tongue feel like it's sparking. It surges out from me in an arrow aimed right at Malachi.

He drops his hand as if burned. Rylan staggers back a step and slumps against the wall. He looks like shit. I *feel* like shit. Tomorrow, I'll be worried about how close we got to the point of no return. I'll torment myself with how to balance the bond so it doesn't happen again. I'll do a lot of things. Tomorrow. "Just leave."

"Little dhampir."

"*Leave.*"

Malachi hesitates, clearly fighting the command. I'll regret this tomorrow, too. I close my eyes so I don't have to see him stalk out of the room, and I almost manage to contain my flinch at the way the door slams behind him.

Wolf shifts behind me and I open my eyes. "I'm angry at you, too."

"Be angry later. You need this."

I ignore his uncharacteristic seriousness and focus on Rylan. "Sit down before you fall down."

"Is that an order?" It's a token of how out of it he is that his question is barely tinged with frost instead of its normal iciness.

I slump back against Wolf despite my best efforts. Damn it, he's right. I need more blood. I'm dizzy and everything feels like it's too far away. "You want to collapse because of pride? Suit yourself."

Wolf presses his forearm to my lips. "Drink."

I do, greedy pulls of his blood into me. I don't know if it's because Wolf's bloodline controls power over blood or if I'm just feeling better already, but I can actually sense it healing me. I take two more pulls and then push his arm away. "That's enough."

"It's not enough." Wolf's arms tense around me as if he's considering restraining me, but he finally lets them drop.

I fight my way to the edge of the bed and stand on shaking legs. Even with Rylan's and Wolf's blood coursing through me, I'm not going to be okay for a bit. But I'm alive and walking around, so that's more than enough.

I stagger to Rylan, stopping just out of reach. For the first time since it snapped into place, the bond is quiet. It won't last; I know that now. I'm still going to appreciate the reprieve.

For his part, Rylan looks just as shell-shocked as I feel. His body has gone back to normal. Vampire teeth. Human hands, not a claw in sight. I hesitate. "Are you okay?"

His smile holds no mirth. "I should be asking you that question." His gaze lingers on my neck. I don't know him well enough to read his expression, but it looks almost tormented. "This fucking bond. I don't lose control. Not like that."

"I'm fine." My gravelly tone threatens to make a liar out of me. I gingerly touch my fingertips to the newly healed skin of my neck. "By tomorrow, there won't be a mark."

"Mina—"

I let my hand drop. I don't want his apologies. I'm not certain that's what he's about to say, but I don't give him a chance. "Come on. We need to clean up." The bed is ruined. Blood soaks the entire mattress. Changing the sheets won't help. I glance at Wolf. "Do you mind airing out the spare bedroom? I think we have some sheets left over from the last shopping trip." They're always on the list since we go through them so often. Blood is a hell of a stain to try to get out, but the real problem is that they keep getting torn up when our bedroom games get rough.

His pale gaze flicks between me and Rylan. Finally, he climbs off the bed and gives a theatrical bow. "As the lady commands."

"It wasn't a—" He's gone before I can finish. I sigh. "It wasn't a command."

"Semantics." Rylan still doesn't sound like himself. The icy distance that I find strangely comforting is nowhere in evidence. He doesn't even argue as I nudge him in the direction of the bathroom.

I'm weaving on my feet, exhaustion pulling at my body, but it feels important to do this. The why matters less than following my instincts in this situation, so I turn on the water, wait for it to heat up, and then give Rylan another nudge.

Again, he doesn't argue. He simply steps into the shower. But he catches my hand and tows me in after him. Neither of us speak. He doesn't comment on the way I scrub the blood off his chest and neck. I don't make note of how his leaning on me suggests that he's nowhere near as okay as he said.

By the time we're done, I can barely keep my eyes open.

Strangely enough, I'm not remotely surprised to find Wolf and Malachi waiting for us. Wolf wraps a towel around me and sweeps me off my feet, carrying me out of the room with quick strides.

Not quickly enough to avoid hearing Malachi's low words to Rylan. "I told you so."

4

I WAKE TO THE SOUND OF VOICES. THE MEN ARE IN THE next room, talking softly. I roll onto my back and open my eyes, staring up into the darkness of the bedroom. It would be the easiest thing in the world to pull the covers over my head and ignore what happened last night. What it signifies. Even if we ran to the very ends of the earth opposite each other, the bond would eat away at us until...

Could it kill us?

I wouldn't have thought it possible, but that was before it physically propelled me across the room to Rylan. Before it made him forget himself enough to partially shift.

I could let the vampires deal with this current mess. They're all older and more powerful than I am. I'm a fool if I think I can stand on equal footing with them in the coming confrontation, bond or no. They will always be stronger, always be more powerful.

If I hide, I'll remain a pawn for the rest of my life, however long or short that ends up being. Dhampirs live longer than humans, but they aren't borderline immortal like full vampires. I have no idea what the seraph lifespan looks like.

The list of what I don't know only seems to grow longer with time instead of shorter.

I sit up and sigh. There's no help for it. The easy way isn't the right way, and I've fought too hard for anything resembling freedom to simply hand off all the decision-making process to others. They might be more powerful, but *I'm* the linchpin in this mess.

Another soundless sigh and I leave the warmth of the bed and pull on the nearest piece of clothing—one of Malachi's shirts. He's updated his wardrobe a bit since we left the house, but he still favors the shirts that look like they'd be perfectly at home on historical romance novel covers. I like them. A lot. I'm swimming in all the white fabric, his tobacco and clove scent nearly as comforting as when he wraps his arms around me.

I'm still angry about last night. It irritates me to no end that I want *him* to comfort me while I'm mad at him. I inhale again, letting the last of my reservations fall away. As tempting as it is to hide from reality, I know all too well the reality will burst through the door without an invitation. Better to deal with things head-on.

The men haven't stopped talking, but with their superior senses, they all know I'm awake and moving around. I pad barefoot out of the spare bedroom, down the hall, and into the sitting room where they've got a fire going.

Rylan is standing by the window, the light of the early morning putting his features in stark contrast. He looks as tired as I feel, his cheekbones a little too gaunt on his handsome face. Wolf lounges on one of the chairs. He's got his leg dangling over the arm like an indolent king waiting to be entertained. Malachi sits on the couch, his elbows braced on his thighs. All three look at me with varying degrees of wariness.

I stop short. "We need to talk about last night."

Malachi holds out a hand, motioning for me to join him on the couch. I almost go to him through sheer habit, actually take a step in his direction, before the memories of last night crash over me again. How he looked like he was going to murder Rylan. How I magically compelled him to leave the room against his will.

I don't know if it's sleep still clouding my mind or if the situation is just becoming too stressful and I'm in danger of shattering. Right now, I need to be calm and collected, an impossible task when every breath feels like I'm drowning, drawing in water instead of the air I desperately need.

I drop into the free chair. Disappointment flashes over Malachi's face, but it's gone so fast, I'm half sure it's a trick of the firelight. I draw my knees up and wrap my arms around my legs. "We're in over our heads. I can't control the bond, and it's putting you in danger."

Wolf snorts. "None of *us* were the one bleeding out last night."

Rylan flinches, a barely perceptible movement I only catch out of the corner of my eye. I ignore it. "That was my fault. Or, rather, the bond's fault. It never would have gotten so out of control if the bond didn't exist and hadn't messed with our control."

"It was Rylan's fault." Malachi's body might appear relaxed, but he looks like he wants to shred something with his bare hands. "He knew there was risk involved with resisting the proximity the bond demands. He played with your life."

"That's enough."

"He's right." The words sound dragged from Rylan. "I knew there was a risk."

I finally look at him. Even now, with the bond mostly sated, I feel the urge to cross the room and press my mouth to his skin. I clear my throat. "I knew the bond was being affected by avoiding each other, too."

"You couldn't know what it meant."

That's about enough of that. I level a look at each of them in turn. "I am not a child who needs others to make the decisions for me or take responsibility for my actions. Maybe I didn't know the parameters of the bond, but there hasn't been a living seraph in three out of four of our lifetimes. None of us have experienced a seraph bond before. As a result, there will be mistakes."

"He almost ripped out your throat." Malachi's staring at me like he wants to wrap me up and shove me into a cage. All in the name of safety, of course.

This isn't an argument I'm going to win. It's written across all their expressions. I didn't expect this seriousness from Wolf, but he's surprised me a lot lately. Or maybe his self-preservation is stronger than his wildness. No one knows for sure what happens if I die, but we're all convinced it's bad.

Better to change the subject and circle back when I have an argument that might actually make them hold still long enough to listen. "You were awfully tense when I came in here."

Suddenly, they all find other things in the room to look at, avoiding my gaze. Alarm bells blaze through my head. "Have they found us again?"

"No. You're safe."

"Don't lie to her, Malachi. She's not safe. None of us are." Rylan's staring out the window as if seconds from stripping and shape-shifting into some animal so he can run as far and fast from this conversation as possible.

If my father's people haven't found us and it's not about last night... What else could possibly go wrong now? I glance from one to the other, finally settling on Wolf. The other two can hold out indefinitely if they decide I need to be left in the dark. Wolf won't. "Tell me."

"I—"

"*Wolf.*"

Malachi's sharp warning is like waving a red flag in front of a bull. Wolf laughs and slouches farther into the chair. "Nothing much, love. Just ways it might be possible to break the seraph bond without killing all of us in the process."

The possibility leaves me breathless. I slump back into my chair, my legs suddenly boneless. "We can do that?"

"Probably not," Rylan says darkly, still staring out the window. "If it could be done, more people would know about it."

Wolf rolls his pale blue eyes. "As I was telling *you*, seraphim were all but legend to most people until this happened.

Just because you've never heard of a way doesn't mean it isn't possible."

Something almost like excitement flickers through me. "How do we do it?" If there's a way to remove the bond, then my chance at freedom isn't gone after all. "What do you know?"

"So eager to be free of us." Wolf laughs again, a high, mad sound that raises the small hairs on the back of my neck. He drops his foot to the floor and straightens. "I know a guy."

"You know a *demon*," Malachi cuts in. His expression is carefully closed down, offering nothing at all.

I blink. Wait for someone to laugh and let me in on the joke. No one does. They're all watching me with devastatingly serious expressions on their face.

Demons.

Demons exist.

I don't know why I'm surprised. Seraphim are, at least according to a number of human religions, the holier counterparts to demons. Considering what my people have done to other supernatural creatures, maybe demons are cuddly do-gooders. I clear my throat, striving to sound like my world hasn't shifted on its axis yet again. "Are demons trustworthy?"

Wolf gives another of those wild laughs. "They're *demons*, love. Demon deals have the reputation they do for a reason. They're an option of last resort, reserved for the desperate."

"Ah." I press my lips together. "Well, we're desperate. How do we get a hold of a demon?"

Rylan frowns as if deciding to be present in the conversation for the first time since I walked into the room. "You're serious."

"Of course I'm serious. I know you think I'm a monster who wants to put a leash on your cock, but I didn't choose this bond any more than you three did. If it's not in play, then I have a chance to actually be free."

"Mina." I hate how reserved Malachi sounds. He's studying me with those dark, dark eyes. "Even if your father doesn't know that you're part seraph, he will hunt you until he's dead or you are. He can't afford to let you escape."

Because if I can escape, supposedly powerless bastard dhampir that I am, then anyone can.

I know Malachi's right, and I hate it. I take a slow breath. "We'll cross that bridge when we get to it. The bond has to take priority."

Wolf is watching me, too. For once, the ever-present mocking amusement on his face is nowhere to be seen. "The cost is always high for demon deals."

I don't say that I'm willing to pay it. I can't, not without knowing what it is. "I'm not prepared to rule out any option until we've fully explored it."

Malachi looks like he wants to argue, but Wolf has already jumped to his feet. "I'll see what I can do."

"*Now?*"

"No time like the present." He strides out of the room without a backward look. Knowing what I do of the man, he might be intent on his destination…or he might get distracted and disappear for a few days, only to show back up having totally forgotten his intentions. Wolf is as wild as his namesake and ten times as unpredictable.

Rylan starts for the door. "This won't work."

"Rylan." Malachi doesn't move, but his gaze tracks the other man. "You need to stop resisting. Last night can't happen again."

"Mind your own business."

It seems like every single conversation we have these days circles back to this fucking bond. I want to rip it out with my bare hands. "It's fine." I continue when it seems like Malachi might argue. "Leave it, please."

"Look at you, already acting like the heir." Rylan's gone before his cold words fully penetrate.

I can't work up even a half-hearted glare in response. Not when he's right. Not when I'm strangely grateful the unnatural peace from last night is no longer in play. *This* Rylan, I understand. When he's cold, he makes sense. Even the feral, out-of-control version of him is safer than the shell-shocked man who shared a shower with me. It's hard enough to keep him at a distance with the bond pulling at me when we actively hate each other. If there's a softening at all...

To distract myself, I look at Malachi, who doesn't seem any happier than he did a few minutes ago. I want to storm out of the room to avoid *this* conversation, too. Unfortunately, that's not a permanent solution. "I'm sorry about last night." I rush on before he can say anything. "Not about what happened with Rylan, though I'm sorry it worried you. But I'm sorry about after."

"Mina, come here."

I almost don't. My reasons for choosing this chair instead of the couch remain, but it's just the two of us now and I miss the feel of his body against mine. I want to blame that on the bond, but I've been drawn to this vampire since before it snapped into place. "We need to talk about it."

"We will." He motions with his fingers again, beckoning me. "Come here. Please."

Please.

Have I ever heard Malachi utter that word? I don't think so. That, more than anything, gets me up and moving around the coffee table to take his hand. He tugs me down to straddle him, but there's nothing sexual in the move. It's as if he wants the comfort of touching me as much as I crave touching him.

"I didn't know I could do that," I whisper.

"I suspected it was possible."

I blink. "You didn't think to say something?"

"Suspecting something and knowing it for truth are two different things, little dhampir." His gaze coasts over my face as if memorizing my features. "I won't say I liked the feeling, but if you hadn't done something, I might have killed Rylan. I...wasn't thinking clearly."

"Malachi." A bitter little laugh slips free. "We are such a mess."

"It's no surprise there's a learning curve on this. There is on all magic."

"I wouldn't know." Up until a month ago, I thought I hadn't inherited any magic at all despite the fact that most dhampir children of bloodline vampires get some kind of magical skill. Based on my father's bloodline, I should be able to glamour people. Instead, I was thought a dud and sent to Malachi as a brood mare.

Apparently my seraph blood stifled or overpowered the vampire genetics. I'm still not sure which is the truth. I don't know if I'll *ever* be sure.

The whole thing makes my head hurt if I think about it too closely.

"Mina." Malachi waits for me to look at him to continue. "We'll figure it out. Together. I'm not prepared to hold missteps against you while you're exploring the parameters of your powers. Do you intend to compel me again?"

"No!" I swallow hard and temper my tone. "Absolutely not."

"That's all that matters. Consider yourself forgiven." He hesitates. "I'm...sorry...as well."

His hesitance makes me smile a little. We really are an unmitigated mess. I glance at the doorway that the other two left through. "I hope Wolf's able to find that demon he was talking about. It could be the solution we need."

Malachi goes tense beneath me. "Are you really that eager to be rid of me?"

EAGER TO BE RID OF HIM? IS HE JOKING? I CRAVE Malachi like a fever in my blood. Even now, I can't help running my hands down his chest, tracing the lines of his muscles beneath his white shirt, so similar to the one I'm wearing right now. "You should be happy there's a chance to negate the bond."

"You're so quick to forget what I said before we left my home."

I sit back and stare. I don't understand why he's angry about this. "Being forcibly bonded is not something anyone wants."

"Don't tell me what I want, little dhampir." He coasts his hands up my thighs, beneath the hem of the shirt, to settle on my hips, tugging me until I'm pressed tightly against him. "We will explore this option if you insist, but I won't allow you to bargain anything you can't afford to lose."

I sigh, the sound almost a whimper as he rocks me against his hardening cock. "The price will be high regardless. That's to be expected."

"All the same."

I should just let him sweep me away with sex like he has every other time my stress winds me too tightly. I frown. "You were never this good at reading me before."

Just like that, his expression shuts down. "You're easy enough to read, Mina."

His lack of tell is a tell all its own. I put my hands on his shoulders and stare down at him. "Malachi, you missed blatant cues when I first moved in with you. Not all of that was intentional, so don't lie to me and tell me it was." When he still doesn't say anything, I press. "I thought the only side effect of the bond was being able to feel proximity. And now apparently my being able to command you."

"The magic you used on me last night might not be linked to the bond. Your father's glamour isn't just changing people's visual perceptions. He can command them, too."

I know that, have experienced it, but somehow the fact that I might be using a *vampire* power never really occurred to me. Still... I shake my head, trying to focus. "Stop trying to distract me. We're talking about the bond."

He finally says, "Feeling proximity to each other is a side effect of the bond, yes."

Careful. So fucking careful. Which means he's hiding something and not even doing it well. "Enough of this." I start to rise, but he clamps his hands on my hips, holding me in place. I glare.

"I'm going to go ask Wolf if he can feel my emotions. *He* won't lie to me." If only because he'll enjoy the chaos the confirmation will bring about.

"Mina."

"Malachi." I match his censoring tone. "I am not a child, and if you hide things from me, I'm going to resent it. Tell me the truth."

His sigh is nearly imperceptible. "Yes, I can...sense things."

"Things being my emotions." The sheer intrusion of it has my chest getting tight. This bond is bad enough. Knowing where they are at all times is horrible. I never thought to ask if it goes both ways, but of course it does. They know where I am without fail. It's how they recognize exactly how far the bond stretches before things get painful.

"Things being your emotions," he confirms. "Not all of them. I get spikes of pleasure or anger or fear. It only seems to be the extreme versions of them."

"I can't feel yours," I say numbly.

He lifts one hand to cup my face, moving carefully as if he expects me to flinch away. "All of us learned to shield a long time ago. It's a necessary skill."

Somehow, this just makes me feel worse. "A necessary skill for vampires and dhampirs with power."

"You have power now." He strokes my cheekbone with his thumb. "I'll teach you, little dhampir."

I want that, but I'm not quite prepared to let go of my complicated feelings about him hiding this. It's enough to make me wonder what else he's keeping from me, supposedly for my own good. "Why didn't you say something as soon as you understood what was happening?" Realization rolls over me. "That's how you knew things had gotten out of control with Rylan last night." It hadn't even occurred to me to question it before now. Vampire senses are incredibly strong, so it's likely they knew we were having sex even without the bond, but now that I think about it, I don't believe either Wolf or Malachi would have come into the room without an invitation. Not when Rylan and I are balanced so carefully at odds right now.

They felt my flash of fear when he bit me and it brought them running.

"Yes." He shifts his hand to cup my neck. "I didn't tell you before because I knew you wouldn't like this new development, and you're already under enough pressure."

Once again the urge rises to simply...let him handle this. I'm outmatched and outgunned and I don't know anything about magic. It would be *so easy* to let Malachi take charge. I can't do it. I close my eyes. "Don't keep things from me again. I realize that I'm hardly an asset right now, but the choices you make affect me, too. I can't make the right calls if I don't know all the info."

I can't make the right calls. How laughable. I haven't made a single fucking call.

"There's nothing else."

I wish I believed him.

Not for the first time, I wish we were just two people who'd met under normal circumstances. I don't even know how that would work. I can't imagine running into Malachi in a coffee shop or on a street or in the thousands of other places meet-cutes happen in fiction. Going on a normal human date? It defies comprehension. What a mess. I slump down against his chest, and he tenses a little like I've surprised him. I close my eyes. "I hate this."

"We're in an adjustment period."

That almost makes me laugh. Almost. "I am magically bound to three vampires who I barely know, two of whom would be only too happy to murder me."

"Wolf likes you."

I open my eyes and lift my head so I can shoot him the look that statement deserves. "Wolf might like me just fine. Sometimes. We both know that doesn't change the truth of my statement."

He shrugs a single shoulder. "None of us are going to hurt you. Last night was an anomaly."

Hurt is such a strange concept. I was a child when I realized that physical hurt is far preferable to the pain someone can cause with their words, with their willingness to lock me away and deprive me of their attention. Compared to that, being beaten is almost a relief. At least I know *that* pain will fade.

The pain and fear I felt last night were massively overshadowed by pleasure. Not to mention the easing of the pressure on the bond between me and Rylan. The cost is more than worth the reward from where I'm sitting, but I don't need to ask Malachi to know he doesn't agree.

"Teach me to shield."

"Tomorrow." He digs his hands into my hair and gives it a light tug. "After we spar."

A groan slips free before I have a chance to stop it. "I *hate* sparring." Even with Malachi's blood having nearly healed my formerly shattered knee, it's readily apparent that I'll never be as fast or strong as he is. Whatever else is true about the seraphim, they're nowhere near as physically superior as vampires are. Against a human? I can hold my own and then some. Against Malachi? I doubt I'll ever be able to. "You always kick my ass."

"You're getting stronger." The way he says it, I'm tempted to believe it's true.

I frown. "I'll never be a match for you."

"Of course not." He gives me a slow grin that has my stomach doing flips. "I'm older and stronger than you." He leans forward until his lips brush the shell of my ear. "You need to learn to fight dirty."

"I *do* fight dirty." I have since I realized I'd never win in a fair fight, a lesson I learned long before I ever met Malachi.

His chuckle is more like a rumble. "You're terrible at it."

"Wow, thanks. That's such an enlightening criticism."

"We'll invite Wolf to spar. He can teach you a thing or two."

I sigh. "I bet. Though it's going to end with me bitten and us fucking."

"Is that so bad?" Malachi shifts against me, pulling me back so our hips are sealed together. He's still hard, but he *always* seems to be hard when we get close. It's a little mind-blowing, but I'm not exactly complaining. I like fucking him. I like *him*. If this situation were different...

But it's not.

He might have enjoyed the sex before we were forcibly bonded when my powers emerged, but if last night proved anything, it's that now he doesn't have a choice. Neither of us do. "It is when the alternative is potentially death."

"Mina, I've wanted you since the moment I saw you." He guides me to roll my hips again, sliding one hand up my spine until my breasts press against his chest and I put my arms around his neck. His lips brush my ear. "Even in a frenzy and half-starved, I had to get my mouth on your pussy. You can't blame the bond for that."

No, but I could blame the whole being-half-starved thing.

I see his point, though. I don't know if I'm willing to accept it, but I see it. I draw in a harsh breath. "We're going to talk to the demon. Getting rid of the bond doesn't mean getting rid of you."

"It better not." His voice lowers, becoming nearly a growl. "Wolf wasn't lying yesterday. I have to make myself walk away from you, little dhampir. All I want is to chain you to a bed and fuck you until you're filled up with me. Until you're pregnant with *my* child."

Oh gods.

I shiver against him. "That, um, is the end goal."

"I don't give a fuck about the goal." He drags his mouth down the side of my neck, directly over where Rylan bit me last night. "I wanted that even before we decided usurping your father was the best option."

I shiver harder. "Oh." It would be so easy to believe him...

Why am I fighting this?

It doesn't matter what might have been because we can only deal with what *is*. And the reality of the situation is that Malachi and I—and Rylan and Wolf—are bonded because of my seraph blood. The reality is also that my father will hunt me—and Malachi, most likely—to the ends of the earth because we escaped his trap. The best way out of a future spent on the run is getting me pregnant so I can take the place as his heir. And then killing him.

Spending time wishing for things to be different from how they are is wasteful.

I tilt my head to the side, encouraging him. "I suppose we shouldn't waste any time."

"Mmm." He nips my neck, nowhere near hard enough to draw blood, and rocks me against his length again. "Take my cock out."

"So bossy," I murmur. I shift back just enough that I can reach between us to do as he commands. He fills my palm and then some, his size massive and familiar. I stroke him. "Hurry."

Malachi ignores me. He grabs a fistful of his shirt that I'm wearing and winds it at the base of my spine, lifting the hem until I'm bared from the waist down. The growl he makes has me whimpering. "So fucking perfect." It almost sounds like he's speaking to himself rather than to me. He palms my pussy, pushing two blunt fingers into me. He's fingered me more times than I can count in the last month, but it feels particularly possessive in this moment. As if he's reclaiming something he thought he might lose.

Something he *refuses* to lose.

"Did it feel good fucking Rylan, little dhampir?"

"Yes," I gasp. I try to rock my hips to take his fingers deeper, but his hold on the shirt keeps me hovering above him.

He idly fucks me, watching his large fingers slide in and out of my pussy. "He partially changed."

It's not a question, but I still feel compelled to answer. "Yes." I clutch at Malachi's shoulders. My thighs are shaking and he's just getting started.

His eyes go a pure, true black and he licks his lips. "Did his cock get bigger inside you?" He wedges a third finger into me. "Did he stretch you until it almost hurt?"

I claw at his shoulders, but I'm not going anywhere until he allows me to. "Yes," I sob out. "It felt amazing."

"I know." He says it so softly, I *know* he's not speaking to me. Just like I know that he and Rylan haven't rekindled some semblance of their former relationship the same way he and Wolf have. *They* might fuck each other nearly as often as they fuck me, but Rylan holds himself apart.

It strikes me that the flicker of jealousy in Malachi's dark eyes isn't directly solely at Rylan for fucking me. It's also at *me* for fucking Rylan.

I release his shoulders and place my hands on my hips. "He grabbed me here. His claws sank into me." There are still little divots in my skin, a reminder that all the blood I consumed went to keeping me alive instead of healing the smaller wounds completely.

"He held you in place while he fucked you." Malachi presses his fingers deeper and then twists his wrist, feeling for my G-spot.

"Yes." This time, when I rock my hips, he lets me ride his fingers. My voice goes a little rough. "He threw me on the bed and held me down."

Malachi exhales slowly. "You liked it."

"I loved it." The truth. I don't know why I love the rough fucking, the near-violent consumption of lust. In the end, knowing why doesn't matter. I love it, and that's good enough reason to do it.

He pulls his fingers out of me, but I don't have a chance to protest because he twists, taking us to the couch with him on top of me. Malachi doesn't give me time to adjust. He spreads my thighs wide and starts working his cock into me. Heat dances on my skin, but no flames appear. He hasn't lost control of his bloodline power since we left his house. I'm grateful for that fact; I love knowing I affect him deeply, but I don't relish the thought of having to flee yet another room because Malachi burned the hell out of it in the middle of sex.

"I like seeing his marks on you, little dhampir." His gaze lands on my throat again. I haven't looked in the mirror since I woke up, but if the pinpricks on my hips from Rylan's claws are still there, then no doubt I still bear a mark from his teeth. Malachi shoves all the way into me and braces himself on his elbows on either side of my body. He's pinning me in place but saving me from the majority of his weight.

He runs his nose over my throat. "I love smelling him on your skin." His tongue darts out to taste me. "This is how it should be. All three of us."

Pleasure courses through me, but my mind trips over what he just said. "You can *smell* him on me?" I shift, but Malachi isn't letting me move. "I took a shower."

"I know." He kisses my neck. "I think it's the bond. Or

because we're all bloodline vampires. Doesn't matter why." Each sentence is punctuated by a slow thrust. "We can scent each other on you. It makes me crazed."

I run my hands down his back and grip his ass, urging him to fuck me harder. "Give me more."

"I'll give you everything." He lifts his head and I catch the metallic scent of blood a moment before he kisses me. He nicked his tongue and his blood coats our kiss, ramping up my desire even more.

More.

I can't get enough.

I suck on his tongue as he fucks me. He shifts his angle and presses his thumb to my clit, working me until I orgasm all over his cock. I half expect him to follow me over the edge, but Malachi has other plans.

He fucks me through my orgasm, his body a cage I don't want to escape. Only as the last wave fades does he slow down, his strokes gaining a leisurely pace that curls my toes. He nips my bottom lip. "They won't be back for a while."

I dig my nails into his ass and lift my hips to take him deeper yet. "Guess we'll have to entertain ourselves."

"Guess so."

We don't stop for a very, very long time.

6

I'M IN THE KITCHEN THE NEXT DAY WHEN I FEEL IT. A
sense of…not exactly wrongness, but an intrusion. I nearly drop
the bowl I'm holding. "What is *that?*"

Instantly, Malachi is on alert. "What is what?"

"There's this…" I frown. "I don't know how to explain it. It's
like an itch I can't scratch."

He narrows his eyes. "Where?"

Without looking, I point nearly behind me. "There. I can't
tell how far."

He doesn't hesitate. "*Rylan.*" Before the sound of the other
vampire's name is finishing echoing through the house, Malachi
has me in his arms and he's moving in that nearly-too-fast speed,
flying through the rooms and out the front door—on the opposite side of the house from where I felt the intrusion.

Rylan lands beside us, and I get the impression that he jumped from the second or third story. His dark hair is a little ruffled, but he's back to wearing a suit and looks freshly pressed. "What's going on?"

"She felt something. Coming from the opposite direction."

I expect Rylan to laugh it off. Why should he take this seriously when he barely bothers to listen to a single word that comes out of my mouth? But his gaze narrows the same way Malachi's did. "Get to the safe house we agreed on. I'll take a look and call Wolf to update him." He pulls off his jacket, quickly followed by his shirt.

I tense. "Wait. I like this house. There's no reason to run if—"

"Rylan will take a look. If he gives the signal, we'll come back." Malachi is already moving, rushing through the trees that surround the house at a pace I could never dream of matching. I have no choice but to cling to him. At this point, I'm just grateful that, for once, I was actually wearing clothing. My shorts and oversized T-shirt are hardly appropriate for the briskness of the weather, but it's better than being naked.

The cry of a giant bird reaches us, and I only need to see Malachi's face to know that it's not good news. "They found us again?"

"Looks like it." He picks up his pace, nearly flying across the uneven ground. "We'll know more after we meet up with Rylan and Wolf."

It took them less than a week to track us down this time. They're closing the gap, and no one can figure out how. Hell, if seraphim and demons exist, maybe witches do, too. Maybe they have some sort of scrying spell. I'll ask Malachi about it after we get out of danger. I don't *think* any of my father's people can match him in size, speed, and strength, but I wouldn't have wagered on my father trapping Malachi behind a blood ward for decades on end.

I could keep peppering him with questions, but the truth is that until we regroup with the others, the only priority is to put as much distance between us and the other vampires as possible. We can't fight, not without risking one of us getting hurt. There's no reasoning with them. They're following orders, and only a direct order from my father will change their course.

This is a race, but I still don't know the parameters. I know *our* goals, but we have no idea what my father knows.

I lift my head and tug on Malachi's shirt. "We need one of them alive."

He glances at me without breaking stride. "That's risky."

"I'm aware. But we need to know if he's pursuing us because he wants you back or if he knows what happened when we broke the blood ward." If he knows I have seraph blood, that I awoke that power, that I'm bonded with not one but *three* bloodline vampires...

That changes everything.

If he can get his hands on me, he'll hold the leash for three of the seven bloodlines. I know all too well the lengths he'll go to get what he wants once we're under his control. The men might be able to hold out indefinitely, but if I have to choose between keeping them alive or doing something really unforgivable, I already know what I'll choose.

My father knows that, too.

"We need to know," I repeat.

Malachi nods. He doesn't turn back, but that's fine. Getting to a secondary location is the primary goal. We know where *they're* headed, and they'll stay at the house for at least a short period of time to plumb it for any information they can. We just have to pick one of them off when they leave. It sounds easy, but I know better.

I lay my head against Malachi's chest and let him carry me away.

Judging by the position of the sun in the sky, several hours have passed by the time he slows and sets me on my feet. I study the little farmhouse in the distance. It's surrounded by rolling fields and looks like something out of a painting. "Is that where we're headed?"

"Yes." He rolls his shoulders. He doesn't look like he's been sprinting at full speed while carrying another person, but he *does* look tired. "Rylan will have gotten word to Wolf by now. They'll meet us here."

"We have to—"

"I know, little dhampir. But no one is going back there until you're secured."

As much as I want to argue, he's right. We fall into an easy jog that eats up the distance at a pace slightly faster than an athletic human could maintain. My knee barely twinges. A month ago, I wouldn't have been able to do this. Not after my father shattered my knee in punishment for an escape attempt. He wanted to make sure I'd never be able to run again, and it was a reality I'd made a tumultuous peace with. Until Malachi gave me his blood.

Bloodline vampires really are something special.

My father always set himself above the rest at the compound, and up until I met Malachi, I thought that was just narcissistic bullshit because my father has some magic. Now I realize how deeply the difference between normal vampires and bloodline vampires go.

Malachi is the last of his line, those who carry the power to control fire. If he doesn't have children, his bloodline will die with him. I glance in his direction. "Do Wolf and Rylan have family?"

He doesn't take his gaze from the farmhouse. "You mean others that are part of their bloodline? Yes. Not many, but yes."

Not many.

Guilt claws at my throat. "Shouldn't they be out procreating or something to ensure their bloodlines keep going? I understand why you didn't, but they weren't trapped behind a blood ward."

"We live very long lives, Mina. There's no rush." The words are right, but there's something off in his tone.

Once again, Wolf's words, Malachi's words come back to me. He wants me pregnant with his babies. It's still a little mind-blowing. A few months ago, pregnancy wasn't even on my radar, and now it's my highest priority. Even that hardly seems real, though. My future is measured in goals right now.

Survive. Get pregnant. Become heir. Kill my father.

Every time I try to think of *after*, my brain bounces off the concept. Pregnancy is one thing. Children is something entirely different. But if I get pregnant, the *goal* is children.

"I'm going to be a terrible mother."

Malachi stops. I don't notice for two steps, not until he reaches out and snags my wrist. "Don't say that."

"It's the truth." I don't look back at him. "I don't know what your childhood was like. Maybe it's been so long that you don't really remember. I'm only twenty-five, Malachi. Those memories are still fresh and bloody in my head." My violent, manipulative father. My ghost of a mother. How does someone come from such trauma without perpetuating the cycle?

"Mina." He tugs on my wrist. When I don't turn, he tugs again, harder this time. I know I could tell him to stop and he would, but I let him haul me back to stand before him. "Look at me."

Reluctantly, I obey, lifting my gaze to his.

He catches my chin, holding me in place. "Do you want children?"

The question makes me laugh. The sound comes out almost like a sob. "What does that matter? The path is set."

"It matters."

No, it really doesn't. Not to me. I try to pull back, but he keeps me easily in place. "Malachi, please."

"Answer the question."

It's a simple question. A vital one, even. Why does it make me want to cry? I close my eyes, hiding from him as much as I'm trying to keep the burning internal. "I don't know. It was never a possibility until it was a decision thrust upon me, first by my father and then by this situation." All true, but not the full truth. My lower lip quivers despite my best efforts. If anyone else asked me this... But it's not anyone else. It's Malachi. "Maybe part of me has always wanted kids, but it was never in the cards. And now that it is—"

"This situation is hardly ideal in that respect."

His understatement makes me open my eyes. "You want kids."

"Of course I want kids." He shrugs as if this is a given. "I always have. Not simply to continue my line. I..." Malachi glances away and clenches his jaw. "I want a family."

The way he says it. Like it's a sin to be ashamed of. Maybe it is in our world, where marriages and children are political right down to their very core. There are no love matches in my father's compound, no matter what some there would like to believe. "I see."

"Maybe it's foolish to want something that so few of our people have, but I want it all the same."

I know what he means even without him explicitly saying it. "There does seem to be a dearth of happy childhoods among vampires."

"It doesn't have to be that way."

I try to picture what he's saying. A happy childhood. I've seen it represented fictionally, but a part of me always believed it to be exactly that—fiction. Even the humans manage to fuck up their kids in astronomical numbers, and most of them are attempting to marry and procreate because of love rather than politics. The odds are not in our favor.

They're especially not in our favor with this current situation.

I don't want to ask the question, but I need to know the answer. "What happens if I get pregnant and you're not the father?" Even with Rylan attempting to stay out of the race to impregnate me, Wolf and I have sex nearly as often as Malachi and I do.

He shrugs. "It doesn't matter to me. I've made my choice."

As if it's just that simple. "If we broke the bond and one of them got me pregnant instead... Malachi, you'd be free. Free for the first time in decades. You should be focusing on that instead of tying yourself to a sinking ship."

"Mina."

Gods, the way he says my name. It makes me shiver. "Yes?"

"I respect your ability to make decisions for yourself enough to stand by while Wolf courts a demon, even though I don't agree with it. Give me the courtesy of returning the favor."

I open my mouth to continue arguing, but I don't have a leg to stand on. He's right. No matter what I think, he's more than capable of making his own choices. I swallow hard. "Okay. Sorry. I just don't want you to end up regretting..."

"Regretting you." Malachi gives me a small sliver of a smile. "Impossible. You've crashed into my life with all the subtlety of a bomb detonating, but it's been refreshing." He turns us toward the farmhouse. "Now, let's get inside and discuss next steps."

And that's that.

I'm completely unsurprised to step through the door and find that Wolf and Rylan both beat us here. Neither of them were weighed down with carrying me or having that conversation out in the field before entering. That said... I glance at Wolf. "How did you know we moved?"

"Rylan caught me on the way back." He hops onto the faded counter and rubs his hands together. "I should have news on the demon front within a day or two. Those bastards like to play hard to get."

Malachi appears in the doorway. "Everything is secure."

"I told you it was." Rylan is staring out the window as if

he'd rather be anywhere but here. I can't exactly blame him, but I won't pretend that his attitude isn't grating on me. Obviously things aren't going to magically change between us just because of what happened two nights ago, but would it kill the asshole to *look* at me?

Malachi moves to lean against the counter next to Wolf. "We can't keep operating like this. The demon deal is a long shot, but even if we remove the bond, it won't remove the threat Cornelius represents. We need to know what he knows."

Finally, Rylan turns from the window. "You want to take one of his men."

"Yes."

"It won't be easy. We'll have to kill the rest of the scouting party."

"I'm aware."

I look between them. "If it's too dangerous—"

"It's not." Rylan cuts a hand through the air. "Malachi and I are more than capable of dealing with a handful of Cornelius's dogs. It will incite him to send more next time, but Malachi's right. We need the information."

Malachi crosses his arms over his large chest. "It was Mina's idea."

"I see." Rylan clenches his jaw and seems to make himself look at me. He might have an expression like he's chewing on rocks, but even he can't mask the heat in his dark eyes.

An answering heat licks through me, but I shove down the sensation. Now isn't the time, and he won't thank me for it. "The sooner we do this, the better."

7

WOLF KICKS OUT HIS HEELS AND GRABS MALACHI'S
shoulder when it looks like the larger man is about to speak. "We
know you don't like leaving the pretty little dhampir alone, but
she won't be alone. She'll be with me."

"That's not the comfort you think it is."

Wolf laughs. "We both know I'm capable of keeping her
among the living. If I'm so inclined."

"My last statement stands." Malachi sighs. "But if you lay
down a blood ward, I'll consider myself comforted."

Alarm blares through me. "No. Not another blood ward."
Not when one of those spells was responsible for keeping Malachi
trapped in that rotting house for far too long.

"Don't worry, love. I don't know which one of my worthless
cousins was greedy enough to be bribed by your father, but wards

are capable of more than just containing. We can keep the enemy out with them." He makes a face. "They're not exactly fun to put in place, though, and feeding from you so soon after Rylan fucked things up is out of the question."

Rylan startles. "That's not—"

"Take the blood from me." Malachi's already turning for the door. "The faster we move on this, the better."

"You're no fun, old friend." Wolf hops off the counter. "But you know what would make it more fun?"

Malachi's sigh is fond. "We don't have time for that."

"There's always time for that."

I listen to them bicker as they move deeper into the house. Judging from the quick look I got at the layout when Malachi whisked me inside, they're heading for the living room. It's fully enclosed, without a single window, so the easiest to fortify. I hold out a hand when Rylan starts to follow them. "They've got this."

"You don't give me orders."

I bite back a sigh. "No, I don't give you orders. But they're about to fuck, and unless you're going to pull that stick out of your ass and join in, you stalking after them is going to be distracting."

Again, that tiny startle. He seems to give me his full attention. "It doesn't bother you that they're intimate when you're not around."

"Why would it? Their relationship predates me." I pause. "So does yours."

"Ancient history." But the way he glances at the doorway gives lie to his words. I don't know what happened with Malachi and Rylan. I haven't asked, and neither of them has offered.

Malachi and Wolf make more sense in my head. Theirs is a friendship that often includes sex, and they hold each other lightly in a way that suggests they aren't heartbroken by the years they've spent apart. As if they've come together and parted over and over again through their lives. I don't have confirmation, of course, but it's there in the way they interact.

Rylan is different.

Wolf doesn't seem to see me as a threat. I'm just another plaything for his amusement and pleasure when he's around. Rylan looks at me as if I stole his only love.

Maybe I did.

"Rylan—"

"No." He shakes his head. "Gods, you're practically beaming your emotions into my brain. Stop it. I don't want or need your pity."

I close my eyes and try to shove the feeling away, grasping for something else to feel instead. Anger lingers just below the surface, just like it always does. I grab it with both hands and wrap it around me like a comforting blanket. When I open my eyes, he's lost that nearly feral look. "Better?"

"Barely."

I glare. "I didn't know I was projecting my emotions. Malachi only just told me before we had to run."

He shrugs, turning for the door. "It's simply another burden to bear."

That's about enough of that. I grab Rylan's arm. He's too strong to move, so when I yank, I end up pulling myself forward instead of him back. He jerks away from me, but I'm not in the mood to let this conversation remain unfinished. I stalk him across the kitchen, barely aware that he's retreating until I have him pressed against the counter.

Only then do I realize what I was doing.

I jerk back. "Sorry."

Rylan catches my elbows, stopping me from backing up. "You want to be a predator? Stop second-guessing yourself."

I yank, but he's holding me too firmly. "I don't want to be a predator." I pull back again. Fail again. "Not with you three."

"I don't fucking understand you." He says it so softly, I almost miss the words.

Just like that, my anger flares hot enough to scald. "Oh, because I'm not playing the part of the monster the way you want? Because I'm just as in over my head as the rest of you? Which part, Rylan? Please enlighten me so we can get past this bullshit."

"There's no getting past some things."

We're so close, we're sharing the same air. I hate that I want nothing more than to press my body against his, to claim his mouth so I can swallow down his poisonous words, can take every part of him into me until we're both a shaking mess.

I want to blame the bond for this. Surely I'm not so twisted as to desire a man who clearly hates me. Unfortunately, the truth is significantly less convenient. The bond is present, of course, but it's not pulling at me the same way it did two nights ago. I am firmly in control. Which means I have no one to blame but myself.

"Let go," I say softly. "We might not be able to control the fact that the bond requires us to drink and fuck each other, but if you really hate me as much as you say, then let me go right fucking now."

Rylan's grip spasms on my elbows. For a moment, his cold expression flickers and I get a glimpse of the feral creature within, the one more in line with the animals he can shift into than the smoothly cultured vampire he normally presents to the world. "I don't hate you."

"Could have fooled me."

He still doesn't release me. "Malachi and Wolf are too young to remember what your people did to ours, but I'm not. It's not something I can release simply because you're not acting like *they* did."

I know this. Of course I know this. He might not have said as much in so many words up to this point, but his hatred goes far too deep to be directed at me personally. I don't blame him for it. That doesn't mean I'm going to roll over for him, either. "I can't change what I am. I don't know if I can change what happened, but I'm trying."

He searches my face. "If Wolf can do what he says, the demon will demand a high cost."

"I'm aware."

Rylan shakes his head slowly. "I..." He takes a slow breath. "I don't want to see you hurt, Mina. I hate this bond, but that doesn't mean I want you dead."

"I know." And I do. If he wanted me dead, he wouldn't have been so panicked when he took too much blood. That strange, soft moment in the shower wouldn't have occurred. Knowing that doesn't excuse his shitty attitude, though. "Let me go, Rylan."

Finally, he releases me. When I don't immediately step back, his lips curl into something that's almost a smile. "If you're not opposed to the idea, I think it'd be wise to ensure the bond doesn't get to the point of desperation again."

"So formal." I tilt my head to the side. "You're saying you want to have sex again."

"Yes." The word is almost a sigh.

"Okay."

Rylan blinks. "Okay?"

"Yeah. Okay." I force myself to take a step back, and then another. "You irritate the hell out of me, and I kind of want to smack you on a regular basis, but I like fucking you, Rylan." Now it's my turn to hesitate. "However, I understand if you don't want to throw your hat into the ring, so to speak. If you want to keep things to anal or oral to avoid the risk of pregnancy, that's okay, too."

Another of those slow blinks. "I don't understand you."

"You don't have to understand me." Part of me kind of wants him to, though. I wave a hand at my body. "No matter what else is true about this bond, babies change things. I'm not going to force you."

He takes a step toward me, and some lingering prey instinct has me backing up. Rylan stalks me across the kitchen, his eyes bleeding silver, his movements going nearly feline. A bolt of heat goes through me when I remember his claws sinking into my skin. I liked that. I liked it a lot. "Rylan."

"You might be pregnant already." He pins me to the counter, the mirror image to what I just did to him. Except he doesn't preserve that last little bit of distance between us. His hips meet mine, and there's no ignoring his hard cock. "It will be weeks before we know."

"Honestly, with the timeline, it's likely to be less than a week." I had my period right after we went on the run, and I tend to be regular.

He leans down and drags his nose over my throat. Directly against the spot he bit me two nights ago. "No reason to deny myself then. Not until we know."

My hands find his chest, but I'm not sure if I'm trying to push him back or pull him closer. "That's faulty logic," I manage.

"I can live with it." He leans back a little. "Can you?"

I shouldn't. No matter how much I desire this vampire, the fact remains that he's got a boatload of baggage when it comes to the seraphim. He didn't choose this bond, and he resents it more than the other two combined. Throwing a child into the mix is a recipe for disaster.

And yet.

And yet I can't stop myself from sliding my hands down his stomach to the front of his slacks. "We shouldn't."

His hands brush my hips and then my shorts and panties fall down my legs in ragged tatters. I jolt and then whimper at the sight of his claws. "Why didn't your claws come out that first time?"

"I didn't lose control then."

My hands shake as I undo his slacks and pull out his cock. "Why are you losing control, Rylan?" I can't tell if I'm trying to taunt him or legitimately asking the question.

"You make me crazed." He digs his hands into my hair and then his mouth is on mine. It's no less vicious a kiss than it was last time, with the bond riding us so hard. The knowledge thrills me even as I get up onto my tiptoes to press closer to him. Knowing that this untamed version of Rylan lurks beneath his icy exterior drives me wild.

He hooks my thighs, his claws dragging across my skin, and lifts me onto the counter. "Can't bite you," he mutters. I barely have time to brace before he goes to his knees and covers my pussy with his mouth. He's just as unrestrained in this as he was in the kiss. I slam back against the cabinets with a moan.

Rylan spears my pussy with his tongue and I freeze at the feeling of it…growing. I stare down at him. "Rylan," I moan.

He fucks me with his tongue, a wicked look in his silver eyes. He knows exactly what he's doing to me, and he's getting off on it nearly as hard as I am. The sheer wickedness of knowing that he's shifting parts of his body while inside me has me sinking my hands into his hair as best I can and lifting my hips to fuck his tongue. "Please."

He moves up to my clit, working me in expert strokes. My toes curl and heat licks through me. I'm dancing on the edge of a truly spectacular orgasm when he shoves to his feet and presses his cock to my entrance. I can't be sure, but I think he might be bigger than last time. His claws dig into the counter as he wedges himself into me in short strokes.

"More." I grab his wrists and he lets me pry his hands off the counter and put them on my hips. "I like your marks on me."

Rylan freezes. A shudder works its way through his body,

and when he speaks, he sounds like an entirely different person. "*Fuck.*"

He jerks me forward, impaling me on his cock, and then his arms are around me. Pain sparks on my ass and a twin prick on the back of my neck. He's holding me entirely off the counter as he drives into me. Deeper and deeper, until it's almost too much and yet not enough.

My earlier near orgasm roars up and sweeps me under. I cling to him as I come, loving the pain as much as I love the pleasure. He thrusts into me almost brutally, only his hold on the back of my neck keeping my head from bashing against the cabinets. "More."

"Take it," I gasp.

And then he's kissing me, claiming my mouth with his tongue the same way his cock is claiming my pussy. He growls against my lips. It's the only warning I get before he orgasms, pumping me full of his come. I swear I can actually feel it inside me, but it must be my imagination.

Rylan nips my bottom lip and shifts to the side to drag his tongue up the side of my neck. Licking the blood from my skin. There's a tiny spark and I know he's healing me with his nicked tongue. I shiver. The urge rises to say something, but I don't know what words to bring forth that won't send us hurtling back into icy anger.

I hold perfectly still as he leans back. He looks down our bodies and watches his cock ease out of me, his expression strange. "Let's get you some clothes."

So we're just…not going to talk about it?

Works for me.

"I didn't have a chance to bring anything." I hop off the counter, and my legs go a little funny.

"I know." He grabs my elbow. Rylan doesn't sweep me into his arms the way Malachi would in this situation. He doesn't make any sly comments like Wolf would. He simply waits for me to find my legs and releases me.

I follow him in the opposite direction Malachi and Wolf went, to the back of the house where the bedrooms apparently are. Rylan pulls out a dress from one of the closets and passes it to me. It's not necessarily something I would have chosen for myself—a floral sundress that reminds me entirely too much of the one I wore that first night I walked into Malachi's home, soaked to the bone and filled to the brim with rage and fear. So much has changed since then and yet so little at the same time. It's not a comfortable realization.

I waste no time pulling off my shirt and tugging the sundress on. It fits perfectly, which just goes further to confirm my suspicion that one of them has been going ahead of us and supplying these safe houses. Every one we've ended up in has clothing that at least mostly fits us as well as food for me.

It's only when I'm buttoning up the front of it that I realize Rylan is still watching me. "What?"

"Nothing." He doesn't turn away, though. "I keep waiting for this attraction to wear off, but it only seems to be getting stronger. It's damned inconvenient."

I laugh. It's the only proper response to that understatement of the century. I run my fingers through my hair. I don't think he got any blood on it. "If it makes you feel better, I don't like you most of the time, but I want you, too."

"Strangely enough, it does." He gives me one of those razor-thin smiles. "Let's check on the others."

I don't have to check on them to know what they're doing. Wolf never hesitates to bring sex into any given situation, and Malachi might pretend that he's the controlled one, but it's plain to anyone who spends time in their presence for ten seconds that he missed the other vampire. "They're fucking by now."

Rylan stops in the doorway. "I know."

I should leave it alone, but I wouldn't be me if I wasn't pushing. "Both of them would be thrilled if you joined in."

His shoulders drop the barest amount. "I know that, too."

I don't ask him why he's holding out. We have enough to deal with without me meddling in affairs that started centuries before I was born. I can't help wanting to smooth things over and give these three vampires what little happiness we can find in this world.

It's not my place.

Apparently I *am* capable of restraint.

I motion to the door. "After you."

8

THE BLOOD BARRIER FEELS STRANGE.

I couldn't feel the one around Malachi's house. I passed over it without even being aware it existed. This is different. I'm not sure if it's because my seraph power has awakened or if it's the barrier itself.

I reach out, startled to discover the air feeling like it gets thicker the closer my palm comes to the doorway into the living room. "Weird."

"Stop." Rylan catches my wrist. "Don't touch it until he lets you in. Knowing Wolf, there will be some nasty surprise if you do."

Through the doorway, we can see Malachi and Wolf. They've lost their clothes somewhere along the way and Malachi is covered in blood. Their bodies move in a rhythm as old as time itself, Malachi thrusting into Wolf and Wolf rising to meet him.

Despite the orgasm I just had, desire heats my blood as I watch. "They're so damn beautiful."

"Yes."

The pain in Rylan's voice drags my attention to him. He looks agonized, so much so that he's forgotten to wear his normal icy mask. It hurts my chest and I rub my hand against my sternum. I don't know how to fix this. I don't even know where to begin. He won't thank me for meddling, either.

When there are no right answers, I go with the only tool at my disposal.

I sink to my knees before him. He tracks the movement. "What are you doing?"

Relying entirely on instinct. I run a single finger along the hard length of his cock where it presses against his slacks. "May I?"

"Mina." He shudders out a breath. "Yes."

I carefully undo his slacks and draw out his cock. Fucking Rylan is one thing. I know I can take most of what he can give me. Giving him head when he might lose control is something else altogether. I'm particularly vulnerable like this. If he shifts or...

It doesn't matter.

Right now, he needs me and I refuse to back away from that need. I hold his gaze and take his cock into my mouth as best I can. Even without partially shifting, he's still large enough that my jaw aches. I push the pain away and hold his gaze, taking him deeper.

His eyes flash silver and he reaches for me before he seems to catch himself. Likely he's all too aware of what his claws could do to my face if he forgets himself.

I withdraw slowly and rub my lips against his blunt head. "Watch them."

"*Fuck.*" Rylan's back hits the wall behind him and he stabs his claws into the drywall. But he does as I say and lifts his gaze to watch the two vampires fucking on the other side of the doorway.

I go back to sucking his cock. He's shaking with the strength of his restraint, and while I appreciate it, a reckless part of me wants that uncontrolled edge he keeps showing me. I crave it on a level I'm not prepared to deal with.

His length prevents me from taking him entirely, so I use my hands to compensate, focusing every bit of my attention on making him feel good. If I can give him nothing else, I can do this. Pleasure. It won't balance the scales of the bond or the mess we're in, but it's something.

Rylan starts thrusting. At first, it's so subtle, I barely notice his hips rising to meet my lips on each downstroke. But all too quickly, he's fucking my mouth. I can tell he's still being careful, still too aware of how much larger and stronger he is.

I look up and pause when I find him watching *me* instead of Malachi and Wolf. We stare at each other and I see the exact moment he snaps. He grabs a fistful of my hair and pulls me off his cock, shoving me to the floor and covering me with his body. And then he's inside me and, gods, I don't know how it keeps being this good.

With Rylan, it isn't sex.

It isn't even fucking.

It's *rutting*.

He thrusts into me so hard, we inch our way up the hallway

toward the living room. Rylan glances up and snarls. He drags one nail down his throat, leaving a long line of blood that makes my mouth water. Then he sinks his claws into the wood floor on either side of my hips, pinning me in place as he fucks me.

I arch up and close my mouth around his throat. The first swallow of blood sizzles through my veins. The second sweeps me away entirely. Pleasure and pain and power. I never knew it could be like this, never knew that I could have anything but pain.

I come hard, so hard that I forget myself and bite his neck. It doesn't matter that I don't have fangs like a vampire. I'm acting on instinct alone.

Rylan curses and then he's grinding into me as he comes. Filling me up again.

I hope he doesn't regret this.

The thought feels as wispy as smoke, wafting away before I can grasp it fully. The sound of footsteps makes me shift to look over our heads. Malachi stands in the doorway, gloriously naked, watching us with a look that I can only describe as possessive. Like we're both his and he's pleased that we've finally gotten out of our own way and closed the circle. Maybe it's my imagination, but I don't think so.

Rylan moves back and climbs carefully to his feet, pulling me up with him. It takes a few seconds to get our clothing back in order, but he doesn't say a word and I'm not about to be the one to break this particular silence.

Malachi nods. "I need to get dressed and then we'll go. Mina, stay with Wolf. He'll protect you." He pulls me into his arms and kisses me. I barely get a chance to sink into it before he's stepping back. "We'll have information when we return."

"Be safe." I try to smile at him and then look at Rylan. "Both of you."

They nod, and then they're gone, disappearing into the growing darkness of the house. I don't think the sun has quite set yet, but it's hard to say without windows to look through. I turn to find Wolf lounging in the doorway. He's pulled on pants, but only barely. They're not fastened and cling precariously to his narrow hips, as if one wrong move will send them sliding down his legs.

He grins. "'Twas Beauty who tamed the beast."

"Oh hush." I eye the blood ward. "Is this going to fry me?"

"Not with an invitation." He reaches through, his hand an elegant offering. "Come here, love. We have things to discuss."

I lay my hand in his and let him pull me through the ward. It sizzles a little against my skin in a way that isn't entirely comfortable, but it doesn't hurt. I touch my lips. "My father's ward didn't feel like that."

"It was keyed to keep Malachi in, not other people out." He shrugs and pulls me to the couch. "Now, be a good girl and keep quiet while the adults are talking."

I frown. I don't know what's going on, but it can't be positive. I dig in my heels, for all the good it does me. He just drags me the rest of the way and half tosses me onto the couch. "What's going on?"

"We're going to have some *fun*." Wolf throws himself down next to me and pulls me against his body. "You wanted to meet a demon, yes?"

Oh no.

I start to sit up, but he catches my shoulder and tucks me back against him. "Wolf, you can't. Not without Malachi."

"Malachi might pass for the leader of our little group, but he won't let you make a deal, no matter what's offered." His eerie blue eyes watch me closely. "Do you deny it?"

I open my mouth to do just that, but I can't. Not without lying. "He's overprotective."

"Exactly."

"I thought you said it'd be a couple days before we are able to make contact."

"I lied." He dips a finger beneath the strap of my sundress, tracing a line down to my breast. He circles my nipple. "It's a shame we don't have time. Soon."

"Wolf—"

The air changes in the room. I don't know how to explain it. It doesn't go cold or hot or anything like that. There's no buzz of electricity like when Wolf brought me through the barrier. It's more like an…aura of danger. Every prey instinct I have demands I go still and silent and hope the predator that just entered the room moves on without noticing me.

"Good girl," Wolf murmurs. He still hasn't taken his hand from my sundress, his middle finger idly tracing my nipple.

A few feet in front of us, in the middle of the room, the shadows gather. They seem to gain weight and height in a way normal shadows most definitely do *not* do. A masculine voice emerges, deep and as decadent as dark chocolate. "It's been a long time, Wolf."

"You always were one for theatrics." Wolf leans back, taking me with him, and crosses his ankle over his knee. "I'm not one of your pretty, desperate women. You don't have to do the whole song and dance with me."

"And yet you have a pretty woman with you." The darkness fades slowly, revealing a man. Except he'd only be mistaken for a normal man if someone didn't have an ounce of self-preservation or a single instinct to their name. Light brown skin, dark hair and eyes, a face so perfect it's actually a little eerie to look at. He catches me staring and smiles.

I flinch. Yes, he might be pretty, but he's easily the most dangerous being I've ever come across. And that's saying something considering the men currently sharing my bed.

The demon doesn't move, but he seems closer all the same. "Or not a woman at all." He inhales slowly and his smile widens. "Seraph. Wolf, things truly are never boring when you're involved."

"What can I say? I'm a gift."

"You are." The demon studies me. It feels like he's crawling around inside my skin. "I thought you smarter than getting snagged by a seraph bond."

Wolf shrugs. He finally takes his hand from my breast and moves it to my shoulder. A reminder to stay in place. "Can you blame me?"

"With this pretty package?" The demon shrugs. "I understand, even if I wouldn't make the same misstep."

Wolf laughs, his high and wild cackle. "Liar. We both know there's one pretty little thing that's turned you into a teddy bear. How are things going on that front, Azazel?"

Just like that, the easiness is gone from the demon's face. "Watch your tongue, vampire. You amuse me, so I come when you call. The moment you stop amusing me, I'll rip your bones from your body, one by one. I'd like to see you heal from *that*."

"Yes, yes, consider me cowed." Wolf waves that away. "Can you do anything about a seraph bond?"

Azazel goes back to studying me. "If I may?"

"By all means." Wolf answers before I can do it myself.

That's all the warning I get before he's in front of me, pressing a cold hand to the center of my chest, right where I feel the bond the strongest. It's not a welcome touch, but he's hardly being untoward. At least on the surface. Beneath the surface is another thing entirely. I can feel his power course into me, thick and smooth. It leaves a prickly taste on the back of my tongue and I flinch.

Azazel moves back slowly, expression contemplative. "I can break it."

"Really?" I don't mean to speak, but I honestly didn't think he'd be able to.

He flashes me a smile that's all charm and no little amount of threat. "Human religion might be more fiction than truth, but they weren't wrong on this one subject. Demons and seraphim are natural enemies, and our powers reflect that. I can dig out a seraph bond."

Wolf narrows his eyes. "Would that mean seraphs can negate demon deals?"

"Careful, vampire. You're playing with fire again."

"Silly me." Wolf tucks me more firmly against his side. "Let's hear it. All the nitty-gritty details."

Azazel is still studying me. "It's not likely to kill the vampires involved, though that's always a possible side effect." He shrugs. "I like you, Wolf, so the cost is my normal rate. Seven years of service."

I open my mouth, but Wolf beats me there. "We'll consider it. You'll have the answer within a week."

"Normally, there's little rush, but I have a pressing engagement in ten days." Azazel gives that dangerous smile again. "Having a seraph on the auction block would be quite the feather in my cap. The others would love it."

"You'll have the answer within the week," Wolf repeats, an edge in his voice.

"So be it." Azazel shrugs and then he is gone, disappearing in a surge of shadows. It takes several long minutes before all remnants of his power dissipate as well.

Only then does Wolf release me and sigh. "Well, that's a dead end."

"What? Seven years isn't that long." Even if I'm not immortal—something I still need to investigate—I'm going to live significantly longer than a human would. Seven years is nothing if it means breaking the bond.

"Here's a hint, love. If it sounds too good to be true, it almost certainly is." Wolf leans his head against the back of the couch and closes his eyes. "Azazel says seven years, but he's not talking about in the mortal realm. He's talking about in the demon realm. That might mean a few seconds gone here, or it might be a few hundred years. There's no way to tell, and he'll lie if you ask him. The way the realms interact when it comes to time passing is one of the few things Azazel's deals can't control."

Panic flickers through me, but I shove it down. "So a few hundred years pass. Who cares? It's not as if I have any ties to this...realm." Later, I'll have a mental breakdown about the fact that there is apparently more than one realm. Right now, compartmentalizing is the name of the game. "You'll all still be alive."

"Maybe." Wolf stares intently at the spot where Azazel disappeared. "But if he's auctioning you off..." He shakes his head. "Malachi would go nuclear. Rylan might be more subtle about it, but he's not going to let you auction off that pretty pussy for his sake."

"What about you?" I don't mean to ask the question. I really don't. But it's out in the air between us, and there's no taking it back.

"What about me?" Wolf grabs one of my thighs and tugs it up and over his lap. He skates his hand up beneath my dress and palms my bare pussy. "I'm a horrible cliché, love. I'm not overly fond of the thought of you fucking any monsters but us."

"But..." My thoughts scatter as he pushes two fingers into me. "But, Wolf." It's nearly impossible to focus while he's slowly fucking me with his fingers, that hungry look on his face, but I give it a valiant effort. "But the bond."

"Eh." He pulls his fingers out to spread my wetness up and around my clit. "No matter how much it triggers Rylan, you're hardly an evil overlord." He uses his thumb to stroke my clit. "If that ever changes, I'll kill you myself."

9

MAYBE I SHOULD FIND THE THREAT OF WOLF KILLING me terrifying. Wolf *is* terrifying. Even knowing him such a short time, I'm painfully aware of the fact that he doesn't bluff. It doesn't make him more predictable, though. He changes direction as easily as the wind.

Still...

"Promise me."

He pauses, his dark brows pulling together. "What?"

"Promise me that you'll kill me if I try to abuse the bond."

He lets loose one of those mad laughs that I've come to enjoy so much. "No. I don't make promises I don't intend to keep."

"But—"

"What if you abuse the bond on accident, baby seraph?" He goes back to slowly fucking me with his fingers, his thumb playing across my clit. "It would be a shame if I had to rip out your throat because of an ill-worded promise. Malachi would never forgive me."

"Can't have that," I say faintly.

"Now you get the idea." He topples me back onto the couch and settles between my thighs. "Ah, this brings back memories."

From the first time we met. I try to glare, but it's half-hearted at best. "You mean when you held me down and drank my blood a few minutes after meeting me?"

Wolf chuckles. "You mean when Malachi extended guest privileges and it infuriated you so much, you welcomed my bite and the ensuing orgasm."

He has me there. I was *furious*. "You would have fucked me then if I gave you half a chance."

"Of course." He lifts himself off me enough to undo his pants and work them down his hips. "Just like I'm going to fuck you now. For old times' sake."

"Uh-huh."

He tugs down my sundress, baring my breasts. "You really are exquisite, love. Perfect breasts. A pussy that's enough to have a partner willing to cage you for eternity." He palms my breasts, lingering over my nipples. "The demon deal is off the table."

"You don't get to make that decision." I arch into his palms. It feels good, but it's nowhere near enough. "I need you."

Wolf wraps a fist around his cock and guides it to my entrance. "This is exactly why. Do you know what kind of monsters they have in the demon realm, love?"

"I didn't know the demon realm existed until an hour ago."

His laugh is a little strained. He's moving slowly, teasing me, sinking inch by inch deeper. "They make us vampires look like house cats. They'll get one taste, one touch of this pussy, and they'll chain you up and never let you go."

I reach down to grab his hips even as I lift mine to take him deeper. "My choice to make, Wolf."

"I'm not a jealous man." He surges forward, sheathing himself inside me completely, and moves down to press his entire body to mine. "I'm not."

I can barely think past how good it feels to have him inside me, but I give it a valiant effort. "Say it again and you might even believe it."

He shifts down a little and bites me. His teeth sink into the curve of my breast. Not a spot where he's going to get much blood, but the effect is overwhelming. I release his hips and grab his head, guiding him to my nipple. "Again."

"Must be the bond," he mutters. "I want to mark you up. Rub my scent all over you." His hands find the spots where Rylan held me down earlier, at my neck and back. "Mark you just like Rylan did. Just like Malachi wants to."

I guide him to my other breast. "Do it."

He does. Again and again and again. Tiny little bites that ramp up my pleasure. Looking down my body and seeing little rivulets of blood marking my skin do just as much for me as the bites themselves. I *love* these marks just as much as I love the ones from Rylan's claws. A sign of mutual ownership, of them claiming me the same way the bond demands I claim them.

Later, I'll worry this is some sort of magic. Right now, there's no room for anything but the feeling of Wolf's little bites in time with his cock sliding in and out of me. Need winds tighter and tighter, arching my body and drawing a cry from my lips. "More!"

He gives me more. Even so, he's not rushing. Time ceases to have meaning as we fuck, our bodies moving in a rhythm as familiar as breathing. With each wave of pleasure, my orgasm edges closer, stronger. When he finally loops his arm under my waist and lifts my hips to find the sensitive spot inside me with each stroke, I lose control completely. I grab his arms and scream. I think I might even black out. All I know is one moment I'm coming so hard the room goes black, and the next I'm blinking up into Wolf's crimson eyes as he finishes inside me.

I'm so dazed, I almost miss the low word he utters. "*Ours.*" A promise and a threat.

The sweat is still cooling on my body when I sense the approach of Rylan and Malachi. They're moving quickly. I don't know what's changed with the bond in the last few days, but I can feel the distance closing in great detail. "They're coming."

"About time. Really, how hard is it to find a group of unsuspecting vampires, kill all but one, and then indulge in a little torture until he tells you everything he knows?" Wolf climbs to his feet and stretches his arms over his head. Even after all the fucking, the sight of him makes my body clench. I try to push the desire down, but from the way his lips pull into a seductive smile, I fail miserably.

I sit up and try to ignore the way his cock is going hard again. "Malachi told me that you can sense my emotions."

"Oh, that." He shrugs. "I don't need magic to know you want my cock again, love. It's called being perceptive."

"I need to learn how to shield."

"Why?"

I blink. "What do you mean, *why?*"

"Exactly what I said." He wraps a fist around his cock and gives a few slow pumps. "Did you ever stop to ask what the purpose of such a side effect could be?"

I start to snap, but it's rare that Wolf decides to go into teaching mode. He prefers to mock and incite instead. I cross my arms over my chest. "No, I didn't worry about why. The fact that it exists is enough for me. I don't need all three of you in my head."

"Ah, but we're not in your head." He grabs my hand and tugs me to my feet. "We're in your heart, and that's something altogether different."

"Don't talk in riddles. I don't have the patience for it."

"Pity." He laughs. Wolf dips down and licks the blood from my upper chest. The sound he makes is nearly a purr. "We're not just eager and willing cocks, love."

"One could argue that Rylan is neither eager nor willing."

He drags a single fingertip over my hip where there's still the slightest pinprick mark from Rylan's claws. It's honestly astounding that they haven't healed fully yet. I've taken blood from all three of them since then, and nothing heals quicker than vampire blood. I wonder if there's something in his claws that slows regeneration—

"Rylan didn't lose control because he hated the feeling of being inside you." He chuckles. "Did you know that when he was younger, he was wilder?"

"I thought he's significantly older than both you and Malachi."

"He is." Wolf shrugs. "But he didn't get that stick up his ass until a little over a century ago."

It doesn't take a genius to put the puzzle pieces together. If I have my dates right, that's around the time of his falling-out with Malachi and Wolf. "What does that have to do with anything?"

"He used to be wilder," he repeats and gives a happy sigh. "We had so much sex, love. The three of us and others we invited in. It was a wonderfully endless bacchanal for years."

"Again, what does that have to do with anything?"

His grin goes wide and sinful. "In all those years, I only saw him lose control of his shape when he was with Malachi and me. Only us. Never when someone else was involved."

Something goes strange in my chest, but I don't know enough to identify the emotion. "That doesn't mean anything."

"Doesn't it?" Another of those careless shrugs. "If you say so."

Malachi and Rylan are almost to the house, which is almost enough to distract me from how this conversation has gone off the rails. "Why shouldn't I learn to shield, Wolf?"

"Oh. That." He palms my breasts. "It's a protective measure."

"Excuse me?"

"When you have strong emotional spikes, all three of us feel it. Knowing when you're afraid or angry is incredibly useful on that note."

Part of me can see his point, but I'm not willing to concede. "Maybe if you chose it. You didn't, so it's invasive as hell."

"Probably." He slides his hands down my sides, his fingers unerringly finding the spots where Rylan impaled me. "Doesn't mean it's not useful. We've got to keep you alive and all that."

"Wolf—"

Movement on the other side of the blood ward. Malachi and

Rylan appear. They're covered in blood and look like something out of a horror movie. I gasp, but Wolf tightens his grip, holding me in place. "Took you long enough."

Malachi lifts his hand. The air wavers a little in front of his palm, and he recoils. "What is this, Wolf? Let us in."

"What's the password?"

"*Wolf.*"

He continues to hold me immobile, his handsome face contemplative. "It occurs to me that you two could have been taken by Cornelius. His bloodline power is glamour, after all. It would be child's play to mimic your bodies and voices and come back here to attack us."

All that is true, but it doesn't account for the fact that I *know* it's them. I grab his wrists and squeeze. "It's them. My father might be able to fool our senses, but he can't fool the bond."

He grins like I'm a student who's said something impressive. "Exactly. It's almost as if the bond does have its uses."

Damn it, I walked right into that. "Even if it does, I'm still going to learn to shield."

"That's up for debate." He finally releases me and snaps his fingers. I feel the moment the blood ward goes down. It's almost like a popping in my ears, strange but not uncomfortable.

Malachi stumbles a little as he steps into the room and true panic takes wing inside me. I push Wolf's hands away and tug my dress back into place. "You're hurt."

"I'm fine." Malachi's actions give lie to his words as Rylan ducks beneath his arm and takes the weight of the bigger vampire. "They were more prepared than we expected."

"My father is a monster, but he's no fool."

"Yes. Which means we need to move and quickly. The more distance we put between the group we just removed and the hounds he'll send next, the better." He looks around the living room as if seeing it for the first time. "What's that smell?"

"Brimstone." Rylan makes a sound suspiciously close to a snarl. "What did you do, Wolf?"

"Who, me?" Wolf pulls on his pants slowly. "I'm sure I have no idea what you're speaking of."

Both Rylan and Malachi go still. Malachi tries to straighten, but he tips to the side and Rylan has to catch him before he falls. I rush to them. "You need blood."

"I'm fine."

"You're about to take a nonconsensual nap, and you just said we need to run." I glance at Rylan. "Please put him on the couch."

For once, Rylan does what I ask without arguing. He guides Malachi to the couch and eases him down. After the briefest hesitations while I figure out the best way to do this, I simply climb into his lap and pull my hair off one side of my neck. "Drink."

"You almost died two nights ago. I'm not drinking from you right now."

"Malachi, shut up and drink." I dig my hands into his hair and guide his face to my throat. It's a token of how injured he is that he doesn't fight me. I flinch a little as his teeth sink into my skin, but then there's only pleasure.

Damn it, for once, it would be really nice if I didn't have a wave of sheer desire overwhelm me at one of their bites. It's useful most of the time, but I can hear Rylan and Wolf conversing quietly behind me, and I desperately want to know what they're saying.

I might as well try to grasp the wind with my bare hands.

With every pull of Malachi's mouth, heat courses through my body. My breasts go heavy and sensitive. My pussy throbs in time with the racing of my heart. Despite my best intentions, I rock against Malachi's hardening cock. He responds by pulling me closer. It's what I need, and yet it's also keeping me from what I need. With us pressed this tightly together, I can't reach down to the front of his pants.

It doesn't matter. I'll orgasm regardless. I'm already halfway there simply from his bite alone. That doesn't change the frustration that blooms. I want him inside me.

I want them all inside me.

The voice hardly sounds like mine, but I can't blame the desire on anyone but myself. I had all three of these vampires only once and it changed the course of my life forever. No matter what else is true, I crave that level of letting go again. The pleasure that overwhelmed me and awoke my powers.

Malachi shifts and growls against my skin, and that's all I need. I orgasm hard, whimpering and shaking and grinding against him. He lifts his head almost reluctantly and drags his tongue over the wounds his teeth left behind. A little spark of lightning against my skin lets me know that he's healed me. He shifts back to kiss me, a slow lingering greeting as if we have all the time in the world.

Rylan curses. "We have to go. Now." His voice goes low and dangerous. "We'll discuss the *demon* once we get somewhere safe."

Just like that, Malachi isn't kissing me any longer. He leans back, his expression carefully neutral. "What did you do, little dhampir?"

10

"WE'LL TALK ABOUT IT LATER—ABOUT ALL OF IT LATER.
Right now we need to move." Rylan plucks me off Malachi's lap,
gives my bloody front an exasperated look, and fixes my dress again.

I consider objecting that I'm not a doll to be moved around,
but I also don't want to have the demon deal conversation right
now. If we need to move, then we need to *move*. Talking now just
means we'll be arguing for hours.

Rylan also shrugs out of his jacket and wraps it around me.
"I'll carry you."

"Actually—"

"Wolf, I know you're not planning on arguing with me after
you just went behind both our backs with this demon. Shut your
fucking mouth."

For once, Wolf shuts his fucking mouth. He hauls Malachi

up, and the bigger vampire looks much steadier on his feet. Not happy, but steadier.

Rylan shoves a hand through his hair. "Colorado. The house in the mountains."

Wolf jolts. "That's a long run."

"We don't have a choice. It's the easiest to secure, and we need time to plan. Jumping states should give us a little more time."

He doesn't seem convinced. "They've found us at each place. It doesn't matter how many layers of subterfuge the properties are hidden beneath; they're able to link it back to us every time."

"They won't find this one. Not with who owns it."

I frown. "Why?"

"This house is owned by a friend," Rylan says. He scoops me into his arms. "We won't travel the whole way on foot." Without another word, he makes for the door. Apparently he's of the same mind as I am; we need to move now and argue later.

He breaks into a run the second we leave the house. As tempting as it is to ask about what they learned from my father's people, I force myself to be patient. It's better to get it all out at once. Maybe when we reach the car...

But no one seems interested in talking once we reach the non-descript black truck waiting behind a gas station. Since Wolf and I are the smallest of the four, we climb into the back seat, and Rylan takes the wheel. Despite my best efforts, the events of the last couple days catch up with me. I lean my head against the cool glass and close my eyes, letting the icy silence roll over me. Sleep follows on its heels and drags me under.

Dawn is creeping over the sky when I open my eyes again. I'm lying down across the seat, my head in Wolf's lap. He's got his eyes closed, though I can't tell if he's actually sleeping. Vampires *do* need sleep, albeit significantly less than humans or dhampirs. Bloodline vampires even less so. That said, I can't remember the last time I've seen any of them catch more than an hour or two. Surely we're all reaching our limits.

Maybe that's why we're headed up the mountain to this place that belongs to a friend of Rylan's.

Wolf shifts his hand to my hair without opening his eyes. "We're almost there."

As tempting as it is to stay in this position and enjoy being casually touched by Wolf, curiosity is more powerful. I sit up and look out the window.

It's like another world.

We're on a narrow road, winding our way ever upward. On either side of us, the banks veer sharply down into canyons. Really, there's barely room for our truck. If we see an oncoming vehicle, I'm not sure how we'll navigate it without someone sliding off the road.

"This is the only road in and out," Rylan says quietly. "The land is difficult terrain, even for vampires. You sensed your father's people before anyone else did."

My skin heats in something akin to embarrassment. "I don't know how I did it. I'm half-sure I imagined it."

"You didn't." This from Malachi. "We would have escaped safely, but your awareness gave us extra time."

"I don't know if I can replicate it." If they're putting their faith in me… As much as I crave being an equal part of this four-some, the reality is that for all my supposed power, I'm still doing the equivalent of learning how to walk. Some things I seem to be able to do on instinct, but that will only get me so far. "I don't want to risk all our lives on the assumption that I can recreate something I don't know how I did in the first place."

"It will be fine." Malachi sounds so damn sure, I kind of want to smack him. How dare he put so much unearned faith in me? If something happens to one of them because of it, I'll never forgive myself.

I don't get a chance to continue arguing because we round a bend and the house comes into view. House. The very term is laughable. It looks like a bunker built into the side of the mountain.

I squint. There are a handful of windows shining in the early morning sunlight, but even so, it's difficult to tell where the house ends and the mountain begins. "What is this place?"

"It's safe. That's the bottom line."

Rylan's answer isn't much of an answer, but I suppose the relative safety is all that matters. *I wonder if it protects against demons.* The thought almost makes me laugh.

Rylan guides the truck to a cleverly hidden garage door that slides open to allow us in. When we drive through, the entire car is encased in darkness as the door shuts again. Rylan mutters something and then a low light flickers to life around the perime-ter of the floor. It slowly gets brighter until I can see clearly. I pick out half a dozen vehicles, ranging from luxury cars that must be horrifically expensive to something that might get mistaken for a military tank. "Interesting friend you have."

"You could say that." We pile out of the truck and Rylan leads the way to the thick metal door. He keys in a code and the light flashes green. "We'll go over security when we get settled."

Inside, I expect something that feels military and spartan, but the door opens into a charming hallway with fountains running the length of it that give the impression of gentle waterfalls. The next door opens into a small room with several more doors. The thick rug swallows my footsteps and the furniture is all high-end, but even I can see the advantage of the layout. Anyone coming in through the garage will be funneled into this room, which is a death trap. There's no room to spread out, no room for tactical advantage for the advancing enemy. Rylan ignores the two doors on the right and leads us left.

Another long hall, another small room with a series of doors.

We do this three more times before we end up in a cozy living room with a giant fireplace and comfortably sturdy furniture. He motions around us. "This is the east wing. While I realize it's not ideal to be in the one without windows, it's safer than the west wing."

"How deep are we?" I look at the ceiling, but it looks like any other ceiling in a nice, if expensive, home. There's no sensation to suggest the press of earth, the weight of a mountain over the top of us.

"Deep enough that we don't have to worry about someone trying to burrow here. It's pure rock around us, so short of dynamite, it's impenetrable. And we'll hear dynamite before they ever get close enough to be a danger."

It really is a bunker.

"The bedrooms and kitchen are through there." He waves at the doors on the other side of the room. "We need to get cleaned up and feed Mina and then we'll talk."

Wolf stretches, his spine cracking loud enough to set my teeth on edge. "Slow down there, Alpha. There's only one leader I accept in this merry little trio, and it's not you."

Trio?

Does that mean I'm outside the hierarchy? I don't know how to feel about that. Then again, I don't know how to feel about a lot that's happened since awakening my power. Why should this be any different?

Malachi shakes his head. "He's right. We're covered in blood and Mina hasn't eaten in…" He glances at me. "When?"

Damn, I was hoping he wouldn't ask me. "I don't remember."

"Thought so." He hooks an arm around my waist and half carries me to the center door. It leads into a room just as luxuriously appointed as the rest of this place. The bed is low to the ground and massive enough to fit several vampires Malachi's size. An open doorway leads into the bathroom. There's another of those clever waterfall walls and a shower with more shower heads than I can begin to know what to do with.

I brace myself for an argument. He's clearly not happy with me; he hasn't been happy with me since they identified the scent of brimstone and realized what Wolf and I have done. But Malachi just turns on the water and faces me. "Are you okay?"

"Yes." It's even the truth. I'm exhausted despite my nap in the car and my stomach is attempting to chew its way through my spine, but I'm as well as can be expected at this point. "Are you?"

He shrugs. "Things were a little more complicated than we expected, but we got the job done." He pulls me beneath the water and sets about washing me with the minty soap available. I almost argue that I'm more than capable of washing myself, but there's a fine tremor to Malachi's touch. I don't know if it's rage, lingering fear for my safety, or simply a faltering control, but I keep silent all the same. Especially since each pass of his hands over my skin seems to calm him. No doubt it's more side effects of the bond.

When we're both clean, Malachi leans down and presses his forehead to mine. "Don't do that again."

"Malachi—"

He keeps going before I can figure out what I'm trying to say. "Don't endanger yourself. Not on our behalf."

"Who says it was on your behalf? Maybe I did it so *I* could rid myself of the bond."

"Mina. Little dhampir." He leans back enough that he can hold my gaze. "It will happen again. Even if you manage to break it this time, the bond is part of being a seraph. I'm not leaving you. I'll just end up bonded to you again."

"No." I try to jerk back, but he tightens his grasp just enough to keep me in place.

"You can't run from this."

"Then I just won't fuck vampires. Simple solution." It's not simple and it's not feasible, though. Not if I want to be heir and dispose of my father. Playing vampire politics will be challenging enough with a strong partner at my side. Alone? It's just adding another layer of complications to the mix because they'll vie for a place in my bed and resent me when I don't give it to anyone.

Another trap.

Another choice, taken away.

I drag in a breath. "Please stop pushing me. I'm doing the best I can."

"I know." He wraps his arms around me and hugs me close. "I don't say this to hurt you, little dhampir. You have to know the boundaries of the fight before you can set foot into the arena."

From the moment we met, Malachi has expected so much of me. Again and again, he's challenged me to find new ways to fight, to utilize every weapon at my disposal. "I'm tired."

"I know."

I allow myself to lean on him for five slow breaths. When I straighten, he releases me easily. I don't feel more centered, but with each path that's removed from my options, my intent becomes clearer. There really is no other way.

Back in the bedroom, I'm not even surprised to find the closet filled with a wide variety of clothing. A quick check confirms that it's in both my and Malachi's sizes. I suspect the other rooms have the same for Rylan and Wolf. "I still don't understand how you were able to outfit so many places on such short notice. Isn't it a concern that doing so will draw my father's notice since he's hunting us?"

"We used an intermediary. He's someone who isn't a known ally to any of us." Malachi motions at the room we currently occupy. "Though we didn't use him for this one."

Curiosity sinks its barbs into me. It's such a welcome distraction from the constant cycle of desire and fear and anger that it leaves me breathless for a moment. After a brief internal debate,

I pull on a pair of leggings, thick socks, and a knit sweater. "Will you tell me about the person who owns this house?"

"It's not my story to tell." He dresses as quickly as I did. I'm mildly amused to discover that his clothing options are more of the same—fitted pants and a loose white shirt. Malachi really is as eclectic as Wolf when it comes to his clothing, even if his style is more understated. Slightly. He turns toward the door. "But if you ask Rylan, he might tell you."

"I will." I follow Malachi back into the living room. One of the other men has gotten the fire going, and the cozy impression of this room only gets stronger with flames sending light dancing across the ceiling and walls.

Wolf is once again dressed in his customary trousers, suspenders, and graphic T-shirt. Rylan surprises me, though. I half expected him to have a suit on, but he's got lounge pants and a knitted sweater. His feet are bare. I stare at them for a long moment, my chest feeling strange. It's such a small thing. Bare feet. People go barefoot all the time. I don't know why the sight of *Rylan's* bare feet has my heart beating oddly against my ribs.

I drag my gaze to the fire. A much safer subject.

Wolf claps his hands and rubs them together in something like glee. "Now. Let's get down to it."

11

WHEN WOLF FINISHES DETAILING THE TERMS OF THE
demon bargain, the silence is thick enough to cut through with a
chain saw. Rylan is so still, I don't think he's breathing. Malachi
keeps clenching and unclenching his fists.

I shift in my seat in the middle of the couch. "We didn't
promise anything."

"And you won't." Rylan cuts in before Malachi can say
whatever he's stewing on. "Those terms are unacceptable."

I straighten my spine. "Everyone in this room is making sacrifices to ensure I become heir so we stop being hunted. I'm willing to make sacrifices, too."

"I swear to fuck, Mina—"

Again, Rylan cuts off Malachi. "There are too many potential pitfalls. Time moves strangely in the demon realms, which is

something Wolf already brought up. Beyond that, we don't know how your seraph bond might work with demons." He shakes his head. "If it tries to bond with whoever bought you at auction, they will kill you before letting themselves be bound. The cost is too high."

"We can bargain on my safety." I don't know why I'm arguing this. Ultimately, he's right. No matter what my feelings on the matter are, if all three of them are in agreement, then I need to listen to their opinions. Rushing forward because I feel guilty is foolish. "There's room for negotiation."

"It won't save you." Malachi crosses his arms over his broad chest. "The demon who kills you will face punishment, but you'll still be dead."

I open my mouth but change my mind before I tell him it's a reasonable risk. Judging from the look on his face, he won't thank me for saying as much. "If you're all in agreement..."

"We are." Malachi's words sound like a threat.

Rylan nods. "It was a far-fetched option at best. The cost is too high."

"You know how I feel, love. The only way I'd agree is if Azazel took you for himself, and he won't. He's focused on another."

I sigh and slump back against the couch. "Then I guess that option's out." Which leaves only the path we're on. Get pregnant. Become heir. Commit patricide. "What did you two find out from my father's hunters?"

"He knows." Malachi says the words so simply, it takes several beats before they sink in.

I push to my feet, earlier exhaustion forgotten. *He knows.* "What does he know?"

"That you're enough seraph to have their power and all that that entails. He suspects you bonded with at least me, if not the others, but he doesn't have a way to confirm it."

This is bad. Really, really bad. "How? How could he possibly know that much?"

"Your magic left a signature of sorts when the blood ward broke." Wolf rubs his temples. "It's not something I considered, but even if I had, it couldn't be helped. Your father isn't old enough to know what you are, but apparently my cousin decided to embrace his ambition further and handed over the information for a hefty sum."

Rylan crosses his ankle over his knee. Of all of us, he looks most normal. Which isn't to say he's relaxed; I don't think I've ever seen Rylan relaxed, even if he's wearing something casual right now. He leans back. "Ultimately, this changes nothing. If he wasn't aware of Mina's bloodline before, he would have become aware once he caught her again. The plan remains the same."

"Does this mean you're going to actually participate?" Wolf drawls. He snaps his suspenders in a steady rhythm, his eyes cold. "Or will you continue to play the martyr and whine about how you didn't want this?"

"None of us wanted this," I say.

They ignore me.

Rylan narrows his eyes. "Forgive me if I wasn't thrilled with how things played out."

"No, I don't think I will. Forgive you, that is."

I glance at Malachi, silently imploring him to step in, but he's watching the other men intensely. Surely he has some thoughts about this? I don't care if Rylan and I have fucked three times in the last three days. I'm not going to compel him to participate in this race to conception. The bond is bad enough; having a child together when he's not fully on board is a particularly nightmarish scenario.

"Don't stop there, Wolf. For once in your life, speak clearly."

Wolf pushes slowly to his feet. His eyes flash crimson. "You're a fucking coward, Rylan. You were full of plans and strategies to free Malachi from his prison, but the moment we found a way through—a way that *you* suggested and participated in—you start crying about regrets. Why are you willing to keep playing the victim and holding yourself at a distance from what you truly want? We are *right here*."

Rylan's eyes have gone pure silver. "Do tell me what I want, since you seem to know."

"Of course I know. You want what we all want." Wolf flings a hand in Malachi's direction. "But that's not the problem, is it? You've pined for Malachi since your falling-out. You were prepared to do what it took to reclaim that relationship. It's *Mina* you didn't bargain on."

"I do believe I've said that myself." For all his icy tone, Rylan looks ready to fly across the room and rip into Wolf with his bare hands.

"Poor Rylan, knocked on his ass by a pretty little seraph and her magic pussy." Wolf snarls. "It must be fucking terrible to love the chains she's unwittingly wrapped around you. That's the real problem, isn't it? It's not that you hate the bond. You fucking *love* it."

Rylan shoves to his feet, but he only gets one step before Malachi's there. The bigger man catches his shoulders. "That's enough."

I tense, expecting a confrontation. Rylan looks ready to commit murder, and from the way Wolf is leaning forward, he's willing to meet Rylan halfway. But Malachi's presence between them shifts the energy in the room. It's still dangerous. So fucking dangerous.

But there's an edge of desire now, where before there was only violence.

"Is it true?" Malachi's words are so low, they're almost lost in the crackle of the fire.

Rylan curses. "Yes."

Malachi drops his hands. "Stop punishing us for what's going on in your head."

Just like that, I can *feel* Rylan's emotions. The conflicting spiral of need and rage. A hurt that goes so deep, it makes my bones ache. Malachi all but ripped out his still-beating heart when he left Rylan. A loss he's never gotten over, one he's never *allowed* himself to get over. He's nursed that wound like the grave of someone beloved, tending to it every single day for so long it boggles my mind.

No wonder he hates me.

He arrived, ready to play knight in shining armor for the man he loves, only to find Malachi wrapped up in me. Even before Malachi gained his freedom, my presence meant Rylan had to throw away a decade's worth of plans and rush to the house to ensure he didn't lose his chance entirely.

I understand all this in the space of a second, and then the feeling is gone entirely as he gets his shields back under control. My eyes burn and I close them to try to keep the tears inside. Rylan won't thank me for the intrusion, and if he thinks I pity him, he'll hate me all the more.

I'm sorry.

Words I can't say. Not if I want this to have a chance to work.

"I'm sorry."

For a second, I think I've forgotten myself and said those damning words aloud. But no, that's not my lips forming the syllables, not my deep voice speaking. I open my eyes to find Rylan staring at me. "I'm sorry," he repeats.

The bond gives a pulse that has me damn near vibrating out of my skin. I scrub at my sternum, but it does nothing to dissipate the sensation. "I understand."

He turns to Malachi, who doesn't release his shoulders. "Things change, Rylan. How I feel about you hasn't, not in all this time. But it was never going to be just the two of us for eternity. I'm not built like that."

Rylan shudders out a sigh. "I understand that now." He glances at me again. "I suppose it's not a bad thing to have an abundance of love."

Love.

Love.

He's not in love with me. He barely likes me. I can't argue something's changed in the last couple days, but it's not *love*. I would know. Wouldn't I?

Maybe that's not what he's saying. Maybe he just means it's not outside the realm of possibilities now. Or something.

He gives another of those deep exhales. "I'm done fighting it. I want everything. You. Mina." He glances at Wolf. "Even this asshole."

"Be still my heart."

Malachi is still looking at Rylan. His shield must be firmly in place, because I don't get so much of an echo of what he's feeling. His expression gives me even less. "On your knees."

Rylan doesn't hesitate. He sinks down to kneel at Malachi's feet. I stare in shock. Even on the night when we awoke my powers, Rylan was hardly submitting to anyone. It never occurred to me that he would submit to Malachi, that he would look utterly at peace while doing it.

"You know what to do."

Rylan reaches for the front of Malachi's pants with shaking hands and undoes them. It's so silent in the room, I can hear his soft exhale as he takes out the other vampire's cock. Malachi knocks his hand away and wraps a fist around himself. He guides his blunt head to Rylan's lips. "No teeth." He doesn't appear to need an answer, because he doesn't stop his forward movement, feeding his cock into Rylan's mouth.

Heat surges through me at the sight. Malachi can be merciless when he's so inclined, and how he is with Wolf—and now Rylan—feels very different from how he is with me. He's crueler, but I know Wolf loves it. Judging from the erection tenting the front of Rylan's pants, he loves it, too.

"They look good, don't they?"

I jolt. I was so busy watching Malachi fuck Rylan's mouth, I didn't even notice Wolf moving to stand behind my chair. He leans over the back of it and rubs his nose against my neck. "They have something special. Always have. Do you find that threatening? You'll never be able to touch it, seraph bond or no."

I might laugh if I could draw a full breath. Does he think he's telling me something I don't already know? I recognized the bond Malachi has with Rylan the moment the other vampire showed up. Just like I recognized the history he and Wolf share. Because of that, when I answer, I'm able to do it honestly. "No. I don't find it threatening."

"What a marvel you are." Wolf hooks the bottom of my sweater and moves back enough to tug it over my head. "We can't let them have all the fun, can we?"

"I like to watch." I bite my bottom lip as he cups my breasts. "Unless you have a better idea."

"I might." He dips a hand beneath the band of my leggings and cups my pussy. I keep my gaze on the vampires before us as Wolf slides his fingers through my folds. Malachi has his hands on either side of Rylan's head and he's thrusting forward roughly, forcing the other man to take every inch of him. Rylan has his hands on Malachi's hips, but he seems to be encouraging the violence of the moment. I catch a glimpse of claws, which only further confirms that.

They're really beautiful together.

"Malachi won't come in Rylan's mouth," Wolf murmurs, the very definition of a devil on my shoulder. He presses the heel of his hand to my clit as he pushes two fingers into me, and then three. "He's saving that seed all for you. He'll let Rylan get him close, and then he's going to come over here and fill you up." He licks the curve of my ear. "And then Rylan's going to do the same as soon as Malachi's finished with you."

I whimper. "But..."

Whatever I was going to say disappears as Malachi pulls back. He traces Rylan's lips with his cock, his eyes gone pure black. "You've denied me too fucking long, and I'm reclaiming what's mine."

"Yes," Rylan whispers.

Malachi grabs Rylan's throat and hefts him to his feet. "I'm going to come inside our little dhampir, and then I'm going to take your ass while you fuck her."

Wolf chuckles against my neck. "You should feel how her pussy clenched at that. She's on board with this plan."

I try to hold still and not lift my hips to fuck Wolf's fingers. "I can speak for myself."

Malachi finally looks at me, his hold on Rylan's throat causing the other vampire to do the same. "Well, little dhampir. Are you on board with this plan?"

"Yes." As if there's any question. I honestly wasn't sure we'd ever get to this point, where we were all in rhythm with each other. It might not hold once we're through and a new day comes, but I won't do anything to tip the balance in the wrong direction right now.

I want this too bad.

"Hold her down, Wolf."

"With pleasure." Wolf moves before I have a chance to protest—though I'm not sure what I'd protest—and grabs my wrists. He guides them up to the corners of the back of the chair.

The position leaves my chest fully exposed and gives me nowhere to hide.

I don't *want* to hide, but I can't stop the instinct that demands I fight being held down. I can't budge Wolf. The knowledge sends a forbidden thrill through me. These three vampires can do anything they want to me, and there's not a damn thing I can do to stop them. I don't *want* to stop them, a fact we're all readily aware of.

They can feel my emotions, after all. There might be a sprinkling of fear, but it only ramps my desire hotter.

Malachi pushes off his pants and stalks to me. He shoves my legs wide, looping them over the arms over the chair. There's nowhere to hide now. I can do nothing but whimper as he rips my leggings down the center seam. He doesn't even bother to push them all the way off my legs, just slides them down to my knees so he has no barriers to my skin.

He guides his cock, still wet from Rylan's mouth, into me. Even with Wolf using three fingers to ready me, my body fights the intrusion. Malachi's just too damn *big*. He plants his big hands on my thighs, pushing them up and back, holding me down as he continues his unrelenting advance.

Watching his thick length disappear into my pussy is almost enough to make me come right then and there. He's so fucking huge. His cock spreads my pussy obscenely, and I can't shake the feeling that he's stamping his ownership onto my very soul.

As if he can sense the direction of my thoughts, he growls. "You might have the bond, little dhampir, but we do, too. You're ours as much as we're yours."

12

OURS.

Gods, that's so sexy. Malachi sinks the rest of the way into me, and I whimper. "Yes." I don't even know what I'm agreeing to. Yes, I am as much theirs as they are mine. Yes, I want this to be equal. Just…yes.

Malachi fucks me like he really does own me. Like he knows my body even better than I do. He unerringly finds the spot inside me that has me going melty and hot, squirming as much as I can while so effectively pinned in place. I try to touch him, but Wolf tightens his hold on my wrists. That, too, only heightens my pleasure.

"Let go, little dhampir." Malachi grips my thighs tighter. "We have all night. This doesn't end when you come."

His rough words cut through the last of my resistance. He's right, after all. I don't have to hold out, because we're not done until *they* are. The strange buoyancy in my chest gets stronger.

Gods, *is* this love? I don't know. It's not like I've had much experience with it or even had a good example of what love looks like.

The relationship between my father and his people, his partners, isn't love. It's control and abuse. The same goes for how he treats his children, even the ones who weren't born disappointments like me.

When it comes to love, I'm feeling my way through a lightless room and hoping I don't fall into a pit of spikes. How I feel with Malachi and Wolf and Rylan is nothing like I've experienced before. Does that make it love? I don't know.

There's too much I don't know.

Malachi shifts one hand to my lower stomach, playing his thumb over my clit. He knows my body *so fucking well.* Even with my head spinning from thoughts of love, my body has no reservations about taking the pleasure he deals and embracing it wholeheartedly. I orgasm with a cry. Malachi keeps up that decadent touch until the waves recede. Only then does he pound into me, chasing his own pleasure. The fire flares hot behind him, the flames licking out of the fireplace for a moment, and then he's filling me up, grinding into me until I've taken every last drop.

He leans down and presses a surprisingly sweet kiss to my lips. I barely have a chance to sink into it before he's moving away and Rylan is taking his place. I tense a little, expecting the same rough fucking we've been getting up to lately, but he coasts his hands up my body, lingering at my hips and sides and breasts, until he lightly clasps my throat with one hand. His eyes haven't gone back to normal, still shining silver in the low light of the room. "I'm done fighting this. Are you?"

There's only one truthful answer to his question. "Yes." I'm done fighting all of it. I could spend the rest of my life railing about how unfair are the turns fate has delivered me. It's even the truth. I've been dealt a rough hand. Bemoaning that until the end of time, though? That traps me in the victim mindset.

It keeps me from appreciating the good things that have been dealt alongside the bad. No matter the events that brought us to this place, I have three bloodline vampire men at my side, all of us aligned in a single goal. I don't need an army to take my father's compound from him, not with Malachi, Wolf, and Rylan.

I catch a glimpse of Malachi coming back into the room, a bottle of lube in his hands. Oh gods, this is happening. My whole body goes tight in response. I twist a little and look up at Wolf. "And you? Are you choosing us, too?"

"I'm hurt you have to ask, love." He gives me his mad grin. "I don't turn down demon deals for just anyone."

This isn't like the night we awoke my powers. We had an agenda and pleasure was the method to deliver the endgame. That's not what tonight is about. Tonight, we're choosing each other.

Malachi closes a hand over Rylan's shoulder. "There's no going back after this."

"There was no going back the moment we chose this method of breaking the blood ward." Rylan devours me with his eyes. "I've adjusted my expectations."

With anyone else, that would be faint praise, if it was praise at all. The way he says it? It's as if he leaned down and dragged his tongue up the center of my body. He drifts his fingertips over my stomach, and I'm not surprised to find them tipped with claws yet again. There's a strange beauty to how seamlessly he shifts between human form and animal. Knowing he could kill me as easily as breathing shouldn't be sexy, but I'm far beyond worrying about what I find sexy with these three.

In my chest, the bond hums in a way I can only describe as happily. This feels so fucking right, I can barely stand it.

Malachi clasps Rylan's jaw with his other hand. "No biting Mina."

"You don't have to worry. I won't lose control again."

He hesitates. "Not tonight. Not when it's still so new. Next time."

Rylan finally nods, though he's still watching me as if he wants to consume me in slow, decadent sips.

Malachi's thumb traces over Rylan's bottom lip. "Bite me instead."

At that, Rylan's eyes go a little wide and a little hungry. "Okay."

Now it's my turn to clear my throat. "Can we, uh, move this to the floor or a couch or something? This chair restricts movement."

"That's the idea, little dhampir." Malachi runs his hand down Rylan's chest to wrap his fist around the other vampire's cock. I bite my bottom lip. Gods, that's hot.

It only gets hotter when Malachi drags Rylan's cock through my folds. Up and down. Up and down. Teasing both of us while he has total control. I try to surge up, but Wolf shifts both my wrists to one hand and coasts his other down my body to press against my stomach, pinning me further.

"Please!"

"Not yet," Malachi murmurs. "Rylan made us wait for an entire month. A few more minutes won't kill either of you."

"It might." I whimper as he circles Rylan's cock over my clit. Every muscle in Rylan's lean body appears carved from stone. He's gripping the armrests of the chair like he might rip them off, but he makes no move to stop Malachi's torment.

"It won't." Wolf pinches my nipple, making me gasp. "You should pierce these. Imagine how much fun we'd have with them. Maybe even get a little chain between the two that I could tug when you're riding my cock."

There isn't enough air in the room. I squirm, and Malachi responds by tapping Rylan's cock against my clit.

Wolf watches avidly even as he moves to my other breast and works that nipple until it's a hard peak. "Yeah, I think I'd like that a lot."

Body jewelry isn't something I've thought overmuch about, but I like the picture he paints. I like it a lot. I drag in a breath, trying to put my thoughts in order. "Wouldn't I heal too fast for them?"

"Pure silver won't let you heal completely." He bites his bottom lip, a tiny stream of blood descending from the puncture. "It would always hurt a little, for as long as you have them."

"Oh." The word comes out as a squeak.

"We'll talk about it later." Malachi notches Rylan's cock at my entrance. "Don't move." All three of us hold perfectly still as he shifts away and picks up the lube he retrieved earlier. He returns to press against Rylan's back. "I enter you, you enter her."

"Okay." Rylan's voice has gone low and gained a rumble.

His cock twitches against me, and I can't be sure, but I could swear it gets even bigger.

But Malachi doesn't move yet. He dips down and presses an openmouthed kiss to Rylan's throat. The arms of the chair creak as Rylan fights to hold still, to submit. His silver eyes are practically creating their own light source now. They only get brighter when Malachi bites him. It's not a gentle one. With me, he's usually careful not to tear the skin any more than necessary, to keep the damage to a minimum.

He's not being careful with Rylan.

The wound is ragged and large, and blood spurts onto my mostly naked body for several seconds before Rylan's healing takes over and the flow slows. Malachi drags his tongue through the blood on Rylan's neck. "Now."

His hands disappear behind Rylan, and I don't need to see details to know he's spreading lube over his length and the other vampire's ass. Rylan moans a little and pushes the head of his cock into me. Knowing that he's mirroring the advance of Malachi's cock into his ass...

"Fuck," I whisper.

"That's the idea, love."

Another inch. Another mixed moan from the three of us. For his part, Wolf seems content to draw patterns in the blood spatter on my chest and stomach, but that won't last. He's not one to sit idly by when there's pleasure on the table.

The sound of wood breaking and then the arms supporting my legs are gone, torn apart by Rylan's attempt to maintain control. Wolf lets loose his wild laugh. "In that case..." Another splintering sound and suddenly the back of the chair is gone, too. He catches me before I fall, using his body to support me. "Hand me the lube, Malachi."

For a moment, I think Malachi might argue, but he hands the bottle over. It takes a little adjustment to get the broken remains of the chair out of the way and move to the spot before the fireplace, but we end up in nearly the same position. Wolf wastes no time working his cock into my ass from below me while Rylan and Malachi kneel between my spread legs. Even though the men like to come in my pussy, Wolf loves to fuck my ass. We've done it more than enough times that I'm making impatient sounds as he slides deeper.

More, more, more. I need more.

Once he's seated his full length inside me, he kisses my neck. Malachi guides Rylan's cock back to my pussy.

He was big before. Even without his bloodline power coming into play, Rylan is large. Having Wolf's cock in my ass as Rylan works into my pussy? He's almost too big. He has to fight for every inch, and his low moans tell me Malachi is doing the same into his ass. Eventually, a small eternity later, he's seated fully within me.

I can't catch my breath. The first initial push was a pleasant warmth, but now I feel like my skin is going to burn right off my body. The sensation only gets stronger when Malachi starts to move. We're all sealed so tightly together that as he braces a hand on Rylan's shoulder and starts to fuck him in slow, deep thrusts, the other three of us rock together with each stroke. I'm pinned between Rylan and Wolf's bigger bodies, spread wide open by their cocks inside me, and none of us can do anything but take what Malachi gives.

The bond flares inside me. Except it's not a flare, not really. What happened that first night together was a flare, overwhelming and near-violent. This feels more like a flower unfurling. "More," I gasp.

Malachi gives us more. He plants his fists on either side of our hips and starts fucking Rylan's ass. Starts fucking all three of us. That's what it feels like. I can't quite explain it, and pleasure makes it even harder to process what I'm feeling, but...

I can feel *everything*.

Malachi's fierce possessiveness, his determination to claim all of us as his in a way that can't be broken.

Rylan's relief, the way this moment feels like all the broken pieces have clicked together in his chest, turning into something whole.

Wolf's joy at finding what feels like home, his anticipation over the chaos and bloodshed to come.

I can feel all of it.

I cling to Rylan—or maybe it's Malachi—as I shatter into a million pieces. This isn't like any orgasm I've had before. It goes on and on, pleasure so acute, it's agony. I can't stop coming, am barely aware of the men losing control in and around me. Something hot and wet hits my neck. Wolf, biting Rylan. Hot pinpricks sear my hips. Rylan's claws. A roar fills the room that sounds like the noise a forest fire makes as it rampages. Malachi.

Higher and higher, more and more. I can do nothing but ride the wave, a piece of flotsam tossed about by a hurricane. There is freedom in submission, and I find it in this moment. My last shred of strength dissipates. I go limp, a marionette with its strings cut.

Someone curses, and everything goes black.

13

I WAKE UP IN A PILE OF BODIES AND COVERED IN blood. For one heart-stopping moment, I think I've killed them, but Malachi groans and shifts, and then Wolf makes a sound that might be his mad laugh if every one of his vocal chords had been shredded beyond repair. Rylan's half on top of me, and I can feel him breathing.

Alive.

I exhale slowly. I feel like I've been hit by a truck, and then they backed over me a few times for good measure. Everything hurts. Not just muscles and bone but down to a cellular level. My throat feels like someone took sandpaper to it while I wasn't paying attention. It takes me three tries to speak. "What the hell was that?"

"Fucking seraph bonds," Rylan murmurs against my throat.

I can't tell if he's angry or just exhausted. "Apparently there's more to this bag of tricks than I realized."

I blink at the ceiling, waiting for his words to make sense. They don't. "Please explain," I manage.

"Later."

As much as I want to argue, he's right. I don't have the strength to form more than a few words at a time. They start to shift, and every one of them is moving like they feel as terrible as I do. What *was* that?

Rylan rolls off me, and I try to sit up. I get as far as planting my hands on the floor and the sight that greets me has me staring blankly. Surely those aren't my hands? Except they can't be Rylan's because I can see *his* hands where he lies next to me. "Um."

"Um?" This from Wolf. He's thrown his arm over his eyes as if even the light of the fireplace is too bright for him.

I flex my hands. They move. Which means they're mine after all. I swallow hard. "I have claws."

"Cute."

I flex them again. Each of my fingers is tipped with a shining silver claw. They're almost pretty, dainty and deadly with a wicked curve that's designed for slicing and tearing. "No, I mean I literally have claws. Like Rylan."

"Funny story…" Wolf lifts his arm off his eyes and flicks his fingers. Sparks dance in the air above him, morphing into a ribbon of flames. It dissipates almost immediately, but there's no denying that it was there.

That puts the strength back into my body. "What the hell is going on?"

Rylan's arm shifts to some kind of large cat and then back to human. "I still have my powers." He frowns. "But I can feel the flames, too. And the blood coursing through all three of your bodies."

Now that he mentions it, I can as well. The fire sounds almost like a siren song. It makes me want to reach out and...

The flames flare up in response.

I silence the thought and they die back down to normal levels in response. "This is bad."

"Is it?" Malachi hefts himself up to lean against the couch. He looks as exhausted as I feel, but there's a contemplative expression on his face that means he's thinking six moves ahead. "This will be incredibly useful."

"If Cornelius gets ahold of us, it will be useful to *him*." Rylan doesn't sound as icy as normal. He's too busy toying with the flames of the fireplace, making them surge and flow. "This is fascinating. It feels so different from mine."

I start to wrap my arms around myself but stop when I scratch my skin with my new claws. "How do I put them away?"

"Concentrate." Rylan's still distracted with the flames. "Picture it and they'll retreat."

How am I supposed to concentrate when my world has just been turned upside down *again*? Having seraph powers is one thing—I still haven't come to terms with it. Having bloodline powers? My throat gets tight and panic flutters in my chest. "I don't know how to control this."

"Mina—"

"I don't have training. I can't shield. I have no experience."

My voice is getting higher and higher with each word, but I can't make myself stop. "This is too much! I'm going to get us killed."

"*Mina.*" Malachi crawls to me and pulls me into his arms. "It will be okay. This is a good thing."

"It doesn't feel like a good thing. It feels like I'm a fucking freak. How am I supposed to deal with this?" I wave my hand, and it's as if my powers snag on every drop of blood in Wolf's body. He jerks several inches to the side. "Oh my gods." I clench my fists and bury my face in Malachi's chest. "I'm sorry. I didn't mean to."

Wolf laughs, the sound a little hoarse. "Kinky."

"It might not be permanent," Malachi says slowly. "Relax. Let's get cleaned up and we'll figure it out like we have everything else up to this point."

"By fighting and snarling at each other?"

His chest moves against my cheek in a soundless laugh. "*Together.*"

The chair is ruined and blood has stained the rug. There's no cleaning this up. I dread what replacing those things will cost, but the men don't seem overly worried about it. When I ask, Rylan gets a strange smile on his face. "The owner of this place has cleaned up worse messes than this. It will be fine."

With *that* cryptic statement, we all head into the master bedroom and take turns showering off. Under other circumstances, it might have turned into some sexy fun, but I'm barely managing to stay on my feet, and the men don't seem like they're doing much better. Malachi orders us into the massive bed before we fall down, and no one argues with his command. That, more than anything, speaks to how fucked up things are right now.

I end up wrapped in a blanket, cuddled between Wolf and Rylan while Malachi reclines on Rylan's other side. It's a strange sort of puppy pile, but it feels effortless. Especially when Rylan idly sifts his hand through my hair.

As tempting as it is to close my eyes and let them comfort me with their presence, we have to talk about this and we need to do it now. I twist a little to see Rylan's face, but not enough to dislodge his hand in my hair. "Did you know this might happen?"

"No." He closes his eyes, his expression strangely peaceful. "But the seraphim weren't exactly sharing the inner workings of their powers with everyone else. The bond was common knowledge at the time, and everyone was aware that it could cause compulsive obedience, but beyond that, it wasn't clear." He frowns a little. "Though it doesn't make sense that it would share powers like this. Plenty of vampires who were forcibly bonded would rather die than stay linked like that. I can't imagine they'd hesitate to use more power against the seraph who held their leash."

Killing the seraph likely meant killing every vampire they were bonded to. "Is that possible even with the compulsion?"

"Yes."

He doesn't need to elaborate. If he says it's possible, then it is. Sharing power the way we have would make it much easier to kill the seraph involved. "Maybe it happened because we chose this. Tonight, I mean. Maybe the bond responded to that willingness."

"That seems likely." Malachi's staring at something off in the middle distance. "In the end, it doesn't change the end goal or the plan. We'll stay here as long as we can. It will give us time to figure out if this is temporary and teach you what you need to know to control them."

That makes me laugh, but not like anything is funny. "It takes bloodline vampires decades to learn to control their powers."

"Who told you that?"

I start to snap back but realize that he's right. My father was my source of all my vampire lore until I met Malachi. It stands to reason that he would keep information close to his chest, even from his children who *did* inherit his magic. Information is just another kind of power, and my father never parts with power willingly. "Well, shit."

"Cornelius really is an asshole." Wolf chuckles. "A month should be more than enough time. Maybe less since you have all three of us helping. You'll be fine, love." He says it with such confidence, I almost believe him.

On the other hand, when has *anything* come easily for me?

"In the meantime, we maintain the course." Malachi looks down at me. Even as tired as he obviously is, there's heat in his dark eyes. An answering pulse goes through me. No matter what else is true, I love having sex with these men. *Love* it.

I...love them.

I won't say it. Not now. Maybe not ever. It's too new and raw and unknown. No matter what we've chosen for the future, the power between us is so precariously balanced. Telling them what I feel is asking for trouble.

Coward.

I ignore the little voice inside me and close my eyes. "Yes. We'll maintain the course."

I don't remember going to sleep, but I wake up with Rylan's mouth on my breasts and Wolf's tongue in my pussy. It feels like a fever dream to glance down and find Malachi's mouth wrapped around Rylan's cock. A fever dream, but so right my heart gives a painful thump in response. This is how it should be. The four of us. Together. This is how it *is* now.

Wolf moves back a little and flips me onto my side. Rylan and Malachi move to adjust, Rylan shifting down to tongue my clit and Malachi moving with him. And then Wolf is pressing into me. "Love your ass," he murmurs against the back of my neck. "Can't neglect this pretty pussy, though."

Rylan chuckles against my clit, and I shiver. "This…"

"Shh, love." Wolf clasps my jaw and urges me back so he can claim my mouth even as he thrusts deeper. "Just a dream."

I reach down and sift my fingers through Rylan's short hair. He's rubbing my clit with his tongue slowly, teasing my pleasure higher. This entire experience feels lazy in the best way. No one is rushing. We're simply giving and receiving pleasure. Each orgasm they deal me feels like a little death that builds on the last one, a slowly rising tide.

At least for a little while.

Nothing good lasts forever. Not even vampire sex.

Eventually Wolf's strokes lose their smooth rhythm and he bites my neck as he pumps me full of his come, setting off a chain reaction of another orgasm from me. I cry out, pinned between his cock and Rylan's mouth. It's too good. I can't take any more.

I don't have a choice.

Malachi eases off Rylan's cock and licks his slit, but his eyes are on me. "Fill her up, Rylan. I want all three of us mixed inside that perfect pussy."

Rylan nods, his eyes nearly glowing. He barely waits for Wolf to pull out of me before he's yanking me down his body and shoving his cock into me. We're still moving slow, still maintaining that lazy vibe, but it feels different with Rylan. It always seems to feel different with Rylan, like he's barely restraining himself from shredding the bedding and driving into me until he tattoos his essence on every inch of my body.

Once again, pleasure rises in a wave. I recognize the feel of Wolf's power sending my blood to pulse in my clit and nipples. I shiver around Rylan's cock, clinging to him as I get swept away yet again. How much pleasure can one body hold? It feels limitless in this moment.

He buries his face in my neck as he comes. I feel the tiniest nick of teeth, but a swipe of his rough tongue and all evidence of it is gone.

Or if would be if we weren't in bed with two other vampires.

Malachi grips the back of Rylan's neck and pulls him off me, his expression forbidding. "No teeth."

"She's recovered." He seems to arch up into Malachi's touch. "Besides, Wolf bit her."

"That's different."

"I'm recovered," I confirm. I'm more than recovered. Now that I'm fully awake, the lingering exhaustion from last night is gone. I feel...really, really good. Like I could run a marathon and then go climb a mountain, and maybe finish off the day with some deep sea diving. I touch my knee. The scar my father gave me is gone, just like the pain and limited mobility are gone.

In fact...

I sit up and look at my body. *All* my scars are gone. How did I not notice it before? I registered that they were fading faster than was humanly possible, but there were still many lingering. At least there were until last night.

I don't like it. Those scars were linked with my memories of surviving. I went through *so* much, and nothing my father and his cronies did could break me. They hurt me, scarred me, damaged my body, but they couldn't break me.

Now, all those scars are only in my head. It feels strange.

I twist to look at Malachi. A sound almost like relief whispers from my lips at the sight of his scarred chest. That, at least, hasn't changed. I want him to tell me the story someday. Would he still do it if the scar disappeared? The thought isn't logical, but I can't shake it. "Come here."

He kisses me, a slow, drugging claiming. I sink into the feel of him, let myself be buoyed by his steadiness. This. This is all that matters. I can face down all the wild magic in the world as long as Malachi remains steady at my side.

He flips me over onto my hands and knees. It gives me a great view of where Rylan and Wolf lean on each other against the headboard. They're not exactly cuddling, but they're not *not* cuddling, either. They watch us with a barely sated hunger.

With vampire blood, there's little to no recovery time. If I didn't have to stop to eat, we could fuck for days, weeks, months. Maybe even years.

Malachi nudges my legs wider and then he's guiding his cock into me. A slow, steady intrusion that has my breath gasping from my lungs. Every time. *Every time.* It always feels like the first time with him, like he's claiming me all over again. "You can take more," he murmurs.

More of his cock?

More orgasms?

I don't get a chance to ask. He braces one hand on my hip and one on my shoulder and picks up his rhythm. At this angle, every stroke slides his cock along my G-spot. I whimper, and my mind goes blank. I'm vaguely aware of my fingertips tingling as they morph into claws, of me shredding the bedding just like I'm sure Rylan wanted to do. He might have restraint. I have none. I can feel my blood surging through my body, a new awareness that no doubt comes from Wolf's bloodline. Part of me screams to control these foreign powers, but I can't think straight with Malachi fucking me like this.

I close my eyes as yet another orgasm bears down on me. I'm so focused on my pleasure, I almost miss the scent of smoke.

Then I'm coming, and I know nothing at all.

14

"YOU HAVE *GOT* TO STOP FUCKING ME UNTIL I PASS out." I watch the smoke waft from the remains of the little fire I apparently set when I orgasmed.

Wolf smothered it with a pillow and now he's trailing his fingers through the smoke with a grin on his face. "Remember when you gave Malachi grief for doing this very thing?"

I groan. "In my defense, he burned a ring around us and nearly collapsed the entire floor. You three might survive a little bit of being burned alive, but I won't."

"You will." Rylan trails a finger over my claws. "I may be wrong, but after last night, I'd wager not much can kill you."

Easy for him to say. I try to frown, but the expression won't stick. I'm too content. "You literally almost killed me...four days ago?" Was it four days? Five? I'm not sure anymore. We hardly kept a regular schedule in the first place, but all the running has messed up my internal clock. Being in a house carved into the interior of a mountain isn't helping, either.

"That was four days ago." He pricks his thumb on my claw and lifts it to press to my lips.

The blood zings through me. My mouth tingles, and I have to work to restrain myself from trying to bite him. My teeth aren't like a vampire's. I'll just gnaw on him without some help from a blade. Or my claws.

Rylan grins as if he can read my thoughts. "Go ahead."

I waste no time scrambling up to straddle his stomach. After the smallest consideration, I lightly drag my pointer finger down the center of his throat, leaving a trail of blood in its wake. Delight courses through me. I don't need the men to cut themselves for me any longer. I can do it myself. I grin and lean down to drag my tongue up his throat.

"Don't get him riled up again, little dhampir." Malachi lies next to us on his back, his head propped on his arm. "We need to leave the bed and do some training."

"I don't want to train," I murmur against Rylan's skin. It's not quite the truth; I know training is vital, both the combat and now magic. But it's hard to remember that with Rylan's hand on the back of my neck, lightly massaging me as I drink from him in little sips.

"Up, Mina."

I groan a little, but I obey. It's only when I'm standing that I get a good look at the bed. "We are going to owe the owner of this house so much money."

"It's fine." Malachi rises and disappears into the closet. He comes back into the bedroom a moment later dressed in a pair of gym shorts and carrying workout clothing for me—leggings, a bra, and a tank top.

I pull the clothing on but pause when Rylan and Wolf make no move to do the same. "Aren't you two coming?"

Wolf drops onto the bed and rolls until he's pressed against Rylan's side. "Oh, someone will be *coming*." He reaches down and closes his hand around Rylan's cock.

"Insatiable," Malachi mutters.

Rylan clears his throat. "We'll join you in a little bit."

Malachi leads the way out of the bedroom, and I can't stop the goofy grin from pulling at the edges of my mouth. I'm not naive enough to think that everyone's worked through their baggage. That's not how anyone functions: humans, vampires, or seraphim. Especially when they have the sheer amount of history my men share. Their issues will crop up again and again as time goes on.

But after last night and this morning, I finally believe we can navigate our way through whatever happens.

We end up in a fancy gym that has everything from free weights to various machines to a nice mat for sparring. I whistle softly. "Wow."

"It's a nice change of pace." Malachi rolls his shoulders. "First, sparring."

This time, I don't bother to complain. He's right that I need this training, and Malachi is an excellent teacher. Even if I want to toss him out a window from time to time because he's so damn unrelenting. This morning is no different.

An hour later, I'm dripping sweat and every muscle in my body is trembling from exertion. Malachi executes a flawless move that has me spinning through the air and landing on my back hard enough to drive the breath from my body. He twists around to look down at me. "You should have seen that coming."

"I did." I wheeze. "Reflexes too slow."

"Get faster."

"Trying."

He reaches down, and I take the offered hand, letting him pull me to my feet. He gives me a slow smile. "You're getting better."

"Don't say 'I told you so.'" I can't quite pull off the grumpy act. My goofy grin keeps peeking through. I press my fingers to my cheeks. "This is ridiculous. I can't stop smiling."

"You look happy."

Happy. The concept is as foreign as love is to me. But if I can feel one, surely it's possible to feel the other? I let my hands drop. "I think I am happy?"

"Are you asking me or telling me?"

"I don't know." I laugh. "I have no business being happy. We still have so much to accomplish. We're nowhere near safe. We—"

"Mina." The quiet command in his voice cuts me off. Malachi takes my face in his big hands. "Life is challenging enough without putting qualifiers on happiness. It passes, just like fear and anger and horror pass. Enjoy the feeling while we have it."

I make a face. "That's not exactly comforting."

"I wasn't trying to be comforting." He leans down and presses a light kiss to my lips. "Now, on to the magic."

Strangely, the magic training is more difficult than the sparring. Malachi sets me up as if we're going to meditate, but his low voice talks me through the process. It feels like trying to bench-press a car. I can *feel* the magic, but it's so overwhelming, I can barely envision wrapping my hands around it, let alone guiding it to my will.

I don't know how much time passes before he calls it quits, but it feels like I've learned nothing at all. "I don't care what you all say. This is going to take years."

"You can already feel the movement of your powers. That's the hardest part."

I give him the look that statement deserves. "If that's the hardest part, I should be able to do more."

"It's the first day, little dhampir. Have some grace for yourself." He holds the door open. "Let's feed you."

"Shower first." I pull the wet fabric of my tank top away from my skin and cringe.

"Shower first," he confirms.

It takes twice as long as it should because we get distracted with each other's bodies, and by the time we make it out, both Rylan and Wolf have disappeared. I eye the bed. "How many rooms does this place have?"

"More than enough." Malachi wraps an arm around my waist, guiding me to the door. "But if we want to reduce the amount of damage we do, we should confine fucking to this room."

Because we're destined to lose control and continue to trash whatever room we're in. I press my hand to my mouth, as if that's enough to hide the grin. "That sounds like a good idea."

"Mmm." He tucks me against his body as we head for the kitchen. "You *are* happy."

He would know. If the lesson earlier is anything to go by, I won't be successfully shielding for some time. "I suppose I am."

"It looks good on you."

We find the other two in the kitchen, Rylan making a pot of coffee and Wolf staring at the fully stocked fridge as if it might jump out and bite him. "Humans and their desire for options. It's food. Why should it need to be so fancy?"

"Spoken like a vampire."

He motions at the fridge. "Pick your poison."

"I'm more than capable of making my own food." I slip out from beneath Malachi's arm and walk to the fridge. As ridiculous as I think Wolf's being, he's right; there are a truly overwhelming number of options here. I grab an apple and wander to the pantry door a few feet away. Thankfully, the owner has a veritable storefront of power bars. I pick a couple and head back into the kitchen.

All three vampires look at me with disbelief.

Rylan raises his brows. "All those options and you choose *that?*"

"I don't know how to cook all that many things and I'm starving, so I don't want to take the time to deal with it right now. Power bars were good enough for me before. I don't see why they shouldn't be good enough for me now."

Malachi's frowning as if solving a complicated problem. "I thought you preferred them because they're easy to carry on the run."

"That is one of the reasons I prefer them, yes." From their expressions, they're not going to let it go, so I feel compelled to explain. "While there are humans and dhampirs in my father's compound, they're hardly a priority compared to the vampires. The food they're provided is designed to keep them alive and healthy so they can continue to act as walking blood banks and, at times, breeders. Power bars were the tastiest of the bunch."

Wolf shakes his head slowly. "That is rather pathetic, love."

"It is what it is." I take my power bars and apple to the counter wrapping around half of the kitchen island and sit down. "Good food matters less than keeping myself alive. That's always been the priority."

"It can still be the priority if you're eating other food." Malachi crosses his arms over his chest.

Rylan pours coffee into a mug and passes it to me. "I'll learn to cook." When all three of us stare at him, he shrugs. "It's a necessary skill if we have someone who consumes food."

"Rylan—" I don't know what I'm going to say, because I never get a chance to finish that sentence.

There's a burst of power in the room and all the shadows seem to surge forth to a center point. One moment, there's the four of us. The next, Azazel stands in our midst. He slides his hands into his pockets and gives the room a long look. "Interesting."

As one, the vampires explode into motion. Malachi grabs me and shoves me between him and the wall, his big body blocking out the rest of the room. I hear Rylan curse and a scuffle. Peering around Malachi's arm finds Wolf pinning Rylan to the counter.

He gives the other vampire a shake. "Focus. He's a demon. If you attack him, he'll slice you to pieces."

Azazel examines his fingertips. Are they sharper than they appeared at first glance? I can't tell from this angle. The shadows move around him almost as if alive. For a moment, I get the impression of a hulking beast with giant horns curving from its head. In the next breath, it's gone, and there's only the handsome dark-haired man who seems to carry an aura of danger on a level I've never experienced before meeting him. Even having been in the same room as he was two days ago isn't enough to make me used to the sensation.

The demon shifts, and the three vampires tense in response. His slow grin says he did it on purpose. "What a charming little nest you've created, seraph. Have you considered my deal?"

"She's not making any deal."

Azazel cuts a look at Malachi. "I didn't ask you." He narrows dark eyes. "Fire-bringer. I'd like to see how you do in *my* realm, vampire. We demons can show you what true fire means."

"Now, now, Azazel." Wolf lets loose his high, mad laugh. "There's no need to prove you're the baddest motherfucker in this room. We're all convinced." Rylan opens his mouth, but Wolf slams his hand over it before the other vampire can speak. "Answer the nice demon, love."

Right. Okay. I take in a slow breath. "I've decided not to make a deal with you." There's only the slightest tremor in my voice to indicate how stressful this situation is.

"Pity." Azazel examines his fingertips again. This time, I'm *certain* they're sharper than they were. They haven't shifted the way Rylan's—and now mine—do. The fingers are exactly the same. Just...sharper. "Ah well. Since we're such good friends, Wolf, I suppose I should tell you that there's a group of six vampires heading up the mountain in this direction. Good luck." He disappears as suddenly as he arrived.

For one breathless moment, we're all perfectly still.

As if on cue, there's a niggling feeling at the very edge of my mind. I didn't notice it with Azazel's presence masking everything, but now there's no denying the fact. It's identical to what I felt last time. I swallow past my suddenly dry throat. "He's right. They're here."

Then Malachi surges forward. "Wolf, with me. Rylan, protect Mina."

"Of course." He sweeps me off my feet before I can take a single step. The house passes in a rush, Rylan sprinting down a hall I haven't had a chance to explore. He ducks into a room filled with monitors and slams the door shut.

I watch him pull down a heavy steel beam to drop into the crossbar over it. "That seems excessive."

"If I were your father, I would send a team from the front and a second, smaller, team from the back." Rylan drops into the chairs in front of the monitors and starts clicking buttons.

I concentrate, but I can only feel the irritation in one direction. "*Is* there a back to this place?"

"Of course." He frowns at the monitors and keeps clicking, flicking through the pictures so fast it makes me dizzy. "Only a fool wouldn't leave a back door to escape from."

Of course. How silly of me not to realize that was the case. "Who *is* this person?"

Rylan's fingers pause over the keyboard. "He was a...friend."

"Was?"

"He died some time ago. His granddaughter owns this house now, and she's responsible for most of the upgrades. For reasons I'm not prepared to get into, she was willing to offer it as a place to stay."

I have more questions, but they'll have to wait. Rylan's stopped on two screens. One depicts the road we drove in on. A single vehicle works its way up. It almost looks like a tank, armored plating beefing up the sides and roof and small windows not offering much in the way of weak points. I've seen that vehicle before. My father owns three of them. He uses one every time he has to leave the compound.

Surely he didn't come here himself?

"It's not him." Rylan shakes his head. "As I said, it's a good decoy, but this is the true strike team." He motions to the second monitor.

It depicts a trio of masked individuals. It's so dark, it takes me far too long to understand what I'm seeing. No trees. No rocks. No dirt. A hallway very similar to the ones we've been traveling since arriving yesterday.

"They're inside."

15

I LEAN CLOSE TO THE MONITOR. "WHY CAN'T I FEEL this group?"

"They must be masking their presence." He doesn't look happy at the revelation.

I could argue that maybe my lack of expertise is to blame, but there's no time to figure out the why. All that matters is that they're in the house and we're outnumbered. "What do we do?"

Rylan clicks a few more buttons. "You're not going to do anything. They're barely inside. It will take them time to get here." He stands and rolls his shoulders. "I'll get to them before that happens."

I'm moving before I register my own intent, shifting to stand between him and the door. "Not alone."

"Mina." He smiles slowly. "No matter what else is true, here

I am the apex predator. Once I'm out the door, hit this button."
He motions to one in the sea of them. "It will shut off the lights."

"Vampires have superior eyesight in the dark."

"They still need some light to be able to see. They won't get
it in here."

Because there are so few windows. I drag in a breath, fear like
a live thing inside me. "That means you need light to see, too."

"Yes, but sight isn't the only way to get around. Smell is just
as useful." He closes the distance between us and kisses me hard.
"Bar the door behind me. If the worst were to happen, there's
a hatch below the desk that will take you out. It's narrow and
uncomfortable, but you'll be free."

If the worst were to happen.

That would mean that Rylan is incapacitated. I drag in a
breath. "If you think that's a possibility, don't go."

"Mina." Gods, the way he says my name. Tenderly, as if testing
it out in the space between us. "No matter what else is true, we are
warriors. We can only run and hide for so long." He brushes his lips
to my forehead. "I care for you. I won't let them take you." Rylan
lifts me easily out of the way and sets the bar across the door aside
before I have a chance to react. Then he's gone, sliding out into the
shadows of the hallway. His body ripples as he changes, shifting
into a monstrous wolf that looks like something out of a nightmare.

I shut the door and wrestle the bar back over the door. It's
heavy enough that I don't know if a human woman could manage
it. If I wasn't terrified out of my mind, I would wonder again
what kind of woman this granddaughter of Rylan's friend is, but
I have bigger things to worry about.

I hold my breath as I push the button Rylan indicated. Instantly, all the cameras go dark. Did I fuck something up? Even as the worry takes hold, the cameras flick back to life, their images taking on a green tint that indicates night vision.

The giant wolf that is Rylan appears and disappears in flashes, running full out down the warren of hallways. He barely pauses at the doors. I can't be certain, but I think he shifts one hand to open them each time. It makes me dizzy trying to track him, so I turn to the intruders instead. They're all dressed in black and wearing masks that hide everything but their eyes, which now glow eerily in the night vision. They could be anyone.

I don't know the layout of this place well enough to figure out where they are, and it's not as if Rylan left a convenient map to track their progress against. All I know is that he's moving quickly, and they don't seem to have been slowed down much by the lack of light.

On the other set of screens, the vehicle is stopped. I catch blurs of movement that might be a fight, but my eyes can't track it to tell for sure. No matter what advantages seraphim might supposedly hold over vampires, their physicality isn't one of them. They're faster and stronger. I can feel Malachi and Wolf through the bond, but all I'm getting is a direction and approximate distance. It doesn't make it easier to tell what's going on.

Trying to follow the action will just give me a headache. I keep one eye on that screen but turn the rest of my focus to the intruders actually in the house. They've gone still. I examine the buttons before me, finally finding one that seems to allow audio. A horrifying howl echoes through the speakers.

Rylan's caught their scent.

I peer at the screen, but they don't seem nearly as terrified as I would be in their position. Being hunted in the dark by a monster, unable to see the threat coming at them.

The staticky sound of a radio. A tinny voice I can barely pick up. "We're in position."

The small hairs at the back of my neck rise as the tallest person in the group lifts the radio and says in a horrifyingly familiar voice, "Round them up."

Father.

Oh gods, Rylan's in over his head. No matter how easily he can cut through normal vampires, all my father has to do is get a word out and he'll flip the tables entirely. He can order Rylan to hold still and cut him into little pieces and there's not a single thing I can do to stop it.

I scan the buttons, looking for some kind of intercom, but it's too late.

On the screen showing the outside, the vehicle explodes. I stop short, staring in horror as vampires emerge from both sides of the road. There's a flurry of blurred movement, a flash of fire, and then everything goes still.

Two bodies fall to the ground, and even in the dark I recognize Wolf and Malachi before the other vampires close in, piling onto them to trap them. "No," I whisper.

"*Stop. Be still.*" My father's voice brings me back to the other screen. He pulls the mask from his face. "Flashlight."

One of the other vampires provides a flashlight and he clicks it on. Right before them, less than ten feet away, is Rylan. His body is low to the ground—obviously my father stopped him right before he pounced—and he quivers as he fights the command.

"Pretty thing," my father murmurs. "You'll make an excellent rug in my great hall."

"No!" They can't hear me. There's no way any of them can hear me.

My father flicks his fingers. "*Sleep.*" He watches with interest as Rylan slumps to the ground. "Bind him with silver." As his people rush to obey, he turns and finds the camera overhead. "Are you watching from some bolt-hole like the rat you are, Mina? All the suffering to come could have been avoided if you'd done the one task I set out for you." He shakes his head. "This is on your head. Now, be a good girl and wait for me. I'll be along shortly."

Something wet and hot slides down my cheeks. I press my fingertips there, strangely surprised to find that I'm crying. All this time and effort, and he's outplayed me once again. If I open the door and turn myself in, he might—

What am I saying?

He won't let any of the men go. Three bloodline vampires in one fell swoop? It's a feather in my father's cap like no other. He won't stop with a blood ward this time. No, he'll want to ensure any progeny of this trio of bloodlines stays within his control. He'll do whatever it takes to make it happen, including drugging and torturing my men.

A sob bursts from my throat and then I'm moving, shoving the chair back and fumbling down at the floor beneath the desk for the hatch Rylan said was there. I can't help them if I'm taken, too. I'm not sure I can help them if I'm *not* taken, but I have to try to fight. They've sacrificed too much for me to do anything else.

I find the hatch and wrestle it open. I can hear my father's voice, vibrating with power, but it doesn't work well long distance. His will presses on me, demanding I hold still and obey, but it's dampened from being conveyed through electronics. Because of that, I'm able to slip into the dark square beneath the desk and pull the hatch closed behind me.

Rylan was right; it's a tight fit. I descend the ladder in perfect darkness, the walls so close, they almost brush my shoulders.

I couldn't feel the weight of the mountain while in the house, but here it's almost overwhelming. Even without seeing my breath, I know it's ghosting the air in front of me. A shiver works its way through my body, and I pick up my pace. There's no telling how long I have before they find the security room, how many minutes it will take them to break down the door and give chase.

Endless minutes later, the ladder ends and my feet find solid ground. I reach around, trying to get a feel for where I am now. My foot nudges something. A box. Inside, I find the familiar shape of a flashlight. I hold my breath, praying to gods I'm not sure I believe in that the batteries are still full.

The light clicks on.

I exhale slowly and take a look at my surroundings. It appears to be a natural cave of some sort, the walls close and slanting. There's only one path forward, so I have to hope that it leads to the exit. Spending years wandering this place, lost, while my men are tortured and bred against their will is out of the question.

The box that held the flashlight also has a thick coat that's only slightly too large, a pair of boots that are also slightly too large, and a pack of bottled water. It's not quite a bug-out bag, but it's close enough. I pull on the boots and coat, instantly feeling better now that I'm not freezing. I glance up into the darkness where the hatch is, but there's no sound or movement. Down here, I'm completely cut off.

Except I'm not really.

I can still feel the men through the bond. Rylan somewhere above and to the right, Wolf and Malachi to the left.

If my father transports them, the bond will react poorly.

Shit.

I pick up my pace, hurrying through the cave in the only direction I can walk. Maybe under other circumstances, I'd marvel at the cold beauty of this place or consider how it makes me feel like I've left our world behind entirely.

It takes less time than I would have guessed for me to see a sliver of light ahead. I click off the flashlight and move forward slowly, all too aware that this might be yet another trap. If my father was able to find the other entrances, surely he could find this one?

Except when I step out into the sunlight and turn back to look at the cave entrance, it's nearly invisible. And I'm standing six inches from it. Someone would have to truly know it was here to find it.

Still...

I consider my options. I know where my father will take my men. He rarely ventures out of his compound to begin with, and it's more than equipped to keep captives. It's hardly the first time he's tried something of the sort.

I suppose I'll have to try to keep pace with them as best I can to avoid the bond lashing at all of us. I'm not sure what will happen if they're taken too far from me, but I don't want them to suffer while we find out.

A branch cracks somewhere off to my left. I react on instinct, crouching down next to a bush and holding my breath.

"I can see you, you know. That's a god-awful hiding spot."

A feminine voice. It's not familiar, but I hardly know all my father's people by voice alone. "If you come closer, I'll kill you."

"Cute, but I don't think so." A woman steps into view. I blink like a fool in response. She's a tall white woman with a mass of wavy brown hair and an athletic build, clothed in what looks like military gear designed to camouflage the wearer. The gun slung over her shoulder isn't her only weapon. I count at least three knifes that I can see, one long enough that it might be termed a sword.

She's also human.

She eyes me. "You're Rylan's seraph."

Surprise flares. I wouldn't have thought he'd tell anyone about my identity or what that might mean between the two of us. "Who are you to him?"

"A friend. Sort of." She lifts her gaze to the mountain behind me. "I take it things went poorly. The alarms have been blaring since those assholes breached my security. Where is he?"

"They took him." I can feel him moving, but there's a slug-gish nature to the bond that makes me suspect they drugged him.

I don't know what drug can incapacitate a vampire, but of course my father is aware of it and has it on hand. "They took all of them."

"Well, fuck."

"That about sums it up." I twist, trying to estimate the growing distance. We have miles and miles to play with, but I'm on foot and they'll be in a car before too long. "I have to go."

She narrows inky eyes at me. "I don't suppose you have a plan."

Not even close. "Of course. I'm not going to let him harm them."

The woman sighs. "I guess I'm at your disposal, at least for transport and the like. Though I'm not storming any castles for you, princess."

I can't afford to trust her, but at the same time, I can't afford to reject any help out of hand. "Why would you help me?"

"My family owes Rylan a debt we can never repay." She doesn't say it like she's happy about it. "Since I'm the matriarch of the family now, that means it's on me to keep balancing the scales."

I eye her. I'm hardly an expert on humans, but she doesn't look much older than me. "Who *are* you?"

"Oh. That." She adjusts the position of the gun across her back and offers her hand. "Grace Jaeger. I'm a monster hunter."

I shake her hand, feeling numb. "Wouldn't you consider me one of the monsters?"

"Definitely." She says it so easily. "But like I said, the whole debt to Rylan thing means you're safe enough with me."

I'm out of options. I run my hand through my hair. "We have to follow them. Do you have a vehicle?"

"Come on."

Her vehicle, if it can be termed such, is an off-roading beast with two seats and yet more weapons. Grace climbs behind the wheel. "Which way?"

I point north. "They'll be heading for Montana where my father's compound is."

"I see." She worries her bottom lip, a small line appearing between her dark brows. "We can't drive this the whole way, but there's a good stopping point a few hours from here that will take us in that general direction."

It will have to do. "That works."

She guns the engine and then we're off, flying over a trail that barely seems to exist. The engine is too loud for easy conversation, which is just as well. I don't know this woman, and all I can focus on is the worry about what comes next.

My father *took* my men.

I close my eyes and welcome the anger that knowledge brings. Better that he'd taken me instead. At least I know how to survive in that compound, though that was back when he actively underestimated me. I doubt he'll make the same mistake again.

Nausea rolls over me in a wave, and I have to open my eyes. What the hell? I press my hand to my chest and try to focus on the area in front of the vehicle, but it doesn't help. Another wave, stronger this time. "Pull over."

Grace glances at me. "What?"

"Pull over!"

She slams the vehicle to a stop, and I barely get out of it in time to lose the power bars and apple I ate earlier. I keep dry heaving for several long moments as my stomach tries to exit my body.

I have never thrown up once in my life. I don't get sick at all, not really. I search the bond as best I can, but it doesn't seem to be originating from there. What the hell?

Another wave of nausea nearly has me dry heaving again.

"You okay?" Grace gives a rough laugh. "You're not, like, pregnant or something, are you?"

Surely not.

Except...

I close my eyes, feeling with my power on instinct alone. I've gotten really good at feeling the parameters of the bond. Searching within my actual body isn't all that different. To be thorough, I scan myself from head to toe. There, nestled in my lower stomach, I find it.

The tiniest, most fragile spark of life inside me.

I open my eyes. "Holy shit."

I struggle to my feet to find Grace offering me a pack of mint gum. "Don't get back in here until you chew through one of these. I'm super sensitive to smell and puke breath is gross."

"Thanks," I say faintly, my mind still spinning.

"Is there a reason you're muttering 'holy shit' at the forest after you throw up?" She sounds vaguely curious, almost like she's asking out of politeness.

If I'm really pregnant, it means I have what I need to fight my father. It would be significantly simpler if I also had my men at my side, but I'll make do. All I need to do is get onto the compound and make a public declaration. It will take careful planning. I can't think about it right now.

I press my hand to my stomach, and the little flicker of life seems to flare brighter in response. I wish I could be happy. This is what we wanted after all. Except my being alone and stranded with some strange *monster hunter* while my men are taken captive by my father was never part of the plan.

"Turns out you were right." I swallow hard. "I'm pregnant."

ACT III
QUEEN

1

I NEVER GAVE MUCH THOUGHT TO PREGNANCY. NOT even when my father sent me to Malachi's home with the intention of sacrificing me, body and blood, to the trapped vampire. At the time, I'd planned on escaping or dying before he knocked me up.

Look at me now.

I slump back against the tub in the cheap motel bathroom. My head spins and sweat slicks my skin. My mouth tastes... Well, best not to think about that too hard or I'll start retching again. I drag myself up to the sink and brush my teeth for the tenth time today. An exercise in futility. I'll be puking again before too long.

As if being sick isn't bad enough, my thoughts feel as fuzzy as the inside of my mouth. I need to be planning, to come up with some idea to free my men, but I barely have the energy to move.

My father has Malachi, Wolf, and Rylan, and I should be coming up with a way to rescue them.

Instead, it's all I can do to navigate the crappy hotel room where I currently reside.

I stagger out of the bathroom to find Grace lounging on one of the two queen mattresses in the hotel room, flipping through channels with a bored expression on her face. I still don't know enough about this woman, for all that she's helped me. She's a white woman with long dark hair and an athletic build. She also seems to want to be anywhere but helping me. Yet she hasn't ditched me. Her pile of weapons is carefully arranged on the desk, and once again I'm left wondering about this one-woman army.

She glances at me and raises her brows. "You're a mess."

"I know." I drop onto the free bed and wait for my stomach to decide if it's going to rebel again. After a harrowing moment, it settles and I exhale in relief. "Did you have a chance to look over the plans of the compound I drew up?"

"Yeah." She sits up. "They're nicely detailed. You have a really good eye for security and what to look for."

Of course I do. I'd been planning on escaping the first chance I got. I had my father's patrols, security measures, and everything mapped down to the smallest detail, and I'd had to do it by memory because if I wrote something down and he found it... I shudder. "At least growing up in that hellhole was good for something. We can help the men." We *have* to help them.

"About that." Grace won't quite meet my eyes. "I'm going to be brutally honest with you—"

"When are you anything less than brutally honest?" We've

only been traveling together for two days, but Grace's bluntness is both a balm and an aggravation. She doesn't lie; she doesn't even bother to cushion harsh truths. I sit up. I'm about to get another of those harsh truths right now. "What's wrong?"

"It's a lost cause, Mina." She doesn't look happy about it. "If I had a trained team, we *might* be able to get in and get out, but the odds already aren't good because of what we're dealing with. By your own estimate, there are hundreds of vampires in that compound. Even if they were only turned and had no powers to speak of, those numbers just aren't surmountable. It doesn't matter that only a third or so of them are trained soldiers. Any vampire is a threat to the success of a rescue effort. Add in the fact that all your father has to do is speak and we lose, and it's impossible."

"No." I shake my head. This isn't right. None of this is *right*. Malachi and I were just talking about plans a few days ago. We should be safe in the mountain stronghold that is owned by Grace's family. We should be prepared to win.

Instead, I'm alone with a woman who obviously doesn't want to help but just as obviously feels obligated to try. And my men? They're currently enjoying the questionable hospitality that comes with being my father's captives. I shake my head again, harder this time. "I refuse to believe that."

"They'll kill us." She doesn't say it unkindly, and somehow that makes it worse. "If you're lucky, they'll kill you, too. If you're not, your father will lock you up somewhere until you birth that little monster and *then* he'll kill you."

I press my hand to my lower stomach where the little spark

of life pulses in time with my heart. "It's not a monster. It's barely a cluster of cells at this point."

Grace opens her mouth but hesitates. When I stare, she finally says, "It's making you weak. You can barely use your powers, and you're sleeping more than you're awake right now."

I drag my hand through my hair. She's right. I haven't been operating at anything resembling normal capacity since I found out I was pregnant a few days ago. I will admit to not knowing much about pregnancy, but it seems like the symptoms have come on far too quickly. I should have *weeks* before I start to see side effects.

Unless you've been pregnant longer than you or the men realized.

I clear my throat. "I know. It's not ideal, but—"

"There are options." She still won't meet my gaze. "You don't have to keep it."

I freeze. My brain knows what she's saying, but it still takes me a few moments to let the offer sink in. Terminate the pregnancy. I press my hand to my stomach. Hard not to be resentful of the little presence that isn't quite a presence. I thought pregnancy was my option to take my father's throne, but I can't even get in there, and I certainly don't have the energy to fight. If I show up and publicly declare myself his heir...

I want to believe it will stick.

I desperately need it to be true.

But there's a chance—and it's even a large chance at this point—that he'll do exactly what Grace says and lock me up until I have the baby and then kill me for all the trouble I've caused. More, my half siblings are hardly going to support my claim. As far as they're concerned, I'm a powerless dud, which means I'm not a legitimate contender for the head of clan.

If I had an army at my back, it wouldn't be a question. I could bust open the front gates, make my claim in front of the entire compound, and take over. No one could stop me. No one would *dare* stop me.

But with just me and Grace? And me being incapacitated more often than I'm not?

She's right to bring up this option, no matter how conflicted I am talking about it. "It's not just my decision," I finally say.

"Actually, it is." She shrugs when I look at her. "Hey, I'm not telling you what to do. I'm just presenting options. Ultimately, it doesn't really matter which way you land on the topic, because it's not going to change the end result. We have no way into the compound that doesn't get us both dead."

I wish she wasn't right. I press the heels of my hands to my eyes, trying to *think*. "There has to be a way." I have no allies. I wouldn't even know where to start looking for them, and it would take far too much time. Grace seems to be a lone wolf. Who the hell could we possibly call for... I drop my hands. "Azazel."

"*What?*"

The familiarity in Grace's tone nearly distracts me, but I'm too focused on what appears to be the only option we have. He asked for seven years of service to break the seraph bond I have with my men. We might not have agreed to those terms, but if he can do *that*, surely he can offer some kind of real help to get my men back. Even if it's the same price, seven years is *nothing* compared to potentially hundreds of years under my father's control.

I might not live that long, but Malachi, Rylan, and Wolf certainly will. It means there's no release waiting in the wings. Just endless suffering. I can't let that happen. I *won't*.

"*Mina!*"

I blink. "What?"

Grace is on her feet and looks like she can't decide whether to shake me or leave the room entirely. She rocks back on her heels. "Say that name again."

"Azazel." This time, I'm paying attention. I see the way she flinches and narrow my eyes. "How do you know that name? Do you know him?"

"No." A sharp shake of her head. "But I know *of* him. I know what he does." The way she speaks, it sounds like she's talking about more than just deals. Like there's an element of sinisterness to it I don't understand. Having met Azazel, I can't say he's anything less than terrifying, but he was rather frank about the terms. There were no hidden catches or trickery. It's more than I can say for how my father operates.

"He seemed fair," I say finally. "Or, if not fair, then honest." He spelled out the terms clearly. Maybe the contract itself would have been a problem, but we didn't get that far. The men drew the line at my paying seven years of service.

"Shows what you know." Grace paces back and forth in the small space at the end of the bed. She pulls her ponytail out and starts braiding her hair in short, agitated movements. "Are you aware of what he does? He rips women away from their families and most of the time they never return."

The way she talks, it sounds like she's speaking from personal experience. I frown. "Who do you know that's bargained with him? And seriously, he only bargains with women? That's kind of...outdated, isn't it?"

"Take it up with the demon." Grace drags her fingers through her long dark hair, disrupting her braid and restarting it. She's long since changed out of the camouflage hunting gear in favor of faded jeans and a plain white T-shirt. Somehow, it doesn't make her less intimidating...or less dangerous. She drops her arms and pins me with a look. "He took my mother."

"You mean your mother made a deal." I don't know why I'm arguing this. I don't owe Azazel anything. Wolf made it extremely clear how dangerous the demon is. If anything, I shouldn't be listening to Grace since she has just as much experience with demon deals as I do at this juncture. I wrap my arms around myself. "What were her terms?"

She turns away. "I don't know. The last time I saw her was the night he came to collect. I know she made a deal, but I've never been able to get more information. I..." She exhales slowly. "I don't know how to summon him. Do you?"

Do I?

I know what Wolf did. It seemed simple enough, at least in theory. His bloodline vampire power is the ability to manipulate blood itself. Thanks to my seraph half, I've somehow managed to acquire that ability, along with Rylan's shape-shifting and Malachi's fire. It *would* be enough...except I got these powers less than a week ago and I've had exactly one training session with Malachi to learn how to control them. Since then, I've barely had the energy to keep up with Grace, let alone try again.

I close my eyes and try to walk back through what Wolf did to summon Azazel. A blood circle that became a blood ward of sorts. I think. He fucked Malachi in it, but I don't know if that's part of the ward or just because Wolf is, well, *Wolf*.

As far as I can tell, after creating the ward, he did nothing at all. Azazel showed up quickly after Malachi and Rylan left, but Wolf didn't even say his name before the shadows went weird and the demon appeared. It has to be the circle. Which is a problem because I don't know the first thing about creating a blood ward. "Do you know how to create a blood ward?"

"Mina, I'm *human*."

Right. Of course. I shake my head slowly. "Then no. I don't think I can summon him." Then again, maybe I'm overcomplicating things? I lift my voice. "Azazel? Can you hear me?"

"Holy fuck." Grace flings herself back against the wall, her dark eyes wide as she searches the room. The seconds tick into a full minute, and we both breathe a sigh of something akin to relief when nothing and no one materializes. Grace glares. "I can*not* believe you just did that."

I can't believe I just did that, either. I shrug, trying to pretend I'm not as shaken as I am. "It was worth a shot."

"It was worth a shot," she repeats, shaking her head. "You are out of your damn mind, Mina." Grace scoops up her backpack from the floor and a small gun from the desk to tuck into her waistband. She pauses with her hand on the door. "Get some sleep. I'm going to see about taking a look at this compound myself. I think it's a long shot, but maybe there's something you missed or something that's changed since you were there that can provide us a way in."

It's not safe for her to go scouting on her own. My father is sure to have sentries farther afield than just the compound walls, and Grace might be human and therefore not seen as a threat, but she's a beautiful human. I wouldn't put it past them to try to snatch her off the street to either be turned or tossed into my father's pool of humans who serve as mistresses and blood banks. "Grace—"

She's gone before I can get my warning out.

I mean to follow. I truly do. But one minute I'm trying to get the energy to stand and move to the door, and the next a wave of dizziness hits me hard enough that I have to throw out a hand to brace myself on the bed so I don't topple. "What the fuck?"

Is this an attack?

I try to push my magic out, to sense, but it's like I'm wrapped in a thick cotton straitjacket. I can't feel anything at all. With a curse, I turn inward. A quick body scan leaves me even dizzier. *Oh no. This is so bad.* I let my hand drop, feeling ill in a way that has nothing to do with morning sickness. I'm not being attacked, at least not from the outside.

It's the baby.

It's draining my magic.

2

I DON'T MEAN TO FALL ASLEEP, BUT LIKE SO MUCH ELSE
with this damn pregnancy, it's as if I don't have a choice in the
matter. One moment I'm cursing my circumstances and the next
I open my eyes to a strange room. It's not the hotel; it's nowhere
near as concrete as that. The whole space feels strangely misty
and uncertain, and yet as I sit up and look around, it also doesn't
feel like a dream. Normally, when I dream, I don't realize it *is* a
dream until I wake.

I feel awake now.

I push to my feet, waiting for a wave of nausea, but my
body feels strangely muted. I inhale slowly and exhale just as
slowly. For the first time in a week, I actually feel like myself.
Nothing hurts. I'm not exhausted. It's enough to make me want
to cry. I didn't realize how bad things had gotten until I was

allowed this reprieve. I swallow thickly. "What am I going to do?"

No use focusing on the problem the pregnancy represents now, though. I have to figure out what's going on. Is this another trap? My father's powers lie in compulsion and glamour; I've never heard him talk about dreams before. This *isn't* a bloodline vampire power at all as far as I can remember. There are only seven of them, each following one family. My father's glamour. Malachi's fire. Rylan's shape-shifting. Wolf's blood. And then air, earth, and water. None of those should be able to influence dreams.

So what is this?

My chest gives a familiar thrum and I don't think. I simply follow it. It's the bond inside me, recognizing—I'm afraid to hope it's recognizing what I *think* it's recognizing. Distance and time have no meaning here. One step seems to launch me forward miles. Or maybe the mist is what causes everything to feel strange. I'm not sure.

In the distance, the mist rolls away and the familiar form of a man stands there. I recognize his pale skin, short white mohawk, and lean frame. The bond inside me thrums happily and nearly jerks me off my feet. "Wolf!"

He turns slowly, recognition brightening his light blue eyes. "Mina."

One step brings me to him. I reach out a trembling hand and press it to his chest. Real? Not real? I can't be sure. He looks even paler than normal, deep circles carved into the space below his eyes. "How are you doing this? How did you bring me here?"

"It's not me, love." He looks around, a frown pulling his dark brows together. "This doesn't feel like vampire magic. Means it's most likely you."

Me or someone else planted us both here. I look around, but there's still nothing but mist. I can't sense danger, but I can't sense anything at all. I didn't feel Wolf before I saw him, and even now, with my palm against his sternum, it's like neither of us are really here. "The bond?"

"That would be my best bet."

That's comforting, though I would feel better if someone had a full explanation. "Is this a dream?"

"It must be. I'm not hungry."

A pang goes through me. It's already started. Of course it has. My father wouldn't hesitate to put them into painful and agonizing situations to ensure he gets what he wants. I swallow hard. "It wasn't supposed to be like this."

"It never is when things go wrong." He shrugs, but his eyes go sharp. "You're close. The bond hasn't bitten us once."

"I'm trying. I knew where he was taking you, so I made sure to follow as closely as I dared." The bond is another problem to the huge stack of them. I found out relatively recently I'm half seraph by accidentally bonding with Wolf, Malachi, and Rylan when my powers unleashed. One of the lovely little side effects of that bond—in addition to these new powers I can't control—is that there's a limit on the distance we can travel from each other before we experience pain. It's worse for the men than it is for me. Distance isn't the only issue, either. Even if I stay within range, eventually the bond will force us closer. There's a physical component that I recently had to navigate with Rylan, and I don't relish the idea of having to do it with all three of them.

I hate it, but so far the only option we've found to eliminate the seraph bond is...

Azazel.

I straighten. "Wolf, I need to know how to summon Azazel."

"No, love. Straights are dire, but not so dire as that." He runs a hand over his short mohawk. "He demands payment up front, and I don't know what will happen to the bond and us if you jaunt off to the demon realm. Even if time passes differently there than it does here, that's quite a bit out of the established distance limits."

He's right. I know he's right.

But so is Grace.

I lift my chin. "I promise I won't bargain away my time like that. I'll think of something else."

"He's a one-trick pony is Azazel. It's seven years' payment. That's the only currency he works in." Wolf shakes his head. "It's not worth the risk."

I grab the front of Wolf's shirt and shake him. Or try to. It's like shaking a brick wall. Frustration blooms, hot and sick, in my stomach. "I have exactly two people to breach the compound. We can't win. Even with the pregnancy, we can't win."

"Even with the *what?*"

The feeling in my stomach gets worse. A pulse that becomes a thrum. I press my hand there and flinch. It's hot. Literally hot to the touch. "What the fuck?" Another pulse, hotter this time. It *hurts.* "What the *fuck?*"

"Mina, love, did you just say you're pregnant?"

I open my mouth to answer, but the mist around us swirls. No, *swirls* is too tame a word. It feels like what I imagine being in the middle of a hurricane is like. Phantom wind pulls at my hair and clothing, so strong it forces me back a step from Wolf. "Tell me how to summon him!"

He shakes his head again. "It's not worth the risk."

The fact that this comes from *Wolf*, who is arguably the most unhinged of my men, should be enough to stop me. To convince me to find another path. Instead, it only infuriates me. I agreed with them on passing on Azazel's last offer. It was the right call, but that was back when we had options.

I'm out of options and out of ideas.

"*Tell me.*" Power thrums through my voice, demanding answers, demanding obedience.

"Damn it, Mina." He hits his knees, and guilt tries to prick me, but I don't have time to feel guilty. He speaks in rough tones. "Circle of blood, charge it with your magic, focus your intent on him and him alone. He'll come."

"I'm sorry."

He shudders, slumping down to his hands and knees. "It's not worth the risk," he repeats. "He'll ask for more than you can safely pay."

It's worth the risk to me. I'd do worse than summon a demon if it means getting my men out of my father's clutches and to safety. "I can handle myself."

"You're making a mistake, love." The mist rises up and swallows him whole. I take a step in his direction, but there's nothing there. It's as if Wolf never existed. If we all survive this, then I'll deal with the consequences of using our bond to force his compliance. Maybe it makes me a monster, maybe he'll never forgive me, but at least he'll be alive.

But only if I succeed.

My body clenches in agony, jarring me from my thoughts. I double over, holding my stomach, and scream.

"Mina!"

I jerk away to find Grace with a freaked-out expression on her face and her fingers digging into my shoulders. She doesn't immediately let me go, though. She pauses, gaze searching my face. "Are you awake?"

"My eyes are open!"

"Yeah, they were before, too." She shudders and releases me, backing up quickly. Like she's scared of me. She glances at the door but then seems to change her mind about fleeing my presence. Instead, she walks stiffly to the other bed and sinks onto the edge. "What the fuck was that, Mina?"

I start to sit up, but my body feels like I've run miles and then climbed a mountain. "Ouch." I press my hand to my forehead, wincing when I realize I'm sweaty. *Really* sweaty. My stomach hurts a bit, but nowhere near like it did in the dream.

I sit up so fast the room takes a sickening spin around me. "I dreamed of Wolf."

"Honey, I don't know what you were doing, but that wasn't normal dreaming." Grace shudders again. "Your eyes were open and you had this aura... It was like some demon possession shit."

"Do demons possess people?" Wolf had said Azazel was a one-trick pony, but that didn't mean there weren't other types of demons out there. As I'm discovering, the universe is vast and has more than one realm. Even in this one, there are more supernatural creatures than vampires. I'm a prime example of that, for all that the seraphim are supposed to be extinct.

"No." She shakes her head. "They can do a lot of fucked-up shit, but possession was invented by the church."

That's right. She'd know, wouldn't she? I'm sure being from a family with a legacy of hunting monsters is handy when it comes to information about said monsters. They must keep records. "How do you know that but not how to summon Azazel? It seems like it should be right up your alley."

"My mother destroyed the records before she made her bargain."

So much emotion in such a short sentence. There are layers of history there, and I should care, but I can barely think past the current mess. When push comes to shove, I barely know Grace. I shiver, the air-conditioning icing across my sweaty skin. Whatever happened to me, it's over. For now. I think back through what Wolf did and didn't say. He'd told the truth when it came to summoning the demon, but his simplified version left a lot to be desired. No doubt that was on purpose since I'd had to compel the information from him in the first place.

Guilt pricks, but I shove it aside. I had no choice. He wasn't going to tell me, and I need this information to have an icicle's chance in hell of saving them. I'll work on earning his forgiveness after I'm sure he'll be alive and free to give it.

I press my fingers to my temples. Wolf said to charge the circle, which confirms my suspicions on why he was the one to summon Azazel. The blood ward *was* vital to the process, which is a problem because I don't know how to charge my blood. I only know how to bleed.

Life has never been easy for me before. No reason for it to break the trend and start being easy now. "Wolf said I need to make a circle, charge it, and then focus to summon Azazel."

"That's it." Grace sounds suspicious, not that I blame her. It sounds too good to be true. Too simple to work.

"Sounds easy. Is a lot more complicated in practice." I shake my head slowly. "Wolf is a bloodline vampire whose specialty *is* blood. He can do things that no one else outside his family can." No one except me, at least in theory. I swallow hard. "It's a power we share."

"You do." Again, the disbelief.

I still haven't told her about my seraph half or my bond with the men. Grace might have some strange allegiance to Rylan—or owe him a favor, as she says—but I don't know how far that, well, grace extends. She's a monster hunter from a family of monster hunters, and everything I've discovered about seraphim to date paints them as monsters even among otherworldly creatures that prey on humanity.

There's a reason they were hunted to apparent extinction by the vampires.

The amount of harm the seraphim did...

I can't guarantee Grace won't decide that I'm too much of a threat, even if I don't know how to use my fledgling powers properly, or even that the little cluster of cells inside me that is a combination of both seraph and vampire will be too monstrous to allow into the world.

I'm not sure she's wrong there, either.

I'm not sure of anything anymore.

"I can't control it," I finally admit. In fact, none of the bloodline powers have manifested since I fled the mountain home where my father had finally caught up with us and taken the men captive. I haven't thought too hard about that, but it has to be because I'm so exhausted all the time. "I'm not even sure how to begin to make it work."

"Well, shit." She slumps onto the bed. "Guess we're back to square one."

A hopeless situation.

I give her a long look. "Why help me? You got me out of there, which is repayment enough for whatever debt your family owes Rylan."

"Undoubtedly." She shrugs. "Honestly, I was going to pay your hotel for a week and then leave today, but now that I know you can summon Azazel—or at least one of those vampires can—you're stuck with me. I need access to that demon."

I don't tell her that her chances of finding her mother alive are low. Maybe they aren't. This world is strange and vast and odder things have happened. It's not my place to crush this woman's hope when I'm engaging in my own long shot.

I need my men back, I need to kill my father, and I need to announce this damned pregnancy publicly where no one can refute it to ensure my half siblings don't hunt me until the end of days just like my father planned to. I need to essentially crown myself queen the same way my father acts the part of a king. None of my siblings are as formidable as he is, but that doesn't mean they're not dangerous.

The only path to peace is through power, and it means taking my father's place as head of the compound...and head of the bloodline.

Ironic, that.

I hold three sets of bloodline powers inside me, but none of them were passed to me by my father.

3

I TRY TO EAT, KNOWING I NEED THE CALORIES FOR THE bloodletting that comes next, but I last all of twenty minutes before I'm in the bathroom, losing my lunch. Hopelessness wells up inside me, deep and dark and all too willing to suck me under.

I've been in bad spots before. I was *born* into a bad spot, a powerless dhampir in the compound my father rules. Normally, dhampir children—those who are half human and half vampire— inherit powers from their vampire parent, at least if said vampire parent is a bloodline vampire. Not me, though. Up until I met Malachi, Rylan, and Wolf, I thought I was defective.

Turns out my mother wasn't all that human to begin with.

I brush my teeth, staring at my reflection in the dingy mirror. I look like shit. Dark circles stain the skin beneath my bloodshot eyes and my dark hair has gone greasy and lank. I've lost weight, too, weight I can't afford to lose. I was hardly at peak health when all this started, though the blood the vampires shared with me seemed to do just as much as...

I stop brushing.

Surely that's not the answer. It would be far too ridiculous a solution. If I managed to drink blood, surely I'll throw it up just like I'm throwing up solid food. I'm not some heroine in a vampire novel. I'm not going from eating normal food and using blood for magic, pleasure, and healing to being on a blood-only diet. It's not going to happen.

I duck out of the bathroom to find Grace gone again. I think she feels trapped in the hotel room. I don't blame her; I'm practically climbing the walls at this point. Or I would be if I had any energy at all.

This is a mess. Worse than a mess. It's a fucking disaster.

I study the bed for a long moment. I still haven't entirely dealt with the fact that apparently I met Wolf in my dreams. I don't know what caused it or what shoved him out of that space, but if I can reclaim it...

I miss them. I miss them so fucking much I ache with it. I wish I could blame the bond for the heightened feeling, but I suspect it's simply that I've gone and fallen for this vampire trio. I desperately want Malachi to wrap me up in his big arms and say it will all be okay. For Rylan to make some snarling, snarky comment about the situation. For Wolf's wild laughter and chaos.

If I can find them in my dreams...

I run my hand over the scratchy bedspread. I'm tired.

Desperately tired. I should still be using this time to practice the magic as best I can.

Instead, I take a slow, careful breath and lie down on the bed on my back. It's too easy to close my eyes. I've been sick and beaten to the point where I'm not sure I'll survive, and I've never felt tired like this. It would scare me if I had the energy to feel anything but exhaustion.

Maybe it's the baby, but maybe that's not it at all. Maybe it's the seraph bond responding to too many days and too much distance between me and my men. If they're suffering similarly...

Sleep sucks me under before I can finish the thought.

I open my eyes with a start. Disappointment sours my stomach—or maybe that's just the baby—when I see the hotel room exactly as I left it. The only difference is the light gone from the windows, replaced by the faded rays of the streetlamp outside.

Grace still isn't back yet, and if she was anyone else, I might be worried, but she can take care of herself. I saw how many weapons she packed away before she left. The woman is a walking armory, and she knows how to use them. She'll be fine.

I sit up and rub my hands over my face. Maybe the dream with Wolf was a fluke. Maybe there are a dozen conditions that need to be met before I can meet like that with any of the vampires. I just don't know enough. I'm in the dark and attempting to feel my way. I don't even have Malachi's support at my back while I'm doing it.

"What the fuck am I even thinking?" I stagger to my feet

and cross to the desk of Grace's weapons. There are half a dozen knives in varying shapes and sizes, and I choose a small one that fits easily in my palm. "I am not helpless."

I'm also speaking to an empty room, which might make me certifiable, but it's better than letting the silence tick out. There are too many things that can go wrong with what I'm about to do. If I think too hard, I'll talk myself right out of it. So I don't. I act instead.

I slice a thin line on my forearm and hold it out away from my body. It hurts, but compared to how everything hurts these days, it's barely noticeable. I turn in a slow circle, leaving droplets of blood behind me, until I'm once again facing the way I started.

My own blood smells savory, which is disconcerting in the extreme, and it only gets worse when I close my eyes and focus internally the way Malachi taught me. I can *almost* sense the magic there, lying in wait. It feels different than it did the last time I tried this, but I don't know enough to guess why.

"Come on, you fucker." I reach for the power with metaphorical—metaphysical?—hands, but it slips through my palms like water. I grab for it again, with the same result. Again and again and again. Nothing. Fucking *nothing*.

I open my eyes as I sink to my knees. My head spins sickeningly, or maybe it's the room spinning. I don't know what's real anymore. Certainly not this nebulous power inside me. I can't even access it without the men present. How pathetic. "Damn it!" I lift my voice, too loud, but I'm past caring. "Azazel! Azazel! *Azazel!*"

"You can't yell my name three times and expect me to arrive."

I jolt, losing my balance and landing on my ass in the middle of the sad little blood circle I created. One completely devoid of power. And yet here Azazel is. I lean back and narrow my eyes, trying to pick him out of the shadows in the corner of the room. I should be terrified. There's nothing protecting me from him, and the menace he seems to carry about him like a cloak is in full evidence right now.

He looks much the same as last time, a man with light brown skin, dark hair, and soulless dark eyes. Though no one with a brain in their head would look at him and think he's something as mundane as a *man*. He's a predator in a way even vampires can never aspire to be.

The shadows lick at his legs as he steps around the bed and stares down at me. "You've called. I've answered. Have you reconsidered the breaking of your bond?" He glances about the room. "Where's Wolf and the others? Did you finally acquire some sense and flee them?"

"What's with all the questions?" My voice comes out slightly slurred and I have to lean back against the other bed when the room shifts again. Damn it, what is *wrong* with me? I blink down at the red stain spreading across my jeans. For a horrifying moment, I think it's the baby...but no, it's nothing as traumatic as that.

I cut my arm too deep.

Or, rather, I haven't had vampire blood in days. A cut that would have healed already a week ago is now leaking blood steadily down to my thigh where I rest it. A lot of blood. "Damn."

"You little fool." He growls under his breath in a language

I'm certain isn't known in this realm and crouches down in front of me. He's no less terrifying up close. Once again, I get the impression that he's somehow bigger than he appears, that horns paint shadows across the motel room behind him. A blink and it's gone, but I can't quite convince myself I've imagined it.

He grabs my arm, moving too quickly for me to jerk away. "This will hurt."

"Wait—" Pain lances my forearm, so sharp and sudden, it draws a scream from my lips. Or it tries to. He covers my mouth with his other hand. Everything gets a little faded, but how in the gods' names does his hand wrap around the entire bottom half of my face?

Something is *not right* with this demon.

"There." Even his voice has changed, deepening with something akin to irritation. "Now you won't bleed out before you can accept my bargain."

I stare blankly down at the scar now carved into my arm. The cut was a straight line. This thing is...not. It's also red and black, twisted, and angry looking like a tree that attempted to uproot itself. "What did you do to me?"

"You can thank me later." He snaps his fingers in front of my face. "The bargain."

"I..." I lick my lips, trying to focus. "I didn't call you here to accept your bargain."

Again that hissing language that hurts my ears. He shoves to his feet. "Tell Wolf to consider the healing a token of our friendship. I have places to be."

"Wait!"

He pauses, but impatience paints every line of his body. "You're wasting my time."

"No." I can't stand. I'll pass out. I'm sure of it. Instead, I try to straighten a bit where I sit. "I want a new bargain."

He exhales slowly and turns back to face me. "I'm listening."

"My father took Wolf and Malachi and Rylan. I want them back."

Azazel considers me for a long moment, then his gaze goes distant. Finally, he shrugs. "Very well. Seven years' service and I'll save them."

My jaw drops. "That can't be anywhere as hard as breaking a seraph bond. Why is the cost the same?" Wolf had warned of exactly this, but part of me didn't believe him.

"I have my reasons."

I open my mouth, but I don't have a good argument. Even if I'm willing to do seven years of service—and I am—the complications presented previously still apply. The men won't like it. More, we don't know what will happen to the seraph bond if I'm whisked away to another realm. Maybe it would be okay.

Or maybe it would kill us all.

He gives that sharp smile. "I'll be back tomorrow. Have your answer by then." He casts a disdainful look at the blood-stained floor. "Next time, use my card." It appears in the air above me, floating carefully down to rest on my thigh that isn't covered in blood.

And then he's gone, melting into the shadows as if he'd never existed.

I lean my head back against the bed and sigh. No good

options. No matter what I try, there are no good options. Azazel was a long shot, but I can hand the card off to Grace. Even if we can't save my men, at least she'll get a chance to find some resolution about her mother. A small win, I suppose.

I close my eyes and concentrate on taking slow breaths. It's starting to look like I really only have one choice. If I can't stage an assault to save the men or sneak them out, there's only one path left, no matter how foolhardy it sounds.

I have to walk through the front gate and declare myself my father's heir.

4

I MANAGE TO CLEAN UP THE BLOOD BEFORE I PASS OUT again. This time, when I wake up surrounded by mist, there's no confusion. I climb to my feet, already looking for whichever one of my men waits for me. Mist swirls at my feet as I start walking, searching the opaque space for familiar forms.

When I see three of them, I almost sob. I break into a run. One step. Two. On the third, I'm among them. Malachi, with his broad shoulders and long dark hair. Rylan, who manages to look put together and vaguely annoyed despite the gaunt lines in his cheeks. And Wolf, all wild eyes and fury.

He's the one who grabs my shoulders. "You're pregnant."

The mist around us seems to dampen the sound, but the other two men go even quieter in response to his words. I don't look at them. I can't. I just give a shaky nod. "I am. I felt it the day you were taken, but I took a test to confirm."

Wolf releases me like I've burned him. "Is that why we can't feel her? I thought it was the drugs."

"It could be both." Rylan speaks from almost directly behind me. Even his voice is raspier than normal. "Not much is known about seraph pregnancy. They always disappeared during those months, and any record of it has long since been destroyed."

"You should have told us."

I turn to face Malachi, but he's not looking at me. He's looking at Rylan, his dark brows pulled together. "If there's a risk to her because of this—"

"Wake up, Malachi. There's a risk to *all* of us. She's not the one currently chained and injected with poison."

My stomach drops. "I'm getting you out." I don't tell them that I'm exhausted. That I can't seem to keep down a single bite of food. That I can't touch the well of magic inside me that only seems to get further and further from the tips of my fingers with every day that passes. All that might be true, but in the end, it's just an excuse.

They're suffering more than I am.

They have more at stake if I fail.

"No." Malachi shakes his head. "It's too dangerous. We'll figure something out."

"Like you figured out a way to escape that house?" He spent a hundred years trapped and slowly starving between sacrifices my father sent him. I can't bear the thought of him suffering through that again, let alone Rylan and Wolf, too. I glare up at him. "Out of the question."

In fact, as I look from one of them to the other, they all show marks of starvation. It shouldn't have happened this quickly; it hasn't even been a week and we all but glutted ourselves on blood before the capture. Yes, we were essentially just passing it back and forth but...

The sinking feeling in my chest gets worse. "You weren't feeding the way you needed to before this."

Suddenly Malachi won't quite meet my gaze. It's Rylan who answers, "I was." Which all but admits that the other two weren't.

I knew he'd ranged farther than Malachi and Wolf, but it hadn't occurred to me that he was effectively working as hunter for our entire group until now. It should have. I take a step back so I can see all three of them. "Feed from me." I don't know if it will work in dreams, but this isn't a normal dream or we wouldn't be able to meet like this at all. Malachi starts to shake his head and I grab his arm. "*Feed from me.* If you want me to find another way, then you need to stay alive and healthy enough to fight when I come for you." I don't know what plan I can possibly come up with on my own, but I'll say anything to decrease their current suffering.

Malachi still looks like he wants to argue. Even Wolf holds back, something serious and worried in his pale blue eyes. I know he's thinking of the last time we met like this and the information I compelled out of him.

Strangely enough, it's Rylan who steps forward. "We don't know what it will do to you. Or if it will work at all."

"Might as well try it." I have been so damn helpless from the start of this. I don't want to be helpless anymore. If I can lessen their suffering at all, even a little, I want to do that. I *need* to do that.

I tilt my head to the side. It's only then that I realize I'm still wearing the same clothes I had on when I fell asleep. It makes a strange sort of sense, but there's no time to think too hard about it because Rylan moves forward, too fast to track even for my dhampir eyes, and bites me.

I expect pleasure.

All I get is pain.

He rears back with a muffled curse, his hand to his mouth. "What the fuck was *that?*"

I drop to my knees and press my fingers to the bite. It's only two pinpricks from his canines, but the pain keeps radiating through me as if he injected poison into my blood. "What's wrong? It's never hurt before."

Rylan removes his hand and there are burn marks on his lips. He shakes his head. "It has to be the pregnancy."

"Or it's this realm." Malachi studies the space above us, though it doesn't look any different from what's around us in every direction. "I'm not prepared to blame the baby. We don't know enough to say for sure."

"For fuck's sake, Malachi, no one is blaming that thing." Rylan swipes his hand across his mouth again, as if he wants to scrub the taste of me right off his tongue. No reason for that to sting, but my logical side isn't online right now. He shakes his head. "Something's off, and it has nothing to do with this realm, if it's even a realm. She might have simply pulled us into her dreams."

"Which means the blood you just consumed isn't really blood." Malachi sounds calm. Too calm. "It might be the seraph bond attempting to protect her when she's already weakened. We won't know until we're back together in person."

"When that happens, *you* can bite her first."

I prop my hands on my hips and glare. "I'm standing right here. Stop talking about me like I'm a child."

Malachi and Rylan both look away, expressions sheepish and irritated in turn. Which is when Wolf speaks. "Did you make a deal, love?"

The breath whooshes out of my body. He's been so uncharacteristically quiet, I almost convinced myself he wouldn't speak about what happened before. I should know better by now. There are few secrets between the four of us, at least when it comes to current events. The past is another animal entirely.

I make myself meet his gaze steadily. "Not yet."

Malachi whips around. "What the fuck is he talking about? What deal?"

"I can explain. I—"

Wolf speaks right over me. "She asked me how to summon Azazel. When I refused to tell her, she compelled me."

I don't like the betrayed look Rylan sends my way. Even worse is the slow anger building on Malachi's face. He drags his hands through his long hair. "We talked about this, Mina. It's out of the question."

"It was out of the question before my father took you three. It's not now." I'm protesting mostly out of spite, though. I can't accept Azazel's bargain now any more than I could before. I sigh. "Look, I'm not taking the deal. I thought he'd give different terms, but he didn't, so we're back to square one. If any of you have any brilliant ideas, I'd love to hear it."

They exchange a look, but no one says anything. I don't

know whether to laugh or cry. The three of them have gotten me out of several messes to date. I can't expect them to do it when they're captive and I'm free. "I'll find another way." I swallow hard, a burning starting in my throat and eyes. "I won't bargain away seven years. I promise."

They don't quite look like they believe me, but that's fine. I deserve the distrust after compelling Wolf. It was the wrong call, but panic got the best of me. That's no excuse, and I won't try to make it one. I lift my chin and open my mouth, but my stomach gives a horrible surge of agony that has me doubling over. "No. It's too soon."

"Mina!" Malachi's hand brushes my back and then he's gone, jerked away into the mist as if a giant hand reached out and snatched him. By the time I look for Rylan and Wolf, they've disappeared as well.

I barely get to curse before the world goes dark. The pain follows me into my waking, cramps that bow my back and have me clamping my teeth shut to keep a scream internal. This time, there's no Grace to help. I turn onto my side and pull my knees to my chest. It feels like something is gnawing away at my insides, dull teeth ripping and tearing and gods, it hurts. It hurts so fucking bad.

Until it doesn't.

I blink through my watering eyes. I can't keep from locking my body, waiting for the next wave of pain. It takes me much longer than I want to admit to slowly unclench and cautiously stretch out my legs. I half expect to find something wrong, but the pain has faded as if it never existed.

But like last time, I'm covered in sweat and feel shaky.

I stagger to the bathroom and take a quick shower, feeling

dizzy all the while. By the time I make it back into the bedroom to pull on the jeans and a T-shirt Grace sourced for me from the local thrift store, I'm almost feeling like myself again.

Well, like the new version of myself who's weak and exhausted and vaguely nauseous at all times.

At least there are no bite marks on my neck, which seems to suggest that Malachi was right about the seraph bond trying to protect me in that dreamy place. I shouldn't take it personally that my blood might be poisonous to my men, but I don't like the thought at all. I enjoy their bites, and not simply for the orgasm that inevitably follows. Exchanging blood has become an intimacy that I don't want to give up.

I glare down at my stomach. "You are a giant pain in the ass."

"Talking to yourself is generally frowned upon." Grace strides through the door and shuts it behind her. She looks as tired as I feel, circles beneath her eyes and her hair escaping its braid. She raises her eyebrows at me. "You look like shit."

"I was just about to say the same thing about you."

She shrugs. "Nothing more than the truth." Grace drops onto the bed across from me. "I don't suppose you have good news? Because all I have is bad."

"Tell me." I have a feeling she's going to get sidetracked as soon as I tell her about Azazel. Beyond that, I've always been one who prefers the bite of bad news before the soothing of good news. My life has had little of the latter until recently and certainly not enough to get used to it.

"He's upped patrols from when you were last there. There are fewer gaps in his security than expected. There was also a large group of vampires who arrived today who seemed to be new, or at least not locals, based on how they were received."

He's pulling in his people. I should have expected as much, but it seems like such overkill, at least until I consider the value and strength of his captives. My father will be taking no risks with them. He wants them locked down and he'll do whatever he has to in order to ensure it. "Well, shit."

"Pretty much." She pins me with a long look. "What happened while I was gone?" She keeps talking before I have a chance to respond. "Don't bother to lie and say nothing happened because I know it did. There are blood stains on the floor and there's still magic lingering in the air."

I glance guiltily at the floor. "I thought I got it all." Wait a damn minute. I whip around to look at her. "Since when can you see magic?" Now that I think about it, she mentioned something about it before, but I was too rattled from that first dream with Wolf to notice.

"Since always. Old family trick. Which is why I know you're not anything as simple as a dhampir, though I'm not going to pry on *that*. This?" She makes a circle with her finger to encompass the room. "Different story. You went into your dreams with those vampires again, didn't you? But there's something else."

I drag in a breath. There's no point in hiding the truth from her. If I can't utilize Azazel, as least I can ensure she's able to contact him. "I summoned the demon."

5

GRACE SURPRISES ME. INSTEAD OF PRACTICALLY TACK-
ling me to get more information, she pulls a sleeve of crackers out
of her purse, hands them over, and waits until I tentatively nibble
on one to start questioning me. "You summoned Azazel."

"Yes. I tried the blood circle and it failed miserably, but
he ended up showing up anyways." I haven't had a chance to
think about that too closely, which was likely best. I can't imagine Azazel noticed every time someone says his name. It isn't
common, but statistically *someone* had to use it occasionally in a
way that had nothing to do with summoning the demon himself,
which meant he was either close or he's keeping an eye on me.
Maybe he was hoping I'd change my mind about the original
bargain and try to summon him without my men around.

The thought isn't comforting in the least.

Another thing to add to the list of worries. I don't *think* Azazel can force me to agree, but he seems overly invested in it. Maybe it's just to mess with Wolf, but I can't take anything for granted now. Maybe the demon simply has a quota of deals to meet. The thought is strangely hilarious.

"Mina."

"Sorry. Right." I shake my head, trying to focus. "He said he could help with getting Malachi, Rylan, and Wolf out, but he won't budge on the terms of the bargain. It's seven years' service in another realm." I sigh. "I can't risk it. It's not even about time moving differently. It's about the bond. It might just flat-out kill all four of us, which kind of defeats the purpose of rescuing them in the first place."

It takes several long moments before I realize Grace hasn't responded. I look over to find her staring off into the middle distance. "Grace?"

"Just thinking," she says slowly. "Did you reject the bargain?"

"He's coming tomorrow to collect his answer." It speaks of long experience that he gives his marks time to consider the offer. It's easy enough to reject something with such a high cost, but given enough time to realize how few options you have? Seven years begins to sound much more reasonable. "It's not going to matter. I might be willing to pay the price of time, but I won't pay with our lives."

"We'll think of something." She still sounds strange, distant, as if her mind if jumping forward a thousand times faster than mine.

Considering how woozy I feel, that's not saying much. I finish my cracker and set the package down, waiting for my stomach to decide if it will hold. I don't have high hopes. Nothing stays down. I press my hand to my neck where Rylan bit me in the dream. It doesn't feel any different, but I can't get the memory out of my head. Even if my blood didn't suddenly become poisonous, my vampires won't agree to drink from me when they see how haggard I look. I hardly have blood to spare at this point.

"We keep saying that, but no solutions are magically appearing." I look down at my stomach. If I had my magic under control... If I could even access it...

Then I think about how fierce Malachi was at the thought of my being pregnant. That was before it even happened. I press my hand to my stomach. If I lose them... My brain tries to shy away from the thought, but I force myself to power through. If I lose them, this baby might be my only connection to them.

Selfish thought. Horrible in so many ways. I still can't shake it.

I squint at the sky lightening through the cracks in the curtains. "What time is it?"

"Early. Five."

Five? I slept through the night, even if I hardly feel rested at all. That seems to be happening more often than it's not. No matter how many hours I sleep, I still wake exhausted. I shake my head slowly. "Wait a minute. It's tomorrow. That means Azazel—"

The lights go out.

"Fuck!" Grace scrambles for the lamp on the nightstand between our beds. It clicks, but the light doesn't come on. "What the hell?"

"Little hunter." Azazel's voice seems to come from everywhere and nowhere at the same time. I twist, trying to see, but even a vampire needs a little light to see. A dhampir needs more yet, and there is none to be had in this room.

"Little seraph." His breath tickles the shell of my ear. "Did you think to trap me?"

Fear surges through me. Azazel has always been scary, but it's nothing compared to what he is now. I try to swallow past the need to scream. "No. No one's trying to trap you."

"And yet you are here with *her*."

"Not for that!" I can't guarantee Grace isn't here for *that*. She's overly interested in Azazel and has good reason to be. She wants answers about her mother. Would she try to kill him, even if it meant I failed?

I don't know.

"Do you know what I do to people who try to cross me?"

I can't move, can't think. Panic bleats through me, as worthless as the ever-present exhaustion weighing me down. It builds and builds, a rising tide that washes away all rational thought. "*Stop!*"

Flames lick at the air around me, Malachi's power manifesting out of my pure desperation. The flames are nowhere near as strong as I've summoned in the past, but they're enough to break the unrelenting dark. I get a glimpse of a monster crouching behind Grace, massive shoulders and arms, horns like a bull coming from either side of its head.

No, not it.

Him.

Azazel.

My flames go out, but this time the darkness only lasts a moment. The light at the bedside table flickers on, weakly doing battle with the shadows seeming to gather in every corner of the room. And there Azazel is, once again wearing his human skin, standing at the space between the ends of our beds, his hands in the pockets of his slacks. His eyes flare red, not quite managing to keep things under wraps. "Explain yourselves. Quickly."

There's no explicit threat tacked onto the end of that sentence, but there doesn't need to be. It hangs in the air, thicker than smoke.

I exchange a look with Grace. She seems shaken but determined in a way that does nothing to reassure me. If she attacks Azazel, neither of us will survive the next few minutes. "Don't do anything foolish," I snap.

Her gaze flicks my way and she tenses. "You took my mother."

"I don't take people. I make deals." He sounds bored. His tone is a lie. From the careful way he holds himself, he's half a breath from attacking us. He turns his attention to me. "I'll have your answer now."

All this mess and I feel like I'm just digging in further. I can't say yes. I'm not sure what he'll do if I say no. "I—"

"I'd like to propose a new bargain," Grace cuts in.

Azazel's interest sharpens on her. "How forward of you."

"I'm just that kind of girl." Her smile is a challenge. "You help Mina get her men back. I'll pay the price."

He sighs. "What do you think you can offer that would replace a half seraph? You're hardly a catch, darling."

"Don't call me darling." She straightens. "I'm the last of the Cel Tradat family. I might only be human, but that means something, even to a monster like you. My family has a long history with the people of your realm. Don't try to pretend securing me in a bargain isn't a coup."

"Calling me names is not the way to get what you want." He

stalks forward, darkness flowing around him. It's enough for me to realize how tightly leashed he kept himself up to this point. He's not even trying now, though he's managed to get control of his form. Either that or there's not enough light for his shadow to betray him.

"Mina won't accept your deal. I will. That already makes me the better bet."

"Hmm." He glances at me, expression shuttered. "You're probably more trouble that you're worth at this point. Not to mention I'll have to suffer through Wolf attempting to summon me repeatedly to demand you back." Azazel shakes his head. "Very well, let's discuss terms."

I can't tell whether Grace looks victorious or sick to her stomach. She lifts her chin. "Rescue Malachi, Rylan, and Wolf, and kill Mina's father in the process. Then I'll go with you."

He chuckles, the sound low and unamused. "You presume you're worth that much, last Cel Tradat or no. Pick one." He pauses. "And you will pay up front."

That snaps me out of my daze. "No. You're not going to take her before you rescue them." *Seven years* under my father's tender care? Unacceptable. "You should rescue them simply because Wolf is a friend."

"I'm a demon, little seraph. I don't have friends."

"How sad for you." Grace shakes her head. "But she's right. What's the point in saving them if they're broken by the time you do? That's a shitty deal."

"Ladies." He sighs again, even more exasperated this time. "I'm under a deadline and I don't have the luxury of this song and dance. I will fulfill my end of the bargain within twenty-four hours of time here. The lovely...Grace...will leave now and come to my realm to fulfill her seven years."

I want to be relieved, but I can't. I *can't*. Too many people are paying debts that should be mine. I press my hands hard to my thighs and look at Grace. "You can't accept. You don't even know what you're walking into. I don't care if..." I hesitate. I doubt Azazel is ignorant of the fact that he made a deal with Grace's mother, but if by some miracle he is, I'm not going to be the one to out her. I clear my throat. "You can't pay this price for us. The cost is too high."

"I'm not doing it for you." She says it firmly but not unkindly. "No offense, but I wouldn't pay this price unless I wanted to."

There will be no reasoning with her, then. I turn to the demon. "I want assurances that she won't be harmed or killed, not by your hand or anyone in that realm. If you can't ensure her safety and comfort, she's not saying yes."

"Mina—"

It's hard to be certain, but I think Azazel actually rolls his eyes. "If you weren't so busy throwing out accusations, I would have already laid out the terms in detail. There are formalities to a demon bargain, after all."

"If you try to trick her—"

"Your opinion of me is truly staggering." He shakes his head. "In three days, you will be auctioned off to one of the leaders of the territories in my realm. You will agree to serve them in whatever way they need, but they will not harm, hurt, or otherwise mistreat you, under pain of death."

I narrow my eyes. "How can you guarantee that? If they harm her, even if they pay a price afterward, she's still harmed."

"I'm a *demon*. My bargains have meanings." He sounds so exasperated, I almost forget to be scared. Almost.

"Serve them in whatever way they need," Grace repeats. "You want me to fuck demons."

"You will not be coerced against your will."

She snorts. "Nice dodge, but by agreeing to this bargain, I'm agreeing to the sex."

Azazel speaks through gritted teeth. "You will allow them the chance to seduce you, but they cannot force you. To do so would qualify as harm."

It sounds like a sneaky loophole from where I'm sitting. I'm about to say as much when Grace shrugs. "Fine. I agree."

"Wait!"

"Perfect." He offers his hand. "We seal it with a kiss."

"Grace, no."

But it's too late. She slips her hand into his. He raises it to his mouth, flips it, and presses a kiss to her wrist. A mark blooms there, black and red, painting itself across her tanned skin in a pattern that seems to shift in a way that defies comprehension.

Azazel glances at me without releasing Grace. "I'll return to pay my end of the bargain tomorrow. Stay out of trouble until then."

Darkness surges and I throw up my hand to cover my eyes. One blink and the room is empty except for me, the shadows returning to the normal faded ones from early morning.

Grace is gone.

Fuck.

6

I SPEND THE NEXT TWENTY-FOUR HOURS IN MISERY. I
still can't keep anything down and I'm so tired, I don't bother to
leave the motel room. Thankfully, I don't have to. Grace paid
through the end of the week, so at least I don't have to be worried
about being kicked out.

Another price she paid on my behalf.

It doesn't matter if she said she was doing it for herself, if she
accepted Azazel's bargain because she was looking for answers
about her mother. She never would have had access to the demon
in the first place if not for me. If anything horrible happens to
her...The fact that she just lost *seven years*...

Everyone is making sacrifices for me. Malachi. Rylan. Wolf.
Now Grace, who's little more than a stranger. Meanwhile, I'm
huddled here on a motel bed, waiting to be rescued. Again. It's
enough to make me want to scream.

I feel the change in the air before Azazel materializes in front of me. It's a strange sort of static electricity, like right before a lightning storm. One moment the room is mundane and ordinary, and the next shadows reign supreme despite the relative early hour.

I won't say Azazel's less scary after all these interactions, but I don't have the energy to cower right now. I just blink up at him as he towers over me. "Took you long enough." Even my voice sounds wrong. Weak and thready.

He frowns. "What's the matter with you?"

"Just special, I guess."

He frowns harder and leans down to coast his hand over my body. He doesn't touch me, keeping a careful few inches of distance between us, but it still feels too intimate. Especially when he hovers over my midsection and huffs out a laugh. "I suppose that would do it. You're cooking quite the little beast in there, aren't you?"

"Don't call them a little beast." The words rush out before I can think. I might have more than a little resentment about the pregnancy, but that doesn't mean I'm going to let this demon talk about the...baby...like that.

"If you insist." His dark brows draw together, eyes lighting almost red for a moment. "Ah, I see. That would do it."

"What are you talking about?" I don't like this. I'm prone and feel particularly helpless, and he hasn't moved his hand away from my stomach. "Back off."

"Your shields are abysmal."

"I'm aware," I grit out. I can't sit up because he still hasn't moved and I don't want to risk accidentally touching him, but I don't like this. Not a single bit. "Get away from me. I mean it." I try to inject as much authority into my voice as possible. I don't know what I'll do if he doesn't listen. I don't know what I *can* do.

"I'm feeling generous after meeting my quota so I'll help you out for free." He presses a single finger against my lower stomach in the gap between my T-shirt and my jeans. It's such a tiny touch. A single fingertip. It still goes through me like a giant bell tolling. The room gives a sickening spin and then another and another before finally settling back into place.

"What the fuck? I told you—" I stop short. I feel different. Lighter. Like I can draw a full breath for the first time in over a week. I'd attributed that claustrophobic feeling to worry about my men, but it was the pregnancy all along? I narrow my eyes at the demon standing over me. "What did you do?"

"Supplemental shield. It won't stop the beast from growing or gaining the necessary sustenance to survive, but it will stop the constant drain of power." He considers. "Think of it as a funnel rather than a waterfall. Better for both of you, I imagine."

"Do you have a lot of experience with seraph pregnancies and the resulting vampire-hybrid babies?" I manage.

"You'd be surprised."

"Can you—"

"You already got this for free. Don't press your luck asking for more." He straightens abruptly. "I'll retrieve your vampires once it reaches full dark. Where do you want them?" He makes a show of looking around. "This place is hardly secure and your father will be searching for them."

I finally sit up. He's still too close, his shadows taking up too much space and making him seem larger than his human form. It's disconcerting in the extreme. "You took seven years of Grace's life and you can't even guarantee that you won't leave a trail for them to follow?"

He sighs. "You continue to press me. It's irritating."

A few weeks ago, having a ridiculously powerful and scary demon exasperated with me would be enough for common sense to take over and silence me. No longer. I lift my chin. "Then maybe you should make better deals. You're supposed to be so powerful. My father is just a vampire. What's that compared to a demon?"

Azazel sighs again, louder. "Fine." He produces a card from somewhere and passes it over. It looks nearly identical to the one from earlier, except it has an address on it. "That's a one-way ticket, so don't use it until you're ready to go."

"Go," I repeat.

He doesn't roll his eyes, but it looks like he wants to. "Yes, go. When you're prepared to leave, hold it to your chest and concentrate. Anything you're carrying will be transported with you."

A sliver of cold works its way through me. Teleportation. Obviously, I knew Azazel could do it since he seems to come and go as he pleases, but to allow someone else to do it independently of him? The thought makes me shudder. It seems risky. Surely there are a thousand things that could go wrong while I'm a disembodied version of myself, winging from one location to another. If that's even how teleportation works. I honestly have no idea.

Riskier than trying to call a cab and leaving a trail for some-one to follow if they know where to look?

No. Not riskier than that.

I finally nod. "It will be safe there?"

"Safe enough." He shrugs. "What happens after that is up to the four of you. My help ends with the transfer."

He looks like he's about to leave, but I find myself speaking before he can pull a disappearing act. "Azazel."

He waits, eyes dark and far too knowing. It would be so easy to let fear silence me, but I breathe through it and say, "If Grace is hurt because of the deal she made with you, I'll find a way to kill you myself." Maybe it's an impossible task, but I'll do what I can to repay that debt.

His lips curve, though his eyes remain cold. "As long as she follows the rules, she'll be fine."

If Grace finds out someone in that realm was the reason her mother never returned, she might murder them. Or at least try. I don't know her well enough to know for sure. Maybe she'll try to kill Azazel himself. The thought has me fighting back another shiver. "She made that deal because of me."

"If you say so. Seems like she was intent on it for her own purposes." He cocks his head to the side as if listening to something I can't hear. "Don't linger here. They'll be searching the area shortly." Then he's gone, sinking into the shadows on the floor as if stepping into a deep pool of water. It's more disconcerting than when he just disappears in a flood of darkness.

I test the floor, now clear of shadows, and it feels solid enough. "Creepy."

I don't know what to think of Azazel's *supplemental shield*, but it's a worry for another day. At this point, I have a *lot* of worries for later dates. There's no help for it. I need to gather what few things I have and get out of here. The card feels strange against my palm, a faint pulse coming from it.

Teleportation.

I shouldn't be surprised that it's possible. In the last couple weeks, I've seen plenty of things that I'd previously thought impossible. With all that said, this feels particularly fantastical. I shake my head and make quick work of packing up anything that could link me to this room. There's the blood on the floor, but I can't do much about that without burning the place down, and I'm not willing to do that. My father isn't able to track from some old blood.

Even he was, he wouldn't have to tear up the carpet in this hotel room to have access to my blood. I left plenty of it behind in his compound over the years, originating with one punishment or another. I shake off the dark thoughts and throw the last few things in my bag.

My gaze tracks to the desk where Grace's weapons are laid out. I can't leave them. When we spoke about deals, Azazel made it sound like time moved differently in the other realm, so seven years might pass in a matter of months or even days. If Grace returns that quickly on our side of things, I want her to have her weapons. It's the absolute least I can do.

As I carefully pack them into the duffel bag she'd brought in, I notice a few of the knives are missing. Two daggers and one that's long enough to be a short sword. I laughed when I first saw it and asked her if she planned on fighting any Spartans. She hadn't been amused.

I didn't even see her grab them during that short conversation with Azazel before she made her deal. Maybe she'd already had them on her. Or maybe she was better at sleight of hand than I could have imagined. I press my lips together. *I hope you know what you're getting into.*

After slinging both bags over my shoulders, I grab the card and examine it. He said I just need to concentrate, which sounds deceptively simple. Everything about magic is deceptively simple.

Just reach for it.

Just imagine what you want it to do.

Just let it do what it's meant to do.

I snort and press the card to my chest. Nothing happens. Of course nothing happens. Why would anything magical I attempt actually work on the first try? I take a slow breath and close my eyes. The desire to leave, to see my men again, whole and healthy, slams into me so hard, it makes me dizzy. I choke on a ragged inhale and the world seems to go sickeningly liquid for half a beat.

When I open my eyes, I'm somewhere else.

I turn a slow circle, taking in the relatively normal living room I now stand in. It looks like something out of a sitcom. Small and cozy with furniture that has a lived-in kind of feel. A staircase leads up to the second floor and I can see the kitchen through the doorway in the back of the room. Another turn shows what appears to be a front door.

The bags go on the low coffee table. I pad to the front door to peer out the windows on either side. I'd half expected to find a street with rows of nearly identical houses, but there is only a gravel driveway leading down a hill into dark trees. Not a single light breaks up the growing darkness, though in the distance I can see what appears to be a town. I exhale slowly. Good. With this house being so isolated, it means there's less chance of innocents getting caught in the crossfire if my father's people find us again.

Less chances of close neighbors asking questions about weird sights and sounds, too.

I do a quick search of the house, but there's nothing worth noting. A few bedrooms with large beds, a deceptively nice shower, a modern kitchen with a fridge and pantry packed with food. I pause there, considering. My stomach is cramping with hunger and I feel a little woozy, but I have energy for the first time since I found out I was pregnant. "Maybe this supplemental shield will help with the morning sickness?" I murmur.

Ten minutes later, I have my answer as I puke up the few crackers I managed to choke down. Damn it.

I drag myself to the living room to dig out my toothbrush so I can scrub the taste out of my mouth. That done, I circle back to the fridge. Food is right out, but I had seen some electrolyte-packed drinks in there. Maybe that will help.

A thud from the living room has me spinning around.

I rush through the doorway to find Azazel standing over my three men as if he just dumped them in a pile. Azazel brushes his hands together as if dusting them off. "Good luck." Then he disappears in a surge of shadows.

I don't hesitate. I drop my drink and rush toward the men. "Are you okay?"

Malachi is at the bottom of the pile, but he throws up a hand. "Stop."

I freeze a few feet away. "What?"

"We're..." He shakes his head, eyes slightly unfocused. His handsome face is haggard and drawn, cheekbones stark. "Not safe."

What they said in the last dream comes rushing back. Somehow my father managed to get them to the brink of starvation in only a few days. In all the chaos, I hadn't had much time to think about it. Now, the truth stares me right in the face, evidence blatant in the fact that all three of them have obviously lost weight. Too much weight. More, they're too pale, their skin stretched tight over their bones. Even Malachi's long hair seems dull and brittle.

I don't move, but I don't retreat, either. "You need blood."

"Not yours," Rylan grinds out. He lifts his head and the gauntness of his cheeks makes my stomach drop. "Need too much."

They can't go hunting like this. They can barely move. If they don't trust me to touch them—or, rather, don't trust themselves to allow me close—then I'll have to hunt for them. The thought fills me with unease, but I'll do anything to keep my men safe. If that means someone else has to pay the price...

Well, it's becoming something of a trend, isn't it?

It's so much easier to make that call for them than it is for myself, though. I would commit unforgivable acts to keep my men with me and safe. I spent a lot of time pretending I'm not just as monstrous as my father, but in this moment, I don't even hesitate. I take a slow step back. "Stay here."

"Mina."

I hold Malachi's gaze. "Stay here. I'll be back."

"*Mina.*"

I don't give him a chance to argue. I spin on my heel and rush back into the kitchen. I had noticed a hook with keys on it by the back door. Sure enough, outside, I find a tiny garage with a truck parked there. It even has a full tank of gas. "Thanks, Azazel," I mutter.

I don't have much experience with driving, but I won't let that stop me. The clock reads midnight as I tear out of the garage and kick up gravel behind me. At this time of night, there's only one option for scoping out victims.

I need to find a bar.

7

I DON'T KNOW WHAT STATE AZAZEL TRANSPORTED US to. I couldn't guess the name of the midsize town I drive into under pain of death. But I manage to find a pair of bars before too long. I park and study them. One is a dive bar with a faded sign that's completely unreadable in the deepening dark, even to my dhampir eyes. The other is newer and already has a crowd of people on the patio surrounded by dangling white string lights.

That'll do.

I glance down at myself. I didn't pause to put myself together before leaving the house—or the motel. My jeans are faded and I've started to wear holes in the knees. My black T-shirt is clean, but with how tired I look, I won't be winning any beauty contests.

How am I supposed to convince people to come with me? How am I supposed to *choose?*

If Malachi doesn't trust himself to drink from me, he must be famished. Rylan and Wolf were no better. There's a decent chance whatever human I bring back to the house will never leave again. That I'll be sentencing whoever I pick to death.

I grip the steering wheel and exhale slowly. I knew the cost when I came here. Waffling and feeling guilty won't change anything. If it's the choice between the men I love or a few strangers? I already know where I stand. It's not moral and it's not right, but I can't bring myself to care. I have not come this far, allowed so much sacrifice, only to balk now.

In the end, it's so much easier than I would have thought.

No one asks for my ID when I walk through the door. Inside is much like the outside: vaguely trendy and ultimately soulless. I could be anywhere. The tables and bar are packed, but everyone seems to be sticking to groups rather than mingling as a whole. I can work with this...I think.

I find a spot at the corner of the bar and order a beer on tap because it's the cheapest thing on the menu. The smell makes my stomach twist, but I force myself to wrap my hands around the glass and take a deep breath. I can do this. I don't have a choice. I just need a moment to figure out a plan.

I don't get a chance.

Two men slide up on either side of me. Too close. I might not be human and even I know that. They're almost touching me, their bodies angled in almost like they're attempting to pin me between them without touching me. They both look rough around the edges, and the alcohol on their breath is even stronger than the scent wafting from the beer in front of me.

I tense. "You're standing too close."

"Haven't seen you around here before, beautiful," the one on the left says. He's got a voice like he smokes a pack a day. He certainly reeks of tobacco.

I half turn to face him. If I were human, I would have missed the movement of his friend at my back. I never would have seen him drop a tablet into my beer. It disappears almost immediately, fizzling out as it descends to the bottom of the glass. It happened *so fast*. Fast enough to make me suspect they've done this before.

The guilt I've harbored since leaving my men behind disintegrates. I'm not one to play judge, jury, and executioner to humans, but if these two think to play predator, I'll show them they aren't the scariest thing in this bar.

It's pathetically easy to pretend to drink the beer. Really, the most challenging part is not throwing up from the scent of it. Halfway through, I let myself list a little to the side. Mr. Right Side is there to catch me, sliding a beefy arm around my waist. "Looks like someone's had too much."

Mr. Left Side chuckles. "Better see her safely home." He even goes so far as to pay for my beer. *What a gentleman.* The bartender gives them a knowing look, which only serves to set my teeth on edge. They *have* done this before. I'd stake my life on it. I mostly keep my feet, but I force myself to half limp, letting them take my weight.

I understand the bartender's look a few minutes later when they haul me out of the bar and we find him waiting around back. He brushes his hands off on his pants. "Let's make this quick. I only have fifteen minutes."

I don't feel guilty at all as I strike.

I might be no match for Malachi and Rylan and Wolf in the sparring ring, but these three are only human. They barely have time to react before I deliver harsh blows to their temples. Not quite enough to kill them—at least I don't think so—but they go down in boneless heaps.

"You fuckers," I spit on the ground. I want to kick them a few times for good measure but if the bartender only had fifteen minutes to get up to no good, then I have fewer than that before someone comes looking for him.

I hurry to the truck and drive it around back. All three of them are still unconscious as I toss their bodies into the bed of the truck and get out of there as quickly and quietly as possible. The drive back to the house seems to take forever, but at least it's easy enough to remember the route.

As I take the dirt road toward the house, I wait for guilt to sweep over me. I didn't hesitate. Even if they hadn't been trying to hurt me, I would have let them think they'd seduced me into going home with them. The end result would be the same. I get no points just because they turned out to be rotten to the core.

The guilt never comes.

Malachi and the other two are nearly exactly where I left them. They've separated a bit, but they don't seem to have the strength to even climb onto the couches. A sliver of fear goes through me but I don't pause long enough to indulge in it. They *have* to be okay. I can't let myself go down a mental road where they aren't. Once they feed, they'll feel better. I'm sure of it. "We're going to stain the rug, but there's no help for it."

Wolf cracks his eyes open. "What did you do, love?"

"What I needed to." No point in explaining beyond that. I go back outside and start hauling the unconscious men inside. It's only as I dump the final unconscious man next to Malachi that I register the fact that I haven't felt the need for a nap since arriving at this house. Before this point, I was taking three naps a day, sleeping more than I was awake. I've been going for hours and still feel relatively fresh.

Apparently Azazel was onto something with that supplemental shield, though I'll be damned before I admit as much to him. If I ever see him again, that is. It's probably better if I don't.

Though I half expect the men to continue questioning me, hunger prevails. Wolf moves first, grabbing the bartender and biting deep. The man groans softly but doesn't stir. Good. It's one thing to attack them when they intended to attack me first. I don't know how I'd feel about them struggling and begging for their lives now.

Then again, these are bloodline vampires we're talking about. Their bites bring great pleasure. After that first contact, no one is fighting anything. They're too busy riding the waves of desire and begging for more.

I certainly was.

It takes less time than one would expect to drain a human body of blood. By the end of it, we have three corpses and all three men look much closer to themselves. I am almost convinced I can see their faces start to look healthier, their gauntness melting away.

Malachi surges to his feet and pulls me into his arms. "Are you hurt?"

My laugh feels a little broken. I'm not the one who has spent nearly a week in my father's not so tender care. I might be permanently nauseous, but the worst I've had to deal with is Grace being cranky in the mornings and throwing up everything I eat. Small things by comparison. "I'm better off than you were."

"Azazel—"

"I'm not the one who paid the price," I cut in. I twist to see Rylan climbing to his feet, almost human slow. "Grace did. She chose it."

He sighs. "I was worried that would happen once I realized who Wolf was summoning. Her mother and Azazel have a history. I thought I could keep the knowledge from her, but this outcome was always likely."

"Who did you *think* I was summoning?" Wolf brushes his hands down his thighs. "There are only so many demons who can cross into our realm and you know it. I can count them on one hand, and half of them haven't been seen in a hundred years."

"Likely because Azazel killed them to corner the market for himself."

"Maybe." Wolf shrugs. He turns to me, uncharacteristically serious. "We're going to get rid of these bodies and then it's time to talk, love."

Malachi's arms tighten around me. "Yes."

They're right that we need to talk, but that doesn't make me look forward to the pending conversation more. There's no strange misty place to sweep us apart when things get awkward, and things are *guaranteed* to get awkward. I compelled Wolf against his will and then I summoned Azazel even though they told me not to. That's not even getting into the whole pregnancy thing.

At least we're back together again. We haven't made any progress with removing the threat my father poses, but he no long has access to three bloodline vampires. To three men I love.

I shiver and Malachi pulls me closer yet. "Sit down, little dhampir. We'll deal with this. You've done enough for now."

It doesn't feel like I've done much of anything at all. I ran when they were captured. I let Grace do all the heavy lifting of recon and surveying my father's compound while I puked up my guts in the motel room. I couldn't even summon Azazel correctly. And then *Grace* paid the price of my bargain. Gods, I even needed Azazel to do some kind of special ward to keep the pregnancy from draining me dry.

I've never felt more worthless in my life. A feat, that. After growing up a powerless dhampir in my father's compound, I didn't think I could sink to lower depths. Apparently I was too optimistic.

But there's no time for self-pity. "I can help."

"You *have* helped." He lets me step away from him, though he runs his hands down my arms and links his fingers through mine. Malachi frowns. "You've lost weight."

"So have you." A deflection, and not even a good one at that. He frowns harder. "Mina."

Wolf and Rylan stalk back through the door. They're moving better now, quickly, less humanlike. It's almost enough to convince myself the last week didn't happen. I know better, though. I step away from Malachi and sink onto the couch. There's not so much as a blood stain on the floor. *Waste not, want not.* I swallow down a hysterical giggle. Shock. It's just shock.

"Don't feel guilty, love." Wolf drops down next to me and throws his arm across the couch at my back. "Humans live so few years. We cut their lives a bit short, but they were always going to be short."

"I don't feel guilty." Not for their deaths. I would wager a small fortune that those three have harmed more people than I care to think about. Now they won't harm anyone ever again. That said, I'm not overly keen on Wolf's blasé attitude. "I might live one of those short mortal life spans. Should we just kill me right now and get it over with?"

"You won't." Rylan perches on the coffee table across from me, close enough that his knees press against mine.

Malachi takes the spot on my other side. For the first time, bracketed in by my men, I can finally breathe again. My voice goes wobbly. "I was so worried about you."

"You got us out," Rylan says, blue eyes direct. "Now tell us exactly how and everything that happened in the meantime."

It takes longer than it should. My ridiculous urge to cry only gets stronger with each point I relay, but their presence gets me through it. By the time I finish, Rylan hasn't so much as moved, Malachi is cursing quietly under his breath, and Wolf's eyes are flickering crimson.

I clear my throat. "Stop it. All of you. You look like you want to comfort *me* and I'm not the one who spent the last week starved and tortured." The starved point is blatant, but I know my father well enough to know the latter is true as well. With three new toys to play with and break, he wouldn't have been able to resist.

"Sound like you've been plenty starved," Malachi rumbles.

"We fucked up, Mina. I'm sorry. You never should have been left alone."

Rylan looks away, something akin to guilt shifting over his handsome features. "I shouldn't have left. My overconfidence meant you weren't protected. I—"

My chest goes hot and tight. "No. We're not doing this. We're not going to play self-recrimination and passing the blame around. If it wasn't my fault, then it wasn't your fault, either. My father outplayed us. Now we have to make sure he doesn't get a chance to do it again." I drag in a breath. "We can't keep running. He'll just catch us again and then we'll be right back where we started." Without Grace to act as convenient willing victim and pay my debts for me. I straighten a bit, feeling grounded for the first time since, well, everything. "We have to strike before he has a chance to regroup."

"WE'LL TALK ABOUT OUR NEXT STEPS TOMORROW."
Malachi doesn't give me a chance to respond before he sweeps
me up and turns a slow circle. "Where are the bedrooms?"

Maybe I should argue, but the truth is I'm crashing fast and
I want to spend some time just existing with them. Azazel promised we'd be safe here, and while I'm not naive enough to expect
that to be true indefinitely, it should be true tonight at least. I
don't even think we're in the same state.

I point at the stairs. "Up."

It's not until Malachi sets me on the bed that I realize Wolf
and Rylan aren't with us. Where did they—

"Ensuring the bodies are never found."

I startle. "I forgot about the mind reading thing." It was still
so new before my father showed up, I'd barely come to terms

with the fact that the men could glean my thoughts since I never learned how to shield. Speaking of... I press my hand to my stomach. "Azazel said my lack of shields were why the pregnancy was draining me so much. He did something, and I feel better, but it's hard to trust him. He said it was a supplemental shield, but I don't know enough to verify it."

Malachi pokes his head into the door leading into what I assume is a bathroom and then comes back to the bed. He takes my hand and tugs me to my feet. "Let's shower."

"Don't tell me you're trying to conserve water." My joke falls flat as he leads me into the bathroom.

"No." He turns on the shower and faces me. "You haven't talked about the pregnancy. Everything else, but not that."

My hand drifts to my stomach but I drop it before it makes contact. "I don't know what to think. It feels like I've been barreling toward this goal, but now that we've accomplished it—or started to, or whatever—it feels unreal. I don't know how I feel." I should feel something, shouldn't I? The people on the compound who'd become pregnant treated it as a rapturous experience that was both deeply emotional and spiritual, right from the moment they realized they'd conceived.

I don't feel anything at all.

"Mina." Malachi cups my chin gently and lifts my face until I meet his gaze. His handsome face is oh so serious, dark eyes intense. "I know we thought this was the only way, but if you don't want this, we'll find a different option."

"Just like that?" The question catches in my throat and comes out jagged. "You told me you couldn't wait to knock me up."

"I know." He shrugs, though his intensity doesn't waver. "But I care about you more than anything else, little dhampir. If you don't want children, then we won't have children."

That's the thing. I don't know what I want. I can barely think about a future without the threat of my father hanging over our heads. His taking Malachi and Wolf and Rylan has only heightened that fear. If I have this baby... If we don't remove my father before it happens...

He could take the baby, too.

I shudder. "I don't have a convenient answer for you, Malachi. I wish I did. I'm not ready to end this pregnancy, no matter how complicated my feelings are about it. It's our only chance."

"I don't give a fuck about the plan," he says quietly. "Do you want it?"

That's the question, isn't it? I pushed back when Grace offered me the same option Malachi is right now, claiming I couldn't make that decision without the men being involved. In hindsight, it feels like an excuse. Not a single one of them would hold making that call against me. I have no doubts about that. "Since Azazel did his magic, I haven't felt so drained and exhausted."

"Mina, that's not an answer."

I know, but I don't *have* an answer right now. I sigh. "I do want it, I think. I haven't really had time to process, and I—" Right here, right now, I can tell him the truth. The awful feeling in my throat gets worse. "I'm afraid to want it. Wanting something is a good excuse for the world to take it away. To have *my father* take it away." I press my hand to Malachi's broad chest. "I dared to want you and look what happened. You spent a week being tortured by him."

"It's fine."

"It's *not* fine." I suck in a harsh breath. "I won't ask you to talk about it if you don't want to, but I'm here if you do." They've listened to my story, but they haven't shared a single thing that happened to them in the time they were captive. I don't have a right to ask them to share if they're not ready, but the big black hole of information makes me uneasy. It's like we're walking on eggshells with each other.

I want to reclaim the easy feeling we'd just reached before my father ruined everything, but I'm not even sure how we accomplished it to begin with. When it comes right down to it, we've only known each other a short time. Things have been uncomfortable and filled with animosity more than they haven't. I shouldn't dare crave something I barely got a taste of in the first place.

Malachi frames my face with his big hands. "It wasn't as bad as you're imagining. I suspect he meant to soften us up, so he focused on isolating us and drugged us with something that made the starvation kick in quicker." His expression is so grave, it makes my chest hurt. "I couldn't think properly, but I worried about you. That was the worst of it, little dhampir."

This time.

If we don't do something about my father, it will be worse next time. He might try to forcibly breed them. The thought makes me shudder. "We have to kill him. We can't wait any longer."

"We can wait to start making proper plans until morning." He shifts his hands to my shoulders and gives me a squeeze. "Just let us take care of you tonight."

"You're the one who's suffered. I should be taking care of *you*."

He smiles a little. "This is how you take care of me." Malachi strips me easily, his big hands gentle on my body. It's not sexual, but it feels like a small eternity since I've touched him. I won't make assumptions. Not with us feeling so raw right now. But I'm only me, and I would have to pass through death's gate in order to not want this man. Maybe I'd even want him in the afterlife.

I don't know how this happened. A few months ago, I didn't even know he existed. Now, he's a cornerstone in my life and I can't imagine going on without him. The strength of that feeling should scare me—and it does—but it's like it can't find purchase in our reality.

I don't know if I believe in destiny, but I can't deny that Malachi and I feel destined.

We step beneath the spray and he pulls me into his arms. It feels so damn good to have his naked body pressed against me. Yes, there's sexual desire, but just touching him reassures a part of me that couldn't quite believe he's here and safe.

A horrible sound wrenches itself from my chest. Malachi hugs me tighter. "I'm here. You're safe."

I bury my face in his chest and sob until it feels like my body will shatter into a million pieces and crumble away to dust. It *hurts*, but at least I know I'm still alive. That he's still alive. We are here together, which is more than I could say twenty-four hours ago. It's like all my fear and rage have crystallized into the tears I shed in that moment. It's a purging.

I don't mean to kiss him. Truly, I don't. One moment, I'm sobbing and the next my mouth is on his and I'm climbing his body to wrap my legs around his waist. Malachi barely hesitates.

He kisses me back like he needs my air to breathe. One step and my back hits the tiled wall. He pins me there so effortlessly, it makes me shake with need. *Yes, this. This is what I need. Please don't stop.*

He breaks our kiss long enough to say in a strained voice, "I can't. Mina, you have to stop kissing me right now if you don't want—"

"Take me." I nip his throat. "I need you. Don't make me wait."

He growls something low in a language I don't recognize and then his big cock presses to my entrance. I'm wet but nowhere near where I need to be for him to plunge into me. It's *work.* He grips my hips and uses short strokes to fight his way into my body. It's not entirely comfortable, but I don't care. I need this as much as he does. More, even.

By the time he sheaths himself to the hilt, we're both shaking and panting. Malachi presses his forehead to mine. "You feel good, little dhampir. You feel like home."

"Bite me," I gasp.

"No." A slight shake of his head. "Not until we know for sure that it's safe." Malachi kisses me, stifling any protest, quick and rough. "I don't need my bite to make you feel good."

It's nothing more than the truth. He cups my ass and moves me up and down his cock, adjusting the angle until he hits all the right spots inside me and my clit rubs against him with every stroke. Immediately, pleasure coils through me. Need sparks low in my stomach, building and building. I missed this. I missed *him.*

"Getting started without us, I see."

He turns with me still in his arms as the curtain is wrenched back to reveal Wolf and Rylan. Malachi raises his brows. "Shower's not big enough for four."

"You look clean enough." Wolf eyes me hungrily. "Take it to the bedroom."

Rylan hands over a towel. "We'll be along shortly."

I give a strained laugh and press my forehead to Malachi's chest. "Sounds like a plan." It means an aborted orgasm right now but more pleasure in the near future. More, it means reconnecting. Maybe after we all get back in bed together, where this connection truly began, we'll be able to banish the strange distance that's cropped up between us since we reunited.

Malachi sets me down long enough to wash me quickly, ignoring my half-hearted protests that I can do it myself. It doesn't take long before we've switched places with Rylan and Wolf. I'm only half dried off when Malachi hauls me back into the bedroom and goes down on his back, me astride him. He plants big hands on my hips and looks at me like I'm his world.

A few weeks ago, I would have doubted this, would have wasted time looking for a trap. Surely no one can fall as hard and fast as we have for each other. I've fallen for the others, too, but with Malachi, it was strangely seamless after our first few initial bumps. I don't understand why he's so sure of me. Or why that feeling is so mutual. I should doubt. I should...

There's no room for should in this world. I almost lost him. I won't waste another moment doubting what we have when proof that it's there is so readily available. I don't know what the future will bring, but we have this now and I won't waste it.

I reach between us and grip his big cock, giving him a stroke and then lifting my hips to notch him at my entrance. It's easier to take him this time. I work myself down his length in a slow, glorious stroke. "You always feel so good."

"I love you, Mina."

My heart lurches and then steadies. Is this the first time he's said it to me? It feels like it. I hold perfectly still, letting the words settle through me. I never thought to find this connection at all, let alone with three men. But it's here, and I won't meet his bravery with cowardice.

I lick my lips. "I…I love you, too."

9

Wolf bounds into the bedroom in a leap that takes him from the doorway onto the bed. The impact sends Malachi's cock even deeper inside me and I can't hold back a moan. Wolf grins. "I missed that sound."

"I missed you," I admit. "All of you."

Rylan joins us on the bed. It's only a king, so there's not a ton of room, but we make it work. He kneels behind me and presses his chest to my back. I close my eyes and soak up the skin-to-skin contact. It feels so good, I could almost be satisfied with stopping here, if not for the steady pulse of desire through my body.

"No biting," Malachi says firmly. "Not until we navigate the new limits."

I tense. "You think my blood's poison like in the dreams." Again, there's no reason for that to sting. If it is, it's some magical quirk and not a reflection of how much they want me, but I can't help taking it personally. Foolish in the extreme, but I'm too emotionally raw to hold back the hurt in my voice.

Rylan shifts my hair off my shoulder and kisses my neck in the exact spot he bit it in the dream. "You're pregnant, Mina. That means you need the blood more than we do. If we drain too much, we could harm you and the pregnancy. Best not to test it while we're...distracted."

Distracted with fucking me.

I try for a smile. "I suppose that's a fair argument."

"So glad you think so." I can hear the smile in his voice.

Wolf appears in front of me with a knife in his hand. "That only goes one way, though."

"Wolf," Malachi warns.

He grins, completely unrepentant. "That little monster growing inside her is half vampire. You can't honestly tell me that a little blood is going to harm it." He jerks a chin at me. "Besides, she looks like shit and she's lost weight."

I blink. "Wow, tell me how you really feel."

"You're even paler than me, love. A little blood will get you back into tip-top shape." He slices a long line across his forearm.

I don't hesitate. I lunge forward and grab his arm, hauling it to my mouth. The first taste is like...I don't have words. I've drank from all three of them before, and their magic is readily apparent in their blood. It was enough to boost my own power and even heal a recent injury. I wouldn't say it's old hat at this point but drinking from them hasn't surprised me since that first taste from each, unique in their own way.

This is different.

The flavor of Wolf's blood explodes against my tongue, sending a wave of pure need through me. I start moving on Malachi's cock, but I keep Wolf's arm in an iron grip. "More," I growl against his skin.

"Malachi?" Later, it will irritate me that Wolf looks to Malachi for guidance instead of taking me at my word. Right now, I can't think past the delicious taste of him coating my tongue and throat.

"Don't stop." His grip pulses on my hips, guiding me to the rhythm that feels the best, long slow strokes that have me rubbing him exactly where I need him. Rylan shifts behind me to run his hand down my stomach and press his fingers to my clit. Another long pull of Wolf's blood and I lose it.

I slam down on Malachi's cock, sobbing my way through an orgasm. It's good. Too damn good. But I don't want it to stop. "More!"

"Mina—"

"More. *Please.*"

Wolf gently pulls his arm from my grasp and then Rylan's is there, blood already streaming. In the back of my mind, a voice whispers that I should stop, that they need their blood more than I do, but I can't. It's like the first taste has peeled away my civilized layers, leaving only the animal beneath. I need their blood, their bodies. I need more.

Malachi moves me over his cock, his expression intense as he watches my face. It's not pleasure alone lurking in his dark eyes. I'm too far gone to nuance it out. Not with Rylan's blood like fire on my tongue. I moan and whimper, drinking deep even as another orgasm bears down on me. It's almost too much, but when has that stopped us?

My orgasm drags Malachi along with me this time. He growls my name as he comes, grinding up into me in the most delicious way. Rylan starts to take his arm back, but I dig my nails in. "Not yet."

"Mina." Malachi sits up and wrenches my mouth from Rylan's arm. I whimper and lunge for it, but he catches me lightly by the throat. His dark brows draw together. "Something's wrong."

"The only thing that's wrong is that you won't let me drink." My gaze snags on the throbbing pulse point in his throat. "Just a little more, Malachi. Please." I hate how wheedling my tone goes, but it's like I don't have control of my body, my tongue. "I'm *famished*."

He glances over my shoulder, conveying something to Rylan. It's *him* who lifts me off Malachi and makes a cage of his arms when I start to struggle. "Peace, Mina."

"Let me go."

"You're not acting like yourself."

I part my lips to command him to let me go, but Wolf is there, pressing his hand to my mouth. There's the tiniest cut there, barely enough to bleed at all and already healing supernaturally fast. But it's enough. It cuts my command off in its tracks.

Concern lines his handsome face. "This won't hold her long."

"Rylan?" Malachi is up and off the bed, moving around behind us. Part of me wants to twist to watch him, but I'm too busy licking Wolf's palm, trying to get every bit of blood I can manage.

Rylan's arms tense around me. "Either her seraph powers are lashing out after the separation...or it's the pregnancy. We have no way of knowing for sure."

"Why not just let her drink her fill?" Wolf switches hands, a new cut on his other palm that he presses to my lips. I moan a little in response and lean forward as far as I can with Rylan restraining me. "She's not going to be able to drain all three of us, and even if she did, she wouldn't kill us."

"Maybe," Rylan says darkly. "Or maybe she'd be glutted and keep going until there was nothing left. It could develop into frenzy."

Wolf laughs, but it's a shadow of his usual mad cackle. "You're thinking demons and werewolves, Rylan. Vampires don't frenzy."

I tense, waiting for Rylan to argue, but he just huffs out a breath. "There's always a first time. I've never seen a pregnant seraph, either. Who knows what happens during that time? They kept their secrets too close. We have no way of anticipating what happens next."

Malachi reappears in front of us. He's tied back his hair and has a knife in his hand. "We can't keep her restrained and gagged. We see this through. It's the only way to know for sure."

"Mal—"

He sends Rylan a sharp look. "We see this through," he repeats.

Something about this should bother me, but I can't think past the fact that Wolf's hand has healed and I've licked it clean. "More."

"Come here, little dhampir. I've got more for you." Malachi leans back against the headboard and motions with his free hand. "Release her."

Part of me expects Rylan to keep arguing, but he curses. "If this doesn't work—"

"Stop thinking so hard and go by instinct." Wolf shifts to kneel next to Malachi. His pale blue eyes take us in, more serious than he's ever been. "Worst case, she takes too much, we wrestle her off him, gag her, and toss her in a basement until we figure things out."

"That is not a plan," Rylan snaps.

"It's more of a plan than *you* have."

Malachi drags the knife down the line of his throat. Too deep. Blood pours down his wide chest to his stomach. Too much blood.

I want it all. My mouth waters. "Let me go."

Rylan releases me with another muffled curse. I waste no time straddling Malachi and licking my way up his chest to seal my mouth against the cut. Pure bliss has me closing my eyes and moaning. He wraps careful arms around me. "Take as much as you need. Everything I have is yours."

I drink in deep pulls. Even through my bliss, I can feel the tension rising in the room with each minute that ticks by. Wolf shifts next to us, fidgeting as if he went to reach for me and stopped himself before he could make contact.

Slowly, oh so slowly, the overwhelming need eases. The cut on Malachi's throat heals, and I give him one last long lick and press my forehead to his shoulder. For the first time since Wolf offered me his arm, my thoughts feel clear. My energy level, though, has plummeted. I can barely keep my eyes open. "I'm sorry," I whisper.

"There she is," Wolf says. He sounds relieved. "Had us worried for a minute, love."

"I'm sorry," I repeat. I can't look at them. I just acted like a monster. I wasn't thinking about them as men and people I care deeply about. The only thing that mattered to me was drinking as much of their blood as I could. "I don't know what that was."

Rylan abruptly stands. "I'm going to make some calls."

Malachi goes still beneath me. I don't have to lift my head to know they're sharing one of those speaking glances that contain entire conversations. His and Rylan's history lends to that sort of thing. They've certainly known each other long enough. A shudder works through Malachi's body. "You're sure?"

"We don't know enough."

"She'll make demands."

"She always does. We'll have to deal with her eventually. Might as well get something out of it in the process."

I don't hear him leave, but the bond I share with each of them tugs as Rylan moves away. Maybe one day I'll be able to pinpoint their location exactly, but for now I just get the vague feeling of increasing distance as he moves away from the house. I sigh. I can't keep burrowing into Malachi's chest like a coward. This—whatever this new complication is—needs to be faced.

"You're not a coward," Malachi says softly.

"Nah, not a coward." The bed shifts as Wolf tosses himself down onto it. "Just a cute little dhampir-slash-seraph in over her head."

I forgot—again—that they can read my mind now. Or at least glean my thoughts and feelings on occasion. Before they were taken, one of the things Malachi and I were working on was teaching me how to shield properly. Another thing to add to the list.

I take a deep breath and straighten. My current exhaustion level feels different than I've gotten used to. It's less feeling sick and unable to function than feeling deliciously sated. That will scare me later, maybe. I press my hand to my stomach. For once, the awful nausea that usually rises after I eat is nowhere in evidence. "The little monster *would* prefer blood to solid food." I can't live on blood, though. At least I'm reasonably sure I can't. All the dhampirs I know lean human in that way.

But then, I'm not human at all, am I?

"Do seraphim eat?"

"I have no idea." Wolf props himself up on one arm next to Malachi. "Rylan will come back with answers."

I twist to glance out the door he left through. He's farther afield now, and he seems to be pacing. "Who's he going to contact?" Silence greets me and I turn to find them looking at each other as if deciding how much to tell me. Irritation flashes. "I would think we're past you hiding things from me."

"It's for your own good."

I glare at Malachi. "I think it's better *I* decide what's for my own good. I'm not a child. Stop treating me like one." When they still hesitate, frustration blooms. "If we manage to kill my father, *I* will take his place. How long do you think I'll be able to hold his throne when you don't treat me like an equal?"

He smooths my hair back, expression intense. "Don't ask us not to take care of you, little dhampir. It's too much to demand."

"You're being unreasonable. I'm not saying don't take care of me. I'm just asking for you to stop keeping information from me. What harm can information do?" The question isn't fair, because information can do a good deal of harm and we all know it. But I am *not* a child.

Still, he relents and drops his hands. "He's contacting his mother."

10

After dropping that bomb of an information piece, Malachi refuses to answer further questions, stating that it's Rylan's business and if he wants me to know, he'll tell me. We end up in the shower again to wash off the blood, but we keep it brief. Later, when I'm tucked safely between Wolf and Malachi, silently tracking Rylan's continued pacing with my mind, I allow myself to think about what Malachi did and didn't say.

I thought these three were the last of their bloodlines. In hindsight, that seems very naive. Malachi, yes. It's known that he's the last one. *Everyone* knows it. But while my father might have extensive information on the seven bloodlines, it's not information he ever shared with me.

Rylan still has family alive.

I open my eyes to find Wolf watching me. Malachi's body

is loose and relaxed at my back. Impossible to tell whether he's actually asleep or if he's merely giving us a measure of assumed privacy. I swallow hard. "Do you have family alive, too?"

"Sure." He shrugs as much as someone can while lying on their side. "There's a few cousins. My parents and sister are no doubt still rampaging through Europe and leaving chaos in their wake."

He says it so casually, too casually. Wolf talks about his family the same way I recited what my father did to my knee to keep me from running. No one keeps their words totally emotionless unless they're hiding something ugly beneath.

Sadness swamps me, even as I tell myself I'm being silly. Surely I wasn't expecting any of these men to have the idealistic childhood of which I was deprived? I know better. My father might be a monster, but there's something to be said about power corrupting. Immortals don't manage to stay alive for hundreds of years by being nice and kind. Doing so is as much as inviting enemies to come in and cut off their heads.

I shiver. "You're not close."

"No." Another of those shrugs. "My parents were even more unhinged than I am. It didn't make for a restful childhood. I haven't seen them since I left a very long time ago. It's better for everyone that we don't congregate often." He won't quite meet my gaze. "I take great pains to ensure I don't cross paths with my sister more than strictly necessary."

I can relate, though it makes me sad. I reach up and cup his angular jaw. "I'm sorry."

"You keep apologizing for things that aren't your fault." His grin is quick and sharp. "Careful, love. Someone might see that big heart of yours and try to take advantage."

"I don't have a big heart." Sometimes I think I don't have a heart at all. All my life, I've never known peace. First, because I was raised in my father's compound as a powerless dhampir, which translated to a useless dhampir. Then, when I was sent to Malachi as a sacrifice, all I could focus on was gaining my freedom. But even that wasn't enough because my father's been hunting us ever since we broke the blood ward around his old house. Every step of the way, I've been looking out for myself first.

Maybe if I hadn't been, Wolf and the others wouldn't have been taken.

"Get that look off your face." He presses his thumb to the spot between my brows. "You could use a little less worrying. Malachi and Rylan are both too brilliant not to figure this out."

The right words but the wrong tone. I frown. "There's something else you're not telling me."

"Wolf." His name is barely more than a rumble from Malachi. A warning.

I sit up. "We *just* had this conversation. Why are you still keeping things from me?"

"I—"

Wolf stretches out and props his head on his arms. "What he's trying to figure out how to bend over backward to avoid saying is that there's a distinct possibility that Rylan's mother will take the questions about seraphim as an excuse to hunt you down and kill you."

I flinch. Judging from what everyone has told me about

seraphim, I can't exactly blame her for wanting me gone, but…
"I'm getting heartily tired of having a target painted on my chest."

"Get used to it, love. Those who remember what your people
did when they held power will either want to use you or kill you."

The walls feel like they're closing in. I hadn't thought beyond
removing my father as a threat. He's been larger than life for so
long, it never occurred to me that there would be others baying
for my blood if they got half a chance. I shudder. "It will never
end, will it? We'll be running forever."

"Eh." Wolf shrugs, totally relaxed. "We just need to kill your
father, convert all his little followers to being *your* followers, and
you'll be set. Our enemies come after you, we'll kill them. They
send others, and we'll kill them, too. Eventually, they'll realize
we're too powerful to fuck with and don't have any intention of
repeating history and they'll leave us alone." He grins. "Except
for the odd assassination attempt to keep us on our toes."

"You are not making me feel better." My voice comes out
reedy. I press the heels of my hands to my eyes. "I thought it
would be over after we kill my father."

Malachi wraps his hands around my wrists and gently tugs
them down. "When you have eternity, you'll come to appreciate
the little things that break up the monotony."

It speaks volumes that they consider *assassination attempts*
to be little things. "I could use a little monotony in my life."

He gives my wrists a gentle squeeze. "You'll have it." He
glances at Wolf and shrugs. "Besides, if it ever gets to be too much,
we can always jump to a realm that's never heard of seraphim.
That would create other challenges, but it's always an option."

I lick my lips. I don't know that I'm ready to abandon *this* realm, but the escape hatch option calms me all the same. "Are there many other realms? More than this one and Azazel's?"

"No one's ever tracked them properly, but there are at least dozens."

Wolf laughs, sounding more like himself. "No one's tracked them properly because they've died trying." He flicks Malachi's hair off his shoulder. "Might be a fun challenge in a couple hundred years when the baby bats are grown and have flown the nest."

I blink. "Did you just call the..." I'm not quite able to call it a baby yet. It's *not* a baby. It's a cluster of cells. "Did you just call it a *baby bat?*"

"It's as good a name as anything."

A reluctant smile pulls at the edges of my lips. "You can't even turn into a bat."

"Rylan can." Wolf makes a show of shuddering. "Freakish thing. Too big. Could probably carry you on its back if you wanted."

I feel the man in question approaching. "I think he's done with his call."

"Spooky."

I shoot a look at Wolf, though I can feel Malachi watching me. There's a tension about him that makes me think he'll lunge forward if I suddenly topple. It's a strange thought, that he'll always be there to catch me. I trust him. I do. But my need to stand on my own is nearly overpowering. "I'm fine, Malachi."

"You're shaking."

I hate that he's right. I lift my hand and study the tremors as Rylan closes the distance between us. He's moving inhumanly fast, and I shouldn't be able to track him so effectively as a result. The seraph bond is freakish.

Too much change. Too much information. Too little time.

Dealing with the long-term effects of the seraph bond will have to wait until we're out of crisis mode, whenever that happens. *If* it ever happens. The thought depresses me. Instead of responding to Malachi's question that isn't a question, I twist to face the door as Rylan walks through.

His expression is a careful mask, giving away nothing. "I spoke with her." He doesn't make us wait, thankfully. He just sighs. "It's...complicated."

"Threat?" This from Malachi. He links his fingers through mine, tense enough that I can tell he wants to haul me back into his arms and wrap me up in himself. I'm not entirely opposed to the idea, but I just got done telling him that I need to stand on my own, so I can't walk back on it now.

Rylan shrugs. "She didn't start making threats, but that's not how she operates. At this point, she'll wait and see, and if she decides she needs to act, we'll hear from her in a decade or so. She *did* give some interesting information."

He moves, strangely stilted, and sinks onto the edge of the bed near me. "When seraphim became pregnant, they would retreat into their fortified locations for the duration. Based on when they'd go missing, it was estimated that the gestation cycle is similar to a vampire or human. Forty weeks, give or take." He looks at me, dark eyes conflicted. "We don't have information on what happens during that time. They would disappear with a retinue of vampire...servants...and reappear with a brand-new seraph baby. Most of the time, the vampires that went with them were never seen again."

Wolf whistles. "Suppose it's too much to pretend they were just moved to different colonies."

"They wouldn't be able to because of the seraph bond."

Damn it. I press my lips together, fighting against the urge to scream that it's not fair. That we deserve to catch a break *for once*. "You think they drain the vampires and kill them during the pregnancy."

"We don't know what to think," Malachi cuts in with a warning glance at the other two. "Seraphim don't drink blood."

"Other ways to drain a victim."

"For fuck's sake, Wolf. Shut up."

Drain them of power, of life, of what makes them *them*. The thought leaves me cold. I was only interested in blood when I lost control earlier, but that's the thing: I wasn't in control at all. If that hunger had switched to more magical things, I wouldn't have been able to stop it. Neither would the men. "You have to leave."

"Absolutely not."

I glare at them all. It's not easy with them arranged the way they are, but I make a valiant effort. "I am not endangering you just because I'm pregnant. That wasn't part of the bargain."

"None of this was." Rylan shrugs. "We work with the realities we have. It might be that you're just mirroring a full vampire more than your seraph half. They need to consume large amounts of blood."

"I've never needed blood before." I was never even offered it until Malachi, so if that was a requirement of living, I would be long gone. "That doesn't make sense."

"It makes as much sense as anything." He doesn't look away. "We are working on theory here. There's no reason to jump to the worst-case scenario."

"That's enough." Malachi's voice has gone harsh. "We all need sleep and then we need to come up with a plan for tomorrow. Everything else can wait."

Until I get hungry again. Or the magic goes weird. Or...

We have been more unlucky than we've had breaks that went in our favor. First we used me to break the blood bond that trapped Malachi, only to discover I was actually half seraph and had bonded with all three men. A seraph bond isn't something that can be reversed.

Then, we finally thought we'd have some time to figure things out, to explore the new powers the bond had allowed us to share, only to have my father show up and take the men.

Then, I find out I'm pregnant, the one way most likely to dethrone my father, only for the pregnancy to be just as freakish as I am. The kind of freak who endangers those I've come to care most about.

It's only as I'm falling asleep that a small voice in the back of my mind points out I didn't immediately throw up the blood I consumed.

That I feel better.

11

I WAKE UP WITH RYLAN AT MY BACK AND WOLF NUZ-
zling my breasts. It's a low, dreamlike adjustment from sleep to
awareness, and I shift against them, enjoying the feel of their
naked skin sliding against mine. They're here, with me. It's not a
dream. They're safe…at least for now.

Rylan cups my hip. "Awake?"

"Yes," I whisper.

Wolf chuckles against my skin. "Good." He moves down, dragging his mouth over my stomach. He nudges Rylan's hand to my
thigh, and Rylan responds by gripping me there and lifting my leg
up and out, opening the way for Wolf. They move seamlessly the
way they always seem to. Even when they're arguing, there's always
this awareness between my men. It speaks to their long history.
Everything about their relationships speaks to their long history.

Malachi isn't in bed with us. I can feel him faintly in the distance, some miles away. He doesn't seem distressed, but... "Malachi?"

"A little morning hunting." Wolf playfully nips one thigh and then the other. "Don't worry about him."

Rylan sighs against my temple. "You can't just tell people not to worry."

"You're right." Wolf laughs, high and unhinged. "I have a better way." Then his mouth is on my pussy.

He kisses me thoroughly, tasting every inch with long swipes of his tongue. He ignores my clit almost entirely, a delightfully aggravating experience as he tastes me. "Missed this," he murmurs against me. I missed it too. I don't get a chance to say it much, though, because he chooses that moment to thrust his tongue into me, making my back bow and drawing a cry from my lips.

Rylan slides his other arm between me and the mattress, hugging me to his body as Wolf ravishes me with his mouth. I can't think, can't move, can only whimper and shake. "I need—"

Wolf sucks hard on my clit, but he stops before I can reach my peak. I cry out in protest, and his laugh goes dark. "Feels good, doesn't she?"

It takes my pleasure-drugged brain a few moments to realize he's not talking to me. He's talking to Rylan, who's gone tense behind me. His arms provide a loving cage that keeps me immobile. He's so still, he might as well have been carved from stone. "Wolf," he snarls.

"Smells good, too." Wolf inhales. He licks a line down my thigh. "Smells *tempting*."

"We shouldn't."

Understanding crashes over me. I know what they're talking about now. Malachi might have instructed them not to bite me, but they want to. *I* want them to. "Do it," I whisper. "Please."

"As the lady commands."

"*Wolf!*"

But it's too late. He snaps forward, quick as a snake, and bites my thigh. I come instantly, crying out so loudly that it's almost a scream. Wolf takes one pull and then another, each one like a pleasurable tug on my clit that only spikes my orgasm higher.

He stops. A little spark of power flares on my thigh where he's cut his tongue to speed my heeling, and then he climbs up my body. He brushes a quick kiss to my lips, too quickly. I'm not his final destination, after all. Wolf shifts just a little so he can take Rylan's mouth.

Rylan moans and his grip on me goes almost painfully tight, claws suddenly pricking my skin as he starts to lose control. They move, pressing close as if they can get to each other through me. It might be enough to make me feel immaterial, but this is what I want just as much as I want them to focus on me. I love that my men love each other. I wouldn't have it any other way.

Wolf lifts his head. "You need it more than we do. Take what she's offering before you lose control and hurt her." His voice goes hard. "Because if your stubbornness causes her harm again, I *will* kill you."

"Wolf, no." My protest is faint. "Don't force him."

"Everyone is so fucking selfless. So damn ready to bend over backward to be polite even though it weakens you." He curses.

"You're too damn shortsighted. One bite, Rylan. You're not going to lose control now, but the same can't be said if you wait too long."

Now it's Rylan's turn to curse. "You're right."

"I know."

Still, he doesn't bite me. I think we're all remembering back at the safe house where Rylan lost control after denying both of us for too long. He bit me too deep. I don't think he would have killed me, even if Malachi and Wolf hadn't intervened, but the memory is too fresh to argue with.

I tilt my head to the side, offering my neck. "I trust you."

"Gods." He speaks low and soft, but the words are lost on me as his teeth sink into my skin. Wolf presses us onto our backs and then his big cock is at my entrance, pushing steadily into me. The first pull from Rylan's mouth has my orgasm rising again, and Wolf working his cock into me only heightens my pleasure.

I want it to be like this always.

Rylan only takes four pulls, but it's more than enough. It's like it incites something within the three of us. A flame. A desperation to be closer, to make our pleasure last longer. A desire for *more*.

He wrestles Wolf and I off him. Wolf lands on his back with me astride him, his cock still buried deep. He thrusts up, laughing in a choked kind of way. "Better hurry, Rylan. Missed this too much to last long."

I plant my hands on his chest and start to ride him. "Yes, Rylan. Hurry." I'm going to come again. It's as if all the misery and suffering from the last week have held back a wave of pleasure so strong, it threatens to sweep me away entirely. I'm not sure I mind. The harsh reality will return all too soon. I want this while we have this chance.

"You can last. Both of you," Rylan bites out. His weight disappears from behind me for a moment and I hear him rustling through the nightstand drawer. He snorts. "The demon *would* ensure we're fully stocked on lube."

"Azazel has his priorities in order." Wolf hooks the back of my neck and tows me close to claim my mouth. Kissing him is rarely soft and never what I expect. This time is no different. His tongue is fierce against mine, filled with things left unsaid. I meet him stroke for stroke, never stopping riding him even as I'm sighing and gasping against his lips.

The mattress dips as Rylan returns to us. I already know what to expect. What comes next. We've done this before. If we live through the coming confrontation, we'll do this many times again. The thought makes me shiver. Rylan palms my ass, that delicious tremor in his hands. "You up for this?"

I break Wolf's kiss to snarl, "Fuck me, Rylan. Don't hold back."

"You heard her." Wolf laughs and then he reclaims my mouth with teeth and tongue.

Rylan doesn't ask again. He spreads lube over me and works his fingers into me in slow strokes. It hasn't been that long since we've done this, but he's nothing if not thorough. When I first met him, I thought he was an unbelievable ass. I still think that sometimes, but beneath his cold exterior is a man who cares far more than anyone would guess.

Anyone except Malachi. And Wolf. And now me.

He presses his cock to my ass. He hasn't always been careful with me in the past—I haven't always *wanted* him to be careful with me in the past—but he's being careful now. Neither he nor Wolf are small men, and the sensation of fullness is almost too much as he seats himself within me entirely. Rylan kisses the back of my neck. "Good?"

"Yes." I can't move, impaled as I am between them, but I still try. "Please. More."

"Love it when you say please," Wolf mutters against my temple. "Rylan?"

"Yeah." Rylan plants his hands on my hips and starts to thrust slowly into me. I squirm and moan, but in my current position, all I can really do is take what they give me. I kiss Wolf's throat, setting my teeth against his skin there. I have no fangs to pierce, but I suddenly want to.

I bite him anyways. Just to do it. His cock jerks inside me and he hisses. "Need something, love?"

"Yes." I stroke his throat with my fingers. A blink and the tips tingle, transforming to claws. Rylan is still fucking me slowly, but I can feel how his attention is now focused on my hand. If I try to rip out Wolf's throat, he'll stop me. I hope. I lick my lips. "Can I, Wolf?"

He tilts his head back as much as he can in our current positions. "Drink your fill, love."

Malachi is on his way back. I can feel the distance closing between us, him racing in our direction in a blur too fast for the human eye to follow. When he returns, he'll make us stop. He laid down very reasonable guidelines fewer than twelve hours ago. Reasonable guidelines that we're flaunting right now.

I can practically feel Wolf's pulse on my tongue, a steady beat begging me to taste. I don't want to wait, and I don't want to play things safe and slow. "Just a little taste." I'm lying and we all know it.

"Put the claws away, Mina." Rylan releases one hip and leans down to cover my hand with his own. "Let me."

I don't want to. I want to draw Wolf's blood, to take it into my body the same way I'm taking his cock right now, to make it my own. What Rylan's saying is smart, though. I don't want to hurt Wolf. I just want to taste him on my tongue. "Yes."

Rylan's skin tingles against mine. I don't know if I've ever felt him use his magic like this before, but it's pleasant. As my fingers shift back to their normal shape, his grow sharp and claw-like. He drags three down the center of Wolf's throat. Not gouging him, but deep enough that it will take some time to heal.

Wolf digs his hands into my hair and guides my mouth to his throat. I hardly need any encouragement. Everything about this feels good, feels *right*. Rylan picks up his pace a little as I drink from Wolf. With how we're arranged, he's essentially fucking both of us. Wolf's grip on my hair spasms and he moans a bit with each pull I take from his throat.

Pleasure builds inside me in slow waves. We're not rushing. It feels like we're spinning a web of desire around each other, each slide of their cocks, each swipe of my tongue against Wolf's throat, the delicious friction of all their skin against all of mine... It all increases the sensation of something magical taking place.

Rylan curses. "Too fucking good. I'm going to—" His teeth sink into my shoulder.

Just like that, I'm coming. I sob against Wolf's throat, writhing through an orgasm that curls my toes. Rylan pulls out at the last moment and a bare second later, his seed lashes my ass and lower back. He barely gets out of the way before Wolf rolls us. His hand is at the nape of my neck again, urging me back to his throat. "More, love. Bite me again."

"Wolf—"

"*Fuck off.*"

Something's wrong, but I'm too far gone to understand what. I wrap my legs around Wolf's hips and urge him deeper as I follow his command. The wounds are almost closed. I won't get as much as I want. *I want...* With the barest thought, my teeth grow sharp in my mouth. They nick my lips, but I don't care. I have what I need now.

I bite him.

He groans, low and deep, driving into me as he comes. Hot blood scours my tongue and I barely have the presence of mind to stop biting him and drink. Each pull makes him drive into me harder, which only makes my orgasm crest again. We're caught in a loop. It's too good to stop.

The door crashes open hard enough to bounce off the wall. The boom startles us enough that we freeze. Malachi stalks into the bedroom, his expression forbidding as he takes in the scene in front of him. I have the presence of mind to remove my mouth from Wolf's throat, but there's no covering up the mess. We're both sticky with his blood and other things. Even the sheets are soaked. "Mal—"

He starts unbuttoning his shirt. "You took too much."

Shame heats my skin. "I didn't mean to." I brush my fingers over Wolf's high cheekbones. His eyes flutter a little, but he looks almost drugged. "What's going on? I've taken more than this before and he didn't act like this."

"Felt too good," Wolf murmurs. "Couldn't stop coming."

It sounds startlingly familiar. It's how *I* feel when they bite me. Pleasure so strong that it overtakes all else. Orgasms that rise and rise and rise until the bite ends. But that doesn't make sense.

I crawl out from under him as Malachi sits on the bed and hauls Wolf up to sprawl across his wide chest. I gingerly touch my mouth. My teeth feel normal, my cut lips already healed. "I don't have a bite like a bloodline vampire. Do bites even work on other vampires? This is impossible."

"When will you admit it, Mina?" Rylan's tone isn't unkind as he sinks onto the bed next to me and wraps a surprisingly comforting arm around my shoulders. "You're not a vampire. You're a seraph. The rules don't apply to you."

12

I DON'T KNOW WHY IT STILL STINGS TO BE REMINDED that I'm not human, vampire, or dhampir. I'm something else, something rare and dangerous and unknown. "I'm aware."

Rylan sighs. "I didn't mean it like that."

"It's fine."

"It's not." He tugs me closer as Malachi offers a forearm to Wolf. Wolf bites quickly and drinks deep. Within a few minutes, he's looking more like himself again. Relief makes me a little woozy. We've exchanged blood before—all of us. It's never been truly dangerous, not like it appears to be now.

No. That's not true. From the moment I met Malachi and then the others, they've been dangerous to me. One bite taken too far could end my life. It's something none of us have really spoken at great lengths about, but we've all been aware of it. This is different.

I've never been dangerous to them.

When Wolf finally sits back, Malachi levels a look at me. "We'll talk about this later. Right now, we need to discuss our next step with Cornelius."

I start to argue that we need to talk about it now, but his rationale makes sense. If we don't survive the fight with my father, it won't matter that I'm dangerous to them, because we'll all be captive or dead. What a cheerful thought.

Rylan huffs out a breath. "Why don't we start with where we are? Did you figure out the state or the town, at least?"

"Still Montana. Best I can tell, it's the next town over from the compound."

"Azazel didn't take us far." Wolf shakes his head, a grin pulling at his lips. "That wily bastard."

Malachi nods. "We won't fly under the radar for long. We have to move while Cornelius is still scrambling to search for us."

Every time he says my father's name, I have to fight back a flinch. He's no demon to be summoned by speaking his name, but I can't shake the strangely superstitious feeling that we shouldn't say it. I swallow past my fear. "Even if I kill him publicly, what's to stop my siblings from finishing what he started? They've all had their powers for years at this point. I won't win in an endless string of duels." Our plan had seemed so reasonable—if a long shot—when we put it together on the run after escaping Malachi's house. My time with Grace poking holes in it has only made me doubt myself. My father is *powerful*. He stopped Rylan, who is a bloodline vampire who can change his entire form, with a single word.

Seraph or no, my father can compel me to do whatever the hell he wants if he gets a chance to speak.

"It has to be public. Witnesses. You have to take control of the entire compound with one shot by killing him and doing it bloody enough that they won't challenge you. He's already primed them to fall in line when faced with a strong leader. We just have to convince them that *you're* that strong leader."

I give Malachi the look that statement deserves. Most of my siblings considered me beneath their notice while I was growing up, and I preferred it that way—fewer people who wanted to kick me when I was down. That might have benefited me growing up, but it hardly primed them to follow me as a leader. "The only chance we have is an attack he doesn't see coming. He needs to be dead before he's able to use his magic. If he gets one word out, we lose. How are we supposed to manage that in public?" Otherwise, we're delivering ourselves right into his hands.

"I don't know yet."

I can't stop my bitter laugh. "Isn't that rather crucial to the plan?" It's not fair to take my frustration out on Malachi. He didn't exactly choose to be held captive by my father for over a hundred years or to be bonded to a seraph when the attempt to gain freedom came with more strings than any of us expected. He needs my father dead just as much as I do.

"Earplugs?"

I'm already shaking my head at Rylan's suggestion. "A few years ago, one of his subordinates tried it. His magic might not work well over electronics or long distances, but normal means of muffling sound don't seem to have an effect." Logically, they *should*, but magic likes to play by its own rules.

"It was worth a suggestion." Rylan gives my shoulders a squeeze. "We'll figure it out."

"We keep saying that, but no brilliant ideas have come." I'm not being fair and I know it, but I can't stop. I shrug out from under Rylan's arm. "I'm going to wash the blood off." I hold up a hand when all three of them tense. "Alone. I need to think."

It's only when I step beneath the water nearly hot enough to scald that my brain starts working properly. I close my eyes and let the worries and mental knots unwind. The men are here. That's already a huge victory and one that shouldn't have been possible if my father had his way. He'll have paraded them before the compound the way he always did in the past with his conquests. Losing them is a blow. Being the one to steal them away *is* a power play that will help establish me as a leader if I manage to kill him.

What they're asking for feels impossible, but they don't have the same history with him that I do. No matter how hard I fight it, my father remains larger than life in my mind. The same isn't true for my men. I need to stop letting my fear control me and *listen*.

By the time I finish my shower, I feel halfway human again. I smile a little at the irony. I might feel halfway human, but I'm not human at all. There has to be some way I can use that. If the seraphim were so feared as a whole, there has to be a reason why. Surely it's not just because when they have sex with vampires, they can bond with them. There must be more.

There has to be.

The men aren't in the bedroom, which is just as well. We

ruined another bed. I stare at the bloodstains and grimace. Someday, when this is all over and we've settled somewhere, we're going to have to invest in plastic sheets on the bed we have sex in and have a strict no-biting rule in the bed we sleep in. I shake my head and pull on a dress from the closet. Like the fridge, it was fully stocked when I arrived. Once dressed, I follow the faint tug of the bond downstairs to the kitchen.

They all look up as I descend the stairs, their expressions varying degrees of wary. Malachi is the one who approaches me. He's always the one who takes that first step, and I'll love him forever because of it.

I clear my throat. "I'm sorry. I shouldn't have snapped. I'm scared, but that's no excuse. You're trying to help."

Malachi takes my hand and tugs me down the last stair and into his arms. "It's nothing. A few sharp words are hardly enough to require forgiveness."

"Still."

He chuckles. "You're forgiven, little dhampir." After one last squeeze, he sets me back. "Shall we feed you?"

Instantly, my mouth waters at the thought of more blood, but he turns to the fridge and that feeling sours. I shake my head. "No. I'm good. I'm not hungry." In fact, I feel the opposite of hungry. I want to fling myself away from the fridge and what it contains.

Malachi frowns. "When did you last eat?"

I start to say this morning, but that's not true. No matter how good it felt to drink Wolf's blood—and Malachi's last night—it doesn't change the fact that it's not *eating*. I touch my stomach. "I'm not hungry," I repeat. When all three of their attentions sharpen on me, I sigh. "I ate... Um." I can't remember. I haven't eaten since the demon deal, I don't think. Maybe the morning after? I vaguely remember being sick. "A day or two."

"Malachi." Rylan says into the silence after my answer. "This isn't outside the realm of possibility. We discussed this. We don't eat. The...baby...is half ours."

"Mina is not a vampire." Malachi speaks softly but he might as well have yelled. "She is not going to be harmed by this pregnancy."

Irritation flares. "For the last goddamned time, *I am standing right here.*" I march past him. "I feel fine, so we're going to chalk this up to some combination of pregnancy, magic, and my strange bloodlines. We have bigger things to focus on. If, at the end of this, we're all left standing, then you can worry and pester me about the pregnancy. First, we need to deal with my father."

Rylan looks like he wants to argue, and I can't see Malachi from my current position but I can feel his displeasure like a flame at my back. Wolf, of course, seems as relaxed as ever. He grins, flashing fangs. "I take it your shower helped."

I nod. "My father has to be our priority. The rest of it can wait. I don't know how we're going to get onto the compound, let alone take him out, but you're right. It's our only option, and we need to do it quickly." I clear my throat and sink down onto the chair next to Wolf. "I'm not going to pretend I have a brilliant plan, but I'm done running." I place the map of the compound I drew for Grace on the center of the table.

It feels strange and a little uncomfortable to sit like this, all of us around the table, but better the table between us so no magic goes funky and we end up having sex for the next three days. I would *love* to be able to do that, but the longer we wait, the higher the chance my father finds us. I don't think there's anything magical about this house. Its location being out of the way and entirely unconnected to any of the vampires is enough to keep us off the radar for a few days, but it won't last forever.

We have to move now. The sooner the better. The vampires disappearing will have disconcerted my father and he'll be desperate to reclaim them. It's likely not enough to make him sloppy, but it's better than nothing.

At least we're not reacting this time. He is. That has to count for something. We have to *make* it count for something.

I quickly update them on the information that Grace passed on. From Grace's information, it seems like not much has changed since I left, aside from increased patrols, and why would it? My father doesn't see me as a threat. He's not going to alter his world because I might be gunning for him.

It's a mistake I hope we can exploit.

"I would wager none of the soldiers he has on-site are powerful enough to be more than a slight inconvenience for you." I point to a spot just south of the main gate. "This is where Grace spent most of her time scouting the place. Because the compound is tucked into a canyon, there are vantage points here, here, and here." I touch each place with a finger.

Malachi takes the pen from me and marks them with a small X. "That will help."

"If you say so." The idea of storming the base with the men is *world's* different from storming the base with just Grace. We should be able to get all the way to the heart of the compound without anyone stopping us.

But that's where it stops being easy.

I stare at the drawing, searching it for anything I've missed. It's as detailed as I can remember, with a few edits from Grace. "The biggest issue is my father's power."

"Yeah. About that." Wolf's pale blue gaze goes contemplative. "He has to speak to use it, right?"

"Yes. He can glamour and the like without speaking, I think. But to use his commands, he has to speak them." I turn to him. "But how do you keep him from speaking?"

Rylan drums his fingers on the table. "Injury would be the easiest way. It won't stick long, not with how old and powerful he is, but even he would take a few seconds to heal a crushed larynx. Maybe up to a minute if someone tears out his throat."

I know my father is powerful, of course. I was raised under his thumb, and I've seen what he does to those less powerful than him. In that compound, *everyone* is less powerful than he is. Still, it feels particularly worrisome to have *these* vampires admit he's a formidable foe. It's not new information, but it still sends a shiver down my spine. "We still have to get close to him to do either of those things."

"Maybe." Malachi sits back, his chair groaning beneath him. "When's the last time you did a ranged attack, Wolf?"

Wolf shrugs, but it's nowhere near the careless body language he normally has. Tension bleeds from him through the bond, winding tighter and tighter. "I haven't had reason to. I'm out of practice."

Malachi hesitates, glances at me, and then sighs. "We should call in your sister." He holds up a hand when Wolf tenses. "I know it's not an ideal situation, but you can't diagnose issues with your blood the way she can. And she's a better ranged attacker than you are by a long shot."

"My sister *poisons* blood." Something almost fearful edges into Wolf's voice. "You're out of your damn mind, Mal. She's as likely to kill Mina as she is to help with anything. There's a reason I haven't seen her in fifty years." He glances at me. "You think I'm a loose cannon? My sister is worse."

He said something to the same effect last night. I'd felt something akin to pity then, but now I don't know what to think. I look between them, taking in their very serious expressions. "It seems like a long shot with greater risk than rewards."

"Mal's right," Rylan says reluctantly. "Lizzie could shoot Cornelius from a mile away and he'd never see the attack coming. It would give us the opportunity to take him out while he can't speak. He's still going to be able to fight, but at least he won't be able to compel."

Wolf's distress flares so brightly, I reach over and cover his hand with mine. He's shaking, just a little, fine tremors that send a surge of fierce protectiveness through me. I look at the other two men. "We're not doing it if Wolf isn't okay with it. It's easy for you to say things will work out and this won't backfire, but it's his family." His family that makes this mad vampire look well-adjusted. I don't know what to think of that. All I know is that I don't want any of my men harmed.

What are the chances of all of us making it out alive?

I don't have an answer for that question.

No one at the table does.

IN THE END, THE TRUTH IS WE HAVE NO OPTIONS.
Unless we nullify my father's ability to compel, any plan we make
is dead in the water. Even dropping a bomb on the compound—if
any of us were willing to do it—wouldn't guarantee my father's
death. He's too old, too savvy. He'd find a way to survive even
that, and then we'd have mass casualties on our heads.

My life was a living hell in that compound, and my father
wasn't the only one responsible for that. But not everyone was a
monster. Not everyone chose cruelty when they could offer kindness instead. I won't say those who showed me kindness as a
child were the majority, but they existed. Even if they hadn't, I'm
not willing to sanction the murder of every adult and child in the
compound. It's too high a cost.

So Wolf phones his sister, Lizzie.

He makes the call in the other room, but even I can hear his side of the conversation, so no doubt Rylan and Malachi can hear both sides. Sure enough, they exchange a long glance. Malachi sighs. "Lizzie is going to be a problem, but we won't let her hurt you."

"Maybe you can fuck her, too, and then the seraph bond will take care of that."

I stare at Rylan. Of all the things to suggest... "Please tell me you're joking."

"Mostly." He grimaces. "It *would* simplify matters, but we'd have to make sure Lizzie didn't kill you during the bonding process, and that's more difficult than you can imagine. She's too unpredictable."

There it is again.

The evidence that they have such a deep history that extends many of my lifetimes in the past. Malachi was in that house for a hundred years, but before that, he was friends and lovers with Rylan and Wolf and others. Maybe even Lizzie. I'm not sure how I feel about that. Not jealous, exactly. Just...strange.

"If you want to know, you can ask."

I jump, startled out of my thoughts by Malachi's low voice. There's no mistaking what question he's talking about. I force myself to meet his gaze. "Were you lovers? Either of you?"

"Not me." Rylan doesn't exactly shudder, but it's there in his voice. "I prefer my throat intact."

"I was, briefly." Malachi holds my gaze. "Does that bother you?"

"I don't know," I say honestly. "I don't think so, but it feels strange. We've been very isolated up to this point, so part of it is that, I think." I'm going to have to get used to the feeling that there are great swathes of these men's history unavailable to me, at least outside sharing stories. We have the future, and that's enough. It has to be. "I guess we'll deal with it as it comes."

Wolf walks back into the room, unhappiness in every line of his body. "She's in LA right now, but she's all too happy to dive into the chaos and do a little murder." His voice goes up on the last part of the sentence, obviously mimicking his sister. "She'll be here in about ten hours."

Every hour is a risk at this point, but this delay is one we can't avoid.

Wolf comes back to the table, but instead of reclaiming his chair, he sinks down onto the floor next to me. He puts his head in my lap and wraps his arms around my waist. I freeze. "Wolf?"

"I'm fine."

He's lying. Now that he's touching me, the bond flares between us, soaked in his misery. I tentatively clasp the back of his neck and massage a little. He responds by going boneless, though his unhappiness doesn't abate. I look at the other two men. "Someone explain this to me. Now, please."

Rylan shifts. "Fifty years ago, Lizzie set Wolf on fire."

"*Excuse me?*"

I know him well enough to recognize that his cold tone is a way of masking his emotions. He holds my gaze and continues. "They had a disagreement and she felt that was a reasonable way to deal with it. He almost died."

The table creaks beneath Malachi's hands. "You didn't see fit to mention that *before* we called her."

I get a sense of Rylan's internal conflict through the bond, but none of it shows in his face or tone. "We don't have any other options."

I keep massaging Wolf's neck and try to think past the fury that burns through me. "Tell her not to come. There has to be another way."

"No other way." Wolf speaks against my thigh. "She's the best. If she helps, it's a sure thing—at least that part of it."

Killing my father is the top priority, but I never expected the cost to be so high. That feels very naive right now, with Wolf feeling so small and human against me. I want to protect him, to wrap him up and keep him safe, and that isn't the world we live in. "It's not worth the cost."

He tightens his hold around my hips. "I'm fine," he repeats.

He most assuredly is *not* fine. Not when he's clutching me like his favorite toy. I look to Malachi and Rylan for help, but they're staring at each other and engaging in one of those silent arguments that I'm not a part of. Malachi is obviously furious they didn't tell him what happened, and Rylan is clearly digging in his heels on his stance.

Huh. Apparently I can read them a lot better now, whether from the experience of being in close proximity for a few weeks or maybe as a side effect of the bond. Their argument ultimately won't change anything. I have to go off what Wolf says. He's my priority right now.

"Feels nice."

I blink. "What?"

He shifts enough to look up at me out of one eye. "Being the priority. Wish it were better circumstances."

Guilt slaps me hard enough to make me shake. "I'm sorry. I know I said it before, but things haven't calmed down enough to talk about it. I'm sorry I compelled you." Bad enough to do it, but then to simply not talk about it as if it's beneath notice? I can't believe I let it get this far. "Maybe now isn't the time to talk about it..."

"Mina."

The shock of him saying my name makes me tense. "Yes?"

"You're strong."

It's such a random statement that I stare down at him blankly. "What?"

"Don't apologize for being strong."

I feel like we're having two different conversations. "I'm not apologizing for being strong. I'm apologizing for forcing you to do something you didn't want to do. Strong or not, it's not right. I love you." The last comes out in a rush. "I love all of you. I don't want to hurt you and I don't want to take your choices away. I shouldn't have compelled you. You *are* a priority to me."

"Seems like a silly thing to apologize for."

"Why would you say that?"

He straightens and wedges himself between my thighs. Wolf isn't as tall as Rylan and Malachi, but he's more than a few inches taller than me. We're nearly the same height like this. He holds my gaze, his blue eyes strikingly serious. "If you hadn't made that call and forced the issue, we'd still be in your father's tender care.

Call me unhinged all you want, but I'm not a fool. I underestimated you." He gives a sharp grin that almost looks like the old Wolf. "Maybe I should be the one apologizing."

"I *compelled* you." Like my father does to those around him. I took away Wolf's willpower and forced an answer out of him.

"Yep." He laughs suddenly. "Gods, love, but seeing you twist yourself up over this is enough to make me feel loads better." He leans up and presses a kiss to my lips. "If you need my forgiveness, you have it."

I sigh. "That doesn't help with your sister."

"Just sleep with her, too, and it will be a moot point."

I frown. "Why is everyone so invested in me adding people to the bond? That's the opposite of what we need if she's as bad as you say." Not to mention three bed partners is *a lot*. I can't imagine trying to juggle the needs of more, let alone one as volatile as Wolf's sister seems to be. No matter what else is true of our little group, the caring between us is real. The men's goes back several human lifetimes. Mine is newer but no less valid. "Besides, even if I could compel her, it only works in spurts. It's not something that I can hold to ensure good behavior."

"I'm joking, love." Wolf shakes his head. "No matter what else is true, I do *not* want to be linked that closely with her. Better to get her agreement to pull this off for us and then to go our separate ways."

I don't have answers. I don't know that I ever have. But we have time and I want to wash away that faintly lost look in Wolf's eyes. *This* I know how to do. *This* is a way I can help. I cup his face between my hands and kiss him. I start gently, teasing his mouth open and delving inside. For once, Wolf doesn't immediately take control. He meets my kiss halfway, but he allows me to lead us.

He tastes so purely *Wolf* that I moan a little. I nip his bottom lip. "Trade places with me."

He moves all at once, surging up and lifting me into his arms. I expect him to do as I say, but instead he whisks us into the living room. I end up on my knees between his thighs, staring up at him. "Wolf?"

"Floor's killer on the knees."

The small act of caring only drives the desire to return the favor all the more. I slide my hands up his thighs. "I'm taking off your pants now."

"Don't let me stop you." But he's the one who undoes the front of his pants and lifts his hips so I can work them down his thighs. It takes a little maneuvering to get them fully off, but it's more than worth it when I reclaim my position with nothing between me and Wolf's body. He's so deceptively beautiful. The aura and mohawk kind of shield that truth, but when I have him like this, there's no denying it.

I can hear Malachi and Rylan still speaking softly in the kitchen. Arguing softly, more like it. I can't do much about that right now. They'll argue and debate and eventually come to an agreement on how to deal with Lizzie and the coming confrontation. I've given them the map of the compound and I'll provide any additional information they need, though we all are aware that it's somewhat outdated, even with Grace surveying the compound from a distance. I can't do anything to help the plan right now.

But Wolf?

I can help Wolf.

I want my vampire back. I don't like the brittle look that's appeared in his eyes. Of the three, he's always seemed the most untouchable, the one who is carefree and more than a little wild. Right now, he seems almost…human.

"Wolf." I lean down and rub my cheek on his bare thigh. "Do you know what I would like right now?"

He sifts his fingers through my hair. Not tugging. Not guiding. Just touching me as if the very contact soothes him. "What?"

"I want to take care of you." He tenses against me so I press a kiss to his thigh. "Will you let me do that?"

"I thought you were going to tell me to fuck your mouth." He gives a low, strained laugh. "Quite the twist there, love."

"Is it so shocking?" They've taken care of me since we met. Yes, there was some circling on whether they wanted to keep or kill me—at least where Wolf and Rylan were concerned—but ultimately that threat didn't last long past the initial meeting. They have bolstered me, have encircled me, have lifted me up to make me stronger.

The very least I can do is return the favor.

More, I *want* to.

Wolf shakes his head slowly. "No. Guess it's not." He smiles slowly, almost looking like himself again. "Very well. Do your worst."

"Oh, Wolf. I'm not going to do my worst." I wrap my hand around his thick cock. "I'm going to do my very best."

14

OF THE THREE MEN, I LOVE SUCKING WOLF'S COCK THE most. He's the only one who is more than happy to finish in my mouth if I'm so inclined. Both Rylan and Malachi were always so focused on not missing an opportunity to impregnate me. I might start like this, with their hard length pressing against my tongue, but it never lasted long before they'd lose patience and haul me up their bodies to fuck me.

Wolf alone let me take my time.

I suck him down, keeping my gaze on his face. He watches me closely, gaze almost predatory. I shiver and take him deeper. The power balance here is a knife's edge between him and me. He could easily overpower me. I hold his pleasure and pain between my lips. I suck hard and am instantly rewarded when he hisses out a breath and lets his head fall back to rest against the couch.

It's not submission. Not truly. But he's letting me hold the reins for now.

The temptation to take him deep, again and again, until he loses control is almost too much to bear. That's not what I want right now, though. I want to make him forget all his worries, to release the stress tightening his shoulders, to get him to focus only on me.

I tighten my grip on his cock just a little and release him with my mouth. He starts to open his eyes, but I'm already moving, licking down his length to play my tongue along his balls. Wolf's thighs go tight on either side of me. "Fuck," he breathes.

I started this process for him, but I can't deny my pure joy at my slow exploration. It's not the first time I've done it, but it's the first time he's given me this much control. His legs are shaking and he's dug his fists so hard into the couch, he's punctured the cushions, but still he doesn't try to rush me.

I keep sucking and teasing, ignoring the ache that blooms in my jaw as a result. It doesn't matter. I can take more than a little discomfort, especially as Wolf's expression goes slack and languid. Finally, when time ceases to have meaning and we're both shaking with need, I move back the smallest bit.

"Wolf." I flick my tongue against the underside of the head of his cock. "How do you want to finish?"

His mouth works for several moments before words emerge. "Come up here, love. I want to be in that sweet pussy when I come."

I give him one last long suck, taking his entire length in, and then release him and climb up to straddle his hips. "Like this?"

"Yeah. Like that."

I sink slowly onto his cock. It feels good enough that I nearly lose myself, but this isn't about me. Not this time. It's about him and what he needs. I work myself up and down his length, rolling my hips in a way that makes crimson overtake the blue of his eyes. "Let go, Wolf." I cup his face with my hands. "I've got you."

He wraps his arms around me and pulls me closer yet. I can't move well like this, but it doesn't matter because he's taking over. He holds me tightly and pumps up into me. I moan. Gods, this feels too good. "Wolf, I—"

He bites me.

I come so hard, I see stars. I'm vaguely aware of him licking his way up my throat and taking my mouth as he follows me over the edge. Each near-violent thrust up into me makes my orgasm surge higher. I'm sobbing against his lips and he's holding me closer yet. Just when it edges into being too much, he slumps back to the couch, taking me with him. I lie there with my ear against his chest and I can *feel* his tension easing. I've never experienced anything quite like it. Is this what the men feel from me without my shields? It's not mind reading. Wolf's thoughts are his own. But I can almost see his emotions. It's strange but not bad. Not bad at all.

I kiss his throat. "Better?"

"Yeah." He huffs out a laugh. "Yeah, I guess it is." Wolf squeezes me. "Take care of me anytime you want, love."

I sense Rylan and Malachi coming closer. They certainly don't make any sound to give away their presence. I turn my head enough to see them standing in the doorway to the kitchen. Rylan looks conflicted but Malachi's face is an expressionless mask. "We have a plan."

Wolf gives me one last squeeze and helps me off him, though he doesn't let me get far. Instead, he pulls me back down onto his lap and wraps his arms around me. I tentatively send out a tendril of awareness through the bond, acting purely on instinct. He still feels calmer, but the inner turmoil beneath the calm surface is causing ripples. There's not much I can do about that, not until we see ourselves through this mess.

He closes me out gently, pushing me away as he reinstates his shield. It's not as impenetrable as a stone wall—I can still get a hint of what he's feeling beyond it—but he closes me out all the same.

"Sorry," I murmur. I didn't mean to invade his privacy. No, that's not accurate. I *did* reach out, but I still have hardly any idea of what I'm doing.

"I dropped my shields. It was practically an invitation." Though there's still a faint tremor in his tone, he sounds more like his old self.

Malachi and Rylan sink onto the couch across the coffee table from us. Malachi leans forward and sets my makeshift maps on the table. "We have a plan." He points to the two buildings near the rear of the compound. I've labeled them as armory and gym. "We'll set fire to both of these. We'll do it during the day so as to minimize casualties."

Rylan takes over. "It should draw most of the guards in that direction, both to put out the fire and to search for who started it. I don't think they're poorly trained enough to leave their posts completely abandoned, but it should alleviate some of the extra personnel." He pauses. "Then you come in through the front gate."

I blink. "That's bold."

"It's the weakest point. More, this conflict is as much about presentation as it is about killing your father. We need witnesses. The courtyard will have to be it." Malachi drags a hand through his long hair. He points to one of the Xs he made near the front. "We'll set up Lizzie here. Will she be able to see the courtyard from this location?"

I peer at the map, trying to hold it up to what Grace and I spoke of. I didn't leave the compound when I lived there, but I spent enough time staring at the surrounding area to know roughly what spot she had indicated. "It's a long shot."

"That's why we have Lizzie."

It seems impossible, but these three men have already proved themselves to be capable of impossible things. "I think so. We'd have to get him into the right position." I close my eyes and picture it. If she's aiming for his throat, he'd have to be facing the gates but at a slight angle leaning toward the shooter's position. "That adds to the impossibility factor, because getting him there will give him more of a chance to compel one or all of us."

Wolf tightens his grip around my waist. "Rylan has an idea, don't you?"

"Yeah." Rylan holds my gaze. "You're going in alone."

"*What?*"

"You're right. Your father's power is a threat while you get him into position. We can't guarantee he won't be able to use it, and if he does, we're more of a liability than a help." He nods at Malachi. "Mal will be setting fires. Wolf and I will go in to the east and west and do what damage to the forces we can. Maybe set a few fires ourselves if we can find a way to do it that won't result in more deaths." His dark eyes are sympathetic. "You were always going to be the one to kill Cornelius, Mina. It has to be you."

My chest threatens to close, but I haven't come this far to fold now. Which sounds great in theory, but the thought of having to face down my father alone makes me want to start running and never stop. I'm not so panicked that I don't notice the way all three of them tense up in response to my emotions. I have to breathe, to think, to process this. "Just…give me a second."

They sit silently as I battle through my instinctive denial. When we were initially talking about returning to that place and doing what was necessary to ensure our safety, at least I had the relative comfort of knowing my men would have my back. Walking through the front gates alone, even if the men won't be too far, feels like too much. I am stronger than I used to be, but I'm nowhere near as strong as my father.

He could kill me.

He'll certainly try.

I press my hand to my stomach. There's only one way to make him pause, and it means giving him information I'd do anything to ensure he doesn't have. It means trusting my men and the plan and myself in a way I don't know if I'm capable of.

Finally, I drag in a breath. "I don't know what will happen

to his compulsion if he's injured." All evidence suggests he needs to concentrate to use his powers, the same as the other bloodline vampires. If his concentration is broken, say by a blood bullet to his throat, the compulsion *should* break.

Am I willing to put myself under my father's control for even that long?

I open my eyes. I can't see Wolf, but Rylan and Malachi look at me solemnly. They know what they're asking, what we're risking. If I die, there's a decent chance it will hurt them, if not kill them. They're asking a lot, but they're putting so much faith in me that it staggers me. We'll only get one shot at this.

We'll either succeed or we'll die trying.

"I'm scared."

"I know." Malachi's eyes go soft. "We wouldn't ask if there was another way."

"I know." I run my fingers over Wolf's bare arm. Really, there's no point in letting panic win. This is the only way. If I think about it, it was only ever going to end like this, with me facing down my father once and for all. "You're both right. There is no other way. I'll do it."

Wolf finally sets me aside, though he laces his fingers through mine. "You'll have to take his head, and you have to do it showy enough to scare people into obeying you right off the bat. Lizzie will start the process, but that's the only way to guarantee that bastard doesn't come back to haunt us and no one challenges you while you're still reeling. Then we burn the body."

I wait for the idea of killing my father to inspire some hesitation or even guilt, but the only thing I feel is grim resolution. It's him or me. If I want a chance at the future, to give my...child...a future, then he needs to die.

Wolf could probably form his blood into a weapon to do it for him. Rylan could partially shift and tear my father's head from his shoulders. Malachi could burn him until there's nothing left to heal.

Theoretically, I'll be able to do all three with the way we seem to be able to borrow powers from each other. But my control has left something to be desired. I don't have the training and while sometimes they manifest, they never do it reliably. Whether the pregnancy was to blame or just my lack of experience is up for debate. I wasn't able to use them even before I found out I was pregnant.

I'll have to do it the old-fashioned way. "I'm going to need a blade," I finally say. "Thankfully, Grace left behind a whole stack to choose from."

"Mina." Malachi watches me closely. "If you don't want to do this—"

"There's no other way." I shake my head. "Let's not waste time trying to find other options. If this is the plan, we need to perfect it."

Malachi hesitates but finally nods. "Let's go over it step by step."

15

WHILE I'M NOT FEELING PARTICULARLY CONFIDENT, AT least I know the steps of the plan by heart after we go through it a few times. Whether or not it will work… I don't know. There are too many things beyond our control, which means too many things that could go wrong. The most important of these, of course, is Wolf's sister.

She should arrive any minute.

Rylan and Malachi went hunting earlier, returning rosy-cheeked and brimming with health. They fed Wolf, but no one offered to feed me. I can feel the hunger stirring—I'll have to eat again before we attack the compound—but I'm just grateful they've stopped trying to feed me human food. The very thought disgusts me. That revulsion will worry me later, when I have time and energy to think about the implications. First, I have to focus on the threat directly in front of me.

Lizzie.

I don't expect to feel her approach. It's been so long since I've been around other vampires, and I certainly didn't feel my father and his people break into the mountain home. This is different. Very different. I lift my head, turning in the direction of the sensation. It feels a bit like what I imagine all the water being sucked out before a tsunami hits feels like. "What is that?"

"Lizzie." Wolf bites out her name. "She's not bothering to shield. She wants us to know she's coming."

Without saying another word, we move into the living room. It's got a clear view of both front and back doors. Malachi nudges me to the love seat that backs a wall with no windows and then pushes Wolf gently down next to me. "Let me and Rylan do the talking."

"That won't work and you know it." Wolf's voice shakes a little, but he's more composed than he was this morning in the kitchen. "She won't be satisfied with that."

I place my hand on his thigh, a fierce protectiveness surging. If this vampire thinks she can come in here and harm those I care about, she'll have to go through me to do it. I squeeze his thigh. "She will not touch you." Something akin to power thrums through my voice. It feels strange, and all three of the men tense in response.

The door flies open before anyone has a chance to comment on it.

I don't know what I expected of Wolf's sister. Perhaps someone like him, who dresses in a style that's Victorian crossed with underground club scene. Someone who feels out of time. Someone fiercely beautiful and wildly unhinged.

The woman who walks through the door looks like a suburban housewife in her dark jeans, cream knit sweater, and knee-high boots. Her dark hair is pulled back into a perfect, sleek ponytail and her makeup is present but tasteful. She's wearing a *floral headband.* She's attractive in a generic kind of way, but she doesn't possess the kind of beauty that will stop people in their tracks. She's devastatingly normal.

At least until I look into her icy blue eyes. There's no warmth there, no soul.

She smiles, flashing fang. "Hello, baby brother."

Wolf goes still beside me. "Lizzie."

She surveys the room, her gaze flicking dismissively over Rylan before lingering on Malachi. "Interesting company you're keeping these days." Her grin never wavers. "Nice to see you out and about, Mal. Silly of you to fall into that trap in the first place."

"Lizzie," he rumbles. "You'd better be here to help rather than cause unnecessary trouble."

"I never cause trouble unnecessarily." She finally looks at me, blue eyes assessing. "So this is the new girlfriend. Welcome to the family, sweet girl." She takes one step toward me and laughs when all three men jolt. "Relax, lads. If I was going to kill her, I wouldn't have walked through the front door."

Rylan makes a vaguely snarling sound that shouldn't have been able to come from a human mouth. "Don't fuck with us, Lizzie."

"Can't blame a girl for having a little fun. Everyone is so *tense.*" She walks over to the chair where Malachi sits and props a hip against it. "Now, tell me who you want me to kill. I feel a tad bit guilty about the little fire incident last time we met, so I'm willing to play nice for the duration." She feathers her fingers through Malachi's long hair. "Besides, I couldn't resist the temptation to see old friends."

She's toying with Wolf. Maybe with me, too. Testing. I might even appreciate how thoroughly she disrupted the room with a few short sentences if the stakes weren't so damned high. "You're not going to be able to kill anyone. We simply need you to shoot him in the throat."

She turns those eerie eyes on me again. When I first met Wolf, his eyes spooked me. Compared to Lizzie, he seems downright welcoming and normal. It's strange to realize that. Wolf has become known and familiar to me in our time together, but I don't think that's a possibility with his sister.

She's fucking terrifying.

Lizzie stops playing with Malachi's hair and straightens. "Explain. My baby brother was sparse on the details."

I open my mouth, but Rylan beats me to the punch. It's just as well. For whatever reason, Lizzie seems less interested in messing with him than with anyone else in the room. He leans forward. "We're going to kill Cornelius Lancaster."

She doesn't seem shocked. She doesn't react at all. "Big game you're hunting. Even with my help, he's likely to kill you all." She laughs, a thread of madness in the sound. "I'm not getting close to that canny old bastard."

"We don't need or want you to get close." Rylan points to the maps on the coffee table. He and Malachi found topographical ones somewhere, so they've overlaid those with my drawings to get a better idea of exactly what we're working with. "You're the best long-range attacker in this realm."

"Flattery will get you everywhere." She scans the map and then looks back at him. "Explain what you want. Then I'll tell you my price."

"You'll be here." He points to the X south of the compound. "It's high enough that you'll have a clear shot of the courtyard." Rylan moves his finger to the X drawn in the compound. "Cornelius will be there. We need you to shoot him in the throat and put enough power behind it to destroy his vocal cords."

"He'll heal fast."

"That's our problem."

More likely, that's *my* problem, but I appreciate the sentiment. Even if I'm the one facing my father, we're all in this together. I lean a little harder against Wolf. He hasn't moved since Lizzie walked into the room, tracking her the way a mouse tracks a cat. It's disconcerting in the extreme.

Rylan sits back. "Will you do it?"

"Sure." She shrugs. "If Wolf comes home."

I'm already shaking my head. "No. That's out of the question."

"Be quiet, little girl. The grown-ups are talking." She turns to Rylan. "You swept him away after that little misunderstanding and it put me in a bad way with our mother. Wolf needs to come home."

"No," I say again. I start to stand, but Wolf clamps an arm around my waist and keeps me sitting. "No," I repeat. "Whatever price you need, *I'll* pay it. Anything else is out of the question."

She raises an eyebrow, looking unimpressed. "What could

you possibly offer me that's worth the risk I'm taking? You're a nobody. If you were someone, I would have heard of you by now."

I'm not about to tell this dangerous woman that I'm a seraph. But that's not the only bargaining chip I have. I catch Malachi's eye and he gives a tight nod. He'll follow my lead. Rylan and Wolf will follow his.

I gently disentangle myself from Wolf and stand. "I'm Cornelius's daughter. His heir."

She narrows her eyes. "You say that, and yet the fact remains that I haven't heard of you. You could be anyone playing dress-up." Her eyes flare crimson for a beat before returning to their normal icy blue. "You don't feel particularly powerful. Smells like bullshit from where I'm standing."

"If you're aware of that much about my father, then you're aware of the stipulations about what it takes to become his heir." A gamble, but she's right. I have little in the way of bargaining power. If we succeed, that will change, but first I need to convince her.

Her gaze flicks to my stomach and her eyes flare crimson again. Lizzie shrugs. "So you're pregnant. That doesn't mean your story holds up. His children would be smart enough to get declared heir before they started sharpening their knives and aiming for that bastard's back."

"I prefer a more direct route." I wave my hand at the three men. "My father has never seen power that he hasn't tried to claim for his own. There's a reason *this* is the stipulation to become his heir. If I try to do this the proper way, he'll lock me up, take the baby, and claim it as his own via one of his mistresses, and likely try to claim the father as well." No need to tell her that he almost accomplished that goal already.

She studies each of the men in turn, finally landing on Wolf. "Is my brother the father?"

It's tempting to lie, but I have a feeling she'll know if I do. I shrug. "I don't know who the father is at this point. We won't know until I have the baby, and that will only happen if we survive what comes next."

"Hmm." She taps a finger to her bottom lip, painted a perfect pale pink. "If you're lying to me, I'll take it poorly."

I think I hear Wolf inhale sharply behind me, but I don't look away from his sister. "I'm not lying."

"So it seems. Not telling the full truth, but not lying." She shrugs. "Ah well, if the little beast inside you is really Radu blood, then our mother will skin me alive if I don't help now. Let me see." She starts for me, and both Malachi and Rylan jump to their feet. Lizzie smirks. "*Relax*, lads. I'll just do a scan. Nothing sinister." She reaches out and presses her fingertip to the back of my hand. A faint tingle goes through my entire body in a wave and she raises her eyebrows. "Interesting."

"What?"

"You don't seem the type to consort with demons, but there's a faint..." She licks her lips, gaze distant. "Cute little shield. The embryo is fine. Powerful little bugger, but too early to know the flavor." She refocuses on me. "I'm in. I'll do what you ask."

I don't breathe a sigh of relief. This was only the first step, and I'm not naive enough to believe Lizzie until she actually shoots my father. "Your price?"

"If you're successful in this cute little coup, you'll owe the Radu family a favor." Her smile goes knife-sharp. "And you will entertain us for a few days in your new compound."

I don't need to look at my men to recognize the trap. If—when—we succeed, that will put me at the head of the Lancaster bloodline. For better or worse, I will be a power whose choices mean something, affect the balance of our world. I lift my chin. It would be smarter to negotiate the favor away and entertain them while promising nothing, but I won't do that to Wolf. He feels the same way about the rest of his family as he does about his sister. Having them in close proximity will be a hellish experience for him. I refuse to put him through it. "I will not be entertaining anyone in the foreseeable future, but I am willing to negotiate a favor, provided it does no harm to me, my men, or my people, either directly or indirectly." Still too wide an offer, but I need her and she knows it.

Her grin widens. "Very well. A favor it is." She turns back to the map. "Walk me through the nitty-gritty details."

I sink back onto the couch as Rylan and Malachi launch into a brief overview of what they need from Lizzie. Fine tremors work their way through my body, the adrenaline letdown nearly making me sick to my stomach. Though I can't hide my physical reaction to the confrontation, I refuse to give in to it entirely while Lizzie is in the room.

Wolf laces his fingers through mine. Through the bond, I feel a wave of gratitude from him. I'm sure Malachi and Rylan will have thoughts about my choice later, but I can only do what I think is right. Rylan seems to have a complicated relationship with his family, but there's no fear there. Malachi has no family left at all. Surely they wouldn't expect me to throw Wolf to the, well, to the wolves?

I squeeze Wolf's hand and listen as the other two men go through an abbreviated version of the plan. I note that they leave out a few key components. Smart. Really, we have no reason to trust Lizzie with all the details. The only thing she needs to know pertains to my father, the courtyard, and her long-distance attack.

She finally sits back and laughs a little. "This should be fun. When do we start?"

"At dawn."

16

AFTER WE GO OVER THE PLAN ONE LAST TIME, RYLAN escorts Lizzie off the property. I keep part of my attention on his presence, monitoring his emotions for any spike that might indicate she's attacked him. It's getting easier to keep track of the men. They all shield too well for me to get much more than a faint impression, but I think that's preferable for everyone. I don't want to invade their privacy, and I look forward to a time when I'm able to get my own shields in place.

If we survive the next twenty-four hours, maybe I'll even manage it.

"We will."

I glance at Malachi. "You know I hate it when you do that."

"It's difficult not to when you're thinking so loudly." He takes my hand and tugs me against his chest so he can wrap his arms around me. Wolf said he needs a little time alone and headed in the opposite direction of both his sister and the town. His presence along the bond doesn't feel as calm as Rylan's, but he's not in a full-out panic state anymore.

This is, I realize, the first time Malachi and I have been alone in quite some time. I run my hands up his chest and look into his dark eyes. "There are more ways tomorrow could go wrong than there are ways it could go right."

"I know." He cups my face and drags his thumb along my lower lip. "But we've survived impossible scenarios already. What's one more?"

"That logic is so incredibly flawed."

He gives a brief smile. "It's the only logic I have."

I don't understand how he can be so steady, so unafraid, so sure things will work out. "Even injured, my father is a significant threat. He's stronger than me, faster than me, and—"

"He's not more determined than you." Malachi holds my gaze. "He'll be fighting for his life. You'll be fighting for so much more." He presses a kiss to my forehead. "We won't leave you to do it alone. All three of us will be fighting our way to you. You just need to survive until we get there."

Survive and prove I'm strong enough to rule.

I tuck myself under his arm. "Lizzie asked a question earlier…"

I don't know if it's the bond or merely Malachi's intuitiveness that has him sensing the direction of my thoughts. "About the baby's father."

"Yes." It's something I didn't even *think* could be an issue, mostly because I've only been focusing on the immediate future and survival. But the fact remains that no matter what magic is capable of, science reigns supreme when it comes to eggs and sperm and the like. Which means that this baby has a single biological father. It's strange to think of it as a baby. I've barely come to terms with the fact that I'm pregnant, let alone what the end result will be.

Still, the last thing I want to do is cause harm if I can avoid it. I just don't know if I *can* avoid it. "I don't want anything to come between the four of us. It feels like every time we find some measure of peace, we get kicked in the teeth and something happens that messes everything up. I don't—" I take a deep breath. "I said I want to keep the pregnancy and I meant it, but I also don't want the baby to be a point of contention."

Malachi smiles gently. "Come, little dhampir. Do you really think so little of us that we'd fight over a baby like dogs with a bone?" He sifts his hands through my hair. "That baby is ours. All of ours. The genetics and powers matter little."

Some tension I didn't realize I was carrying leaks out of me. I press my forehead to his chest and let him hold me for a few beats. "I want this to work."

"I know. It will."

There's plenty for me to fear. I should focus on what happens tomorrow, for one. But I can't help spinning out a future with several children, with a *family* that's built on love and respect instead of fear and threats. I have a chance at that future with Malachi and Rylan and Wolf. We just have to survive long enough to take it.

"Okay." I lift my head. "Okay. Thank you."

"I love you." He says it softly, as if it's a simple truth and not one that rocks me every time those three little words leave his lips. "I love them, too. We are a unit, Mina. All four of us. I know this hasn't been an easy journey and it's not likely to get easier, but we *will* prevail." His hold on me tightens before he seems to force himself to relax. "We will cut down anyone who threatens our future. *Anyone.*"

With that kind of promise, what can I do but return it? I go up on my tiptoes and press a kiss to his lips. "Starting tomorrow, with my father."

⁓◦❧◦⁓

I half expect a night that feels like our last night in this world, but everyone is sober and distracted. Malachi keeps his arms around me, but both Rylan and Wolf pass by with casual touching as we settle down for the night. They're all too wired to sleep, but I can feel it pulling at my eyelids, a tyrant lord demanding their due.

"You need to eat."

It takes me a moment to realize Malachi is talking to me. "I'm not hungry." It's not strictly true. My stomach is empty and craving blood, not food. But considering how Malachi's reacted to *that* fact so far, I don't think he'll welcome the news. Not to mention part of me is scared to feed that way again. What if I lose control? Our plan is too carefully balanced to have one of the men out of commission because I went too far and drained too much.

"Little dhampir." He shakes his head. "I might not understand what's going on, but that doesn't mean I'll allow you to go without."

"You can't harm us," Rylan says from where he's just pulled

on a pair of lounge pants. "We're stronger than you and there are more of us. If you get out of control, we're more than capable of handling it."

I blush. I can't help it. "I get overwhelmed."

"That's just practice, love. All baby vamps get a little wild." Wolf flashes fang. He's not quite back to normal—I don't think he will be until we're done dealing with his sister—but he's a bit more of his wild and charismatic self.

"Come, Mina." Malachi practically carries me to the bed and drops onto it with me in his lap. He holds me with my back to his chest and offers me his arm. "Drink."

"Are you sure?"

"Yes. I'll not have you weak simply because we don't understand what's going on. Obviously you're taking blood the same way a full vampire does. We'll not deprive you."

I press my fingers to my lips. "What if my teeth change again and I do damage?"

"Try to control it."

Considering I still don't know *what* is going on with me, trying to control it is a laughable objective. Still, for them, I will attempt it. "Okay."

"Your claws."

It takes a moment to realize he's speaking to me, to understand what he wants. I close my eyes and concentrate, trying to envision my fingers changing to claws the way they've done in the past. For a beat, nothing happens, but then a faint tingling starts at my fingertips. It's tempting to open my eyes, but I resist, focusing on that feeling, on expanding it until my nails shift.

When I finally look down, the tips of my fingers have morphed to dainty claws. They're small, but they're sharp. "Could I do more?"

"This is how training starts." Rylan leans forward to examine my new fingers. "You have to work up to a full shift, because if you panic halfway through…" He doesn't quite shudder, but the feeling is there in his voice. "It won't kill you, but it's a painful and scary experience. Better to wait until you master this first."

The thought of being stuck in some half-transformed state makes me feel vaguely ill. "I don't know if I'll ever be ready for that."

"You will." He says it with a quiet confidence that makes me take it as truth. Maybe someday I'll be able to shift into a giant wolf the same way he can and we'll run together. The thought pleases me. It's not something I would have sought out as an ultimate dream before now, but I want it. Another part of our future that I will fight to be able to experience.

I drag a single claw along Malachi's forearm. Not deep enough that it won't heal easily, but it also won't close immediately. He presses his forearm to my mouth and I drink greedily. The first explosion of his blood against my tongue feels so right that I moan. This. *This* is what I've been craving.

Drinking this time isn't the frenzy from before. I can feel that monster inside me, pressing up against my skin, but Malachi's blood sates it before it has a chance to crave more. Or maybe I just haven't depleted the energy I got from the last feeding. This is all so new, it's impossible to say for sure.

All I know is that I lean back a few minutes later, sated and sleepy. "Thank you."

"Sleep now." Malachi's words rumble through my back. "We'll look out for you."

I want to stay awake. I do. But with his blood thrumming through my veins, my body has other ideas. My blinks lengthen and deepen. I'm aware of Rylan reclining on the bed next to us and Wolf flopping on top of him with a casual intimacy that makes my lips curve.

Together.

We're together.

This is how I want it to be.

Always.

17

WHEN I WAS DRAGGED FROM MY FATHER'S COMPOUND and tossed in a car to be delivered to Malachi, I never thought to return. I wasn't supposed to live this long. I can admit that now, crouched precariously high in a tree and looking down over the familiar walls and buildings.

He planned for me to die by Malachi's hand. A convenient snack that got his powerless dhampir daughter out of his hair and kept the trapped bloodline vampire alive. Malachi and I were never supposed to get along, to fall in love. We were never supposed to join up with Wolf and Rylan and break the blood ward, awaken the powers no one thought I had, and come for my father's head.

It's happening now.

There's no going back.

"Can you make the shot, Lizzie?" Malachi's hand is warm where it's wrapped around my bicep. I'm not in danger of falling, but he's taking no risks. I don't move with the same supernatural grace as the vampires, but my balance is better than it's ever been. A good thing, that. I'm going to need every advantage I can come up with for the pending confrontation.

Lizzie is in the next tree over. She's wearing high-end workout leggings, a long-sleeved shirt, and a puffy vest. She's added a soft headband to her ponytail today. She looks like she should be jogging in some carefully curated park...except for the rifle slung across her back.

She narrows her eyes at the compound. "I can make the shot. This is well within my range."

I blink. I know this is why we risked asking for her assistance, but the compound has to be a mile away. Maybe more. "Even for your powers?"

She smirks. "Yes, little girl. Even for my powers. You get him where I can see him, and there won't be much left of his throat when the hit lands."

We estimated a timeline based on the worst-case scenario. Even so, getting my father out into the courtyard is going to be a risk. *He's going to compel me.* That's the one thing we haven't spoken about, that no one's addressed directly. To keep my father complacent enough for Lizzie's attack to land, I have to lose. There's no guarantee that his power will break when his concentration does, but I'm not one of his followers, happy to follow his instructions and open to compulsion. I will be fighting it every step of the way.

It will break.

It has to.

And that's when I'll strike.

"Then we move." Malachi scoops me into his arms before I have a chance to tense and drops down to the forest floor. Rylan and Wolf land soundlessly on either side of him. There's no need to speak. We went over the plan one last time before leaving the house. They'll deposit me just outside the sentry lines and I'll wait ten minutes while they circle around to their respective locations.

At that point, I walk into the compound to surrender myself and seek an audience with my father. Then the fires start. That should draw the extra soldiers away from the courtyard. My father will suspect the truth—that the three vampires are attacking—but he still views me as a powerless dhampir. He won't have reason to keep security around himself because he's never needed help to deal with me before.

I'll only have one chance.

The first faint hint of sunrise is fighting back the dark of the sky when Malachi sets me carefully on my feet. He hugs me tightly. "This isn't goodbye."

It might be. It's easier for things to go wrong with this plan than it is for them to go right. None of that matters now. We've come too far to turn back, which means this isn't the time or place for doubts. I pull him down for a quick kiss. "I'll see you soon."

He steps back and then Wolf is there, whisking me into a dip and planting a kiss on my lips. "Give them hell, love."

And then there's Rylan. He takes my hands and looks down

at them for a long moment. "Fear and pain can help motivate a change. Not panic, though. It's a fine line." He squeezes my hands. "You are *never* defenseless, Mina. Not with our powers flowing through your blood. Trust them and trust yourself." He kisses me quickly. "Stay alive."

There's a beat of hesitation, as if we're all waiting for someone to speak up, to call the whole thing off. The temptation is there—I won't pretend it isn't—but I stay silent and so do the men. One by one, they turn and melt into the trees. I track the growing distances between us for a few moments and then turn toward the compound.

I breathe the cold mountain air and allow myself to feel all the conflicting emotions being back in this place brings. Anger and sorrow and a strange sort of bittersweet nostalgia. Things were more bad than good while growing up under my father's tender care, but there were small spots of light in those first twenty-five years of my life.

My mother is a hazy, distant one. She died when I was still young, one of my father's many mistresses to be felled by the very purpose he had them in the compound to serve: birthing another dhampir. My father is obsessed with his progeny, with his bloodlines.

It's why he took my failure to manifest powers personally. That and the fact that I was determined to push back against his authority every chance I got. I smile a little, though it feels wrong on my face. We've been working toward this endgame since I was born. Now that it's time to act, my nerves ease and my path remains clear.

If I fail, I won't be the only one to pay the price.

I press my hand to my stomach. So much has happened in the last few days, there were moments when I actually forgot I was pregnant. It's far too soon to see physical changes, and with Azazel's temporary shield in place, most of the worst of the side effects have passed.

Should I get pregnant again, I'll have to figure out how to shield on my own. I shake my head and check my watch. I'll worry about the future tomorrow. Right now, I can't afford to be distracted. I take one last breath and start walking toward the compound.

I expect to be stopped. There aren't many sentries outside the walls, but only a fool wouldn't post at least a few people in the forest surrounding the compound. Vampire senses only stretch so far, after all, and an early warning system can mean the difference between life and death in a confrontation. My father is many things, but a fool isn't one of them.

He must really see me as less than a threat. It's the only explanation for why I'm able to walk up the dirt road to the compound gates. They're large enough to drive a truck through...and they're ajar.

"Quite the welcome," I murmur. The urge rises to turn and flee. If we meant to set a trap, my father certainly intends the same.

I lift my chin and push open the gate. Inside, it's exactly the same as I remember. Low square buildings, all in a uniform gray. Nearly indistinguishable from each other. Rationally, I know a year hasn't even passed, but it feels like several lifetimes since I last moved about in this place.

Since no one appears to stop me, I walk through the low buildings that serve as gatehouse and a place for the wall guards to rest between patrols, especially when the weather is intense. Both seem to be empty.

I see the smoke before I scent the burning: three large plumes stretching to the heavens. All three of my men have their shields locked up tight, so I only get the faintest impression of fighting as I step into the courtyard. I turn my focus from them. Now's not the time to be distracted. Not when I have my own part to play.

I stretch out my arms. "Where are you, Father? I've come to negotiate."

This all hinges on him coming to me. If he goes to fight one of the men first, we're in trouble. He could compel them to fight the rest of our group. It would hamstring the other two men because of their desire not to hurt the compelled person. It would ruin any chances I have of succeeding because I am no match for any of them. No, I *have* to make sure he comes to me instead.

I turn a slow circle, arms still outstretched. "I've come to take my place as your heir. You got your wish." I raise my voice. "I carry a bloodline baby. Will you honor your terms, or will you take the coward's way out?"

I feel him before I see him. He's circled around behind me, which is exactly where I want him now that I'm facing the front gates. I turn slowly as he walks out from between two buildings. For such a monstrous man, my father looks nearly as normal as Lizzie does. Silvering brown hair, vaguely attractive features that would be forgettable if not for the charisma he exudes wherever he goes. He weaponizes it now. It presses against me with a force that nearly sends me to my knees, getting stronger with each step he takes in my direction.

He smiles benignly. "Come now, Mina. You must know that you can never be heir. My people will never follow you."

"Let me worry about that," I grit out. He's not even compelling me, but it's hard to speak. Each breath burns as his magic seems to seek a way inside. I hate that feeling, like each inhale gives him a little more power over me, like even now, he's worming his way into my brain. "Will you keep your word?"

He shakes his head and tsks. "How am I to even know you're my child? You have no bloodline powers to speak of. You look exactly like your mother. Who's to say she didn't betray me with some other man to beget you? None of *my* children are such a constant disappointment."

How can his words still sting after everything he's done? I drop my arms. "So you'll break your word."

My father moves closer. His expression remains benevolent, but his words only get uglier as he lowers his voice. "I don't know what game you're playing at, you little bitch, but it won't work. Losing the three bloodline vampires was a temporary setback, and now you've returned them to me. If you truly *are* pregnant, then I'll happily cut that baby out of you the moment it can survive on its own." His smile drops. "You, of course, will not survive the process."

Over my dead body,

I glare. "You're making a mistake. Name me as heir—"

"*Kneel*, slut." His power slams into me, forcing me to my knees. "I don't know how you managed to find *three* of them, but I commend you on being so willing to open your legs to fulfill my aims. I suppose we'll find which is the father once the child is born." He leans down a little, more power infusing his voice. "Are you actually pregnant? Be honest."

"Yes," I bite out. I couldn't have lied if I wanted to. I *hate* this feeling. Like I'm a puppet to his whim. I'm screaming inside my head, but no sound leaves my lips except what he wills. It doesn't matter that he's done this to me before; it's not something I'll *ever* get used to.

If our plan succeeds, I'll never have to experience it again.

"The fires. Your men are responsible?" I clench my jaw and he drops the charming act, his brows drawing down. "*Answer me.*"

"Yes."

"What is their plan?"

I was still a teenager when I learned the trick to dealing with his ability to use glamour to wrest answers from unwilling mouths. With most people, he seems to make them want to tell the truth so that they surrender their knowledge willingly, to please him. With me, he's always used brute force. It hurts, but there is some room to maneuver, depending on how vague his questions. "Start fires."

He stares down at me as if he wants to rip my head from my shoulders. "What is their plan? *Be specific.*"

I fight against the push of his power. To do anything else is out of the question. I don't know what Lizzie is waiting for, but I will buy as much time as I need to. I taste blood and grin up at my father. "To start fires," I repeat.

He clenches his hands into fists and releases them slowly.

"And after they start fires?" He bites out each word like he wants to rip into me with more than power.

"Fight."

"I swear to the gods, I will kill you now, child or no, if you don't stop being so damned difficult." When I don't answer, he throws up his hands. "Well?"

"That wasn't a proper question." A little bit of blood leaks from the corner of my mouth. I'm not sure where it comes from when he does this. There's no cut or obvious injury, but I always bleed when I fight him.

I sit back on my heels and look up. A wave of dizziness passes over me, but when it clears, I nearly sob with relief. A little red dot appears on his throat. "Father?"

"*What?*"

"I hope this hurts." My hand goes to my boot, to the long knife in the sheath there, both courtesy of Grace's bag.

"I changed my mind. You die—"

His throat explodes.

18

I SURGE TO MY FEET BEFORE THE BLOOD MIST HAS A chance to fall. My father is old. He'll heal far too quickly to hesitate now. It's why we couldn't risk a shot to the head. If he's still able to speak, he'll put a stop to any attack before I have a chance to finish it.

His power still lingers in the air, but it no longer feels like it's chaining me in place. I lunge at him, taking him to the ground even as he tries to stop the bleeding. His mouth moves, but no words come out. How many seconds do I have? Thirty? Twenty? *Ten?*

Fear gives me strength as I hack at him with the knife. One strike hits his hands, another, and then they're finally out of the way. It takes one glance at his throat to drive home how little time I have. It's knitting together before my very eyes. "No!" I bring the blade over my head and thrust it down, intending to impale his neck. It will be impossible for him to heal if there's a knife in the way.

I don't make it.

He catches the blade in the palms of his hands, the blade sliding clean through and catching on the hilt. Shock freezes me for a single heartbeat, and then it's too late. He wrenches the knife away. The momentum sends it spinning away from us. I follow the trajectory as horror rises with the realization that it lands too far away. If I go for it, he'll be healed by the time I get back to him.

Rylan's voice rises from the back of my mind, memory, or something else.

Never defenseless. Never weaponless.

Do not panic.

I scream as my father strikes up at me. Instinct has me lifting my hands to keep him from hitting my face. In my fear, I almost don't notice the tingling that spread from my fingers down through my hands. I shove back at my father and blink down as blood sprays where I make contact.

My hands are...transformed. It's not like before. There are no dainty claws that are sharp but ultimately less than useful in a fight. No, my claws look like Rylan's when he's a wolf. They're huge and wickedly curved and achingly sharp.

My father's eyes go wide. *No,* he mouths.

"*Yes.*"

This time, when I attack, it doesn't matter that he's trying to fight me with his bare hands. A blow from me, and there are no more hands to speak of. Another swipe and his throat is gone entirely. I keep going, fear driving me, until his neck is entirely gone and his head rolls away from his body.

Only then do I stop attacking, sure that he can no longer hurt me.

Only then do I look up to realize the courtyard is no longer empty.

My father's people and many of my half siblings stand around the edges. To a person, they stare at me with fear. I push slowly to my feet and several of them flinch away from me. I hate it. I never wanted to rule like this, but the men are right. Fear is the only way to ensure I survive this coup and keep surviving. There aren't any soldiers present, which is just as well. The men will take care of them. It's up to me to sell this once and for all.

I grab my father's head and hold it aloft. Someone cries out in horror. I ignore them and turn a slow circle, meeting as many gazes as I can manage, holding them until people look away. I lift his head and raise my voice. "I am my father's heir by virtue of the babe now growing in my womb. I am now the head of the clan by virtue of his death. Challenge me now or take a knee."

One of my brothers, William, steps forward. He opens his mouth but stops speaking as fire pours from my palm, turning our father's head to ash. I hold his gaze as I turn the fire on the body next. It burns hot, hot enough to flash dry the blood coating me, hot enough that the people closest take several large steps back. William shakes his head and sinks to one knee.

Fear truly is a powerful tool for a leader. The thought makes me vaguely ill, but there are no depths I won't descend to in order to protect the people I care about. I don't want to slaughter my way through my half siblings, but I'll do it if they force my hand.

William's taking the knee starts a waterfall effect, though. One by one, all the people around the courtyard kneel and bow their heads. I turn slowly, but not a single one of them will meet my gaze, let alone challenge me. *Thank the gods.* I refuse to let the relief show on my face.

Instead, I rotate to face William and lift my voice. "Gather everyone. It's time to make an announcement."

He doesn't look happy, but he nods. He turns to several people next to him. "Make the call."

It takes fifteen minutes for everyone in the compound to reach the courtyard. My hands still haven't returned to their normal shape and I'm still covered in my father's blood, but it's just as well. Again, not a single person challenges me as I declare myself the leader.

There will be challenges later, both martial and subtle, but it will take them at least a few days to gather their courage to try. A few days is all I need to cement my place here. I won't pretend that dueling will be easy, but after facing down my father, I'm not as worried as I was before. None of my half siblings' powers are as strong as his were. I can break their compulsions, which means I can win the fight.

There's another matter to attend to first, though. "Allow me to introduce you to my partners." I fling a hand over to where I feel Malachi, Rylan, and Wolf waiting. They leap over the bystanders and land at my back, a flashy move that almost makes me smile, especially when everyone gasps. Truly, my father's people are already conditioned to fall in line behind a strong leader. I have no intention of becoming a tyrant like my father, but I am not above taking advantage of the rotten foundation he left.

I will give them the strong leader they crave. Unlike my father, though, I won't abuse my power over them. I fully intend to be a queen they'll grow to love over time, or at least respect.

"You will obey these men as you would me." I wait for the murmured assent before continuing. "Now, go back to your homes and rest assured that you are safe. Your lives will not be negatively affected by this change in power." I hate that I find myself pitching my tone to mimic the way my father talked in public, that I'm using his cadences to ensure obedience from these people. I never set out to lead, but if I walk away and allow William or one of the others to take over, they will hunt me the same way our father did. I've made myself too much a threat to do anything but take my father's place. It's the only way.

"Do *not* force me to make an example of you." I sweep my gaze over them. "Go. Sleep. We will rebuild after everyone rests for the day."

The men fall behind me as I turn and head deeper into the compound. It's only when I take a familiar turn that I realize I'm walking back to my old room by habit and that it's not appropriate for me to sleep there if I'm supposed to be leading. It's just as well. That tiny room holds no good memories for me, and it's nowhere large enough for the four of us.

With a sigh, I veer in the opposite direction and make my way to my father's home. Stepping through the front door, even with my men at my back, feels like being launched into a past I want no part of. My knees buckle.

I never hit the floor.

Malachi scoops me up. "Bathroom?"

I try to speak, but no words come. Rylan brushes a hand over my head. "I'll get a shower going." He disappears through a doorway leading deeper into the house.

Wolf surveys the room. "I hope you're not attached to any of this." I shake my head mutely and he smiles. "Let Mal wind you down and we'll take care of the rest. You did good, love."

Malachi carries me through the house to the large bathroom Rylan found. Steam already curls through the air, and I take what feels like my first full breath in hours. We did it. We actually pulled it off. My father is gone and I am now the leader of this compound. *Holy shit.* I don't even know how to process that. I don't even know where to begin to start. "Oh gods." My body starts to shake, violent tremors hitting in waves. "It hurts." I don't know what I mean, only that it's true.

"I know, little dhampir. I know."

Rylan stays long enough to use his claws to divest me of my clothing and then he leaves, shutting the door softly behind him. Mal steps beneath the spray without setting me down. "Breathe. You did it. The worst of it is over."

"I never wanted to lead," I whisper. "I just wanted to be free."

"Freedom in our world comes at the price of power. This was the only way." He hugs me tightly. "Can you stand?"

"I think so?"

He sets me carefully on my feet and washes the blood from my body and hair. When he gets to my hands, he examines the claws. "These are impressive."

"I don't know how I did it. I just heard Rylan's voice in my head and then the magic obeyed."

"Sometimes it happens like that. Close your eyes." I obey, and he keeps speaking in that low, calm voice. "Envision your hands as they normally are. Not a claw or bit of fur in sight."

My eyes fly open. "I don't have *fur*."

He grins. "Now you don't have claws, either."

Sure enough, he's right. I wiggle the fingers of my very human hand. They look just like normal, feel just like normal. How strange. "That was easy."

"I did say it would get easier."

"I didn't think it would happen this fast." I take a deep breath and look at the door. "They're going to expect information and announcements and official things tomorrow."

"Yes. But you're not doing it alone." He presses his hand to my lower stomach. "You have us. I meant what I said last night. We will make this place the safest spot in the realms to raise our children. Anyone—*anyone*—who threatens us won't live long enough to regret it."

There was a time when I might say that's too bloodthirsty, but that time and that person are long gone. I nod. "Then I guess we best get started."

"Tomorrow, Mina."

When we leave the bathroom, clean and exhausted, it's to find that Rylan and Wolf have gutted the house. I look around with wide eyes. How did they possibly move this quickly? The living room is completely empty except for a plain mattress with what appears to be clean sheets sitting in the center of it. "What's this?"

Wolf saunters through the door. "Couldn't do the whole place in the time we had, but we figured you didn't want to be surrounded with memories of the monster." He eyes the mattress with distaste. "This is the largest we could find on short notice."

My lower lip quivers at the thoughtfulness of this. I *don't* want to be in this house, faced with the memory of my father, especially when it takes less than no effort to conjure how warm his blood was against my skin, how easily his flesh gave way to my claws. I shudder. "Thank you."

"Anything for you, love." He flops down onto the mattress.

Rylan steps into the house and shuts the door firmly behind himself. "I don't expect trouble tonight, but we'll keep an eye out for it." He frowns at Wolf. "Get off those clean sheets until you've had a shower."

"Right. Whoops." Wolf rolls easily to his feet and moves past me toward the shower. He brushes the backs of his fingers on my arm and then he's gone. A few seconds later, the shower starts up again.

Rylan comes to stand before me. "How are you doing?"

"I'm shaky and exhausted and overwhelmed." I try for a smile. "But we're all alive, so I'm good. Really good." I hesitate. "Lizzie?"

"Gone. I'm sure she'll be circling back at some point for that favor, but the Radu family will be doing what the rest of the clans are now that you've taken over." At my questioning look, he gives a wry smile. "Watching. Evaluating. Traditionally, there's a year grace period when someone ascends to head of clan, so we have that long to bolster our defenses and alliances and ensure we're too strong to reckon with."

"Oh," I say faintly. I've never heard of a grace period, but my father has ruled for a very, very long time. He was also tight-fisted with information as a way of controlling people—something I intend to change. I drag in a breath. "I guess we need to get started on that soon."

"Tomorrow," Malachi says firmly. "Everything can wait until tomorrow. Right now, we're going to hold you and we're going to celebrate the fact that we're alive and we won."

I find myself smiling slowly as he leads me to the bed. "I kind of like that plan."

"I thought you might." He smiles down at me, and for the first time since I met him, it's completely joyful and free of reserve. "I love you, little dhampir."

"I love you, too."

"Forever."

I go up onto my toes and kiss him. "*Forever.*"

19

FOUR YEARS LATER

I SMELL SMOKE AS I TURN DOWN THE HALL TOWARD the nursery. "Not again." I pick up my pace, sprinting the last few steps and throwing open the door, power at my fingertips and ready to quell the fire. The sight that greets me stops me short.

Rylan is sleeping in the rocking chair, the twins in his arms. They're still little, only three months, and they seem to have taken it as a personal challenge to see how ragged they can run the four of us. I'm more tired than I could have thought possible, but it's a good kind of tired. They're sleeping for once, so *they* aren't the source of the smoke.

No, the source is Wolf and Asher sitting on the floor across from each other, shooting little fireballs at each other. I start to yell a warning when Wolf sends one spiraling at our three-year-old, but he sends a little burst of power to fizzle it out well before it makes contact.

Then he turns and gives me an unrepentant grin. "He's even better at fire than you are."

"Mama!" Asher jumps to his feet and sprints to me, moving so quickly I barely get my arms out before he throws himself into them.

I spin him around twice and cuddle him close. "Hello, Trouble." I press a kiss to the top of his head, covered in dark curls. "Let's move this to the living room so the twins can sleep." I eye them. "Do you think it's wise to move them?"

"Rylan won't let them fall." Wolf hefts himself to his feet. "And you know what happened last time we tried to move them when they were sleeping."

I wince. Hours of sobbing and a particularly sleepless night. "We leave them then." Hopefully all three of them take a nice long nap. I turn and carry Asher out of the bedroom and down the hall to the living room. In the years since I took over the compound, everything's changed. Gone is my father's overbearing style, replaced by grounded, cozy furniture in pleasing colors. This house feels like a home for the first time in my life, and it's not solely because of the redecorating.

Malachi walks through the front door as we settle on the couch. He's dressed in a pair of jeans and a gray T-shirt and he's never looked better. He grins at the sight of us. "Someone said they smelled smoke, and I figured it was Asher getting up to no good."

"Wolf was supervising."

He glances at Wolf. "I bet he was."

We fully expected Asher to develop only one power, courtesy of whoever was his biological father, but in the last six months, he's shown evidence of all four bloodline powers that flow through his veins. We still don't know if it's courtesy of the bond I share with my men or because of some seraph quirk, but I'm already attempting to prepare myself for the chaos that will come when the twins start manifesting their powers. I hope we survive it.

Malachi crosses to press a kiss to my lips, then Wolf's, while he ruffles Asher's hair. "The twins?"

"They're taking a nap with Rylan."

His grin widens. "He does have the magic touch with them." It's true. They sleep better for Rylan than for any of us, though even that isn't saying much.

Next to me, Wolf clears his throat. "I heard from Lizzie."

I turn to look at him. "What? When?" She stopped by the compound exactly a year and a day after I took over the leadership, claiming it was to say congratulations for building a strong, stable community. In the three years since, she hasn't shown her face...or claimed the favor I owe her.

"Earlier."

I search his face for any evidence of distress and send a tentative probe along the bond. Wolf cracks his shields for me, allowing me in far enough to see that his calm isn't an act. I ease my magic away from him. "What did she want?"

"To call her favor due." He holds up a hand. "I'm fine. Things are different now than they were four years ago. We have people."

It's certainly true. While there was a small exodus of people in the weeks after I took over, the majority of the compound citizens stayed. In the time since, we've built up something special. The fear that originally held them in sway has given way to mutual respect and admiration. Wolf's right. We're stronger than we've ever been. Still, Lizzie presents a complication. "What favor?"

He gives a mirthless smile. "She wants us to entertain the Radu clan for a week."

"No. Absolutely not."

"Yes." He covers my hand with his. "You already have her word that they won't cause harm to any of ours. We'll get it from my mother as well. It will be fine."

I narrow my eyes. "You're taking this rather calmly." Far more calmly than he did when Rylan's mother came to visit. I shudder a little at the memory. She didn't do anything out of line, but I've never met a scarier person in my life. I'm not eager to repeat the experience with Wolf's mother. "I thought you'd want to avoid it."

"I thought she'd be here within the second year. The fact that we've had this long is a boon." He shrugs. "Like I said, we have people."

I twist to catch Malachi's eye. "How do you feel about this?"

"He's right. We're too strong to fuck with."

"Fuck with," Asher says.

I shoot Malachi a murderous look. "No, baby, those are grown-up words and only grown-ups are allowed to use them."

"Fuck, fuck, fuck." Asher wiggles out of my arms and practically bounces from one piece of furniture to another. "Fuck!" He sends a tiny fireball shooting at a painting I bought during one of our trips last year.

Malachi snuffs it out quickly. "That's enough of that." He gives me one last kiss and scoops up Asher. "It's bath time. No more fireballs, no more bad language."

Asher gives him a look like he might test this new boundary but ultimately decides bath time is more important. He smiles like a perfect little child who wasn't just shouting expletives and shooting fireballs. "Yes, Daddy."

"Thought so." He stops in the doorway. "We have time to figure out the Radu stuff, but don't worry, little dhampir. There's nothing to fear."

I take a slow breath and let it out as he disappears down the hall. He's right. I take Wolf's hand and squeeze it. "You're really okay with this?"

"More or less." He shrugs. "It was bound to happen at some point. No matter how crazy my family is, they value children. They just want to poke their nose into our business and test our defenses a little. Nothing will come of it." He makes a face. "The same can't be true when the children are adults, but that's a bridge we'll cross when we get there."

"Hey, I love you." I wait for him to look back at me. "If they come here and cross the line, then we'll kill them and you never have to deal with them again."

Wolf lets out that glorious laugh that I love so much. "There's my murderous woman." He pulls me into his lap. "I love you, too. We'll get through the visit without murder." He grins, bright and sharp. "But I appreciate the sentiment all the same."

I never thought to end up happy in this compound. I certainly never thought I'd have built a life with three men. But...I've never been happier. The thought of living a life that stretches for hundreds of years used to scare me, but each day now brings something new and wonderful. Even the bad stuff isn't world-ending because I'm not facing it alone.

I'll never have to face it alone ever again.

And neither will my men.

EPILOGUE

THE DEMON REALM

EVERYTHING WAS IN ITS PLACE.

Azazel surveyed the room one last time. The low stage stood at the front of it, just wide enough to fit five humans standing side by side. The room was arranged carefully, seating grouped just far enough away from each other that it made a confrontation less likely, all arranged in a half circle equal distances from the stage. Politics bored him, but they were necessary to navigate from time to time.

Like now.

After tonight, he would have what he wanted most. In addition to that, all four leaders of the other territories in this realm would owe him a favor. The women had been prepped and the contracts were good on their end. All that was left was to auction them off, get the second set of contracts signed and those bargains cemented.

Then he could focus on his reward.

Thane was the first to arrive, and he came alone. He nodded to Azazel and sank into the low pool built into the floor. The dark water hid the tentacles taking up the lower half of his body and nearly matched his dark gray skin.

Next came Bram, his wings tucked tight against his body. He eyed Thane and made a wide, pointed circle around his pool. Air and water rarely got along, but this was ridiculous. He finally sank into the backless chair ready for him. "This better be worth the trip, Azazel."

"Oh, it will be."

Thunderous footsteps signaled Sol's arrival. Azazel knew for a fact the dragon could tread silently when he chose, but why bother with that when he could shake the building instead. He stalked through the door, glanced around, and made a beeline for the stool with a divot in the back to accommodate his thick tail.

Rusalka, of course, was last. She always liked to make an entrance. She came through the door with her hair floating in an uncanny current. Flames burned beneath her flesh, so bright in places, it almost hurt to look at her. She was nearly as tall as Sol and had the most human body of all of them...as long as one ignored the fiery skin that would burn anyone who touched her without permission. He'd seen it happen before, and she'd laughed while the poor bastard died at her feet.

"Thank you for coming. I think you'll find tonight's offerings to your taste." As if any of them had tastes for *this* kind of offering. Humans in their realm were few and far between; he had brought most of them over years ago. They—and their bloodlines—were a rare enough commodity to get all these leaders in the same room for the first time in generations. "The price will be the same regardless."

"I'm sure." Rusalka draped one leg over the other, her cloven hoof tapping the ground. "We're not giving our lands up for a piece of ass, Azazel. Be serious."

"I don't want your lands." Being the ultimate leader of this realm would be more trouble than it was worth. "I want peace. The constant warring is draining our resources faster than we can replenish them. You all know that or you wouldn't be here. It's time for a new generation of leaders to do things our way." He motioned to the doorway on one side of the stage. "The peace offering."

One by one, five women filed out onto the stage.

Azazel turned to the gathered leaders. "Now, we make our selections."

Don't miss
WICKED BEAUTY,
the sinfully sexy story of a modern-day
Helen of Troy, Achilles, and Patroclus.

1
HELEN

"I AM SO FUCKING LATE," I MUTTER UNDER MY BREATH. The hallways of Dodona Tower are blessedly empty, but that only makes the clock ticking down inside my head worse. Tonight is the night everything changes. The night when I stop being a pawn in other people's games and finally gain the agency I've craved ever since I was a little girl.

And I can't believe I'm fucking *late*.

I pick up my pace, barely managing to resist the urge to run. Showing up out of breath and flustered to an Olympus party is even worse than showing up late. Appearances matter. It's been a long time since Olympus experienced anything resembling traditional warfare, but every day, little battles are fought and won using the most mundane things.

A carefully designed dress.

A sweet word hiding a poisonous sting.

A marriage.

I duck into the elevator that will take me up to the ballroom floor and barely resist the urge to bounce on my toes with impatience. Normally, I wouldn't give a damn about any of this. I make petty rebellions an art form.

Tonight is different.

Tonight, my brother Perseus—-Zeus, now—-is making an announcement that will change everything.

Less than a week ago, Ares passed away. It was hardly unexpected—-the man was old as dirt and had been knocking on the doors to the underworld for three months—-but it's opened up an opportunity that's usually only seen once a generation. Of the Thirteen, Ares alone is open to absolutely anyone. A person's history, connections, finances don't matter. You don't even have to be Olympian.

You simply have to win.

Three trials, all designed to cull the wheat from the chaff, and the last person standing steps up to become Ares. One of the thirteen people who create the ruling body in Olympus. Each handles a specific part of keeping the city running smoothly, but more importantly to me, no one can compel any of them to take an action they don't want to.

Not even Zeus can force the hand of another member of the Thirteen—-or at least that's the theory. My father never paid attention to those sorts of niceties, and I doubt my brother will now that he's inherited the title. It doesn't matter. If I'm Ares, I'm no longer daughter to one Zeus, sister to another, a spoiled princess with no real value beyond her pretty face and family connections.

Becoming Ares will set me free.

The elevator doors open, and I hurry in the direction of the ballroom. The long hallway has changed since the last party, the dour, dark drapes that hung floor to ceiling on either side of the doors replaced with an airy white fabric that has silver threaded through it. It's still not welcoming, but it's significantly less oppressive.

I'm curious who made *that* design call, because Perseus sure as fuck didn't. Since he stepped up as Zeus after our father's death, the only thing my oldest brother cares about is running his business and ruling Olympus with an iron fist.

Or at least trying to.

"Helen."

I stop short, but recognition brings a relieved smile to my face. "Eros. What are you doing out here lurking in the shadows?"

He steps forward and holds up a tiny jeweled bag. "Psyche forgot her purse." He should look ridiculous holding the purse, especially considering the violence those hands have done, but Eros has a habit of moving through life as if he's untouchable. No one would dare say a word and he knows it.

"What a good husband you are." I take the last few steps and press a quick kiss to each of his cheeks. I haven't seen him much in the last couple months, but he looks good. Eros is one of the most gorgeous people in Olympus—which is saying something—a white guy with curly blond hair and a face to make painters weep at its perfection. "Marriage suits you."

"More and more every day." His gaze sharpens. "You've pulled out all the stops tonight."

"Do you like the dress?" I smooth my hands down my gown. It's a custom piece, the golden fabric molded to my body from shoulders to hips before flaring out the slightest bit. It's heavy with a subtle pattern that's designed to catch the light with every move. A deep V dips between my breasts, and the shoulders have been shaped into sharp points that give the slightest impression of military bearing. "It's a showstopper, as my mother would have said."

I ignore the twinge in my chest at the thought, just as I always do when my mind tries to linger on the woman who died far too young. She's been gone fifteen years, having suffered a *mysterious* fall when I was fifteen. Mysterious. Right. As if all of Olympus didn't suspect that my father was behind it.

As if I didn't know it for certain.

Pushing *this* thought away is second nature. It doesn't matter what sins my father committed. He's dead and gone, just like my mother. I hope he's been suffering in the pits of Tartarus since he drew his last breath. When I think of his death, all I feel is relief. He died before he could marry me off to secure some bullshit alliance, before he could cause even more of the pain he seemed to enjoy inflicting so much.

No, I don't miss my father at all.

"She'd be proud of you."

"Maybe." I glance over his shoulder at the doors. "Maybe she'd be furious over what I'm about to do." Rock the boat? Fuck, I'm about to tip the boat right over.

Eros doesn't miss a beat. His brows rise and he shakes his head, looking rueful. "So it's Ares for you. I should have known. You've been missing a lot of parties lately. Training?"

"Yes." I brace myself for his disbelief. We might be friends, but we're friends by Olympus standards. I trust Eros not to slide a knife between my ribs. He trusts me not to cause him undue trouble in the press. We hang out on a regular basis at events and parties and occasionally trade favors. I don't trust him with my deepest secrets. It's nothing personal. I don't trust *anyone* with that part of me.

On the other hand, everyone in Olympus will know my plans very shortly.

I square my shoulders. "I'm going to compete to become the next Ares."

"Damn." He whistles under his breath. "You've got your work cut out for you."

He's not telling me he thinks he can't do it, but I wilt a little all the same. I didn't *really* expect enthusiastic support, but being constantly underestimated never fails to sting. "Yes, well, I'd better get in there."

"Hold on." He surveys me. "Your hair is a little lopsided."

"*What?*" I lift my hand and touch my head. I can't tell without a mirror. Damn it, I'm going to be even later, but it's still better than walking into that room out of sorts.

I start to turn in the direction of the bathroom back toward the elevators, but Eros catches my shoulder. "I got it." He opens Psyche's purse and digs around for a few seconds, pulling out an even smaller bag. Inside, there is a bunch of bobby pins. Eros huffs out a laugh at my incredulous expression. "Don't look so surprised. If you had a purse, you'd have bobby pins stashed, too. Now, hold still and let me fix your shit."

Shock roots me in place as he carefully fixes my hair, securing it with half a dozen bobby pins. He leans back and nods. "Better."

"Eros." I gently touch my hair again. "Since when do you do hair?"

He shrugs. "I can't do more than damage control, but it saves Psyche some trouble when we're out if I can help like this."

Gods, he's so in love it makes me sick. I'm happy for him. Truly, I am. But I can't help the jealousy that curls through me. It's not about Eros—-he's more brother to me than anything else—-but at the intimacy and trust he shares with his wife. The one time I thought I might have that, it blew up in my face, and I still wear the emotional scars from the fallout.

I manage a smile, though. "Thanks."

"Knock 'em dead, Helen." His grin is sharp enough to cut. "I'll be rooting for you."

I drag in a slow breath and turn for the door. Since I'm late, I might as well make an entrance. I straighten my spine and push both doors open with more force than necessary. People scatter as I step into the room. I pause, letting them look at me and taking them in at the same time.

This room has changed since Perseus inherited the title of Zeus. Oh, the space is still functionally the same. Shining white marble floors that I can barely see beneath the crowd, an arching ceiling that gives the impression of the ballroom being even larger than it is, the massive windows and glass doors that lead out to the balcony on the other side of the room. But it still feels different. The walls used to be cream, but now they're a cool gray. A subtle change, but it makes a difference.

Most notably, the larger—than—life portraits of the Thirteen that line the walls have different frames. Gone are the thick gold frames that my father favored, replaced by finely crafted black. I would have to get closer to verify, but each looks like they might be custom, unique to each member of the Thirteen.

Perseus didn't make these changes, either. I'm certain of it. Our father might have been obsessive about his image, but my brother doesn't give a fuck. Even when he should.

I start through the crowd, holding my head high.

Normally, I can identify every single person who attends a Dodona Tower party. Information is everything, and I learned from a very young age that it's the only weapon I'm allowed. Some people meet my gaze, others stare at my body in a way that makes my skin crawl, and still others all but turn their backs on me. No surprises there. Being a Kasios in Olympus might have its perks, but it means being born into generations-old grudges and politicking. I grew up learning who could be trusted—no one—and who would actually shove me into traffic if given half a chance—more people than is comforting.

But this party isn't a regular one, and tonight is not a regular night. Nearly half the faces are new to me, people who have arrived from the outskirts around Olympus or been ferried into the city by Poseidon for this special occasion. I don't stop moving to memorize faces. Not everyone here will be nominating themselves as champions; plenty of them are just like the majority of the people here from Olympus. Hangers—on. They don't matter.

I don't pick up my pace, moving at a steady stalk that forces people to get out of my way. The crowd parts for me just like I know it will, whispers following in my wake. I'm making a scene, and while half of them love me for it, the rest resent me.

Everyone has pulled out all the stops tonight. In one corner, my sister Eris—-Aphrodite, as of three months ago—-is laughing at something with Hermes and Dionysus. My chest gives a pang. I would like nothing more than to be with them now, just like I am at every other party. My sister and my friends are what makes living in Olympus bearable, but the last few months have driven home the new differences between us. It wasn't so noticeable when Eris was still Eris, but now that she's also one of the Thirteen...

I'm getting left behind. Being sister to Zeus and Aphrodite, friend to Hermes and Dionysus? It doesn't mean shit. I'm still a piece to be moved around on someone else's board.

Becoming Ares is my only opportunity to change that.

I catch sight of the Dimitriou clan in the opposite corner, Demeter with three of her four daughters, as well as Hades, husband to Persephone. Like everyone else, they're dressed to perfection. The fact that Hades and Persephone are here only spotlights the importance of what's to come. Every member of the Thirteen is present to stand witness to the ceremonial announcement of the tournament to replace Ares. Eros appears at his wife's side, and the way her face lights up at the sight of him... I turn away.

The throne is my destination.

Well, the pair of thrones—two more changes our shift in leadership has caused. Gone is the gaudy gold monstrosity our father used to love, replaced with a steel sculpture that's attractive but oh so cold. Kind of like Perseus himself.

The second throne is a daintier version of his. Callisto Dimitriou sits on it, a beautiful white woman with long dark hair dressed in an elegant black gown. She's staring at everyone gathered below her as if she'd like to shove each one of us through the huge glass doors that have been opened to let in the balmy June evening air. I doubt she'd stop there, though. More likely, she'd love to see us tossed right over the balcony.

Why my brother chose *her* to be his wife, to become Hera, is a mystery to everyone in Olympus. They certainly don't seem to like each other. Their marriage reeks of Demeter's meddling, but no matter how I dig or pry, I've never been able to find a proper answer. I suppose it doesn't matter *why* Perseus married her, only that he did.

I drop into a quick curtsy that *almost* manages to be polite. "Zeus. Hera."

My brother leans forward and narrows a cold look in my direction. While Eris and I take after our mother's coloring, Perseus is all our father. Blond hair, blue eyes, pale skin, and a ruggedly attractive face. If he put any effort behind it at all, he'd be good—looking enough to charm the whole room. Unfortunately, my brother never excelled at that type of skill the same way the rest of my family does.

Not Hercules. He was as bad at playing the game as Perseus.

I shove the thought away. There's no use thinking about Hercules, either. He's gone, and as far as most of Olympus is concerned, he might as well be dead. No, that's not right. People talk about the dead. They pretend Hercules never existed in the first place. I miss him nearly as much as I miss my mother.

"You're late." Perseus doesn't lift his voice, but he doesn't have to. The people nearest us have gone quiet, tense with the possibility of seeing Kasios family drama play out. I can't resent them for that. I've given them plenty of fodder for gossip over my thirty years.

"Sorry." I even mean it. "Time got away from me." The temptation to overprepare isn't usually one I fall victim to, but there's nothing usual about this situation.

Perseus shakes his head slightly, his gaze tracking the rest of the room. "I'm making the announcement soon. Don't wander off."

I bristle, but there's no point in taking it personally. Perseus talks to everyone as though they're a small child or a dog; he has since we were little. I might understand that it's just the way he is, but his preferred method of communication is already breeding resentment among Olympus's elite.

That's not my problem, though. Not tonight. I give him a bright smile. "Of course, dear brother. I wouldn't dream of it." After the announcement, people will have a chance to put their names forward to become champions, which will enter them into the tournament for Ares's title. The window to put a name forward doesn't technically close until dawn, but from what I understand, it's rare for there to be latecomers, so I want to make sure I'm on hand to get my name in before anyone can think to stop me.

I turn to study the room, though I can feel my brother watching me. Probably worried I'm going to embarrass him further. Another night, I might even see that as a challenge, but right now, I have my eyes on the prize. I will not be diverted.

After tonight, everyone will know that I'm a force to be reckoned with.

It doesn't take long for the rest of the Thirteen to drift over, taking up positions on either side of my brother and Callisto—-Hera. She looks bored with this whole process, but she's the only one. A current of excitement surges through the room. I know Perseus just wants stability for Olympus, but this fanfare will be more than that for the city. It will give them something to cheer for, an event to raise civilian morale—something that has wavered recently.

The Thirteen might rule Olympus, but ultimately they are only a handful of people. Without the support of the greater population, that power is in name only. There has only been an uprising once in our history, a few generations back after a war between the Thirteen decimated the city, but it was brutal enough for us to know we never want it to happen again.

Things work best when the current members of the Thirteen play the celebrity game. When someone takes over a new title, they decide how they want to craft their image and run with it. Some—like Demeter, the last Aphrodite, Hermes, and Dionysus—go hard, using public opinion to further their respective goals. Poseidon and Hades have never played the game, though. Hades by virtue of no one on this side of the river knowing he existed until recently. Poseidon because he garners enough goodwill by being one of the few who can come and go across the barrier that surrounds Olympus freely, which means he imports anything industry in the city can't create for itself.

A bunch of new members of the Thirteen in a short time means uncertainty, and in uncertain times, anything is possible. Even revolution.

My brother will do anything to ensure that doesn't happen.

The crowd presses closer, and I angle myself away from the front of it, shifting close to where Dionysus stands. He's a white man about my age with short dark hair and a truly impressive mustache that he's grown out just enough to curve it up at either side of his mouth. It should look ridiculous, but it's Dionysus. He makes ridiculous an artistic statement, from his peppy attitude to his brightly colored suit. He grins at me. "Ready for this?"

My stomach is twisted into half a million knots, but I smile back. "Of course. There's bound to be drama, and you know how I love that." *I* will be the drama shortly.

A light over Perseus brightens as the camera crew takes up positions across from him. This event will be broadcast to the greater city, which means the impressions champions make, starting now, are vital. Ares doesn't technically need civilian support to do their job, but being popular with the citizens helps smooth the way.

My brother straightens to his feet. He doesn't have the commanding presence our father did, but he *does* have the ability to make it seem like he's looking right into a person's soul. He uses that now, his icy gaze shifting over the people gathered before landing on me. Something flares there, something I don't recognize, but he moves on before I can identify it.

"You all know why we're here." He doesn't raise his voice, but he doesn't have to. My siblings and I were trained to speak in public from a very young age. To be perfect symbols of our perfect family line. "We're here to honor the passing of Ares. He served the title for nearly sixty years, and he's gone far too soon." Nice words. Meaningless words. The last Ares was, quite frankly, a dick.

Perseus turns to the other part of the room. "Tonight, we begin the process of finding our next Ares. Tradition states that three trials will be issued, the first of which you'll know in two days' time. The winner of the three challenges will become the next Ares." A weighted pause. Again, that strange look passes over his face.

It's the only warning I get.

Perseus looks at me, something akin to sympathy in his blue eyes as he seals my fate. "And marry my sister Helen."

ABOUT THE AUTHOR

Katee Robert is a *New York Times* and *USA Today* bestselling author of contemporary romance and romantic suspense. *Entertainment Weekly* calls her writing "unspeakably hot." Her books have sold over a million copies. She lives in the Pacific Northwest with her husband, children, a cat who thinks he's a dog, and two Great Danes who think they're lap dogs. You can visit her at kateerobert.com or on Twitter @katee_robert.